THE GUARD OF LOTHFORIAS

BLOOD AND WATER: BOOK ONE

PARKER ATLAS YAW

ORANGE DOOR BOOKS

The Greater Continent

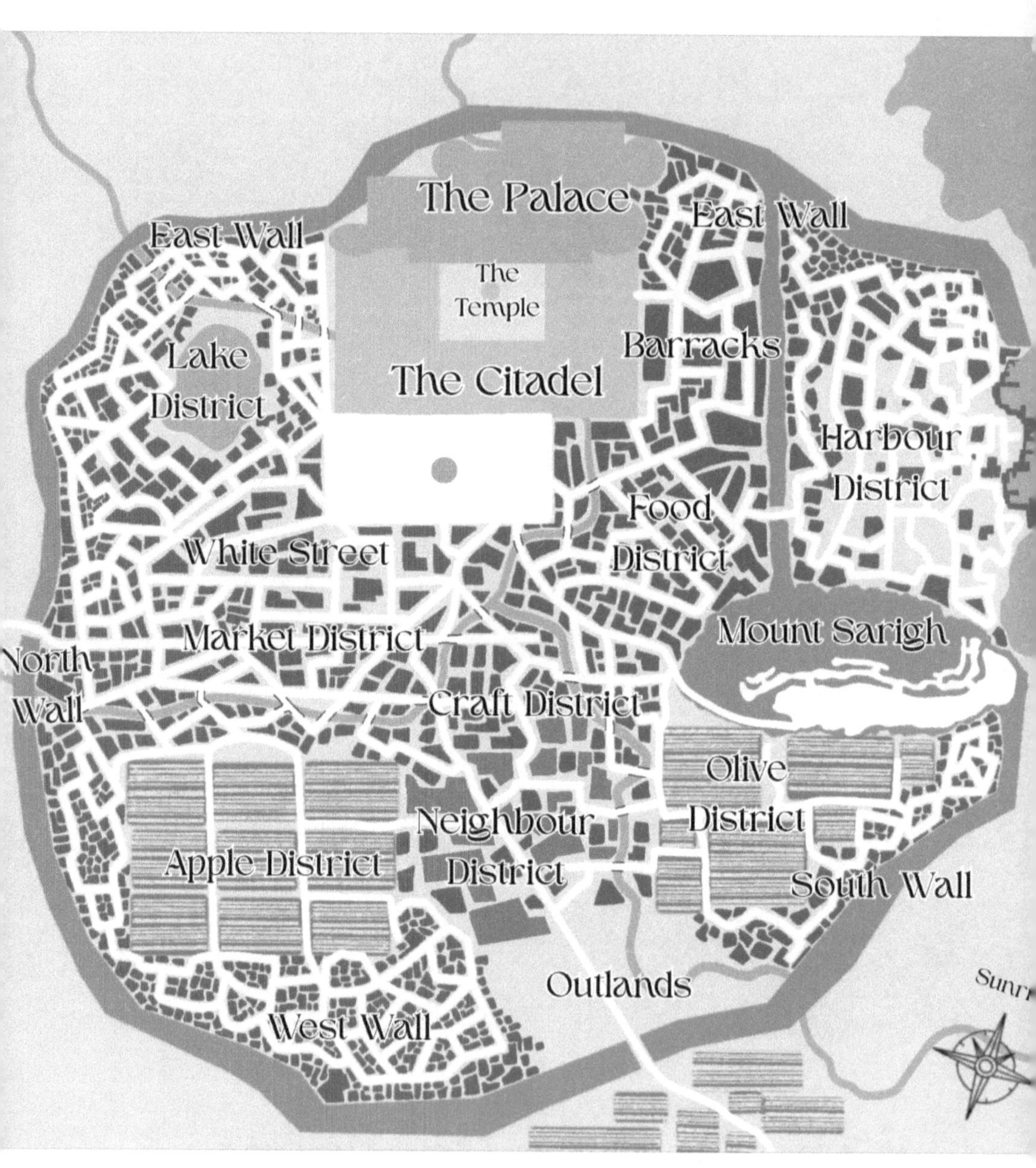

The City of Lothforias

CONTENTS

To those who don't break, and those who do.

Returning

CHAPTER ONE

ELIN

I DON'T KNOW HOW to go home. What does home even mean?

I quickly stepped off the skiff to allow the other passengers to disembark, adjusting my grip on the pack slung over my shoulder. "Fair winds," I told the ferrywoman as I passed.

"Even trails," she replied gruffly. As I started down the wharf, I heard the same exchange behind me half a dozen times before the skiff was finally empty and the ferrywoman began to push it back down the river with her long oar.

When I reached the end of the wharf and set foot on solid ground, I stopped to let my eyes wander down the long, winding path that led to the city. **Two years...** I wondered how much Lothforias had changed. I wondered how much I had.

I felt someone's hand on my shoulder. Gentle touch, but rough texture. I looked back at the woman who had just caught me and the dour man at her side. She smiled up at me. "Excuse me, son," she started. "Are you travelling to the city?"

"I am, mother."

"You're welcome to walk with my husband and I, in the interests of safety and good conversation."

"I can promise safety," I assured her as I touched a hand to the knife on my belt, "but I'm afraid if you're hungry for good conversation, you'll starve."

She laughed, resting her other hand over my heart. "I rather think I'll have my fill. I'm Edda Lahd— and this is my husband, Ruce."

The man wore his hair cropped so close to his head he seemed bald, and my eye was drawn to the linen wraps that snaked up his forearms. I could see delicate stitching on them, words too small to make out and flowers embroidered into the fabric. He held out a weathered hand and I took it firmly. Strong, confident, unassuming. "Pleasure, father."

He regarded me curiously, but didn't voice the first question that came to him. Instead, as we began walking the well-trodden path through the forest of tall cedars, he asked, "What brings you to the province, young man?"

"I've been... searching for something, for a while," I answered carefully. "And you?"

"Our home was destroyed. We, like so many, are hoping to find refuge in the capital."

"I'm sorry."

"What of your home, son?" Edda asked.

"I don't know... It's been over two years since I set eyes on Lothforias."

"You were born in the capitol?" Ruce said in surprise. "Then this is a return home for you."

"A return, yes... but I'll be as much a stranger in the city as the two of you. My family... my family would hardly recognise me," I murmured to myself.

As we had been walking, though my tone was light and my posture lax, my eyes were scanning our surroundings constantly, never still for more than a moment. Some may have called it paranoia, but I called it vigilance— and who could argue with me after my caution proved warranted, after the glint of metal in foliage gave me the hairsbreadth of a warning before we were surrounded.

It was enough time to draw my knife, but the blink of an eye would have been enough time for a Guard of Lothforias— even a banished one— to draw their knife. I unsheathed it with one hand and caught Edda's wrist in the other, pulling her to stand between me and Ruce as our attackers leapt from the bushes. Ruce, at least, wore a dagger on his hip. Edda was entirely unarmed. Once I could see them clearly, I knew there was no reason to fear. Their movements were clumsy, uncoordinated, and showed no training— but outnumbered five to one is never the time to get cocky. Better handle this quickly anyways...

"Drop the blade, boy," one of them spat, her own knife long and undulating and flecked with rust (blood looked much the same once the air dried it, but I had far less faith in her ability to wound an opponent than I did in her poor maintenance habits).

The small kills quietly.

"Please don't hurt me," I stammered out, flinging the knife weakly onto the ground in front of me. Her eyes followed its arc and I took the opportunity to curl my fingers back and drive the palm of my hand into her unprotected nose. I felt it break with a satisfying *crack* as her head snapped back from the force. Using my momentum, I spun, lashing out with my other fist to send our next nearest assailant to the ground.

She hit the dirt with a thud and didn't stir, but the first woman was groaning quietly as she pushed herself to all fours, blood spurting from her nose. I would need to deal with her again before this was over, but I figured I had a minute to play with the others before Broken-Nose was back in the fight.

I shook my hands out and raised them in loose fists to hover just below my chin, turning on the two young men who stood a few feet away from me. They were hesitating, despite the fact that they were armed and I was not. **Smart boys.** As I stood waiting, gravity slipped my left sleeve down a few inches— not enough for my opponents to see the brand I had been covering, but judging from the intake of breath that came from behind me, enough for Ruce and Edda to see it.

"You gonna stand there all day?" I asked with a grin. "Or you gonna come over here and let me hit you?"

That did it. All it took to override their common sense was a touch of anger. The nearest one swung at me and I ducked, feeling the cold air of momentum. Momentum I used to yank him over my shoulder by his tunic, slamming him into the ground with a *whoomph* that stole the breath from his lungs and left him gasping.

The second boy was smart enough to draw his weapon, but not smart enough to scare me. As he came in close with his dirk to swing at me, I caught his wrist cold, stopping him and holding him fast. With my other hand, I slammed the blade from his grip and kicked out his knee, sending him to the ground screaming.

I turned as Broken-Nose staggered to her feet, slamming my palm into her ear in a way that set her head ringing. She spun awkwardly and tripped into the dirt, groaning.

1, 2... 3, 4. Someone else should have tried to kill me.

I turned, looking for the last attacker, but found her sprawled on the ground, dazed and nursing a broken wrist.

"What happened to her?" I asked in surprise.

"You did, obviously," Ruce said with a vague gesture, his arm still wrapped around Edda. "You must have lost count."

"Heat of battle," Edda said with a gentle nod. "Thank you, young man, for saving our lives..."

As I glanced between them with narrowed eyes, the forest went quiet again but for my breathing. Ruce crouched to grab the knife I had discarded, looking up at me curiously as he offered it to me.

"Thank you, father..." I said slowly, my heart racing from the thrill of confrontation but my head spinning because I **knew** I hadn't touched that last attacker. "...We should get moving again if we want to make the capitol before nightfall."

CHAPTER TWO
RUCE

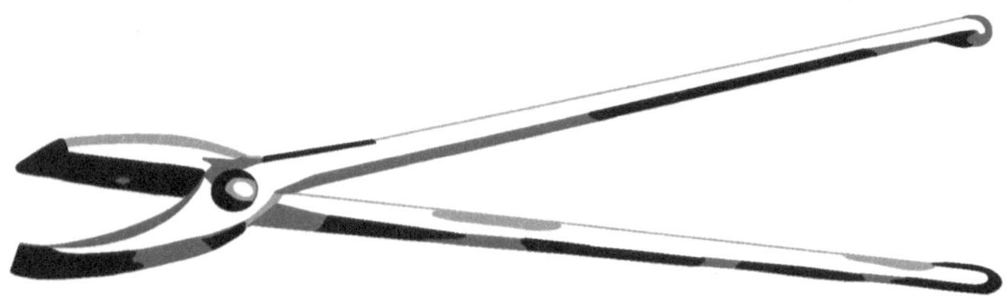

I NOTICED IMMEDIATELY WHEN Edda began to fall behind, each of her strides making up only half of mine or the boy's, and it seems so did he, as he quickly turned to her and held out a hand. "Mother, let me take your pack."

She gave him a tired smile and shook her head. "No, I don't wish to burden you, son. I'll manage."

He stopped in the middle of the road, bowing to her with a dramatic flourish. "On my honour, mother, I cannot allow you to suffer under such a weight."

I scoffed, "Well, you can't dishonour the boy, Edda," and she giggled, allowing him to shift the weight of her pack onto his free shoulder.

We started walking again, passing the time with friendly but surface conversation. Every so often, Edda would look over at me with a furrowed brow before turning back to the trail. After thirty years of marriage, she didn't need to speak for me to know what was going on in her head.

She was thinking of the boy who walked beside us, the brand we had both noticed when he was fighting off our would-be muggers. We may have never travelled to the capitol before, but even in our remote village, one was familiar with the Sentinel of Lothforias, the mark of honour worn by each of the city's trained Guards. That didn't warrant Edda's concern, though— the Guards were heroes, known for their compassion and bravery and devout loyalty to the Goddess of Lothforias. There was no call to be afraid of him. No, her face was drawn tight because the boy beside us could hardly be twenty. Too young to have served in the Guard for eight years, as the lines beneath his Sentinel told us.

It was not long before we came to the main road, the white walls of Lothforias rising up in the distance. The three of us wove our way into the crowd of refugees slowly moving into the city, ambling along at the snail's pace of bureaucracy until we finally caught sight of the gate. Only one of its double doors was open, heavily flanked by Guards with narrowed, calculating eyes that raked over every refugee desperate for shelter before allowing them entrance.

As we got closer, we watched the Guards pull a young man forward, yanking his sleeve up to bare his forearm and turning it over in the light. Satisfied, they released him and let him pass into the city.

The boy beside me, our protector on the road, suddenly tensed at the sight. "No, no, no." He turned and tried to fight his way against the flow of refugees fruitlessly, something caged and desperate in his eyes.

I caught him with a firm grip and put my arm around him, leaning close to whisper, "It's alright."

"They're looking for me," he protested, struggling to flee.

"Keep your head down, walk with a limp."

"What? What are you talking about? Why-"

"Do as I say, boy."

As we reached the front of the line, the nearest Guard peered at us. "What would they call you that know you?"

My wife stepped forward. "I am Edda Lahd, seamster. This is my husband, Ruce, metalworker."

"And- our son, Elin, apprentice," I quickly added.

Edda's eyes flicked over to me as I said the name, startled and hurt. *Dreya*, she looked just like him... our boy. His eyes had looked just as scared that day, as fire licked at the walls of our smithy and smoke stole our breath. I couldn't save Elin... but I was going to protect this boy beside me.

Edda understood almost immediately and looked back at the Guard with a gentle smile. "Our village was destroyed in a raid, our home burned. We come seeking refuge."

Another Guard stepped forward and nodded to 'Elin'. "He could be the right age."

The Guard questioning us nodded and reached out, taking 'Elin' by the arm. At the touch, he winced and cried out very convincingly. The Guard's grip weakened enough for Elin to slip free and Edda quickly put a motherly arm around him.

"What's happened to him?"

"Our son was burned in the fire," I quickly explained, and Elin's eyes flicked up to mine appraisingly, the corner of his mouth ticking up at how quickly I went along with his deception. "He's still healing."

"Apologies," the Guard said gruffly, stepping aside and waving us through. Edda took my hand, keeping her other arm around Elin as we set eyes on the beautiful city of Lothforias for the first time.

CHAPTER THREE

EDDA

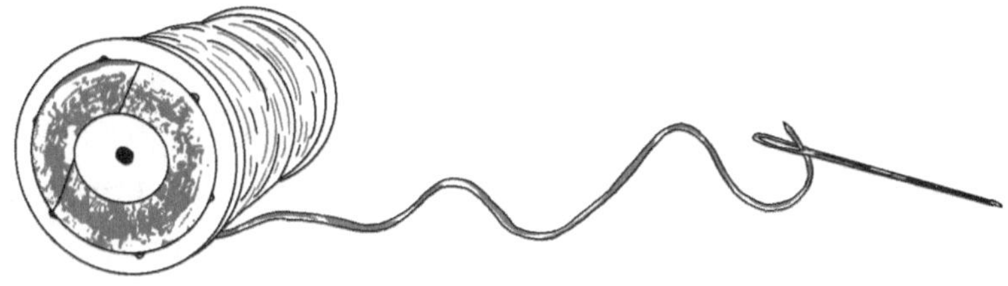

"FOLLOW THE YELLOW MARKERS, mother," the Guard said to me as we passed. "They'll lead you to the cutaway on Mount Sarigh, in the Olive district. It's full of refugees who will help you get settled. Once the sun sets, a Guard will come to take you to the city square. The Captain wishes to address the refugees."

"Thank you, son," I said sweetly, tugging Ruce and 'Elin' along quickly to get away from the Guards with ever-shifting eyes.

The city was a blur of sights, sounds, and smells as we moved through what looked to be a very large market which stretched out over several blocks. As we drifted down the street, I was overwhelmed by the smell of spices coming from a nearby stall. Vendors called out to us as we passed, holding up beautiful jewelleries and fabrics to catch our attention.

"Fresh fruit! Fresh fruit!"

"Authentic Stangrey trinkets! Your children will love them!"

"Spices from the Three Cities! Turmeric, cumin, sumac! Anything your heart desires!"

"This way," the boy said quietly, guiding Ruce and I into a narrow alley. By the time we reached the end of it and came out on another street, the dizziness of the market had faded and we were alone. "Thank you," the boy sighed, glancing between me and Ruce. "I know you didn't have to-"

"Nonsense, sweetheart. You protected us; it's our turn to protect you," I told him.

"I don't know why you've returned," Ruce added, "or why you're hiding... but I trust you have a good reason."

"I don't suppose you'd tell us your *real* name, though," I sighed.

The expression that crossed his face told me I 'don't supposed' right. "Thank you for helping me get into the city," he said finally, "...but it's better for you to stay out of this. Follow this street and it will take you to the Olive district. You'll see-"

"You're not coming with us?"

He faltered in his explanation, turning back to me. "Coming with you?"

"If we let you leave us now, what will you do? Do you have somewhere to go? What if your plans go wrong? Will someone protect you?"

As I asked the questions, I saw panic rising in his throat. "I'll- figure it out; I always do. All I need is to find the Captain... I'll be okay," he promised, turning to leave.

Ruce caught the shoulder of his shirt in a firm hand. "The Captain of the Guard is addressing the refugees in the city centre tonight; at least stay with us until then." The boy was about to refuse, but Ruce pressed. "What if you run into another Guard before you get to him? Will they think twice about throwing you out of the city? Or worse? I don't know what happened, but I know this: if the Guards of Lothforias see you as an enemy, they *don't* show mercy."

I didn't need to ask my husband how he was sure of that; I already knew.

"If things go as planned tonight," Ruce continued, "great. We'll see you on your way, glad to have met you. But if they don't, you're going to need somewhere safe to go. All I'm saying is… our home will be safe to you for as **long** as you need it."

The boy shakily inhaled, his eyes locked onto my husband. "Okay."

"Okay." Ruce let go of him and gestured down the street. "Now, lead the way, 'Elin'."

Elin looked between us with a strange mixture of amusement and gratitude, and then he turned and led us down the street again. We quickly came upon the markers again, following them until the streets became winding and inclined rather than flat city blocks. I glanced back to see the city below us as we moved up the cliffside. We came to a large ledge that stretched and curved around the cliff to where we could no longer see it. Above us, the openings marked with yellow paint, dozens of caves peppered the cliffside. Refugees moved on ladders and steps carved into the rock, weaving in and out of caves with sacks of grain, blankets, pitchers of water. There was one word for the energy here, among hundreds of people from different places bringing different traditions and skills to work together— community.

A nearby Guard caught sight of us and stepped forward, pointing up at a nearby cave. "There is an empty dwelling there for your family, mother. Please make use of the community food stores at the base of the stairs."

"Thank you, daughter." I touched a hand to her shoulder as we moved up the steps and into the cave she directed us to.

Elin ducked inside and I followed him in, my eyes adjusting to the dimness quickly. The dwelling was sparsely but solidly furnished— gifted, like everything else in this place— with three carved rooms going off deeper into the mountain. The main room held a table and chairs, a fireplace, and the makings of a modest kitchen, with a pool of water in the corner fed by a constant trickle through a small section of the ceiling that had been cut away. The room to the left was home to nothing but a clothing chest and a pile of straw for livestock. The bedroom was directly off the back, lit only by a flickering torch. In the right corner, at an angle and moving deeper into the mountainside, was an ice room, for keeping food and medicine cold. It was the only room with a door.

"There are only two beds," I said slowly. Elin brushed past me and set my pack onto the first bed, moving to the side room to tuck his own pack into the corner where straw was piled.

"Oh, Elin, you take a bed," I insisted.

"No— mother, that bed is entirely too comfortable. I'd never fall asleep."

I laughed and nodded, starting to become accustomed to his manner of caring. "Well, I wouldn't want that."

"Elin," Ruce began, "you mentioned that you had family in the city. Would they want to know you had returned?"

Elin turned away, his throat bobbing with emotion. "I'm... not sure. Uh- Besides, the- the walk to the cemetery is long and it'll be dark soon; we need to leave for the city centre shortly."

"I'm sorry, I-"

"So am I."

"What?"

"Was Elin not the son you lost?" he asked, gently but matter-of-fact-ly. "I think we fit together in the way that amuses fate the most— me a son without parents, you parents without a son."

There was nothing left to say after that, and the sun was about to set, so I rose up onto my toes to kiss his forehead and turned to unpack.

When a horn sounded outside, Ruce and I watched as Elin knelt before the pool of water, cupping his hands under the flow. He took a drink, then raised his arms to tip the rest onto his head, drops of water bouncing off of his curls and peppering the shoulders of his cloak. "Faith my reservoir," he murmured to himself.

It was a ritual I had seen before, on the occasions members of the Guard of Lothforias had passed through our village. An offering to the Goddess who had built the city's protective walls.

"That horn was notice to gather in the city centre. A Guard will be coming to bring us there soon."

Elin pushed himself to his feet, turning to lead us out of the dwelling. As I made my way down the steps to the main ledge, he held out a hand to steady me. A crowd quickly formed around the Guard who came up the path, and once we had all emerged from the caves, he led us down the mountain path and into the heart of Lothforias. The sun had just started to set during the trek down the cliff and was kissing the sky an uncertain orange. As we walked, we were surrounded by more and more people as hundreds of us made our way to the square to hear from the Captain of the Guard.

"Are they all refugees?" I murmured to my husband.

Finally, the street in front of us opened up to a sea of people so large it became a thing itself, hands becoming the crests of waves and cheers the sound of water breaking on the rocks. Lanterns were hung from posts and rooftops, bathing the square in a warm light.

"Well, I'll be…" Ruce breathed, gaping at the mass of refugees. There must have been thousands. "Well, I'll be…" he started again, but I never found out **what** he'd be. I don't think he knew either.

Elin, Ruce, and I stopped at the foot of the statue in the centre of the square, a tall woman in a long flowing dress. She had two sets of arms stretching out from her shoulders, the hands of her upper arms cupped in front of her like she was trying to catch rain. The lower arms were down by her sides, holding a hammer and a chisel. The engraving at the base read *Foria Gria.* "Goddess of the Walls." I looked with interest; it had been over thirty years since I'd set foot in a city, and out in the country where Ruce and I had lived, worship wasn't the same. We'd given thanks to the river and the rain, but here, she had a name— Lady *Foria*, in falling and flowing water.

"Elin, if she's a Goddess of water," I murmured to the boy, "why does she look like a stonemason?"

"She is; water is one of the greatest carvers of rock, and she built the city's walls with her own power; pulled them from the earth."

"Oh," I said mildly. "Understandable, then, why she looks so strong. She'd need muscles for that kind of work."

Elin laughed, shaking his head. "I need to get closer if I have any chance of seeing the Captain."

Ruce nodded and we followed the boy past the statue, gently pushing our way through the crowd with the occasional, "'Scuse me," or "Pardon us, folks". When we stopped, we were within spitting distance of the citadel's walls. From the front of the crowd, I could now see three people spaced out on a platform beneath the balcony who were facing us. Interpreters, Elin told me. Interpreting what?

All at once, the square fell silent as the doors of the citadel balcony opened, a dense man with a scar across his face striding out to lean against the railing lit by strong torchlight. Beside me, Elin stopped breathing.

"Welcome," the man said in a booming voice, "to our new citizens. I am Captain of the honoured Guard of Lothforias, Jove Owaines." The three interpreters in front of the crowd began gesturing as he spoke, and some of the people around us had their eyes fixed on the movements, nodding along as though they were following a story. They were deaf, I realised. I had heard about a language spoken with the hands, but living most of my life in our remote village, I had never seen it before. "My Guards and I will keep you safe as you integrate into life in our beautiful city, and we are proud to have you here! I know many of you come to us desperate and looking for a brighter future, and we *will* provide this, if only-"

His eyes passed over us and caught, his voice dying in his throat momentarily. His jaw went slack as he locked eyes with Elin, out of the thousands of people in the square, and Elin stared back boldly.

Jove cleared his throat and smiled. "-If only you do your part to help us keep this city beautiful and prosperous!"

For the rest of his speech, Jove's eyes never came near us again. His entire body was tense, his hands clenched white on the balcony railing as though he had been struck by lightning, and it had been the boy beside me that did that to him.

"For the glory of Lothforias!" Jove shouted, pumping his fist in the air as cheers came up from all over the square.

He turned to leave, stopping to whisper to the Guards that flanked the doorway, subtly pointing in our direction. They stiffened, scanning the crowd and calling down to the Guards in the square below. They began moving through the crowd towards us and hurt and confusion crossed Elin's face as he looked up at the balcony.

I felt his hand on my shoulder. "I'll be home, Mother," he promised.

"Be safe," I pleaded.

And then he was gone.

THE
LIE

CHAPTER FOUR

JOVE

SEVERAL SETS OF FOOTSTEPS echoed in the hall of the citadel as my Guards hurried behind me.

"Captain, we sent men to arrest him, but he vanished onto the roofs," my right said breathlessly. "Lieutenant al Abbas pursued. What do you think he's doing here?"

"Should we tell the king?" my left asked.

"No!" I snapped, hurrying to regain my composure as the two of them startled, stopping in the middle of the corridor to look at me. "This doesn't need to concern His Majesty just yet," I said with a dismissive gesture. "Are we or are we not the Guards of the most powerful city on the continent?"

"We are, Captain Owaines. Apologies."

"It's already forgotten. Now; we have discussed what to do if that traitor should return, yes? Double the Guard around the city centre, enforce a curfew, and find out how he got into the city," I instructed my right. Turning to my left, I said, "Speak to the gate watch; find out if a lone young man was granted refugee status and where they sent him. Then find him and bring him to me— use whatever force is necessary. Do not forget how dangerous he is. He was the best Guard I had ever trained before he tried to murder the king. Understood?"

"Yes, sir!" they chorused boldly, each hammering a fist over their heart in salute as I turned to my study. I looked back to close the doors behind me, making carefully measured eye contact with both of them as I did.

"Do not let me down." I let the slam of the doors punctuate the statement, and then I was alone.

I leaned against the doors heavily, my shaking breath taking years to leave my chest. ***That damned boy is going to ruin everything...***

I spun quickly, my nervous energy turning to electricity as I paced. I'd sent out warnings to the gate watch as soon as I received word that the boy had succeeded in his quest and was returning to the city with the venom of a four-fang serpent.

I should have known better than to send him after the antidote two years ago. I had intended it as a wild goose chase, a suicide mission, but he really was the best student I'd ever had. Of ***course*** he would be one of the only people in the world who could survive the hunt for a four-fang. I'd just wanted to keep him quiet, to get him out of the city, to give him false hope that he could make up for his 'mistake'. I knew if I had just banished him without a purpose to consume him, he would dwell on King Bazzeri's poisoning, and he would eventually come to realise that he was not to blame. And when that happened...

I caught myself rubbing my throat unconsciously and swallowed thickly. I remembered all too well what he was liable to do to someone who threatened the city, and I had no desire to be the blood on the end of his blade. Better, I'd thought, to distract him, to send him off in search of a cure that he could never find.

But here he was, with an antidote to the poison I had risked my life to acquire and slip into the king's wine. He was so close to ruining everything. If he had the chance to speak to any of my Guards... if they realised he wasn't the traitor I claimed, but one of the most brave and devout of their ranks... if he managed to get into the palace and actually give Bazzeri the cure... What if Bazzeri recovered his strength and learned what I had been doing? I would-

No. I shook my head and dispelled my nervous thoughts, anchoring my hands on the desk to stop my pacing. All I had to do was kill the boy. It would take many lives, I knew, to match his skill, but every Guard who died at his hand would merely add to his villainy in the eyes of the city. No, this was good. This could be salvaged.

My eye caught on the painting of *Foria* that towered up behind my desk. In the small, dark room, she almost seemed to be looking down at me sadly— not unlike a mother who'd caught her child in a lie.

"Oh, shut up," I hissed at the canvas.

CHAPTER FIVE

RUCE

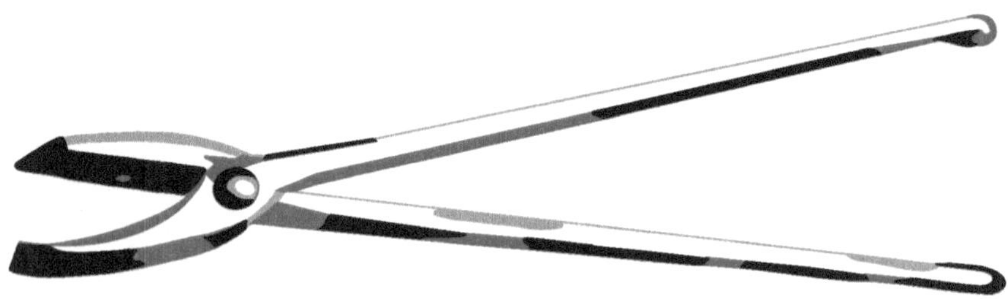

THE DWELLING WAS DARK and silent when we returned. Edda's hand squeezed in mine anxiously as we came upon the cave, and her pace quickened as she ducked through the doorway. Elin had vanished into the crowd at the city square some twenty minutes ago, and my wife's breathing hadn't steadied since.

"He's not here," she murmured to me.

"He will be," I reassured her, rubbing her shoulders gently. "He will be. We should make dinner; I'll start a fire."

I crossed the main room of the dwelling to kneel in front of the hearth, but when I glanced back, Edda hadn't moved.

"*Habi*, I'm sure Elin will be hungry when he gets back."

That stirred her from her daze, and she moved towards me as if pulled by a taut rope connecting her to the task. "Right. Dinner."

After I finished building the fire, we worked side by side at the counter in silence, our kitchen dirks slicing through vegetables from the community stores with a series of heavy *thunks*. I kept glancing up at the opening of the cave, as if Elin would have appeared in the five seconds since I last checked.

The square had been in chaos after that Captain had seen Elin, and there were rumours swimming through the crowd as we were ushered back to our dwellings—the most popular being that someone had made a rude gesture towards the city's Goddess and then fled—but no one had any inkling that Elin was involved. What was that boy into?

Edda dished out three bowls of *cousa* soup and we ate at the table, the tension buzzing in the air between us. "He promised he'd be home," she would tell me on occasion.

"I know, *Habi*."

By the time we finished dinner, Elin still hadn't come home and Edda couldn't quiet her hands, so she took to a seaming project as her foot tapped a frantic beat into the dirt.

Finally, he ducked into the dwelling, and Edda was instantly up and across the room, looking over him tenderly. She brushed his hair back with a quiet intake of breath, seeing a wound on his temple that was sticky with blood. He caught her hand as her fingers shook over his forehead. "I'm fine, Mother."

"Sit," she ordered. "Eat. I'll get a cloth. Ruce?"

He moved to sit at the table, where she had left his portion of food, and I rose to grab a piece of *yoran* root from my pack, deftly breaking it in half. I handed it to Edda, who dipped her cloth into the cool salve hidden inside.

Elin ate silently as she tended to his cut, and when he finished, he pushed himself to stand and kissed her hair. He started towards his room and Edda caught his arm.

"You're going to tell us a story someday, aren't you, Elin?" she implored, struggling to keep her voice steady and passive.

He glanced back. "Someday, Mother," he promised, "but I'm tired."

We were learning that, with Elin, honesty came in trickles, watered down. The boy must have been dead on his feet. Edda stood up on her toes to kiss his forehead and then shooed him off to bed.

She slowly drifted back to sit next to me, her head falling to my shoulder.

"Expensive thoughts, *Habi*?"

"Wondering," she said to me, "what that boy of ours could be caught up in... Wondering how we can help. I don't want him to come home bloody," she sighed. "Whatever this is... I want to protect him from it."

"I don't know that we can, Ed. But at the very least, you have plenty of experience stitching up wounds."

"Yes," she mused, lacing her fingers through mine, "thanks to another boy too brave for his own good. You were always too willing to give me practice."

||

Edda's brows were scrunched in concentration as her shaking hands brought the needle up to my arm. She drew back, pulling a strand of her frizzy hair off of her forehead where it had been stuck with sweat.

"I really don't think I should be doing this," she huffed. "I mean, surely there's a more suitable physician around than a seventeen-year-old girl with no training."

"It's just a cut," I said with a roll of my eyes. "You're too soft."

"You're too rough," she shot back angrily. "Just... hold still."

She moved closer again, but her hand shook violently. I caught it in mine and looked up at her. "Hey. It's alright. Just take a breath and steady yourself."

She looked at me for a long time, then slowly inhaled and exhaled. She scooted closer on the fallen log and grit her teeth, making the first stitch before she could overthink it. I clenched my jaw, holding in any sounds of pain. She was scared enough as it was.

The moment she was finished, she leapt up from the log, moving to the nearby stream and scrubbing her hands raw to remove the blood.

"Are you alright?" I asked as I pulled my shirt back over my head.

"Fine," she sighed shakily. "I just don't like it."

"You should get some rest. I'll take first watch."

Without another word, she moved to her bed roll and wrapped herself up. She was so tired she was asleep the moment her head touched the ground.

I clipped my sword back to its place on my belt, moving to sit against a nearby tree. I settled in and glanced over at Edda's sleeping form, wondering when we'd be able to stop running.

CHAPTER SIX

ELIN

EDDA AND RUCE'S VOICES were a soft, intermingling hum from the other room, muffled by the curtain Edda had hung in the doorway to give me some semblance of privacy. My fingers fumbled at the fasten of my cloak, eventually thumbing the toggle free. The cloak fell from my shoulders to drape over the chest beside my makeshift bed. I groaned as I bent over to unlace my boots, tugging them off clumsily. I finally fell to the straw with a soft rustle, sighing in exhaustion.

Do it, traitor!

I squeezed my eyes shut, rolling onto my side as the dull pain in my head turned into a roar.

||

On our way to the city square that night, I had scanned the streets carefully, reminding myself of every alley and every support tendon. The tendons stretched between the roofs of dwellings and shops, a strong braided wire that anchored the buildings of the city to each other and made them sturdier.

When I fled the square, I immediately ducked into an alley and hauled myself up onto the nearest tendon, knowing most of the Guard were not trained to traverse rooftops. In the dark, and forced to follow the pattern of narrow streets as they were, I lost them quickly— even if I moved clumsily from two years of missed practice. Finally feeling the safety of solitude, I dropped down and started making my way back to the Olive district. I couldn't return to the dwelling yet, not willing to risk discovery, but there were several empty shops I knew I could hide in until the sounds of the city began to lull. Unaware that I was still being followed, I walked down the main streets at a comfortable pace.

She had seen me a few blocks past the city square, tailed me across rooftops, dropped down from a tendon like a ghost and cornered me in the alley behind the *sahlab* shop we used to visit after training.

"It's really you," she breathed. Her face was wavering and uncertain in the torchlight, but I would have known my best friend blind.

"Riadh!" I practically sighed in relief, letting all my defences down as I surged towards her. "I'm so-"

The blow had taken me by surprise; I hadn't even seen the brass stave in her hand until it was cracking across my temple and sending me to the dirt. "How dare you come back here?" she spat. "How dare you set foot in the city after what you did?"

"Ri," I pleaded as blood streamed past my eye, "it was a mistake! One I've spent the past two y-"

"What you did to my father was a **mistake**?! I **trusted** you!" In her anger, she advanced, brandishing the bloody stave. "I will not make that mistake again. Captain Owaines told us why you've returned; I will **not** let you finish your task."

"Riadh, you have to!" I begged her, my head still spinning from the blow. "This is the only way it can all be put right!"

Something changed on her face as she stared down at me. "...You really believe that, don't you?"

"**Yes**. I have dedicated my life to finishing this mission; nothing else matters."

"Very well."

With that, she struck. If something in her tone hadn't unsettled me, my reaction would have come too late, and as it was, I couldn't fully avoid her stave. What should have been a crushing impact still ended up a glancing blow to my ribs, sending waves of pain radiating through my chest. My foot shot out for her knee, destabilising her and giving me the moment's respite I needed to regain my footing.

She was lunging at me again almost immediately and I ducked, using her momentum to push her past me and send her to the ground, but she caught my arm and dragged me with her. We struggled, fighting for her weapon in the dirt, until her stave flew from her hand and bounced off the wall, sliding further away from us. She slammed her elbow into the side of my head, gaining purchase, and fought to pin my arms down with her knees as she reached for the stave.

I took that momentary distraction to knock her off balance and draw my knife, pinning her to the ground and holding the blade to her throat. "Stop!" I ordered. "Stop fighting!"

She stilled at the sensation of cold metal, her eyes darkening. "Do it," she hissed. "Do it, **traitor**."

My brows pinched and I drew back, the knife inching away from her. She swallowed thickly as I gave her space, staring up at me in shock. "I'm not a traitor," I told her. "But I can't have you following me."

I pushed myself to my knees and sliced her thigh open before she could attack me. She screamed in shock and pain.

"It's shallow; put pressure on it and you'll be fine. Don't come after me or you'll bleed out." I staggered to my feet and backed out of the alley as she stared up at me with utter confusion. "I'm sorry, Ri." I turned and sprinted into the fading light.

||

I sighed, laying back in the straw and shifting to get comfortable. Why had she looked at me like that? Did she really think I was a traitor? After **everything** we'd been through together-

I blinked, sitting up. What had Jove told her, for her to look at me with such hatred? When my mistake allowed the king to be poisoned, he had no choice but to banish me— but he had given me a way out. He told me he couldn't be seen to forgive me, even by the other Guards...

told me that unless I could somehow find the antidote and deliver it to him personally, he could not revoke my punishment and the Guard of Lothforias would always keep me from entering the city. I had kept going these past two years knowing that if I could only find the antidote and give it to him, cure the king and save him from the weakness of the poison, I would be forgiven. But this...

He had lied.

He had told them that I tried to kill the king, that I had returned to-

I will not **let you finish your task.**

Riadh thought I had come back to the city to kill her father, not to save him. Nothing else could explain her anger towards me, her willingness to cut me down.

I weakly lifted my hand to the reassuring coolness of the vial that hung from the cord on my neck. For two years, I had thought of little else but the venom I now held in my hand. So many sleepless nights in the desert trying to figure out how I had messed up, so many blistering days risking my life trying to figure out how to make up for it... And my entire plan had hinged on him— on the man who had raised me and trained me and treated me like a son— taking me in his arms and telling me I was forgiven. I had known something was wrong, in the square, when no one else had recognised me and he sounded the alarm anyways, but I had tried to convince myself that he was just playing the part... making sure that, if anyone else had noticed me, he still appeared to be upholding the laws of the city. What else would I have thought? I trusted him.

And he had **lied**. He'd branded me as a traitor, an attempted murderer. Didn't he want the king cured? Didn't-

...Didn't he?

CHAPTER SEVEN

RIADH

I GRITTED MY TEETH as the needle worked, careful hands sewing up the gash on my thigh. I had torn a strip of fabric from my clothes and tied it above the wound to stem the bloodflow and limped my way back to the citadel.

"Lieutenant al Abbas," Captain Owaines said as he entered the room. "I take it from your injuries that you found him?"

"And lost him," I spat angrily. "All I know is he went south from the *sahlab* shop."

"Which could have been a misdirect, you know how he is. We're lucky you weren't more badly hurt. There's no telling what that boy will do... When you've recovered some, I need you to meet with the emissary from Stangauer. I don't want them hearing about our... trouble, so I need you to distract them. I'd do it myself, but-"

"'I can't stand that Djanson,'" I said in unison with him, making my voice gruff and deep. He cut himself off as I continued. "'I don't trust him as far as I can throw him.'"

He gave a short laugh. "I'm that predictable, am I?"

"When it comes to diplomatic meetings? Yes."

"I've sent Guards to establish a curfew and search the city for the boy. I'll let you know what turns up. Remember— Stangauer isn't to know he's returned."

"Yes, Captain," I nodded as he started out of the room. "Are you done?" I asked the healer that knelt before me, glancing down at my leg.

She nodded. "Almost, Lieutenant. You should be careful, though, for a few weeks. Too much strain will pull your stitches."

I looked down at the sutured wound in distaste. It would slow me down, keep me from joining the search for my **old friend**.

My eyes fell to the section of my shirt I'd torn off to make a tourniquet. He owed me a new *kara*— though that was the **least** of what he owed me, after his betrayal.

I stood, changing into the new clothing that had been brought for me, and started down the corridor towards the meeting room. When I entered, I did my best to hide my limp, so the emissary would not know something was wrong.

Tor was waiting for me on the verandah that overlooked the harbour. He was a parrot of a man and looked right at home against the colourful backdrop of the harbour market.

"Tor!" I beamed as I caught sight of him. I was, actually, somewhat happy to see him. As overwhelming and performative as his personality could be, he had been a great help over the years and, if not a friend, I at least considered him an ally.

"Riadh," he smiled back, embracing me. "Can I assume I've been summoned to discuss the disturbance during your Captain's speech last night?"

"Yes, unfortunately this meeting isn't just to catch up and drink tea."

"There will be tea, though?" he interrupted conspiratorially, giving a charming laugh.

"Of course, Tor. I'll take any excuse I can to steal some tea. Please, sit. There's no need to get business over so quickly that we can't chat, is there?"

"Absolutely not," he said as he joined me at the table. A servant stepped into the room behind me with a tea tray and set it before us, serving up two steaming cups.

I sipped my tea with a controlled expression, having become accustomed enough to the bitter taste after years of diplomatic meetings with Tor Djanson. He, like most Stangreys, loved his tea. I, like most Lothforians, did not— but it was a bridge I could cross to respect his culture and gain his support.

"I strolled through the marketplace a few days ago," he told me as he rested a hand on my arm. "The repairs went so swimmingly you can't even tell what happened there. It looks more beautiful than ever."

"It does. Our people are so grateful for the help you provided during reconstruction. It's done wonders for morale and commerce."

"When Lothforias succeeds, we both succeed. We're a team in this, doll. Now— our tea is ready, I'm ready; tell me about the incident in the square last night. Was it scandalous?"

"Oh, **such** disrespect," I lied, doing my best to match his gossiping tone. "A foreigner— Lithdreyan, though I'm sure you'd guess— made **such** a rude gesture towards Lady *Foria's* statue in the middle of Captain Owaines's speech. He led our Guards on a **wild** chase through the city before we finally caught and expelled him."

"Those Lithdreyans," he scoffed. "Such a lack of tact. You know, I've heard rumours, doll, that they may be behind your... troubles."

I looked up at him with a measuring gaze. "We've found no proof of that, but I wouldn't put it past them. You know how long there's been bad blood between our two nations. The last confirmed attack was on the city of Cessiri almost forty years ago, but you know they didn't just stop. You'll... keep me apprised of the rumours?" I asked, laying a hand over his arm.

"Of course, doll. As long as you bring the tea."

I laughed. "Thank you, Tor. Well, I don't want to keep you from your duties; I know you're due back to report to your king any day now."

"I leave in the morning, yes. But I'll see what our informants can dig up, and when I return next month, we'll chat again."

"Always great to see you, Tor."

"Likewise," he said as he pressed a kiss to both my cheeks. *"Ha det."*

"You too."

He bowed and exited the room, and the moment the door swung shut, I dumped the rest of my tea into the potted plant next to me.

"Drink up, kid."

I strode out of the room, letting the empty-headed smile fall from my face as I rounded the corner. Something fruitful **had** come from that meeting, as unexpected as that was. I'd had my suspicions that Lithdreya might be behind the attacks, but to hear similar thoughts from an outside source... This was something I could take to Captain Owaines.

Chapter Eight

Edda

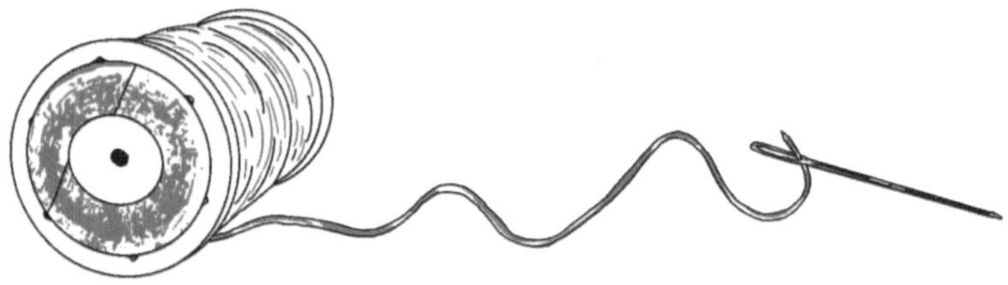

"Elin," I called, "breakfast! Anyone of able body has been asked to aid in the harvest for the next three weeks! The Guard will be up soon to fetch us."

"Coming, Mother!"

He ducked between the curtain that separated his room from the main, smiling at me as he laced up his sleeves.

"Good morning."

"Good morning, Elin. You'll let me check your forehead before we leave."

"Yes, Mother." He moved next to me and started slicing the bread I'd set out on the counter. "Is Father well?"

"Fine, and he'll **get moving if he knows what's good for him**!" I called into the bedroom.

"I'm coming, woman," he huffed.

"What was that?"

"I love you."

"That's what I thought I heard," I said with a smile as he ambled out into the kitchen, pressing a tired kiss into my hair. "Grab the cinnamon," I asked.

"Grab it yourself, crank."

I poked him in the ribs and he laughed, reaching up to the shelf above my head to get the small glass jar I needed. Elin grinned beside me as he watched the exchange in his periphery.

I reached for the cinnamon and Ruce pulled it back past my arm's-length. "*Kahve*," he said simply.

I crouched down to the shelves under the counter and grabbed the bag of *kahve* beans, holding it out to him. He warily reached for it, never breaking eye contact with me, then suddenly snatched it and pushed the cinnamon into my hand as if we were engaged in a tense hostage exchange.

"Thank you, *Habi*," he said mildly as he turned to the table.

CHAPTER NINE

EDDA

THE GUARD LED US down the cliff at a gentle pace, the sun just peeking over the horizon as we started our descent. Ruce was yawning loudly beside me, still waiting for the effects of his *kahve* to grant him a divine burst of energy.

"Elin," Edda said to me quietly, "you're from the capitol. What is the harvest?"

"The city has many crops, but we've arrived during the fall harvest season, so we'll likely be helping with its most famous— golden apples, olives, pomegranates, and goddess grapes."

"Goddess grapes?"

"Pure white grapes that taste of lemon and sparkling wine. It's said that *Nora Gria*, the Goddess of the stars who guides travellers at night, let drops of starlight fall from the heavens. Wherever they fell, grapes began to grow that taste like no others, and can survive the harshest deserts."

I gestured to the ground below us as we worked our way down the side of the mountain, drawing Edda's attention to the fields that stretched on to the horizon, a dark, striking green against the desert soil. Even from a distance, we could see the wide variety of crops sectioned off into plots creating a mottled sense of green.

As we grew closer, the smell of fresh fruit overwhelmed me and reminded me of my father's rough hands and cheerful voice as he sang and worked the land. He was never too quick-witted, and never ashamed to admit it, but his hands were steady and sure and he knew how to care for the apple trees and protect them from greenflies. My brother and sisters and I would walk barefoot with him through our small field as he taught us how to tend to the trees— barefoot because that was the best way to feel when the soil was too wet or too dry. "The trees don't wear shoes," he would tell us, "so why should we? In order to care for the trees, we need to feel what they feel." He'd scoop the littlest of us up onto his shoulders to help us pick the apples, taking our tiny hands in his to show us his tricks.

"Elin," Edda asked, setting a hand on my shoulder, "are you alright?"

I quickly wiped my eyes, smiling back at her. "Fine, yes. The wind just blew some sand into my eyes."

CHAPTER TEN
RUCE

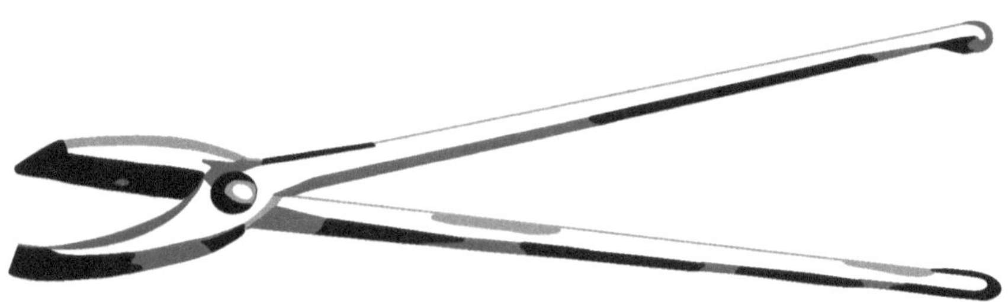

I HAD WORKED THE land before, with my grandfather when I was a boy, but it had been many years and my hands were clumsy on the apples, squeezing too tight and bruising the delicate fruit that smelled like something out of a fairytale. Elin quickly came over and reached his hand up to cover mine, showing me how to twist my fingers around the fruit to catch it right, how much pressure to break it from the branch without damaging the tree.

He'd shed his shoes almost immediately, walking deftly around the orchard barefoot, ducking under branches with a smile that made the morning that much warmer. In moments like this, he really did look like the son we had lost... his dimples and the set of his shoulders and his tanned skin from working under the sun. If it weren't for his honeyed curls, I might've been convinced that he had always been our son.

"We need to colour his hair."

"What?" Edda asked, straightening her back and wiping sweat from her forehead as she looked up at me.

"You and I have dark hair— well, you more than me now— and his is much lighter. If people start looking for him, they might question it."

She nodded. "I'll darken it later."

"Hm? What are you doing to my hair?" Elin asked from a ladder a few trees away.

"Cutting it all off of your head."

"Pity," he said mildly. "I rather like my hair."

CHAPTER ELEVEN

EDDA

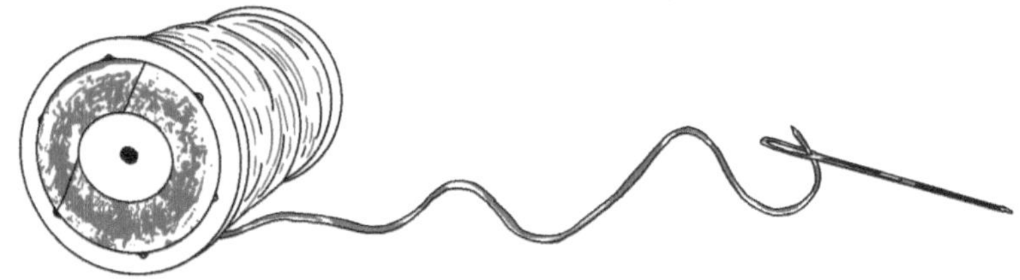

I WIPED MY HAIR back from my forehead with a huff, the heat and sweat making my curls more wild than usual.

"Alright, Mother?" Elin asked, holding a hand down to me. "Do you need help?"

"Thank you." I let him help me up the steps that were carved into the rocky hill, reaching the dip in the stream where fresh, cool water flowed past us. The other workers all took their turns to sip from their cupped hands, sighing contently. We had all started the day with full waterskins, but after hours under the hot sun, if they weren't dry, they tasted of nothing but leather— and sometimes, thirst was preferable.

Ruce offered an arm to steady me as I joined him beside the stream to drink, but I glanced up at Elin. "Are you not thirsty?"

"I'm fine, Mother," he answered, his voice slightly scratchy from dehydration. Thirsty, then, but not drinking. Instead, he crossed his arms and turned to scan the horizon, watching over us as we slaked our own thirst.

As I lifted handfuls of cool water to my lips, I remembered Elin's ritual, water spilling over his curls a small offering to the Goddess of the walls. I looked around at the other workers crouched over the stream. Some were refugees, but not all— some had lived their entire lives in this very city, but not one of them practised the same ritual. It was then that I realised why Elin refused to drink. Only a Guard of Lothforias worshipped in that way, and Elin would not expose himself like that; nor would he forget the ritual and let himself drink from the stream.

On the pedestal in the square, I had seen the phrase, "of flowing and falling water". This was *Foria Gria*'s domain. Elin would not drink from a stream or a fall without his ritual.

Once I had finished drinking, I unstoppered my waterskin and, dumping the dregs of leather-water from the bottom, dipped it into the stream. The cool water rushed over my hands, swelling the waterskin until it was full once more. I sealed it again and held a hand up behind me blindly for aid. There was a clumsy bumping of hands as Ruce and Elin both moved to help me to my feet.

"Thank you, boys." As our little crowd finished drinking, we began to amble back towards the city. "Elin," I sighed, "could you carry this for me? Now that it's full, it's too heavy."

I held out my waterskin and he looked up at me, the corner of his mouth ticking up. He took the strap over his shoulder and brought up the rear of the party. Moments later, I heard the quiet squeak of the waterskin unstoppering.

||

"Where are we going?" I asked Elin, who had ducked down for me to whisper in his ear after I touched his arm in question.

"Public baths, Mother. There are several around the city."

"Public?" I asked askance.

"There are separate sections for men and women, don't worry."

"Oh."

"Many people take the time to socialise at the end of the workday. And after working out in the hot sun, the cool water is a welcome reprieve."

"What if you're... uncomfortable undressing in a crowd?" I asked in concern, glancing at Ruce.

"There are a few smaller rooms at the back of each section, for those who need privacy. Washerwomen, for example, choose to preserve their modesty for religious reasons, and some veteran soldiers who don't want war wounds on display."

We followed the crowd to the inner-city, finally stopping at a wide building with windows all along the top of the walls. I could hear friendly voices echoing off the tiles inside as people laughed and chatted about their days.

Elin led us inside to a room that spanned the width of the building. People were milling about, saying hellos and goodbyes, before splitting off through the two separate doorways.

"Mother, you'll go into that room," Elin told me. "We'll meet you out here when we're done."

I ducked into the room, finding a long pool with steps down every few feet. The room was beautiful, with tiled mosaics creating lush vegetation and goddesses all along the wall.

"I recognise you," a voice said from my left. I turned and saw a woman with coiled brown hair undressing. She stood next to a row of shelves, where she neatly folded each article of clothing as she removed it. "You moved into a dwelling on the Sarigh cutaway just the other day, yes?"

"Yes. I'm Edda," I said, reaching out to shake her hand. I moved to a nearby shelf and shucked off my dress.

"Basma. Anything you need, let me know. I've been living up on the cutaway for a few years and I've got the run of the place."

Together, we stepped down into the pool and I sighed in relief at the cool waters. "I must say, the city has been a bit disorienting. There's... so much life here, you know? And the idea of a public bath-"

"You came from a small village, did you?" she laughed gently. "Not used to the hustle and bustle?"

"No," I said frankly. "The city is beautiful, though. So many colours and people. I think I'm going to like it here."

"I'm certain you are, and I know having a community will help. The cutaway is a very close-knit group. We have meals together, parties, shared rest days... You should come, get to know everyone— and bring your family. We'll be happy to have you."

"Thank you; I'll take you up on that."

"You've been helping with the harvest?" she asked. "I myself work for the harbourmaster hauling fish," she sighed as she leaned back further into the water. "You'll find your place in the city fast enough." She flexed her hand and my eyes were drawn to the fish-hook scars on her knuckles. "There's something for everyone."

"Where did you live, before you became a refugee?"

"I was actually born in Lithdreya, but spent my childhood in the city of Cessiri," she sighed, "so I've been a refugee most of my life." My stomach dropped as images of fire and violence washed over me. "I was only five when the city fell, so I don't remember the attack, but I know nowhere really felt like home until I made my way here a few years ago."

"I... I understand the feeling."

Chapter Twelve

Elin

"ELIN, AREN'T YOU EXHAUSTED?" Edda sighed, glancing up from the table at me. "You've been working all day."

I paused, letting my sword fall but catching it before the tip hit the dirt. When we'd gotten back to the dwelling, I had ducked into the ice room, where my sword was hidden behind the door, and started drilling. "I haven't been working with my sword. I need to keep myself sharp, Mother."

"Then you should stop letting your elbow drop," Ruce grunted over the rim of his icemilk.

"Pardon?" I straightened and turned to look at him.

"You have a bad habit of dropping your elbow before you strike. It's a rookie mistake."

"I've been training with a sword for ten years," I scoffed.

"Yes, and over the past two years while you've been roaming... what, the *Denuda* Wastes, judging by the red dirt on your boots— fighting desert dwellers and thieves, I'm sure your sword was a bit too conspicuous, so you took to knives. But the moment you come up against a competent swordsperson, they'll leave you bleeding in the dirt."

I went to speak but stopped, slowly nodding. "You're right. I... I haven't used my sword in far too long, and I didn't notice, but if-" *If I went up against Riadh again...* "It could have gotten me killed." I started to turn away, but my brows furrowed of their own volition and I looked back up at him. "What kind of metalworker are you?"

"A tired one," he said in a friendly, unhelpful manner. "Goodnight, Elin."

"G- Goodnight," I said quietly as I watched him leave.

"His hair, Ed," Ruce called back.

"I'm going," she sighed, looking up at me with tired eyes. "Elin, carry me to the counter so I can darken your hair."

I laughed, resheathing my sword and tucking it into its spot inside the ice room, and moved to the small kitchen counter in the main room. Edda rose from her chair with a groan and joined me by the counter. "Grab the *kahve*; if I bend over, I'm not getting back up."

She quickly brewed a potent cup of *kahve*, heaping a few extra scoops of grounds and some powdered walnut into it when she had finished, and gestured for me to join her at the table. From the gifted hodgepodge of dining table chairs, she chose one with a low back and turned it so it rested against the table, setting a bowl behind it. At her direction, I sat down and tipped my head back to rest in the bowl. She mixed a piece of ice into the *kahve* and moved over to me, slowly pouring it into the bowl. The ice had cooled it enough that the heat was merely comforting, not scalding.

"How long do I have to sit here?" I asked Edda.

"Until you smell better," she joked sweetly, moving out of my field of vision— which was limited by the fact that my head was tilted up towards the ceiling.

"Mother?" I asked again.

"The answer will just upset you, Elin. Sit there until I come to rinse it out of your hair."

"Why do you get to seam while I'm stuck with my head in a bowl?"

"Because I'm not a fugitive, *hayati*."

"Hmph." I crossed my arms, adjusting how I was sitting to get more comfortable in the chair.

"I think, dear Elin, this is the first time you've actually looked like a child since I met you. Who knew you could pout?"

"I'm not pouting," I shot back, uncrossing my arms. "I'm... I'm-"

"Pouting."

I huffed, letting my eyes fall closed, and listened to the fire crackle in the hearth. I swear it was only seconds later when Edda touched my shoulder and shook me gently, but the *kahve* had lost much of its heat.

"Time already?"

"Already," she murmured. "Come let me rinse it out."

Compared with the warmth of the *kahve*, the water in the pool was startlingly cold as it seeped into my hair. Edda sat beside me, humming softly as she ran her fingers through my wet hair. I imagined the ever-expanding halo of dark brown that flowed from my hair into the pool as she worked. It was comforting, her hands and her voice... familiar.

"My hair used to tangle into the worst knots," I told her, "and my mother would sit me in her lap and sing to me while she worked them out."

"My boy," she smiled, "liked to explore the forest... would come home with all manner of sticks and bugs and leaves wrapped up in his curls. It would take ages to pull them all out... But he would always bring me something back; berries and flowers, and-" her voice caught for a second as she touched the pendant she wore. It was a smooth river stone with a hole through it, and it had been strung onto a flax rope. "He made it for me, when he was five..."

"When did you lose him?"

"Oh... hardly a month ago. Sometimes, it takes me a minute to remember that- that he's not going to walk through the door."

"I'm sorry... I hope you always remember his voice."

"Oh, I remember every breath he's ever taken. Let me get you some linen to dry your hair, *hayati*."

CHAPTER THIRTEEN

RUCE

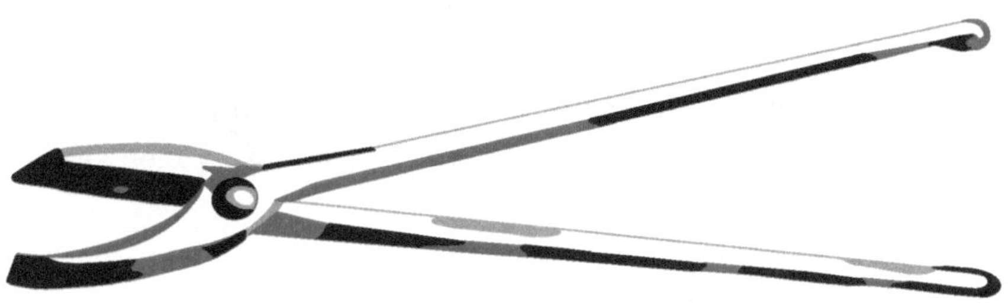

"Ed," I called, "if the Guards arrest you for lazing about, I won't wait for you."

There was quiet grumbling and something that sounded a lot like cursing from the bedroom and soon, Edda appeared in the doorway, rubbing her eyes as she glared at me without feeling. "We both know they couldn't hold me," she shot back. Her curls were wild and frizzy and impossibly high off her head from violent sleep— violent, I knew, because she had kicked me thrice in the night.

She stubbed her toe against the counter and swore under her breath, her hair flying wildly as she caught herself from falling. I smiled over at her. **Absolutely beautiful.**

"What's baking? Smells amazing."

"*Ka'aq,*" Elin told her, glancing up from the hearth. "Flatbread filled with white-brine cheese and covered in sesame seeds. It's a favourite in the city; my older sister learned to make it from a street vendor she was engaged to."

He gingerly lifted it from the cooking stone with a cloth and brought it to the table, setting it on a plate.

"How long have you been awake, Elin?" Edda asked. "This must have taken ages."

He gave a one-shouldered shrug as he cut into the bread, setting out portions for each of us. I turned to let Edda handle his sleep habits and grabbed the bag of *kahve* from the counter. I froze as I lifted it, peering down in to see that there was barely any left.

"Where did all of the *kahve* go?!" I asked incredulously, glancing at my family.

Edda's eyes slowly shifted to Elin and I followed her gaze, finally taking the time to consider how much his hair had darkened since the night before.

"No," I murmured in a voice filled with grief.

"Ruce, I'm sorry, but-"

"Don't talk to me."

"Ruce-"

"It's fine," I said ambivalently, setting my lips into a pout as I slowly drifted to sit at the table with them. "This bread had better be delicious," I informed the boy next to me, "or I'm putting you up for auction."

"We can get more *kahve* at the market, Father," he informed me gently.

"I know, but I don't want to be nice yet. I'll get over it soon."

"How soon?"

I considered. "Fifteen minutes."

"That's much quicker than usual," Edda grinned. "He must really like you, Elin— when I finish his *kahve* it takes at least half an hour for him to forgive the betrayal."

CHAPTER FOURTEEN

RIADH

I TIPPED THE WATER into my hair as I felt my thirst ease, looking up to the clear blue sky. Clear, but hiding something— my instincts told me it was going to rain.

I pushed myself to my feet, stepping back from the fountain. "Faith my reservoir," I murmured to myself.

This temple had become one of my only safe spaces, after the betrayal... A place I could come to remind myself that the Goddess was still with us; that good could still find me.

Around me was the buzz of quiet conversation as Guards talked together, strolling through the courtyard while a gentle breeze moved through their ranks. I had mixed feelings about the crowd. I was never alone here, but I was never alone here. Usually, I was grateful that I could worship the Goddess in the company of the other Guards, but right now... I hated people. I wanted nothing more than to be so alone that I could scream without disturbing anyone.

Much of my frustration was due to the limp I still walked with, but the effect of the crutch I was forced to use shouldn't be discounted either. I had been confined to the palace after taking a certain... shortcut... caused me to pull my stitches. The short walk from my quarters to the temple in the palace courtyard was the only thing keeping me from going insane.

I caught sight of Hakim entering the temple and waved, catching his attention. He altered his course to join me by the fountain, taking a drink and spilling the rest of the water in his hair before speaking. "How can I serve, Lieutenant al Abbas?"

"You've been put in charge of taking census, yes, Corporal?"

"I have."

"Report on the Lithdreyans in the city."

"We've had some difficulty tracking, with the flood of refugees seeking protection over the last few weeks, Lieutenant. Officially, five Lithdreyans have moved into the city, with roughly thirty others coming in on day passes before returning to the desert. The problem is, we only know about the people who came through on days when the gates were open to Lithdreyans, only the people who declared themselves. Since the attacks around the nation started, we haven't been able to keep track of the people coming in. We can't ask the same questions to verify identity or we'll have people clustered outside the city for days."

"I see."

"I'm sorry, Lieutenant, is there something you're looking for?"

I realised I was clenching my fists and released a breath. "No, just... I was curious. Think nothing of it. Have you seen Captain Owaines?"

"In the temple?" he asked. "Not in years; I think he had a meeting in the citadel, though."

"Thank you."

I started out of the temple as quickly as I could manage, beelining for the nearest corridor that connected the palace to the citadel. I made my way down the stairs, grimacing at the pain that went through my leg.

"Captain Owaines!" I called as I entered the hall of craftsmages, catching sight of him talking with a woodcarver nearby.

"Lieutenant al Abbas..." he said cordially, "you're supposed to be resting."

"When we have assassins and killers loose in the city? I don't think so."

"You have news?" He followed me further away from the craftsmage to give our conversation some privacy.

"Only suspicions, Captain, but the emissary from Stangauer has heard rumours. He told me that radical Lithdreyans are responsible for the attacks. And the Guard at the gate has been overwhelmed; there is a chance Lithdreyans slipped through."

"Rumours. Chances. Riadh... this city has managed to avoid the attention of the *Menagerie* thus far. If-"

"Unless we haven't! You don't-"

"If we were to blame Lithdreya for our troubles without evidence-"

"That's not what I'm suggesting, but it's worth investigating. Don't you agree?"

"Your father has rejected war with Lithdreya, and we can't spend resources investigating our citizens and risk weakening our defences. That **will** draw attention. We must show strength."

He started deeper into the hall of craftsmages and I followed him urgently. "Captain-"

"Hey, what are you doing?!"

I turned to the panicked voice, but before I could process what was happening, I was thrown back by a sudden and violent force. I was sent sprawling as the citadel shook and rumbled in the wake of a huge sound. Sections of the floor gave way, pieces of the ceiling crashing to the ground. Within moments, I was blinded by the thick dust filtering through the air.

I coughed violently, clearing my throat as I pushed myself to stand.

"Captain? Captain!"

CHAPTER FIFTEEN

ELIN

EDDA HANDED HER NEWLY filled waterskin up to me so I could take a drink, then cupped her hands into the stream and took a long sip.

We had spent the day working the olive trees, trying to stay under their branches as often as possible to hide from the punishing sun. My throat was so dry I could hardly clear it to speak by the end of the shift, so I was grateful for the water. The thirst reminded me of my time searching for the four-fang in the Lithdreyan desert, so I was quick to quench it.

Edda stood, turning to me. "Now that I know you cook... We should make dinner together tonight. Hm? Something fun?"

"Could we use these?" I asked, tipping the opening of my satchel towards her to reveal several glistening pomegranates, apples, olives, and clusters of grapes.

"How did you- We never left the olive orchards today. You-"

"I have my ways," I said with a smile. "Have you ever tried pome-granates?" I murmured to her.

She glanced side-to-side and then shook her head, grinning at me like a little kid. "Oh, I can't wait, Elin. Tonight, we'll feast like kings!"

I couldn't keep the smile from dying on my face and she saw, stepping forward and touching my arm. "Elin-"

"I'm fine. I-"

I staggered forward as the ground suddenly shook, a boom echoing from the centre of the city. For several moments, it felt like the world was collapsing. Ruce dove for Edda and me, pulling us to the ground and sheltering us in his arms. All we could hear was earth moving and people crying out.

Then the ground went still and slowly, gently, as we pushed ourselves to stand, stone dust began to filter through the air from the citadel.

"Was it an earthquake?" someone asked.

"No," I answered instantly. "It was an explosion."

Edda and Ruce looked up at me in shock.

"The city was attacked."

CHAPTER SIXTEEN

EDDA

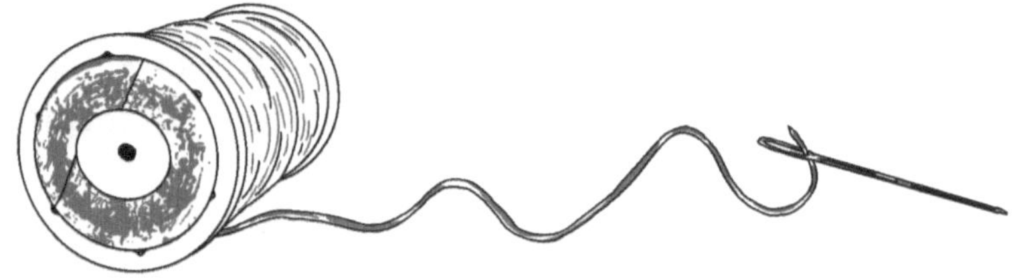

"PLEASE STAY IN YOUR dwellings for the night," the young Guard told us as he tried to hide the panic in his voice. "We will return in the morning with news and instructions. I know that you must be scared, but we **will** keep you safe. Please help us to do that."

I turned towards our dwelling to realise that Elin was already gone. He hadn't said another word after the explosion, his face ashen and distant.

Ruce took my hand and led me inside. He only locked eyes with me for a moment, but I could read him perfectly. **What has that boy gone through?**

Elin's satchel had been dropped onto the table, the fruit he had been so excited about only a little while ago treated carelessly, absentminded-ly.

As we moved further into the house, I caught glimpses of Elin in the ice room, his sword flashing violently in the light. He had drilled last night, of course, but there was now an intensity to his movements that wasn't there before. He seemed almost possessed by something now. Ruce glanced over at me again but said nothing, simply picked up a slightly-bruised pomegranate and began to cut into it so he could start on supper.

I moved to stand next to him, purposefully angling myself so the ice room was out of view— as if not being able to see Elin would keep me from worrying— and slowly, side-by-side, Ruce and I fell into a clumsy rhythm.

I jumped at a loud clang from the ice room, the apple in my hand almost slipping from my grip. And that was when Elin started to sob.

CHAPTER SEVENTEEN

ELIN

I WAS TEN, THE first time it happened.

Every day, I worked the fields with my father and my siblings, and every night, I dreamed about protecting the city like the brave Guards I saw when we went to the market. In my free time after dinner, I would cut branches to shape and pretend they were swords, waiting for my birthday to come so I would finally be old enough to join the Guard.

The day I turned ten, my parents looked at me differently, like they knew what I was planning— even though I'd never been brave enough to tell them what I wanted. But they didn't say anything either.

Every year, on the Day of Pledging, the city would gather together to watch citizens devote themselves to the Guard of Lothforias. Anyone over the age of ten was allowed to make the pledge, but very rarely did anyone under sixteen choose to do so.

The night before the Pledging, my father called my name quietly, asking if I was awake, before he came into the curtained-off room where I laid down every night.

He called to me again, but I was too scared to answer. Once, when I was much younger, I had told my father how amazing and brave I thought the Guards were. My father never raised his voice, but he shouted at me then that I was a fool, that to fight and kill was not an honourable thing, that the way to put good into the world was through mundane magic like he did. He pleaded with me then, to find anything else. If I were not happy being a farmer, to seek an apprenticeship with any of the craftsmages in the city— smithing, carving, singing, anything but fighting.

I knew what he would say to me that night, that he would try and convince me to stay... So I pretended to be sleeping, and he pretended to believe me.

In the morning, we ate and dressed silently, and when it came time to leave for the Pledging, my mother had to coax my father to stand and leave the house. With that look in his eyes... I don't know if he would have gotten up at all otherwise. He might have sat at the table for the entire day, the sun slowly twisting the shadows all around him until he sat there in the dark.

When the entire city had gathered in the square, the Captain of the Guard stepped out onto the balcony beside her husband, the king, smiling down at us all.

She began gesturing passionately, signing to the crowd below.

"We are here today," the king translated, "to bear witness to the bravery of our faithful Guards, and to invite any who wish to join their ranks to pledge themselves to the service of Lady *Foria* and her city. Any of you who share this desire, step forward."

One by one, several grownups and teenagers made their way through the crowd to the raised dais beneath the balcony. From it rose up a small spring of fresh water, and as each person stepped up, they took a sip from cupped hands, lifting the rest to spill over their hair and shoulders.

I moved to join them and felt my father's clawed hand digging into my shoulder.

I looked back at him, my brow furrowing in anger, and he seemed to come back to himself, slowly prying his fingers from my shoulder to let me go, though he looked at me like he would never see me again.

I brushed past the crowd of onlookers, finally reaching the dais. A Guard looked at me in shock before offering me his hand to step up. A ripple of voices moved through the crowd as I knelt before the spring, the startlingly cold water running over my hands before I took a sip and let the rest fall into my curls. I didn't need to look up at the archway that led into the citadel; I had long since memorised the engraved words. "Faith our reservoir..." I murmured.

As I stood and joined the Pledged, the Guard at the dais called out, "Does anyone else wish to pledge their service?"

"I do," came a hard voice from behind him. I turned to see Princess Riadh stepping into the square, her chin held high as she made her way up to the dais. She was only a few months older than me. I looked up at the balcony, searching the faces of her parents for the horror I had seen on my father's... but both the Captain and the king were looking down at her with pride.

After making her pledge, she came to stand beside me as the square filled with cheers for those of us who had joined the City Guard.

As we were ushered from the square by the Guard at the dais, I caught sight of my father's face in the crowd one last time. Grief. My shoulders hunched against their will.

The Guard moved to walk beside me and Princess Riadh, glancing down at us both. "It's been a while since we had anyone so young take the pledge, but I can see that the two of you already know what you're meant to do with your lives. It's customary for an Instructor to handle initial training... but I'd like to make an exception for the two of you and oversee your training myself."

"You're-"

"Lieutenant Jove Owaines," he said as he held out a hand to me. "Pleasure."

After that, the days blurred together as Riadh and I were taken under his wing, given special instruction. It had only been three months before I won my first match against a Guard of fifteen years, and Riadh was right beside me. She had a cold, hard shell, but as we trained together, she slowly began to let me through her defences. The Day of Visiting was quickly approaching, and she made me promise to introduce her to my family during the festival.

I was nervous to see them after leaving the way I did, but every night before I fell asleep, I rehearsed in my head what I wanted to say to my father. I wanted to tell him that I hadn't been angry, I just didn't want to see him disappointed in me. I wanted to tell him that I had learned so much about how to fight, and I wasn't going to be a monster, I was going to be a protector. I wanted to tell him that I had been handpicked by Lieutenant Jove Owaines himself, and that he believed I would one day be Captain of the Guard. I wanted to tell him that there was a way to fight— and kill— with honour.

I wanted to tell him so many things… but then it happened.

I was with the other Guards who had been assigned to the city square, helping to prepare for the festival that would start in less than three hours. Riadh was meant to be helping too, but had instead been amusing herself by seeing how many hook flowers she could sneak into my hair without me noticing. She had reached nineteen before the ground suddenly shook and sent us sprawling.

From all around us, several large booms echoed across the city, sending dust and debris flying into the air. I watched heavy plumes of smoke rise up from the outer parts of the city, including the farmland.

"My family," I breathed, and then I was sprinting through the streets, ducking past injured civilians and manoeuvring over rubble. I finally reached the edge of the city blocks as I stared out at what had once been fields.

The world around me was on fire, desperate and pained wails rising up through the smoke. I staggered in the wreckage, trying to orient myself in the place I had spent most of my life, but nothing was still standing. The miller's house, the sheepherder's pasture, the baths… Everything was gone.

Something snapped under my foot and I looked down at the broken wooden sign with a symbol of a cleaver. ***Khafiz and Son.***

I quickly moved again, knowing that my family's house had stood just beyond the butcher's. "Mother! Father!" I stumbled, catching myself on rough brick and bloodying my hands. "Miriam! Ismael?! Pali, Fatima, can anyone hear me?! Can anyone-"

A woman's hand peeking out from under a fallen wall, pale and limp and wearing my mother's ring.

I staggered back, afraid to keep looking— to find Fatima's unseeing eyes, or Miriam's hair matted with blood— and lost my balance.

I fell, catching myself on elbows and hands, and as I saw what I tripped over, my stomach leaped into my mouth and banged against my teeth, demanding to be let out.

Ismael's favourite toy lion laid on the ground, its maw delicately touched with a few drops of blood.

Riadh caught up to me then, as I was sobbing and holding that little fabric lion, and threw herself to her knees to cling to me.

"I'm sorry," I breathed, "I'm so sorry..."

CHAPTER EIGHTEEN

RUCE

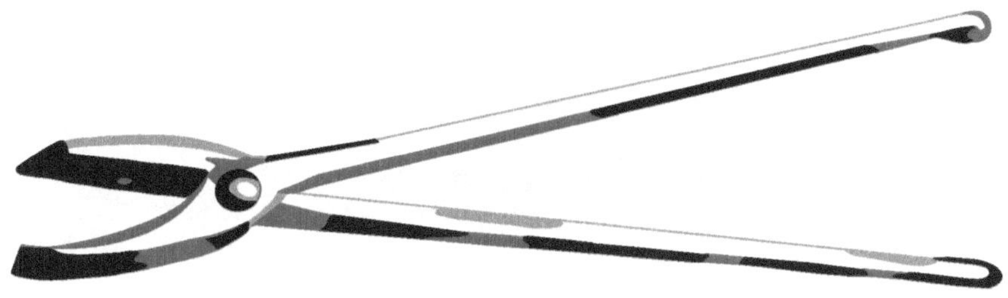

I MOVED INTO THE ice room, but Edda was a moment faster than me and already on her knees hugging the boy by the time I caught sight of him. She was clutching at him like he was dangling off a cliff, so desperate and tight, and holding his head to her shoulder.

"I'm sorry," he sobbed, "I'm sorry. I- I didn't-"

They were covered in shadow for a moment as I stepped forward, kneeling to pull them both into my arms, my thumb rubbing circles against Elin's shoulder.

"It's okay, *hayati*," Edda promised him. "We've got you. It's okay…"

CHAPTER NINETEEN

JOVE

THE CITADEL WAS IN chaos, the world swimming in the heat of the fires that still hadn't been put out. Thousands of years of our history had been damaged, and several lives had been lost in the attack. Healers ran past me to tend to the wounded, shouts rising up for help as Guards and craftsmages lifted chunks of rubble to free injured friends.

I turned, catching the eye of my Lieutenant, and beckoned her over with a curt motion. "Casualties?" I asked stiffly, pausing only to give her time to reach me before I started down the corridor.

"We're still counting," she told me, doubling her pace to keep up. "But so far, seventeen wounded, three missing, four dead— all from the craftsmages except for one of our own who attempted to stop the attack. Our production of armour and weapons has slowed to a crawl. Emissary Djanson is waiting in the meeting hall."

"Send a team to notify the Guard's family, find a way to make up production, and-"

"Deal with Tor?" She nodded. "You never can stomach his pleasantries, even when he's trying to give us money."

"Before you go, get that cut checked out." I nodded to the gash on her temple. "I shall inform the king of what's happened."

Riadh caught my arm, her face twisting in concern. "How is my father, Captain? Has his condition changed?"

"I'm sorry, Riadh, but you know the only thing that could restore his health is a tonic of the same venom that poisoned him."

"Have you received word from the squadron you sent into the Lithdreyan desert?"

"Dead," I lied. No squadron had ever been sent. "Just like the last. The search is so dangerous... I fear we will never claim the venom of the four-fang and save your father."

"Please send me, Captain. I promise I will not fail, I promise I will bring back the tonic."

"I can't, Riadh."

"Why-"

"Because you are not only my Lieutenant, you are our princess. One day, when you are ready, we will need you to lead this city. I will tell your father you are thinking of him."

She ducked her head and turned away, hurrying down the hall to follow my orders as I faced the doors leading to the king's bedchambers.

I nodded to the Guards flanking both sides and they ushered me in, closing the doors once again to give me privacy. The curtains had long been drawn in this room, so the large windows gave no light. Silence and sickness seemed to linger in the air over the king's bed, where he had laid for the past two years and three months, slowly losing more and more of his strength.

I approached Bazzeri's bedside and smiled to myself as I fell into a bow. "Your Majesty," I said reverently.

His eyes were distant and lazy as they worked their way up to my face, unable to focus. His lips moved clumsily, mumbling and working to speak but only managing to be unintelligible.

"Don't task yourself, old friend, please... I've merely come to inform you of recent events. There was an attack on the city, earlier today...

Many craftsmages were wounded and killed. We're working to begin production of weapons and armour anew. However... Your Majesty, I-I'm sorry to have to tell you this. But your daughter was responsible for the gap in our defences. You know I was hoping for her to succeed me as Captain of the Guard, but after what's happened... I don't know if she's suited to being a leader. I've tried to train her, to be a good Captain for her as her mother was for me, but since you were poisoned, since she was betrayed— I think it might be too much for her."

He looked up at me, eyes sunken and exhausted but full of concern, and struggled to clear his throat. "When... When the time comes, can she become queen?" He broke into a fit of coughing and I quickly helped him to sit up, raising a cup of water to his lips.

"Your Majesty, she must. You have no other heirs, and who could you entrust the throne to but your own flesh and blood?" I set the cup back down and helped him to lay back against the pillows. "Rest, Your Majesty. Once I have handled the invaders, I will come to you again and give you an account. I shall take care of everything."

I faded from the room, trying my best not to think of how much I had changed... of the person I had been before this all started.

CHAPTER TWENTY

EDDA

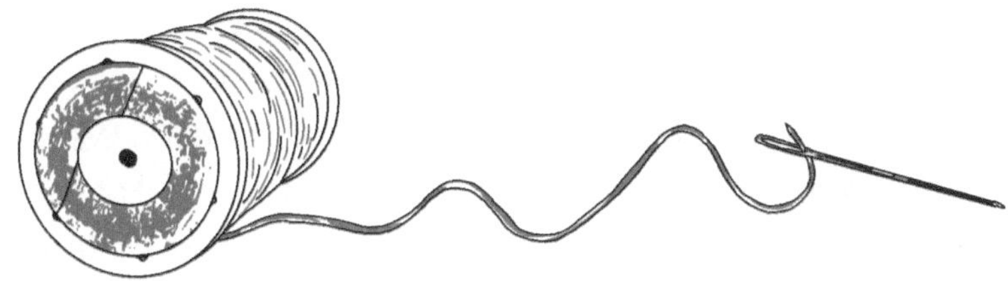

"HE SHOULD STAY HERE today, to rest. He's in no state to go work the fields," I murmured to Ruce. "The poor boy hardly slept at all last night, and he didn't touch supper."

"I agree with you, *Habi*, but try stopping him." He nodded to Elin's room, where through the gap in the curtain I could see him lacing up his *lahat*. The boots were still touched with red dirt in places. When I met Ruce, his boots had been covered in that same dirt.

"Elin," I called gently, turning my head away so he wouldn't know I'd been hovering, "are you going to eat breakfast?"

"I'm not hungry, Mother."

"You-"

He ducked through the curtain and started outside, where the other refugees were beginning to gather.

I sighed, quickly grabbing my satchel and tucking the remains of our breakfast inside. "That boy is going to eat something," I huffed. "He has to."

"Ed-"

I followed Elin outside and Ruce had no choice but to trail along after us. The other refugees were chatting quietly as they gathered in the centre of the cutaway, but suddenly they all fell quiet. I stretched up on my toes to see why and caught sight of several Guards at the front of the party. They began to move through the crowd and Ruce and I instinctively locked hands and drew closer, trying to block Elin from view. Why were they here? Were they looking for him?

"What was that explosion yesterday?" one of the refugees asked, and everyone began to speak at once, panic rising up in the crowd.

One of the Guards held up her hands and they all fell quiet once more. "The explosion was an attack on the city by raiders. We are working to catch them, but many of our craftsmages were killed and injured in the attack, and the Lieutenant has sent us to recruit more workers to help us defend ourselves. Please, wait patiently so we can ask each of you what your mundane magics are and determine whether the city will be best served by your working the fields or returning to specialisation. Thank you."

"What are mundane magics?" I murmured to Elin.

"Your crafts; the skills you use in your work."

We hovered at the edge of the crowd until one of the Guards approached us. "Your mundane magics?"

"I am a seamstress, and my husband is a metalworker."

"What kind of metal do you work, father?" she asked Ruce.

"We fled from Jezzine-on-the-Meander."

Elin looked up at him in surprise, but quickly schooled his expression as the Guard voiced the question he shared. "Meandering Steel? You can make weapons and armour?"

"Of unparalleled quality, daughter," he nodded.

"And you, mother, you trained at-"

"Jezzine Silver Academy, yes."

"Then we are in desperate need of craftsmages of your ability. Can you start work in the citadel today?"

I began to nod, but Elin stepped forward and held up a hand. "One condition. For our wages, instead of coin, you pay us in materials and free use of your smithy and seaming table."

"What?"

"We're in a new city looking to establish our skills. Coin means little to us— worth only our next meal, not our future. We need to build our names, and we escaped to Lothforias with nothing but our lives. My parents are incredibly skilled craftsmages, and one day you may walk past them in the Hall of Statues, but we need to build their reputation in this city."

"It simply isn't possible... Use of the craftsmage centres is valuable, and combined with the cost of materials-"

"Wages in materials, and we return three percent of every profit until our time is paid," Elin shot back.

The Guard slowly looked over at me. "A shrewd son of yours, mother. Apprenticing with you?"

"My husband, and we're quite fond of him too. Are the terms amenable?"

"'*Asabat*. Material wages and access to craftsmage centres with the condition of three percent profit until such a time as your use is paid back."

She held out a hand and I shook it. "'*Asabat*."

CHAPTER TWENTY-ONE
RUCE

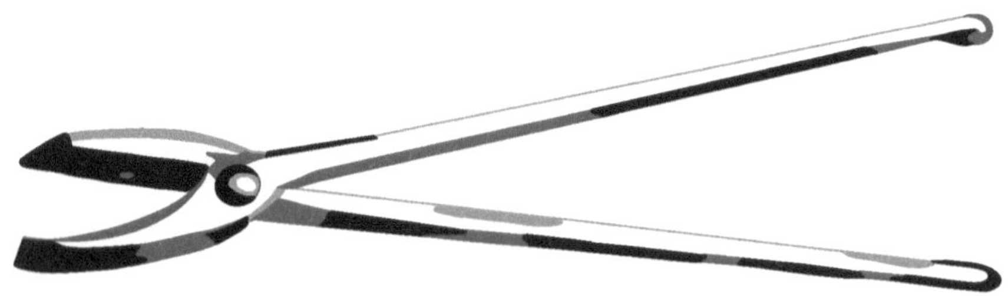

"IT LOOKS JUST LIKE our smithy at home," I said with some humour as I looked through the soot and debris. "Grab me that bucket, will you?"

Elin was quick to comply, though his eyes wandered around the craftsmages hall.

"What are you thinking, son?" I asked him quietly as he set the bucket in front of me, its handle partially broken from the explosion.

"Nothing," he said innocently, "just admiring the beauty of the citadel, Father."

"And what beauty would that be?"

"Look at those crates," he told me, "being carried inside. Isn't the craftsmageship interesting?"

I followed his gaze, squinting to see the crates that had caught his interest. "What of them?"

"Well, they must be quite sturdy indeed. Those crates are designed to carry soft linens, but look how the men carrying them strain under their weight... Just interesting, is all."

"What do you think is inside?" I asked, dropping my casual tone.

"Nothing good. I'm wondering how the raiders smuggled explosives into the citadel... wondering if they're too good for manual labour."

"You think-"

"I do. And I think you're going to send me on an errand and cover for me if the Guards ask where I've gone."

"You'll be careful, of course— or your mother will kill me."

"I'll be back," he murmured, vanishing into the shadows of the hall a moment later.

I searched for him for a minute fruitlessly, then turned back to the smithy and began taking stock of the tools. Most of them were beyond repair, but the material could be reused. The biggest problem was the forge itself, which was still half-buried by what used to be the back wall. The stone floor was covered in cracks and burn marks and discomforting stains that looked brown but were probably once red.

When we were first ushered into the citadel, we were led past carts covered in white sheets and piled high with something— later, I realised it was bodies— and through tented areas where healers were bandaging wounds until we finally reached the craftsmages hall. It was large and echoey and beautiful, but marred by the recent attack. There were mosaics on the walls that had become unrecognisable, beautiful statues and carvings that were irreparable, and right in our path was a small fabric animal that must have belonged to a craftsmage's child. Elin had looked like he was going to vomit at the sight, and Edda quickly caught his arm and guided him through the hall faster. When we reached the smithy, the Guard bid us goodbye and led Edda and the other seamsters further into the hall to find the seaming tables.

Now I was alone, in the wreckage of an explosion that had killed metalworkers and destroyed their smithy. With all the soot around, it was clear that the thatch in the roof had caught fire after the blast. Fire...

My son died in a place just like this.

Chapter Twenty-Two

Elin

I QUIETLY EDGED DOWN the hall, following the footsteps of the men with crates as they echoed off the walls. Maybe I was just being paranoid, but something was off... Foreigners in the citadel with crates that were heavier than they should be the day after an attack? It was definitely worth investigating.

This isn't your job anymore, a part of me hissed. The part that wanted to be angry at the Guards, at Riadh, at Jove.

"It's always my job," I forced out, murmuring it over and over again like a mantra.

I turned the corner and stopped dead, looking from side to side. I knew they had come this way, but now they were just... gone. I slowly stepped forward, realising something about the hallway. Obsessed with symmetry as the ancient masons were, this hallway had one torch out of place— and from sneaking around the citadel complex with Riadh as children, I knew that meant there was an entrance to the Catacombs behind it.

I gingerly lifted the torch from its sconce, trailing its flame along the wall as I kept a careful eye on its peak. Suddenly it was sucked toward the wall, pulled by a current of air. I dug my fingers into the crack and found a seam that eventually gave way. A section of the wall swung inward and revealed a steep staircase going down into the bowels of the citadel. I moved to replace the torch before I followed them down, but I was startled by a sudden, "Hey!"

I turned, seeing a Guard striding towards me. "Craftsmages aren't permitted to be in this hallway, and-" She stopped short as she saw the secret entrance to the Catacombs. "What do you think you're doing?" she asked me, her voice dangerously low.

"I think the men who caused the explosion yesterday went down here. They were carrying a crate, but it was too heavy to-"

"Is that the best you can come up with?" she scoffed. "You're one of the refugees, aren't you? They just let you waltz into the citadel, and now you're looking to steal from us."

"No, that's not-"

"I know exactly what you are," she spat, taking me by surprise as she struck me with an armoured backhand. I was sent sprawling, catching myself and burning my hands on the rug. The knot keeping the vial around my neck came loose and it skittered across the floor, but the slam of the door to the Catacombs covered the sound of glass on stone. "If I catch you outside the hall of craftsmages again, you will not like the consequences. Get back to work."

She turned back down the hall, leaving me dizzy on the floor of the citadel. I slowly reached up to touch my hair where she hit me, my fingers coming away bloody. ***Mother is not going to like that***, I thought with a sigh as I picked myself and the vial of venom up off the floor.

CHAPTER TWENTY-THREE

EDDA

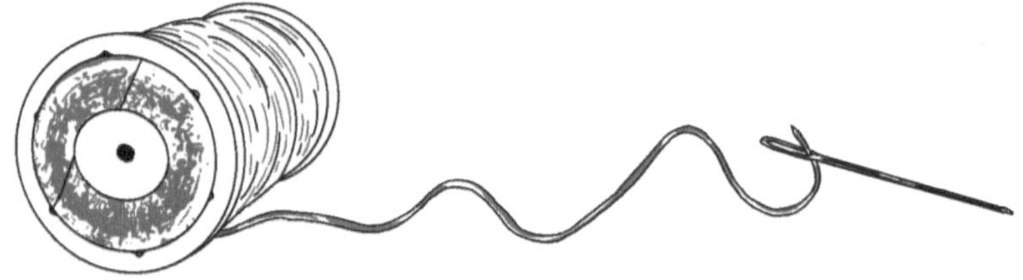

THE SEAMING TABLES, DEEP in the citadel and made of dense wood as they were, had been largely spared from the damage of the explosion. There were several pieces of rubble from the ceiling that must have fallen during the blast, but the tables themselves were still usable.

At the front of the room was a tall, slender woman, dark-skinned like my Ruce, who introduced herself as the high seamster— though what that might be, I could only guess— and taught us the "stitches of power" that were worked into the under-armour of the Guards to protect them.

I loved seaming, and once I set to work, the time passed quickly. I worked many tunics, drilling into my mind each stitch exactly as it should be done, so that I might replicate the technique at home for Elin. The stitches, the high seamster had told us, were the language of the seaming Goddess, *Setcha Gria*, and invoked her magic.

The city's gods were all craftsmages of some sort, creators or warriors or farmers. People who practised those same crafts, I'd figured out, were also considered craftmages, though they only used "mundane magic" for the most part. There were a special few, Nassir— the man sitting beside me— said, who became so skilled at their craft that their magic was no longer considered mundane, and they were honoured in the Hall of Statues.

"My son mentioned that place to me," I nodded. "What is it?"

"It's just around the corner. Would you like to see for yourself when we break for lunch?"

"Yes, I would," I answered immediately.

And so there I stood, staring up at two dozen statues that were each four times my height. Elin had told the Guards that my husband and I might stand among them some day. The statues flanked the hallway, standing tall and impassive in flawless marble, their surfaces scrubbed clean and polished— all except one.

I slowly approached the statue of the swordsman, blackened and marred by ash and soot, as though it had been burned. The features I could make out were unmistakable to a mother who had studied her boy's face to understand him— it was my 'Elin'. I crouched to wipe grime from the pedestal, which bore the title *Oren Anit*. The Mage of the Sword, I translated. The name had been scratched away angrily, and I could hardly make it out.

"Harun Rachid," I murmured quietly.

"We don't... we don't say that name," Nassir told me stiffly. "Not anymore."

"Why not? What happened?"

"He poisoned the king and fled in the night," he spat. "He betrayed the city and left us weak. The king's illness made the raiders more brazen. If he hadn't betrayed us... I wouldn't have had to bury my wife."

"I hope you always remember her voice," I said quietly, stepping back and looking up at Elin's statue. **There must be more to it... There must be.**

I worked much slower the rest of the day, pricking my finger constantly in my distraction. I was trying to reconcile the boy I knew with the boy Nassir had told me about… and I just couldn't. I knew there was a part of the story I was missing, because Elin—Harun, whoever—wouldn't do something like that. Unless… Maybe he hadn't always been the boy I now knew. Maybe something had changed him, made him kind… something like regret.

"Stop that," I hissed at myself, shaking my head.

Or maybe he had just been playing us from the beginning. Maybe he had returned to finish destroying the city and was using us to do it.

"That's not true. My instincts tell me he's a good person, and I refuse to doubt that for even a moment."

"Edda," Nassir said to me as he leaned over, "you are muttering to yourself. If you're going to think out loud, at least have the courtesy to speak up enough that I can eavesdrop."

"I'm just worried about my son. We're refugees," I told him, "and my son went through something traumatic… but he won't talk to me about it, and I don't know how to help him. He's… he's something like a stranger, honestly."

"My Malia doesn't talk to me either; not since we lost her mother… Did your boy lose someone he loved? The grief that comes from that… you feel it in a language we were never taught to speak. Sometimes it's beyond words. Sometimes you just need to hold them."

I didn't say anything. I didn't think anything needed to be said. We both fell silent and we didn't speak for the rest of the workday.

||

"Mother, are you okay?" Elin asked, glancing up from his dinner. He had been quiet the whole walk back from the citadel at the end of the workday, and the entire time he helped me make dinner— but then, I had been quiet too.

I slowly took a breath before deciding to speak. "Tell me something, Elin. I don't care what it is, I just want to listen…"

He looked at me for a long time, his mouth stuttering over what to say as he turned pages in his mind, searching for something that was real but not painfully so. Eventually, he failed.

"The explosion yesterday... the rubble, it- it reminded me of my family. Of the way that I lost them." That was where he stopped, his fingers drumming, stuttering, over the table as he looked at me.

I pushed myself to my feet and rounded the table, coming flush against the chair as I carefully pulled him towards me, wrapping my arms around him. He exhaled shakily as his head fell against my chest, his hands fisting in my dress. I gently carded my fingers through his hair to soothe him, but my hands quickly brushed over dried blood.

I looked down at him, frowning as I tilted his head to the light. "Do I want to know how you got this?"

"Probably not," he said with a teary laugh.

"Oh, Elin, what am I going to do with you?" I sighed. "You should get some sleep, *hayati*. We're going to have another long day tomorrow."

Ruce nodded. "While you were off admiring the citadel's craftsmageship, I got the smithy back in working order. Tomorrow, I'll start teaching you how to work Meandering Steel..."

Elin did his best to contain the grin that was dying to conquer his face as he stood. He started to his room, then stopped, his hands moving to the cord that hung around his neck. He pulled it over his head and I caught sight of a small vial filled with a strangely-coloured liquid.

He moved to the fireplace, drawing his knife with purpose. He used the blade to lever a brick from its place, scouring out a small depression behind it in which he placed the vial and cord. He carefully slid the brick back into place, glancing up when he realised I was watching.

"For safekeeping," he said lightly with a one-armed shrug. "This city's lousy with thieves."

"Of course. Goodnight, Elin."

"Goodnight, Mother."

A little while later, from my chair in the main room, I could hear Elin's quiet snoring as I crafted a tunic from the fabric I'd been paid in. The Lieutenant who had overseen my payment looked at me with interest as she handed me the fabric. "Jezzine Silver Academy?" she'd asked. "My subordinates told me of your credentials, and your husband's. When I first learned a deal had been made to pay wages in material, I was astounded... but craftsmages of your skill do indeed warrant such exception. I thank *Foria* that you took refuge in our city."

The fabric was a lovely olive colour, strong but soft. As the tunic took shape, I worked stitches of power into the seams, hiding them from sight so a stranger might not realise they were looking at the under-armour of a Lothforian Guard.

"*Habi*," Ruce told me, "you don't need to finish that tonight. It's late; come to bed."

"You see these?" I asked, holding the tunic up to show him the intricate stitches by the seams. "These are used to protect the Guards of the city. They're the language of *Setcha Gria*, the Goddess of seaming. The high seamster said it turns normal fabric into a carapace, strong enough to block a knife strike."

"It's for Elin," he realised. "You're worried about him."

"Aren't you? After everything you went through when you were his age, can you tell me you aren't worried about him?"

"Yes," he promised, crouching in front of me and clasping my hands in his. "I can, Ed, because I trust him. He isn't... like I was. He's certain, and he's **good**. He is more steadfast and driven than a boy his age has any right to be. He is going to get hurt, but I know that he has thought about what he's doing, and he has made the decision that it's worth it."

"It may be worth it to him, but it's not to me. He shouldn't have to make those decisions. He's just a boy!"

From the other room, we heard Elin stir in his sleep. Ruce looked up in the direction of his room, speaking more quietly. "You know that's not true, *Habi*. He's not **just** anything."

"There's a statue," I said quietly, "honouring that boy as a Mage. It was made years ago... He was a hero to these people when he was—what, fifteen? Children... children shouldn't grow up like this. He should've had the time to be **just a boy**. He shouldn't be involved in-"

"In what?"

"Oh... I- I don't even know where to begin, Ruce. You wouldn't believe the things Nassir told me about him..."

FORGING

CHAPTER TWENTY-FOUR

ELIN

I LOOKED UP AS there was a knock on the door. "Harun?" Riadh asked gently, padding in with a plate of food. "How are you feeling?"

"I'm fine," I told her, going back to my sword drills. The nearest post of my bed was full of nicks and slashes from my training.

"It's only been a week, Harun, since the-"

"I know," I said sharply, trying to push the memories from my head. They swirled about all the time, dripping into my consciousness without warning and turning my stomach. My mother's limp hand, Ismael's favourite toy bloodied and torn... "And yet," I told Riadh, "I'm fine."

She huffed, coming to set the plate on my desk. "I'm trying to help, Harun."

"If you want to help, then spar with me."

"What? How would that-"

"I need to be better. Next time, I'm going to be able to protect this city. Whatever it takes, I'm going to be stronger. That's what I need right now, not comfort."

"You're serious. That's what you're thinking about right now? Harun, you have to let yourself grieve. You-"

"If you're not going to help, will you leave me alone? My sword skills won't improve if I stand here chatting."

She sighed, stepping back. "I'm not going to indulge this. Tell me one thing, Harun; when is it going to be enough? When will you be satisfied?"

"When they make me a Mage."

||

A hand on my shoulder stopped me, my sword dropping to the dirt as I turned to look up at Jove Owaines. "Lieutenant," I panted, "do you need me?"

"You should take time to grieve. You're working yourself too hard, son."

My jaw clenched against my will and he caught himself, glancing away.

"I... I'm sorry, Harun. I didn't-"

"Harun!" Fatima giggled, "kick it back!"

I squeezed my eyes shut, speaking harshly to dispel the memory of my sister's smile. "None of the other Guards are taking time; some of them lost people as well. Why should I be any different from them, Lieutenant?"

"Because unlike them, you're just a boy."

"Then let me get back to training, and I'll fix that. Let me train with my sword and leave me be."

"Harun-"

"Harun," my mother laughed, "you're a mess!"

"This- is something I can do right now, Lieutenant. This is-" My voice shook. "This is the only thing I can do. Please don't take it from me." My jaw was tight, working, and my hands would have trembled if they were not around my sword.

"...You would be better served by sparring with an opponent who will fight back, then," he sighed, glancing up at the post I had been abusing. "Riadh! Centre ring!"

"Thank you, Lieutenant."

||

For two years after that, I sparred with Riadh every day, until we knew each other better than we knew ourselves. Then, Lieutenant Owaines set us against older opponents. There were laughs, the first time I stepped into the ring, from the men and women who stood watching... but they went silent after I disarmed my opponent with three blows.

"Again," Lieutenant Owaines called, nodding to another Guard. She stepped into the ring gingerly, looking me up and down. I understood her confusion, because I stood a head shorter than her, and her arms were each as thick as my head, but that had also been true for my last opponent— and he was still picking himself up off the dirt.

That fight lasted a few seconds longer than the first, and then Lieutenant Owaines was pointing to two of the Guards standing outside the ring. "Again."

They advanced on me together, edging out to the sides to divide my attention. Riadh took a step forward to fight alongside me, but Lieutenant Owaines held up an arm in front of her.

"I didn't tell you to step into the ring."

"He's outnumbered."

"I know. It's his job to fix that." He looked up at me in question, a glint in his eye, and I nodded curtly.

I lashed out suddenly, taking one of my opponents on the cheek and sending him to the ground with a thud. His hand flew to the cut, staunching the flow of blood, and I turned to my other— now only— opponent. She was shorter than most of the Guards, strong and squat and dense like Lieutenant Owaines.

She studied me with eyes narrowed to slits, wary of my blade still touched with blood. She took her sword in a two-handed grip and dug her foot into the ground to lunge towards me. I deflected the strike, and then started the dance. Our blades glanced off each other, the sound of metal striking metal ringing out into the courtyard almost to a beat.

Slowly, surely, my opponent began to give ground under my assault, her feet edging closer and closer to the ring carved into the dirt.

Her face was grim, her brows pinched, when suddenly her eyes flicked to somewhere behind me. I turned, catching sight of the opponent I had injured for only a moment before his fist connected with my jaw. I was unconscious before I hit the ground.

||

Hours later, Riadh paced the room angrily as I sat holding a cool cloth to the bruise on my jaw. "I can't believe he did that," she huffed, her hands clenching and unclenching. "That wasn't a fair fight." She turned and thrust the training manual at me, pointing to a section of swimming text. "It says right here. Look!"

"That's way too many words," I said belligerently. "I'm not reading that."

"It's Rules of Conduct for the training of recruits. The minor provision specifically states-"

"I'll win next time," I told her.

She spun on me, her fury suddenly directed at me. "***Next*** time?! There shouldn't be a next time! If we told my mother what Lieutenant Owaines had done-"

"No! I'm not going to get any stronger if people keep treating me like a kid! That was the first time I've learned anything in months. It won't happen again."

"Harun-"

"Harun, will you help Ismael get an apple? He can't reach on his own," my father told me.

"I ***have*** to become stronger than them. Than all of them."

She looked up at me like she was seeing me for the first time. "You really meant it, then. You want to become a Mage. Harun, ***no one*** in the history of the city has ever been skilled enough with a sword to be named a Mage. It just doesn't happen."

"It will. Someday."

Chapter Twenty-Five
Ruce

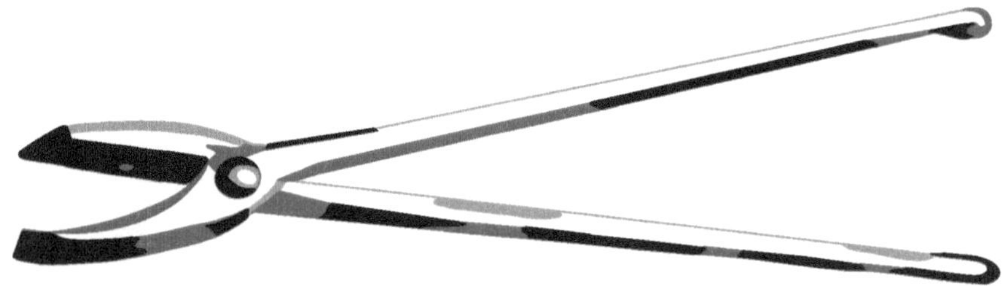

"THERE YOU GO, ELIN. Ah- slowly... slowly. Okay, pull it out now."

He stepped back, pulling the sword from the barrel of oil. Of course... when it emerged, it looked more like an octopus than a sword, all curled in on itself and warped.

"I'll get it next time," he promised. "Show me again."

"You're doing great, son. Remember, you've learned in a few days what took me a few years."

"Well, my teacher's okay," he said as he smiled up at me. "But I should get most of the credit."

I laughed, coming up to take the 'sword' from him. "I'll melt this back down to reuse; start from the beginning, with-"

"Folding the steel three times."

"Exactly. And you'll know you've done it correctly if it looks like-"

"Waves."

"Get to it."

||

When I had just started learning to work the forge, I was uncertain and shaky. I didn't trust myself or the decisions I made, and Tri could see it.

She drilled me ruthlessly, giving me no time to hesitate or question myself. She had taught me to forge weapons, yes, but the most important lesson she gave me was to trust myself.

I'd ruin a blade and shy away, instinct preparing me for punishment, and she'd just lay a hand on my shoulder and say, "No time for regret, boy. Try again."

She took a sixteen-year-old boy who thought he was a monster and turned him into a metalworker, hammering out my doubts and shaping me into the man I was today.

At the end of a long workday, after I'd been standing over the hot forge for hours, she'd simply pat me on the cheek and walk out of the smithy, calling over her shoulder, "See you in the morning, boy."

"Bright and early, Master Tri," I'd call back. The only answer would be the tap of her cane against the cobble as she made her way back to her dwelling.

||

Hours later, Elin finished shaping his second sword, dipping it into the oil with a *hissss*. "Slowly, slowly..."

The sword emerged from the water unmarred. It wasn't perfect, but my boy had only been apprenticing for three days. With that in mind, it was exceptional work.

Elin seemed different when we were working the forge. Only one other place was he as quiet and focused and driven— and that was when he was drilling with his sword in the early hours of the night, hidden in our ice room to avoid prying eyes. I watched him move around the smithy, murmuring steps to himself as he worked. Every action was sure, decisive, even though he was only just learning the craft. That was why I told Edda I wasn't worried, when she asked. His certainty.

I turned back to my own work, a partially-finished sword that I had hammered out to the right shape. I now needed to grind down the blade until I had the cross-section I wanted. I moved to the grinder, setting the blade against the coarse edge of the wheel. I was about to start working the pedal with my foot, but I felt a presence behind me and glanced up to see Elin peeking over my shoulder.

"How are you going to shape it?" he asked me, studying the blade.

"How would you shape it?" I tilted the blade towards the light.

"I don't know," he said eventually, his brows furrowing. "I don't know how you're supposed to choose."

"Feel it. Look at the sword and decide what it's going to be; that's all there is to it. No right or wrong, just different swords."

His eyes ran up and down the length of the blade and finally he nodded. "Convex grind with a double fuller," he said decisively.

"Double?" I asked with a smile. "You're getting fancy on me."

"It looks better than a single— and with a blade that thick, you want to make it as lightweight as possible without compromising strength."

"And a convex grind will do what to the blade?"

"The cutting edge will be more dull than with a flat or concave grind, but the blade will be stronger too. Great practise sword."

"Good. Show me." I held out the blade and he blinked in surprise.

"What? You want me to-"

"You decided the grind. Now make the sword."

His fingers twitched for just a moment before he reached out and lifted it by the handle.

I stepped back from the grinder and stood at Elin's side, quietly directing him as he moved the blade over the rough belt of the wheel, but it was largely unnecessary. He knew what he was doing.

In the small smithy, the heat was all-enveloping and sweat stuck his hair to his forehead. I was more used to the heat myself, but as I stood watching him work, even I felt my face growing damp.

Finally, he stepped back, wiping his forehead as he looked over the blade. "Satisfied?" I asked.

He looked up at me for a moment, fighting not to ask for my approval, and eventually said, "Yes. It's good."

"What's your next step?"

"Heat."

I nodded and he moved to the forge, laying the blade down on the grate. He stoked it slowly, gradually bringing up the heat. I drew breath to remind him how far to heat it, but I stopped, deciding to let him lead. Moments later, he glanced back at me. "I need you to heat a piece of scrap to orange to warm the oil so I can lattice the sword when it's done."

I smiled, nodding quickly. "Yes, sir." I moved to the task efficiently, drawing out the hot piece of scrap and dipping it into the barrel of oil to heat it. If a tempering blade went into cold oil, it would warp and become brittle. The oil needed to be cool, but not cold, and it was a delicate balance. When I finished, I stepped back to watch Elin work.

He peered into the light of the forge, crouched by the opening, and waited until the blade had been heated to a red-orange before pulling it out. He took a single breath and held it as he took the plunge, dunking the blade down into the oil that would cool and harden the steel. Before I could remind him, he started spinning the blade in the oil, counting out the half-minute it would take to cool.

"Now what?" I asked as he removed the flawless blade from the oil.

"It has to temper— for two hours."

"At two well-songs, yeah?"

"No— just one." He looked up at me and grinned. "You were trying to trick me."

"One well-song. Get to it."

He moved back to the fire in the forge, which hadn't yet begun to die down, and he held his hand out over the heat, mumbling the well-song to himself. He yanked his hand back before he had finished, glancing up at me. "It needs to cool a bit longer. Then we can temper."

Two hours later, we had finished tempering the blade, and Elin set it on the stone table to cool. I came to look at the sword over his shoulder, smiling as the blade began to fade from orange to silver as heat left it. Meandering Steel was singular in appearance, black and silver warbling together as layer upon layer of folded steel strengthened the blade. "Beautiful," I told him, laying a hand on his shoulder. "Absolutely beautiful."

He beamed up at me, quickly looking back at the sword he had made. "All that's left now is to let it cool overnight and then finish it, right?"

"Yes, sir. What grit are you gonna go to?"

"400."

I looked up at him with an appraising eye. "You've got high standards, son. I appreciate that."

"You boys still working?" a voice called from outside the smithy.

I glanced up at the dark hall, waving to the lone Guard that was on watch. He approached, looking at the sword in front of us with interest. "Just finishing up a blade."

He whistled in appreciation as he turned it over. "Are you selling your pieces yet?"

"Are you buying?"

"If they're all as beautifully done as this one, then yes. You do wonderful work, father."

Elin hid a small smile, turning away from us. I clapped him on the shoulder, pulling him back into the group. "This sword was made by my boy, actually. We should be getting home to his mother, but in the morning, stop by to tell us your needs. We'll see what we can do— and tell your friends we're selling."

CHAPTER TWENTY-SIX

ELIN

We were sprinting through the corridors of the citadel, chasing a would-be assassin. I'd stopped him from lighting the fuse on the small box of black powder he'd smuggled into the palace, but rather than be captured, he turned and ran. As we reached a fork in the path, Lieutenant Owaines shouted, "We'll pursue! You cut him off in the square!"

I nodded, turning down the corridor on the right as Lieutenant Owaines and Riadh took the one on the left.

I ducked through the crowd in the hall of craftsmages, shouting, "Move aside!" It was mostly unnecessary, though, because the sight of a Guard with their weapon drawn was enough to make most people duck for cover.

When I reached the city square, I caught sight of the assassin just ahead and started towards him. As he caught sight of me, in panic, he yanked a woman up to stand in front of him, holding his blade to her chin.

As Lieutenant Owaines and Riadh caught up, I held my hands out, staying very still to keep the assassin from killing his hostage.

"This isn't going to end well for you," I told him. "You're surrounded, and killing her isn't going to give you a way out. Let her go, and you'll keep your life. If you tell us who sent you, we may make a deal."

"Death before betrayal!" he seethed, bringing his knife closer to the woman's throat and walking backward. He edged closer to the statue of Lady *Foria*, protecting himself from being flanked.

"Okay. Okay…" I glanced at Riadh, who subtly moved the hand that was down by her hip. A fist, then a cutting motion. *Kill him*, she was telling me. *Quickly*.

She stepped forward and drew his attention, speaking in a firm voice. "How is this going to end?" she asked. "It's up to you. You have the chance to **make a move** and **help us** get you out of this."

"I'm not getting out of this!" he shouted hysterically.

"I know," Riadh said, her eyes shifting to the hostage, who immediately bit the assassin and flung herself free from his grip. Before he could react, I was on him, driving my knife up through his rib cage.

He staggered back, gasping as I withdrew my knife. He fell at the base of the statue, his blood spilling over the cobblestones and soaking into the cracks. He shuddered as his last breath left his body, unseeing eyes staring up at the Goddess.

I turned to the young woman and caught her arm gently. "Are you okay?" I asked.

She had to look down to meet my eyes and she gaped at me. "I… th-thank you, *Oren*."

I nodded, glancing at her companion. "Make sure she gets home okay."

I looked back at the man I had just killed and Lieutenant Owaines clapped me on the shoulder, coming to embrace me. "Impressive work, *Oren*. Fearless as always."

||

I moved through the city square, on my way to meet Riadh at the *sahlab* shop, and a small group at the base of Lady *Foria's* statue caught my attention. The washerwomen, dressed in their pale blues, were kneeling on the cobbles scrubbing blood out from between the cracks.

For a moment, I stood there and watched, their towels wringing pink as they worked. I didn't feel any guilt about what I had done, and I wondered if I should. I had taken a man's life yesterday, but I had slept just as soundly as every night before.

I turned away and kept walking. They were doing their jobs, just like I had. As I passed, every eye in the bustling crowd turned to look at me as though there was a celebrity in their midst. I didn't mind the respect, but the attention made me want to be invisible.

I made my way down the side streets to avoid any more eyes on me, finding Riadh waiting outside the shop. "Took you long enough," she huffed jokingly. "My time is very valuable, you know, and I don't like waiting."

"My apologies, Your Highness, I promise to be punctual in the future."

"Good," she said as she wrapped an arm through mine. "You're buying."

"Not on your life."

||

When I finished sanding the blade down smooth, Ruce came to stand beside me and look at my work. "Adequate," he said flatly.

I looked up at him and his straight face morphed into a grin.

"Beautiful," he corrected earnestly. Only then did I allow myself to take pride in the work I had done.

I had slept heavy the night before, my entire body stiff and sore from the day working the smithy, but when we came back this morning, I found it just a bit easier. I knew, as I worked day after day, that I was getting used to it.

This work was different, harder, than waiting tables at- ***Don't do that***, I told myself. ***Don't think about the watering hole. Don't dwell on it. You can't go back... whatever was there is gone now.***

"Elin," Edda called from the other end of the hall, "come help your mother carry her things."

"Coming!" I leapt up from the bench and ran to offer her my empty arms.

"Thank you, *hayati*. Did you learn much today?"

"You should see the sword we made, Mother, it's beautiful. And one of the citadel's Guards commissioned a sword— from **me**."

She touched my cheek and smiled. "Putting your father out of business, are you?"

"It's not my fault he's a natural teacher."

"That's right," Ruce said gruffly. "And it's a family business, Ed. The boy's success is my success. Let's get back to the dwelling; I'm starved."

||

A little over an hour later, we had returned home and eaten a rich meal together. I moved to the ice room to do my nightly sword drills and Ruce called, "Hold up there, Elin."

I turned to see him rise from the table, puttering around with his pack for a moment. Finally, he pulled out a wrapped object shaped like a sword— which made sense, as it turned out to be the sword we had finished earlier today.

"You'll do more good with a sparring partner," he said simply as he came to join me at the entrance to the ice room.

"Father-" I started hesitantly.

"You're not gonna hurt me. Don't get cocky, boy."

"I'm- I wasn't-"

"Oh, you weren't, were you?" he asked with a smile. "I may be old, but I bet I can still give you a decent fight."

"Of course, Father," I said carefully, accepting that I wasn't going to change his mind. I stretched out my hand around the handle of my sword, telling myself to be careful, to go easy on him so I didn't hurt him. And that was how I ended up in the dirt moments later with a deep nick in my blade.

Ruce offered me a hand to stand and I grinned up at him. "Oh, okay," I nodded as he picked up my sword and held it out to me. "This is gonna be fun."

Edda gave a long-suffering sigh as she turned back to her seaming work. "Be careful, boys."

I sized Ruce up once more, playing over in my head how he had disarmed me, the unassuming expression on his face, how his feet had stayed planted the entire time. **Confidence**. Fantastic— it had been so long since I'd crossed swords with someone who knew what they were doing.

||

I stepped forward and offered a hand to Riadh, who had been sent panting into the dirt as her sword skidded across the ground.

"Don't help me," she huffed, pushing my hand away. She groaned as she got up, twisting her arm to see the fresh cut. "Lieutenant Owaines must be proud of his protegé."

"Are you really mad?" I asked.

She sighed. "No, Harun, I just-"

"Play with me, Harun!"

"Oren."

She stopped, looking up at me. "What?"

"It's *Oren*, now."

She scoffed and gave a low, tilting bow. "**Yes**, Your Majesty."

"Riadh-"

"Don't follow me. Now I am mad at you."

CHAPTER TWENTY-SEVEN

RUCE

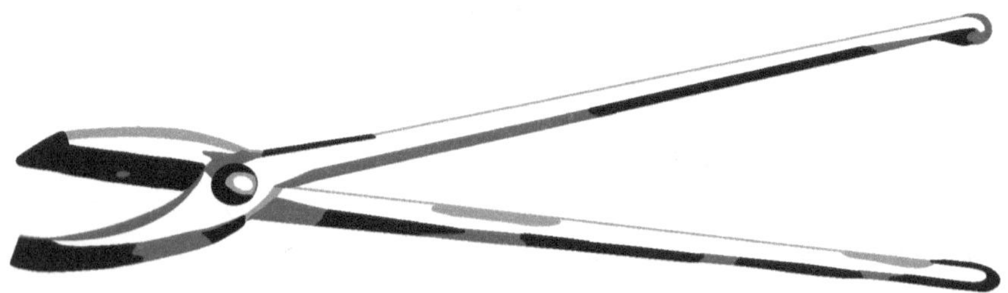

ELIN AND I WERE both sporting a number of bruises and the odd cut or scratch when we finally moved towards bed later that night, but we were both satisfied.

As I sat down on my bed— I had pushed it up against Edda's the first night here— and unwrapped the linen from around my arms, I felt Edda staring at me with that look of hers; one skillfully arched eyebrow, a smile playing on her lips that couldn't decide if it was genuine, threatening, or disappointed.

"I can hear you thinking," I informed her over my shoulder as I rubbed at my forearms. The linen always chafed by the end of the day, but I had no choice but to wear it. I looked down at my arms as my fingers brushed over the intricate pattern of dots to soothe my irritated skin. If anyone but Edda were to see the scars, I knew what they would think. **Spy. Traitor. Killer.** "What's wrong?"

"I didn't tell you about the statue so you could send him to bed bloody."

"Surface wound," I shrugged. "And the boy held his own, *Habi*. You said you were worried about him... but he knocked me on my ass a few times."

"I assumed it was your age showing," she said without venom. I reached over and poked her in the ribs with a scoff.

"Well, it was not. I'm just saying, if he can hold his own against **me**... Why are you worried?"

"Because he's come home bloody twice now, and he won't tell us why. You may trust his judgement and his **decisiveness**, but do you trust him to come to us when he needs help? After what happened to his family, do you really think he would be willing to risk our lives like that?"

"No," I sighed. "I don't. If he needs our help... we'll have to make that decision on our own. Play it by ear— just like we did last time."

A mix of emotions washed over her face as she was brought back to the first time we'd met, some thirty-five years ago. She ran her fingers over the scar on her palm absentmindedly. "That was different. The things we had to do..."

"I'll do them again, no hesitation, if that's what it takes to keep our boy safe."

"So will I," she said so quietly it was almost nothing.

||

The city was on fire.

The heat was blistering on my skin, the ash so thick it muffled my footsteps. My skin was covered in the grime of fire, my sword slippery in my hand from the presence of blood.

The city shifted and changed in the fire. After all this time, I didn't remember what it looked like; I just remembered the flames and the screaming.

People sprinted through the streets, fleeing from attackers, assassins. Edda was among them, her image made sharper in memory than it had been on that day. Her curly hair flew wildly as she urged children out of burning buildings, screaming the names of her family.

I started towards her, wanting nothing more than to help, when the ground gave out beneath me and I was falling.

I landed, air forced from my chest as I picked myself up. I was standing in front of our forge, back in Jezzine. "Elin?" I called, turning to find him. "Elin!"

Figures moved past the window; attackers, assassins. Flame suddenly licked at the walls and smoke burned my throat.

"Elin!"

"*Aba!*" he called desperately, his voice hoarse. "I can't get out!"

"Elin! I'm coming!" I moved through the smithy, struggling to take every step as fire ate away at our life. Flaming support beams fell in front of me, blocking the path to my son. I kept going, coughing harshly as it became harder to breathe. My head spun from the smoke and I stumbled. "I'm coming, Elin! I'm here!"

"*Aba!*"

I wheezed, unable to take a single breath. My limbs wouldn't obey me, my vision blurring and darkening. "Elin..."

||

"Ruce, this is the third time I've tried to wake you! If you don't get up, we're going to go without you and our new neighbours will be *very* offended."

I groaned, pushing myself up on my arms and freeing my face from the pillows enough to respond. "Tell them I'm an inhospitable old man."

"I will, and they'll believe me because I'm charming and pretty, and then no one will want you to come to any parties or eat any of their food."

"You know," Elin says absentmindedly, "I heard that Basma Lembahd makes the *best* sweet bread. Samhid said it practically melts in your mouth."

Moments later, I was dressed and standing in the doorway. "Well?" I asked my family. "What are we waiting for? That sweet bread isn't getting any younger."

Edda grinned at me, looping her arm through mine, and the three of us made our way out of the dwelling and down the steps to the main section of the cutaway. There were mismatched tables and chairs and cushions scattered around wildly, and several of the tables were heaped with a variety of food that only came from several cultures meeting in the same place. It made sense; refugees had been trickling into the city from just about everywhere over the last few decades, ever since Lithdreya had become more aggressive in their raids. No one else in this city was to know why, but I did. Everything had changed after Bishera had become the new Quiet, the overseer of *Al majowan*. She was ruthless and blood-thirsty and bold as they came, and unlike her predecessors, she didn't care for subtlety. In the last several months, *Al majowan* had only grown more bold.

"Edda!"

We turned as a woman embraced my wife tightly. "Basma," she beamed. "You must meet my family. This is my husband, Ruce, and our son, Elin."

Basma quickly and eagerly grasped our hands in greeting. "The city has been stirring with talk of you... Edda, you never told me your 'small village' was the famous Jezzine-on-the-Meander. A metalworker and a seamster— Tali will put the two of you to use. Have you met my wife yet?"

"We haven't had the pleasure," Edda answered, and Basma locked arms and dragged her across the cutaway with Elin and I in tow.

"Tali," Basma called as we approached a group. "This is my wife, Tali Lembahd. She's become something of a leader for our little community over the last several years."

Tali reached out a hand and I shook it, then she moved down the line as Basma introduced my family. She was a hard-muscled woman, several scars spanning her arms and face.

"It's an honour," she told us. "I'm sorry I haven't had the chance to introduce myself; we've had our hands full carving new dwellings for all the refugees." She muttered under her breath in Lithdreyan and I looked at her in surprise.

"You're from Lithdreya?"

"Don't hold it against me," she said easily. "I served as a soldier in the People's Army, until too many of us were scattered or imprisoned to continue the fight. I may have been born in Lithdreya, but I spent years of my life fighting the cruelty of *Al majowan*. If your family ever needs anything during your time here, or if you are capable of lending us your skills, you can find me in the stonemason's hall, if I'm not at my dwelling." She kissed Basma quickly before walking away, calling over her shoulder, "We're short on chairs!"

"Please," Basma said, "come sit with us and I will introduce you to your new neighbours."

"As long as I get an introduction to your sweet bread I've been hearing about, I'll be happy."

She laughed, holding out a hand to guide us to sit. "I can handle that."

Chapter Twenty-Eight

Riadh

I MADE MY WAY out of the city centre, taking the sharp left that cut through Barrier Ridge. The ridge was steep and impassable, almost tooth-like as it stretched from the ground, spanning the gap from Mount Sarigh to the East Wall, where a smooth transition had been carved between the ridge and the Goddess's stonework.

The path to the harbour was a narrow, shadowy scar in the ridge, steep and twisting as it wound down the slope and finally opened to the crisp sea air.

I inhaled deeply, shielding my eyes from the sun as I searched for the Rejohanese envoy ship. They had come from across the ocean as part of an ongoing trade negotiation, and as always, Jove would not be bothered with the 'trifles of diplomacy'. I accepted it philosophically, though, because Jove had never been skilled at haggling.

He had never had the patience for it, and Harun hadn't had the teeth, and only one of those things seemed to have changed.

||

"I don't like it," Harun had said to me in undertone as we walked the familiar path to the harbour. "These traders have sailed for months. They know their goods are worth almost a **hundred**. To offer **ten**? It's an insult."

I shook my head. "It's part of the game, Harun. Vendors and merchants come to the table expecting to compromise, expecting to negotiate. If you just blindly take what they offer you, you're going to get swindled."

"We're bartering with crown money, why not just pay what the steel is worth?"

I rolled my eyes. "Because your generosity will bankrupt this city within a week." I pushed him forward, guiding him towards the captain of an iron trader. "Remember," I hissed, "haggle. Be ruthless."

"No, no, no. I am **very** ruthful. This is not going to go well."

"Don't be a dittering old man, you're a warrior!" I scoffed.

He sighed, stepping forward and catching the attention of the ship's captain.

"Pardon, Captain. I'm in need of smithing steel, weapon grade."

The captain beamed at him, a charming and friendly smile, and I sighed internally, knowing this wouldn't end well. "Then you've come to the right place... Private?"

"Corporal," Harun answered quietly, and the captain's eyebrows shot up in respect.

"Apologies, Corporal... but this is opportune, as a warrior such as yourself will clearly see the superior quality of our steel." He held out a sample and Harun turned it over in his hands, taking in the weight and sheen.

"I need seven *shekh* worth."

"A hundred and twenty *darai* would be reasonable, but out of respect for your position, what say I give it to you for a hundred?"

Harun cleared his throat, glancing back at me. "I... I would say eighty is more than fair."

"Oh," the captain said painfully, miming a dagger thrust into his heart. "Corporal, you wound me. Let's call it ninety six and be done, eh?"

I wanted him to argue, but Harun shook his hand. "'*Asabat*."

My palm slapped up to my forehead in exasperation. They exchanged money and goods and Harun turned back to me, unwilling to meet my eye.

"I know," he said to me.

"Oh, what a naturally skilled negotiator you are! What was that steel worth, you said? A hundred *darai*? And how much did you talk him down? Was it an entire **four** *darai*? Impressive, Corporal... Impressive."

"If you wanted a good deal, maybe **you** should have done the negotiating. I don't **want** to underpay, Riadh."

"Ah," I laughed, clapping him on the shoulder, "I'm just happy you didn't take his first offer and **overpay**. We'll work on it."

"I don't want to work on it."

"This is why you always lose at *bita*."

"Good. I don't like *bita*."

||

Rejohan was a mountainous country to the northeast, and for centuries, we had been separated by far more than just the ocean between us. Four months ago, an envoy ship had been sent with a message asking to open negotiations. We had agreed, and our agreement took a month to arrive. Then it was another month for the envoy ship to make port to deliver the Changing Emperor's offer. Last month, they had returned with our response. And now, I was once again sent to negotiate with their envoy. Tedious business, and just as well Jove refused to do the negotiating— he was of the mind that a knife to someone's throat made the whole thing go much faster.

"Lady Hinata," I called in greeting as I approached the ship. The Emperor's niece was dressed in traditional formal clothing, as always, in a delicate purple robe that covered everything but her collarbone and her hands. "Glad to see you made it through the storm unscathed. How is Their Majesty, the Changing Emperor?"

"Hopeful that our negotiations will soon bear fruit. It is difficult, haggling from across the sea."

"Well, we would be happy to host them, should they wish to continue negotiations themself."

She scoffed, shaking her head as she tied up her long black hair. It looked difficult, in her wide-sleeved robes, but she navigated the dangling fabric easily.

"The Emperor cannot leave the nation unguarded for the months of travel it would take, Princess, but they assure me that they are invested in the outcome of our negotiations, and I have been given the authority to make decisions. Their Majesty does not wish to continue with this tortoise pace of messages delivered by ship."

"Wonderful. Then, perhaps you would like to come into the city with me and we can sit somewhere comfortably. We have a teahouse trained in both Stangrey and Rejohanese styles-"

"Perhaps, in the spirit of cooperation, I might immerse myself more in your culture today? I understand that most Lothforians have no love for tea, and only drink it out of respect for their allies."

I smiled at her, shaking my head. "I can't say I would choose it, no. I would be honoured to bring you to my favourite *sahlab* shop, Lady Hinata."

"Lead the way, Princess Riadh."

||

Hinata studied me over the rim of her mug as she gently sipped her *sahlab*. We had come to an impasse in negotiations, both of us dancing around the true value and risk of our positions.

"I must say," she told me, "that you are everything the haggler you're rumoured to be."

"I am only working in the best interests of my people, as are you."

"Then let's cut the niceties of tradition and get right to it. I am willing to offer no more than a twenty-seven percent tax on goods sold in your harbour—on the condition that you lift the ban on our import of *myiaki*."

"I can't just lift the ban, but I am willing to come up with a system to ensure that only tainted *myiaki* is stopped on the way in, and as a compromise, how about a twenty three percent tax?"

"Fair enough... but I will need something else from you."

"And that would be?"

"A recipe for this wonderful drink."

I grinned at her. "I think we can work something out. Do we have a deal?"

She shook my outstretched hand, bowing her head to me. "We have a deal."

"In my country, we say *'Asabat*, or 'pledged'."

"Then *a-sab-at*, Princess Riadh."

"*'Asabat*, Lady Hinata," I said in reply, bowing to her as she had done to me moments before. "Your ship will need restocking before you may leave for Rejohan. Perhaps you would join me and my Captain for dinner?"

"I would be honoured."

CHAPTER TWENTY-NINE

JOVE

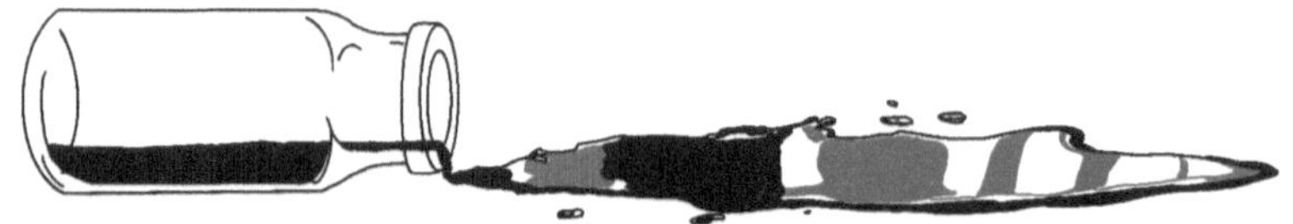

SHE HAD ALWAYS BEEN smarter than me, and unafraid to show it. As I fell into the dirt, Jazhara laughed, her hands moving quickly. *I win*, she told me. *Again.*

"That's because you're cheating, Your Highness," I told her.

She quirked her head to the side and slowly signed to me. *You accuse the princess of cheating, Sergeant? Treachery.*

"Yeah, yeah, help me up."

She pulled me to my feet, grinning. *Again?*

"You'd like that, wouldn't you," I grumbled. "How are you so much better at this than me? You only joined the Guard a year before I did."

Dedication, she said smugly.

"Whatever. I'll get it. Walk me through the attack again."

She started to draw her sword, but something behind me caught her eye. I turned, seeing another Guard moving into the courtyard.

"Eschel," I asked, "what is it?"

"He's here."

Jazhara and I locked eyes and she huffed. *And?*

"And... your mother has requested your presence to welcome him."

She signed curtly and I turned away, snickering.

"I... I'm not going to tell him that," Eschel said timidly. "I think he would have me executed."

Fine, Jazhara sighed. *I'll pass along the instructions myself.* She started out of the courtyard and glanced back. *Coming, Jovey?*

"To meet your future husband? A pack of wild dingoes couldn't keep me away." I slung an arm over her shoulder as we walked, turning my head to her so she could read my lips. "Go easy on the guy, yeah? Those Cessirine boys are softer than you and I. You have to be delicate."

Delicate, she laughed. *I'll grind him into dust.*

We reached the throne room, where Jazhara's arrival was heralded, with a confused, "and friend" tacked onto the end.

Standing near the throne was a boy a bit older than us, and he turned when the herald spoke, smiling widely. He adjusted his glasses carefully, stepping forward to hold out a hand. "Hello, Princess. Bazzeri Douren. It's an honour to finally meet."

Jazhara turned and smirked at me. *Pampered. Think he's ever seen a sword in his life?*

I snickered.

"My apologies, My Lady," Bazzeri continued as she turned to him once more. "I do not understand your language. But, if you have the patience to teach me, I am eager to learn. My hands are clumsy, but I am an attentive student, and devoting my time to learning to hear you would double my dedication."

Jazhara's lips parted in surprise as he bowed his head towards her.

Yes... she signed slowly. *Yes, I'll teach you.*

I translated, holding out a hand. "Jove Owaines, Sergeant in the Guard of Lothforias and your future wife's closest friend."

"A pleasure. The Queen has told me of your recent victory in the Silver Mountains." He turned to Jazhara and smiled. "I would love to hear of your journeys, My Lady. I have travelled very little myself, but I long to see the kingdom, and I think you will be a captivating storyteller, when I have learned to understand."

||

Preparations for the Day of Visiting were underway, and the city was buzzing with joy knowing that the festival was around the corner.

I had been tasked with going to the merchants in the market who were providing food and candles and games for the festival and ensuring they would be ready. If I hadn't, I never would have seen Harun's father among the crowd, bartering for a child's dress.

"Mr. Rachid," I said in surprise as we bumped into each other.

Anger crossed his face as he recognized me. "Lieutenant," he said tightly. "If you'll excuse me."

I caught his shoulder, moving into his path. "We'll see you tomorrow, yes? The festival? I know Harun is looking forward to seeing you, to showing you what he's learned."

"I want to see nothing of what you've made him," he spat.

"That's funny," I said gently, "because all I see is what you've made him."

His brows furrowed in confusion.

"Oh, I'm teaching him to fight, but I had nothing to do with his kindness, his wit, the dedication he gives to every task I set him. He's not changed just because he knows how to hold a sword now. He's still the boy you raised... and he is earnest in his desire to keep this city safe. If he were my son... I couldn't be prouder."

His eyes dropped, a glimmer of recognition in them that told me he recognised the boy I had described. I knew Harun had been the exact same way when he went to work the fields with his family.

"He's already saving lives..." I continued. "The market fire a few weeks ago? He didn't think twice before running into danger to save a little girl who was trapped. She is home, safe, with her family because your son is kind, and brave, and certain of who he is. He told me you were angry at him, for joining the Guard... but I hope you come to see him tomorrow. He deserves to see the pride on your face that I see now."

He cleared his throat, his eyes slightly watery though he tried to hide it. "You... you must think very highly of him, Lieutenant."

"Believe me, Mr. Rachid, when I tell you that boy is going to save so many lives... I imagine, one day, he'll be leading this city. He already has the heart for it. Come, let him show you."

He slowly nodded. "I... I will be there. Thank you, Lieutenant."

CHAPTER THIRTY

ELIN

"Hurry up, boys," Edda called. "We don't want to be late for dinner."

"Who are we visiting with, again? And why?" I asked. "How do we know them?"

"Nassir is a friend of mine, a fellow seamster in the citadel. We're eating with him and his daughter, Malia, because they want to welcome us to the city and because I promised that we would."

"But we don't know them," I complained.

"Yes, well, if we ever actually make it to their dwelling tonight, we'll fix that, chat and break bread together."

"I don't want to have to play with a little girl, Mother."

"She's only 'little,' Elin, if you think of yourself as such. She's a year older than you."

"Even worse," I muttered as I moved past Ruce, tidying up the smithy from the day's work. I ducked down to grab a small bundle wrapped in cloth from the bottom shelf when his back was turned, tucking it into my satchel.

"Follow your father's example; he's looking forward to making new friends."

"As long as this one doesn't ask to borrow my tools," Ruce grumbled.

Edda rolled her eyes. "Will you ever let that go? You're holding a grudge against a dead man. You understand that, yes?"

"It's what he would have wanted," Ruce said haughtily.

We started out of the city centre as a family, but instead of turning left, as we usually did to go home, we went right down the street which would bring us to the inner city where Edda's friend lived.

"What do we even talk about?" I asked her.

"Elin," she laughed, "you're acting like you don't know how to charm people— and I know that's not true, because you charmed us the moment we met. You know well how to make friends."

"Doesn't mean I have to like it."

"Just give it a chance; who knows, maybe we'll play some *bita* together to break down the wall."

"Oh, great," I said cheerily. "Something I like less than 'chatting'."

CHAPTER THIRTY-ONE

EDDA

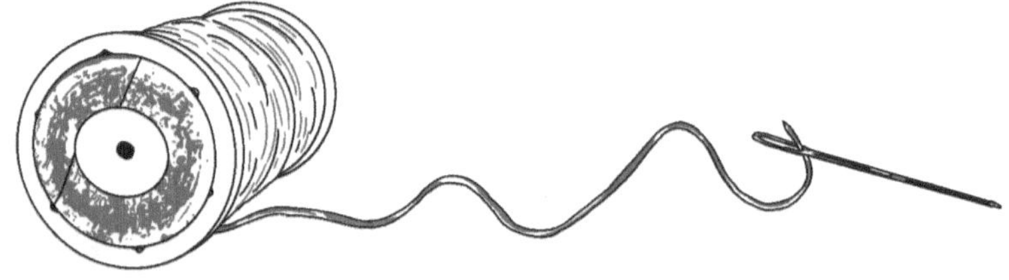

"EDDA," NASSIR SAID WITH a wide smile, stepping forward to embrace me. "This is the family I've heard so much about. Ruce, and Elin, yes?"

"It's a pleasure to meet you, father," Elin smiled, shaking his outstretched hand. "My mother speaks very highly of you."

Ruce and I shared an amused glance as Nassir beamed at Elin, instantly charmed. "As she does of you, Elin. Come and meet my daughter, Malia. She's of marriage age, not unlike yourself."

I stifled a laugh at the grimace that crossed Elin's face.

Nassir put an arm around Elin and led us all inside the dwelling. It appeared, at first, to be structured much the same as ours, with three rooms branching off from the main, but there was a door to each room, and as I looked up, I saw that there were two further stories to the house.

Each had an open centre, forming a square of clear sight to the top of the house, which was made of touched glass.

In the fading light of the sky, its colours filtered down and danced on the walls in pockets, washing a spot on the wall red, turning a stave in the balcony blue, trailing yellow down my arm. I hadn't realised how wealthy Nassir's family was, but then I kicked myself. **Bayouth**. I should have remembered that name... There was a noble house in Cessiri with that name. An enduring branch, must be.

A young woman smiled at us as we entered, her hips swaying slightly as she continued to set the table. She really was a beautiful girl, all warm smiles and ample curves. I had looked much like her when I was younger, at the age when I left my home and made my way to Jezzine-on-the-Meander with Ruce.

"Wonderful to meet you," Malia said— with a smile, of course, always with a smile. Nassir had told me that, since her mother's passing, she hid herself, and I couldn't see it; not until I realised the smile was the hiding place. Happy, light, shallow smiles that didn't take any effort or thought, or offer any insight into what she was feeling. The same way my Elin hid behind strength, she did behind smiles. "Malia Bayouth."

"Elin Lahd," my boy said as he took her hand.

"Good. Your hands work," she said playfully, using her grip on his hand to pull him into the kitchen. "Help me set the table."

Perhaps they would be good for each other, if my son could move past the irritation he'd had earlier at the thought of socialising.

Our dinner was delicious, cooked by Malia— who had been apprenticing with her mother before an attack several months ago took her life.

"How many attacks have there been?" I asked sadly. "How long has this been happening?"

"The first was... some ten years ago, with many subsequent attacks averted by brave members of our Guard," Nassir sighed, "but after the king was poisoned, these raiders only got bolder. The attacks have become more frequent, more deadly. We no longer celebrate the Day of Visiting, because we can't risk lowering our defences."

"What is that?"

"Guards and recruits used to be given a day off from training to spend with their families," Elin explained. Nassir and Malia glanced up at him in surprise and he quickly shrugged. "I've been reading, trying to learn about the city's culture," he lied easily. I held back a laugh; I hadn't seen that boy read a single word since we met. Far more interested in action than books.

"He's correct. It was once a wonderful festival, the entire city celebrating together in the square... hook flowers and lights everywhere, the sound of laughter, and the smell of good food," Nassir sighed. "I hope we are safe enough, one day, to celebrate it again."

"We will be," Elin said. To a stranger, it sounded like well-wishes and hope, but I knew it was a promise; a decision. Ruce told me our boy had already begun investigating the raiders during the workday. We shared a glance.

"Onto happier things," Nassir said with a smile. "Ruce, the wrappings on your arms are curious. I don't believe I've seen anyone else dressed in such a way. Is this a fashion coming from Jezzine?"

Ruce shook his head with a smile and held up a forearm to show off the linens. "I've worn these every day for... oh, thirty years now? When Edda started her apprenticeship at the Silver Academy, she had to practise her new stitches on scrap linen to make her hands steady and sure. She started at one end, adding a piece of embroidery every day... At first, they meant nothing, just flowers and fancy stitches. But as time passed, and we fell in love, she would stitch me notes, embroider animals from stories I had told her... These wrappings are five years of work that tell me how much she loves me."

"Well," I laughed as warm attention turned to me, "I was never one for writing love letters." I intertwined my fingers with Ruce's, running my other hand over a delicate lion stitched onto the linen.

"That's beautiful," Malia said.

The rest of the night passed quickly, warm and happy and full of laughter.

||

After we'd returned to our dwelling, I glanced up at Elin, who was hovering at the table with his satchel.

"You know," I told him, "Nassir mentioned to me that his daughter is looking to marry. He was wondering aloud if you might be a good match."

Elin looked up at me in horror. "You told him no, right?"

"Well, Elin, he offered three cows. Where else are we going to get that kind of offer?"

"Mother-"

"Of course I said no, *hayati*," I promised with a laugh as I ruffled his hair. "I would never speak for you, though I do think the world of Malia."

"She's nice," he said quickly, "but I'm not... I have work to do," he said finally. "I'm not the kind for settling down with. She wouldn't be happy, and neither would I."

There was so much truth and vulnerability behind that statement that I didn't press any further, just glad that he had told me something real. "Why are you just standing in the middle of the room, Elin?" I asked to change the subject.

His hands wrung about the strap of his satchel for a moment before he reached inside and thrust something onto the table. "I- I made something," Elin told Ruce. "For you."

Ruce looked up at me for a moment as he reached out, unwrapping the bundle of cloth to reveal a beautiful knife that gleamed in the candlelight and a leather sheath, likely bartered from another craftsmage. His eyes filled with tears and his mouth scrunched up as he looked down at it.

I remembered the day our son had made his first weapon, presenting it to his father with a smile that still needed a tooth. The blade was far from perfect, but that didn't matter. It was made and given with love, and so to Ruce, it was flawless.

When we had come to Jezzine several years before that, Ruce had melted down the weapons he'd carried his entire life and turned them into horseshoes and bowls, things that did more than take. Though he'd learned under a master how to make weapons, he refused to carry one, to be the same person he was before. But when our boy had given him that knife, Ruce had proudly strapped it to his belt, where it had hung ever since.

"Elin," he told the boy we'd taken as our own, as he buckled the knife into place next to the first, "it's beautiful. I love it, thank you."

Elin beamed, turning towards his room sheepishly. "Goodnight."

"Goodnight, Elin."

He reached the doorway and stopped, half-hidden by the curtain. "Oh, and Mother?"

"Hm?"

"I'm worth at least five cows." With a dry smile, he disappeared into his room.

Chapter Thirty-Two

Elin

"So you're really doing it? You're really going to fight them again?"

I glanced up to see Riadh leaning against the barracks door with her arms crossed angrily. "I'm not going to lose this time."

"*Lose*? Harun, I'll be happy if you're conscious by the end of the fight!"

"I'm not going to lose."

"Well, I'm not going to just stand by and watch you take a beating because you have something to prove."

"Then don't come."

"Fine," she shot back. "I won't."

"Fine."

||

Half an hour later, I stepped into the ring opposite my opponents. They weren't as wary, this time... Our last encounter had instilled them with confidence.

"Begin," Lieutenant Owaines called.

"Don't worry, Harun," the woman said. *Harun, catch me!* "We'll go ea-"

I immediately lunged forward, my sword jarring against hers and sending pain up her arm as she staggered back. I spun and struck at the man with my palm, his head snapping back as I broke his nose.

His partner was immediately on me again, our swords clanging together in a discordant melody, but I made sure to keep her between me and Broken-Nose so he couldn't take me by surprise. Out of the corner of my eye, I noticed Riadh peering out from behind a wall, her face tight with concern.

My opponent made a large overhead swing and I ducked, catching her by the wrist and throwing her over my shoulder as I stole the sword right out of her hand. Her momentum sent her gasping to the dirt as the *thud* stole her breath. Broken-Nose had gotten to his feet, slightly dazed. I pressed myself to the ground, sweeping his legs out from under him. As he joined his partner groaning in the dirt, I pressed a foot to his chest, bringing my swords to hover just below their chins.

"Thanks," I hissed, "for going easy on me."

They only coughed and wheezed in response.

My eyes flicked up to where Riadh had been watching and she slowly shook her head, a smirk fading onto her face.

||

Three years later, I stood in the same ring staring down five opponents. They were each armed with a sword, but before he had left, Jove told me I was only allowed to use my staves— which was fine with me. The fights were over too quickly, otherwise.

"Begin!"

Three minutes later, I was looking down at a groaning heap. I lifted a hand to my cheek, where one of the younger guards had managed to cut me. I crossed the ring and holstered my staves against my back, offering him a hand up. He took it quickly, bowing his head to me as he stood.

"I'm sorry, *Oren*. I didn't-"

"What's your name?"

"Hakim, sir. Private Hakim Sadir."

"Don't ever apologise for doing something right, Hakim. Next time we spar, I expect you to land **two** hits on me."

"Yes, sir!"

I strode out of the courtyard, feeling a touch against my head as I reached the corridor. I ran a hand through my hair, quickly pulling out a pointed purple hook flower. "Have you been skulking in the rafters all day?" I asked as I kept walking.

Riadh quickly dropped down to keep pace with me. "Best view in the house."

"You were watching the match, then?"

"Oh, that's what that blur was? I blinked and it was over."

"I know," I groaned. "Riadh, I'm so bored. Jove keeps giving me new challenges to keep things interesting, but I can't remember the last time I was **actually** challenged by anyone but you— and we know each other too well by now to be surprised."

"You want a new challenge?" a gruff voice asked.

We turned, seeing Jove standing behind us with crossed arms.

"Lieutenant!" Riadh said in surprise. "When did you get back from your Immersion?"

"Just a few minutes ago. And it's Captain now, remember."

"Yes, Captain," she said quietly, and I watched her disappear behind a stoic face. It had only been a month since her mother was killed in the Lithdreyan border raid, but whenever I asked, she told me she was fine. That it didn't hurt anymore. I knew she was lying, and I knew exactly what she was feeling... but that was the one thing I'd never learned to do— talk about something real.

"I want the two of you to meet me in the courtyard at dawn. I have an idea to get rid of your boredom," Jove told us.

"Yes, Captain." We turned away and started down the corridor.

"Ah— Lieutenant, if I might have a word?" he continued. He hadn't publicly named a Lieutenant yet, so I didn't know which of the Guards in the courtyard he was addressing.

"*Oren*," he called after me. "I was speaking to you."

I stopped in my tracks, looking back at him in surprise. "What?"

"I need to confer with my Lieutenant. If you'll walk with me?"

I glanced at Riadh with wide eyes and she grinned at me, nodding in Jove's direction. "I'll see you later... **Lieutenant**," she purred with a bow.

I turned back to Jove, but he had already started walking. I jogged to catch up, glancing over at him. "You were gone longer than we expected. What delayed you for over two weeks? Did something go wrong with the Immersion? Do you need-"

"No, just a border skirmish," he assured me. "I spent the month bathing in the Goddess Falls, honouring my fallen Captain and queen, and when I emerged for the last time, the mist from the falls mingled with the sunlight and gave an auspicious omen of colour like touched glass. Everything went well. But on the way home, we faced some trouble at the Lithdreyan border."

"Lithdreya?" I asked. "Why did you pass by our sister nation? That would have brought you through the desert..."

"Did I say Lithdreya?" he asked quickly. "Apologies; I'm still preoccupied with the attack that killed my best friend. I meant the Stangrey border."

I nodded. "I'm sorry, Captain. I know how much she meant to you..."

"Jazhara was my mentor, *Oren*. Everything I've taught you, I learned at her side."

"Then I'm grateful, because you've taught me much."

"I may still have something to teach you," he said enigmatically. "I suppose we'll see."

Chapter Thirty-Three

Riadh

"Captain!" I called as I caught sight of him, sprinting to catch up.

"Lieutenant al Abbas, excellent idea to seek craftsmages from the newest refugees. Our production is almost up to where it was before the attack. And the emissary from Stangauer departed yesterday without issue."

"Thank you, sir, but that's not what I'm here for. I've been thinking about the recent attack, about how the explosives were brought into the citadel."

"Yes?"

"One of our Guards mentioned that she caught someone trying to enter the Catacombs... I think that-"

"Lieutenant," he sighed, holding up a hand to stop me. "I hate that it's come to this, but you are too emotionally involved. As much as I want revenge on Lithdreya for your mother's death, there is no evidence they are behind these attacks, and you are not thinking clearly. Even if those old tunnels weren't half-collapsed, it's a maze down there. No one— not our enemies, and not us— could navigate through them reliably enough."

"But sir-"

"Your fears are unfounded. I don't know how they got into the citadel, but we won't find them by getting ourselves buried alive. We'll find them by following protocol and strengthening the Guard at the entrance."

"Yes, sir." I bowed my head in parting and turned back down the corridor, slipping into a side hall that was symmetrical but for one torch. "I guess I'll have to find them myself."

Chapter Thirty-Four

Jove

"Jazhara, you're cheating!" I huffed.

She dusted off her shoulder in amusement. *Winning,* she signed to me. *Maybe you just don't recognise it.*

Bazzeri laughed, patting me on the shoulder as Jazhara swiped several of my pieces from the board. "There, there, old friend. I'm sure you can summon more soldiers."

"Oh, don't you start. You've got half the deck!" I tried to sound angry, but I was laughing at that point too. It was late in the evening and the three of us were sitting around a table in their chambers.

This was my favourite place in the world... When we were younger, I had never been allowed in here. The son of a butcher, merely a Private, wandering freely about the palace? Jaz had never cared about those things; I was her best friend. If I couldn't come to her, she'd come to me.

So we spent our teenage years running around the city, every place that felt like home to me, every place she had never been. We'd haggle for fish straight off the ships in the harbour and climb up Mount Sarigh to the caves, cook them over a fire and burn our fingers because we were too impatient to let them cool.

After Bazzeri arrived, things started to change. Jazhara was busier, teaching him everything he wanted to know, the way we had once taught each other. I resented him, at first, because he was marrying my best friend, taking her away from me, but I couldn't ignore how happy he made her.

Then one day, a normal day like any other, a scout came with a frantic message. **Cessiri burns.**

We rode out at once, files upon files of Guards swarming out of the gates to rescue our sister city. We didn't think twice.

So many lives were lost that night, so many changed forever. I was hardly nineteen myself, and the things that I saw...

Our Captain died in my arms while the *Menagerie's* Crocodile, their precious *Tannin*, laughed. My ribs were broken, I knew, but all I could feel was my Captain's blood soaking my hands. *Tannin* towered over me, and if I'd had a moment to think, I never would have picked up my sword, but anger moved faster.

My bloodied fingers had hardly closed around the grip of my sword before the Crocodile's dagger sliced my face open. "Stay down, boy," he hissed with a toothy smile. "It'll hurt less that way."

I tried to push myself up when a swift kick set my ears ringing and my vision blurry.

The city burned around us. Children were crying, mothers screaming, brothers bleeding out in the dirt... And I was going to join them.

Tannin grinned down at me wickedly... Always smiling, always reveling in the blood. His was the last face I would ever see. He slowly raised his sword, his eyes never leaving my face, taunting me to move, to fight, to make it fun for him... But every breath felt like I was underwater, drowning, dizzy.

Someone let out a primal roar and Jazhara was leaping onto his back, driving her daggers into his shoulderblades. They struggled, bloody and animal, and I realised that it was Jazhara roaring. I'd never heard her voice before... raw, unpracticed, honest. Her hair whipped through the air as *Tannin* tried to throw her off, but his movement became sluggish, jerky. Finally, he staggered forward and **thudded** into the dirt.

Jaz stumbled over to me, holding my face in her hands in worry.

"I'm okay," I promised her as my head swam and my chest screamed. "I'm okay..."

You're going to have a scar, she told me. *You'll have to beat the ladies off with a stick.*

I laughed at that, but the movement sent stitches through my ribs, reminding me of the broken bones I had suffered.

Jazhara set a hand on my arm, stirring me from memories. *It's your turn*, she told me, but as she studied my face, she frowned. *You okay, Jovey?*

"Fine," I nodded as I looked through my hand of cards. "I was just deciding on my strategy to beat you two. Jaz, I need you to surrender your northern territory to my cavalry force," I told her, holding up a soldier card.

She swore, looking over the board and her shrinking lead, and Bazzeri laughed. "She's going to make you pay for that, Jove."

"Actually, Bazzeri, you're going to pay— this is for you, sir," I said with a grin, handing him a tax card.

"You're going to bankrupt me!" he said incredulously. "I thought we were friends!"

"You should know there are no friends in *bita*, Your Highness."

After we returned from Cessiri, the Guard needed new leadership. Both the Captain and the Lieutenant had been killed, so Jazhara and I stepped up to fill their shoes. Then, I was no longer the son of a butcher, I was the Lieutenant of the honoured Guard of Lothforias, and I went where I pleased. And so Bazzeri, Jazhara, and I dined together every night, playing cards and drinking a little bit too much, and life was good.

She was right, that the women of the city found my scar and my stories **rugged** and **dashing** and **handsome**, but nothing ever felt right... How could I find a woman I loved more than Jazhara?

||

"I am glad we still hold to tradition, my old friend," King Bazzeri said to me as he shuffled through the cards in his hands. I pretended not to see the tears in his eyes, just as he pretended not to see the tears in mine. "I think that to lose you too would have made my wife's death all the more unbearable..."

"She loved you, Your Majesty," I said in a broken voice. Jazhara's chair sat empty beside us, and all at once, the table felt so much bigger. "You and Riadh were her everything..."

"I don't know what I would do without your support, Captain. It seems we are always losing good people to these border skirmishes with Lithdreya." He set down a soldier card wordlessly and I surrendered my western territory, but our hearts couldn't have been farther from the game.

"About the border raids-"

"Who have you decided to name as your Lieutenant, Jove?" Bazzeri asked, looking up at me.

"*Oren*, Your Majesty. I know he is young, but-"

"So were you and Jazhara. I think he will do well; my daughter speaks highly of his character."

"He is a credit to our creed, Your Majesty. Now, about Lithdreya-"

"My daughter has closed herself off... She tells me she is fine, but-"

"Bazzeri!" I shouted, slamming my fist onto the table.

He stared at me, taken aback by my outburst.

"We need to go to war with Lithdreya. No more standing by, playing on the defensive, as they strike at our borders and burn our outlying villages. We have the strength, if you just give me the authority. I will lead our soldiers to war and we will avenge Jazhara's death."

He shook his head sadly. "Jove... I cannot. I know how much you wish to raise a sword against them, but I do not wish to answer blood with blood. If we don't reach for peace, this never ends."

"I could end it," I said sharply, throwing a locust card onto the table and swiping the pieces from the board with a violent swing of my arm. "Your people starve to death; I win." I pushed myself up to stand and started out of the room angrily.

"Jove, where are you going? Come, sit with me. Let us share a drink, for her sake."

"I'll drink alone," I spat. "If you really want peace, you can't have loved her the way I did. You have to be willing to do **whatever** it takes."

His chin jutted out in anger. "Perhaps I didn't, because I will not let my grief turn me into a monster. I'll see you after your Immersion."

CHAPTER
THIRTY-FIVE

EDDA

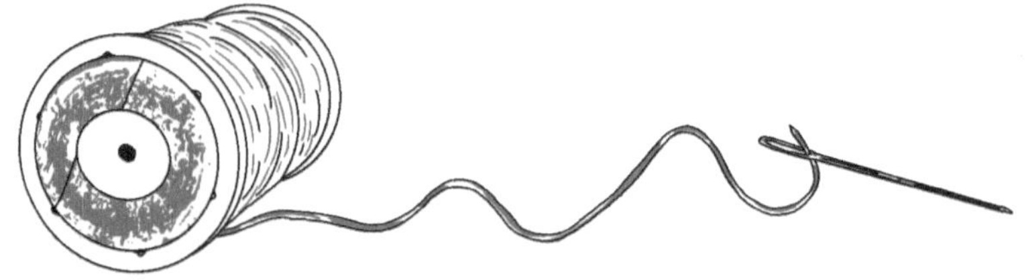

I sat up, looking over the seams once more before I called out to Elin. "*Hayati*, come try this on!"

He ducked out of the ice room after quickly tucking his sword away, Ruce following patiently. "What?"

I held up the olive green tunic and he unwrapped his *kara* and pulled his under-shirt over his head, setting them to the table. I held in the sharp breath that wanted to escape me as I saw the marks peppering his body— forget his Sentinel brand. Long scars from swords and knives, gouge marks in his shoulder, burns like acid. Newer wounds, cuts and bruises... He was far too young to be marred like that.

When he turned back to me, I made sure I had stopped staring, instead offering him a smile as I held out to him what I had made. As his hand closed around the tunic I offered him, he frowned, rubbing the fabric between his fingers. "This feels like-"

"A carapace. I learned the stitches of power, and I thought it might help you get home in one piece the next time you do something dangerous. I know they're only worn by Guards of Lothforias, so I hid the stitches in the seamwork inside."

"I... Thank you, Mother," he said with a smile, pulling it on and slipping his thumbs through the slits in the sleeves. I watched as he put the *kara* overtop, wrapping the hanging tails into place— one over his shoulder, one around his waist— and tied them where they met at his hip.

The style of the *kara* was to bear one's arms and shoulders, but Elin was always mindful of his brand and never left his room without an undershirt to keep it hidden, so when he pulled his *kara* on now, the sleeves of the carapace tunic were visible. The fabric almost shimmered, like the shell of a beetle.

"A perfect fit."

He ran his hands down his chest, grinning. "I didn't think I would ever get to wear a carapace again, after-" he cut himself off, shaking his head. "Thank you," he said again.

"I know how much this city means to you, and how much it must hurt to be unable to honour your traditions. If there is anything else I can do, anything else from the uniform I can replicate-"

Elin started to speak, then shook his head. "I don't... I couldn't even describe to you how to make the *venaq*... This is enough, Mother. This is perfect."

||

It was only the next morning that the Lieutenant approached me with a request.

"Pardon, mother," she said with a smile, "my boots have torn and I need them replaced. There's no one I would rather trust the job to than our seamster who trained at Jezzine Silver."

I shook my head in apology. "I'm not a cobbler, Lieutenant al Abbas. I don't know how to make shoes. You-"

"I call them boots, but..." she set the pieces in front of me and I held one up to study. They were made of leather panels interspersed with fabric, laced up the back with holes for the front of the foot and the heel to come through. Upon inspection, the material at the sole was different—slightly hardened. The 'boots' looked as though they were meant to come up just below the knee.

"These boots have stitches of power in the leather at the sole?" I asked.

"Exactly. *Venaq* come from Stangauer, where they are used by trapeze artists and climbers for the aid they offer when walking across tendons and standing on thin surfaces. They enable more precise balance and easier grip than the standard *lahat*."

"*Venaq*..." I said slowly. "I'll get to work."

"Thank you, mother."

"Looking at the pattern, I should be able to make you a new pair before the end of the workday, as long as I have the proper materials... though I may need to make multiple attempts to get it right," I lied.

"I'll see to it."

CHAPTER THIRTY-SIX

ELIN

"Your mother said she would meet us," Ruce told me as he led me through the market, "with Nassir in tow to help."

"Help with what?" I asked, ducking under an over-exuberant vendor showing off his wares.

"Well, you can't sleep on a pile of straw forever. We've gotten some commissions, so we have spending money."

"Father, you don't have to-"

"You would deprive your mother and I of the joy of taking care of you?"

I fell silent, pouting for a moment as Ruce used my own trick against me. "Thank you," I said slowly.

"Ruce!" We turned to see Edda and Nassir waving at us through the crowd. "Packed here, isn't it?"

"Nassir, good to see you." Ruce took his hand and embraced him in greeting.

"Happy to be of help. My friend's shop is just down this street; she is the best in the business, guaranteed."

We followed him into a brightly-lit shop and the old woman behind the counter beamed at him. "Siri!" she said with a laugh.

"Nala," he grinned. "How've you been?"

"Well, and yourself? I hear Malia has had great success with her apprenticeship."

"Yes, she finished a few weeks ago. Now, Nala, my friends here are in need of your services. This young man has been sleeping in the hay-room of their new dwelling, and it's stunting his growth. See the way he slouches? He's shrinking! He was taller when I met him!"

I glanced over at the shopkeeper, certain that I wasn't shrinking.

"We'll get you taken care of. Follow me."

The next twenty minutes were spent haggling. Or, in my case, bored out of my skull watching Nassir and Nala spar.

Nala offered a price and Nassir easily shot back a number less than half the original offer. Nala feigned offense and gave a number tangentially lower than her first, and Nassir replied with a number just as distant from **his** first. This went on for what felt like hours, with the two slowly closing the gap between their two offers, until it seemed Nassir had had enough. He threw up his hands and scoffed, starting to walk out of the shop, and Nala called him back, promising the high quality of her goods. He stopped in the doorway, unmoved, and she gave a number that leaned slightly more towards her offer than it did his. He came back to the counter and made an offer a little bit lower, and she nodded. "*'Asabat.*"

He shook her hand. "*'Asabat.'*"

As much as the ordeal ground at me— I had never seen the point in haggling over spare change— it also reminded me of Riadh. She told me once that she had been born haggling, and while it painted an amusing picture, I could easily believe it.

I wondered what she was doing right now... wondered if she ever thought fondly about me, just once and a while.

Chapter Thirty-Seven

Riadh

"What's this for?" Harun asked, glancing over at Captain Owaines. "Trapeze?"

"You two told me you were bored; you asked for a challenge. You're not going to spar the way the others do anymore." He nodded to the seamster who had been waiting in the courtyard when we arrived, and she stepped forward and offered us each a pair of something.

I turned them over and Harun looked up. "What are they?"

"*Venaq* boots. Put them on."

"Boots?" I asked incredulously. "But they're missing the toes!"

"And the heel," Harun added, sticking his hand through the hole and waggling his fingers.

"Better for balance and grip," Captain Owaines informed us.

We both looked over at the ropes which had been woven into a net with wide holes.

"You want us to spar while standing on that net?"

"You'll need to have perfect balance and footwork to keep from falling. Hopefully that's a suitable challenge," he told Harun with a wolflike grin.

"Yes, sir," he smiled back, his eyes alight with excitement. He quickly sat on the steps down from the corridor and pulled on his pair of *venaq*, lacing them up tight. He pranced around the courtyard for a minute as he got used to the strange feeling, then hopped up onto the net and stood, wobbled, and immediately face-planted.

"Start with just being able to move around on it. Then we'll go to sparring."

I warily joined him, the world swaying underneath me and sending me to my knees, where I quickly got tangled in the net. Within a few hours, though, we were finally able to stand without flailing our arms. In a few days, we were chasing each other around— and we only fell when we got too excited.

We spent a little over three months sparring on the net before we were as confident there as we had been on the dirt. The next morning, we came out to the courtyard to find that every other rope had been removed from the net. We got used to it again, and then we were only given four ropes all parallel to each other to spar on. Then three, then two, and finally we were fighting each other balancing on the same taut rope.

Captain Owaines had been right, about the *venaq*. They made me so much more light and responsive.

One day, after I had just turned seventeen, the courtyard had been filled with round wooden posts one foot high, half a foot in diameter. Harun leapt up nimbly and sprinted across the courtyard, jumping from post to post like he was made of air. I was wobbly for a few minutes when I followed him up, but by the end of the day we were playing tag, chasing each other across the posts and laughing like we were still children. Sparring came easily.

After that, the posts gradually got a little bit higher and a little bit thinner. Finally, it came to the two of us sparring on posts five feet high and four inches around, with the other Guards all jeering from the ground where they watched. Every so often one of us would fall, but we usually caught ourselves partway down the post, clambering back up and regaining our footing. Only once did I actually hit the ground and do any significant damage. A dislocated shoulder and a ban from sparring for two weeks.

It didn't keep me from chasing Harun around our sparring ground, though. The fall had just made me more determined to keep working at it— and it paid off. By my next birthday, neither of us would ever fall off the posts. We abused our newfound power on occasion, treating cupboards, railings, and occasionally the shoulders of the Guards as shortcuts to get around. Two years after my mother had been killed, I was finally laughing every day again— and it was because of my friend. Because of Harun.

And then he ruined everything.

Now, I stood alone in the dark of the Catacombs, peering down at the sewage tunnel below me. When the Jezzine seamster delivered my new boots, I had immediately slipped them on and gone back to the hallway I entered the Catacombs through, checking that I had my chalk and my wits.

I wanted to reach the corridor on the other side of the sewage tunnel, and there had once been a thin bridge here (I remembered playing *ghalem* games with Harun) but it had since crumbled. Every so often, along the sewage tunnel, a thick braided wire ran across it, anchoring the support columns that ran down its length. Now I stepped onto one of these, my feet sure and swift as I worked my way over the water.

Chapter Thirty-Eight

Jove

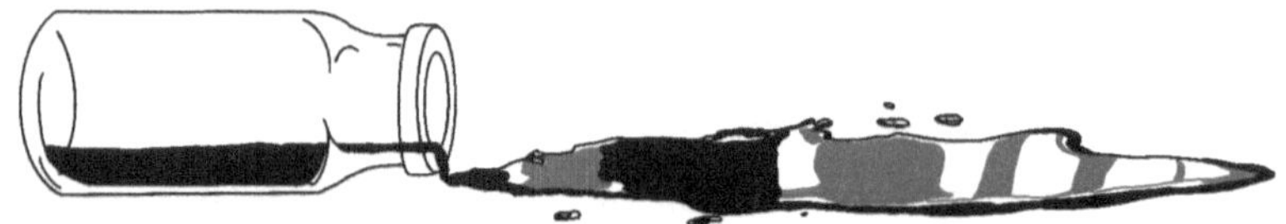

I STEPPED INTO THE room, bracing myself against the stale air of sickness. Bazzeri was sitting up against a wall of pillows, one of his servants spooning food into his mouth. He was one of the only servants I allowed to attend to the king now— not because, like some of the others, I trusted in his loyalty to me, but because he was unable to speak. During the fall of Cessiri many years ago, his tongue had been cut out by Lithdreyan Initiates. Now, he took pride in serving the king, and he could never whisper some truth in his ear that would ruin my plans.

"Your Majesty," I said with a deep bow. "I'm sorry to be the bearer of bad news... but your daughter-" I shook my head and sighed.

"Tell me," he said weakly.

"She... she has abandoned her duties. Instead of leading the Guards in protecting the city, she is absent. She disappears for hours at a time, without telling anyone where she is going... I worry more and more that she would not be fit to- No, I shouldn't."

"You worry... what will happen when I pass. You worry about when she is queen."

"She can't be blamed for this, Your Majesty. I just fear it's too much for her. She has gone through so much in her young life. She lost her mother, almost lost you, and her closest friend betrayed her. Now she believes the same enemy who killed her mother is attacking her people, and she just... she broke. It's not her fault. The crown is a burden on anyone, and someone who has experienced such loss so young... her weakness is not her fault."

"You will keep me informed, Jove... of her actions? Perhaps-" He coughed harshly. "I will need to... make other plans. Can you ask her to come to me?"

"I will try, Your Majesty, but you know how she has been in the past. She hasn't sat by your bedside even once..."

Chapter Thirty-Nine

Elin

"Watch that heat," Ruce warned from across the smithy.

"Sorry," I yelped, turning to the forge to stamp some of the fire. The blade had started to glow almost white in my distraction.

"Something very interesting outside the smithy?" he asked.

I pointed with my chin and he glanced across the hall at the woman who kept shooting me dirty looks.

"A friend of yours?"

"She caught me sneaking around the other day. And she wasn't... well, she didn't seem to like refugees."

"She struck you?"

I gave a shrug, turning back to the forge. "Maybe... maybe she was just worried because of the attacks. Maybe she thought I was one of the people involved, and she was just protecting the city. She is a Guard, after all. She wouldn't just-"

"Elin," he said slowly as he came to lean against the wall near me, "not everyone... Not everyone is like you. People can be selfish and cruel— even those who are supposed to protect you. Just because she's a Guard... it doesn't mean she's like you."

"Well, she's **not** like me, because I'm not a Guard. I-" I huffed. "I was banished from the city, Ruce. I'm not like them, I'm-"

"Better," he said solidly. He looked up at me with an expression that dared me to protest. "Set that blade aside to cool overnight."

"Yes, sir. What do we need to make now?"

"That depends," he said lowly. "Of all the weapons Guards of Lothforias are trained to use, which are you most comfortable with?"

"What?"

"Edda gave you armour, but you need to be able to protect yourself— and we both know the blades you carry are inferior to what we could make here."

The gouges his sword left in mine could attest to that.

My eyes fell. "I... I had to make do, after I was banished."

"You don't anymore. Tell me what you need."

||

"You're bankrupt!" Riadh said triumphantly, dropping a tax card to the table. "My armies conquer your last territory. Pay up."

Anahid groaned, reluctantly unclipping her dagger from her belt. "That's not fair. You've won five times in a row. You must be cheating," she complained.

"Maybe you just need to be more cutthroat," Riadh said smugly.

"Come on, can't we call off the bet? You already have a dagger."

"Oh, I know. Hand the dagger to *Oren*, please."

I looked up in shock. "What?"

Most of the Guards had weapons that had been forged specially for them, as gifts from family members or spouses. As an orphan, and the son of farmers besides, I'd had to make due with whatever weapons the Guard armory could spare. Lieutenant Owaines had gifted me a sword in secret, but the rest of my kit was standard: unadorned, ugly, and slightly rusted— though I quickly fixed that last.

Anahid held her dagger out to me, far less annoyed as she came to the same realisation I had. This was probably the nicest thing I'd ever hold in my hands.

"Well, if I had to give Pierre up to someone, at least it's the prodigy," she said with a rueful smile.

"Pierre?" I asked as I looked up from the beautifully-made dagger.

"He's foreign. My mother commissioned him from a Stangrey smith. I love foreign men... Take care of him."

"Another hand?" Riadh asked, and Anahid quickly stepped back from the table.

"I'm gonna head to bed before you take my armour," Anahid sighed, "and if the rest of you have any brains, you'll join me."

The other Guards grumbled, slowly fading away from the table with muttered 'goodnight's and 'sleep well's and 'I'll keep my money's. I hardly noticed, once again looking over the beautiful weapon in my hand. Riadh elbowed me with a grin. "We make a heck of a team, don't we? You play weak and lure them in so I can go in for the kill?"

"We both know I wasn't 'playing weak,' Riadh. I just suck at *bita*. You can't really give this to me," I told her, holding out the dagger.

"I order you to accept my gift, *Oren*, as your princess."

"You know I don't care."

"Okay, then as your best friend."

"Ugh... Fine. You got me."

"And now that you have a good weapon on your hip, you've got me," she said cheerfully. "I heard Jove's sending us on a training mission in a little over a week, so you'd better get practicing with **Pierre** if you're going to have my back."

CHAPTER FORTY

RUCE

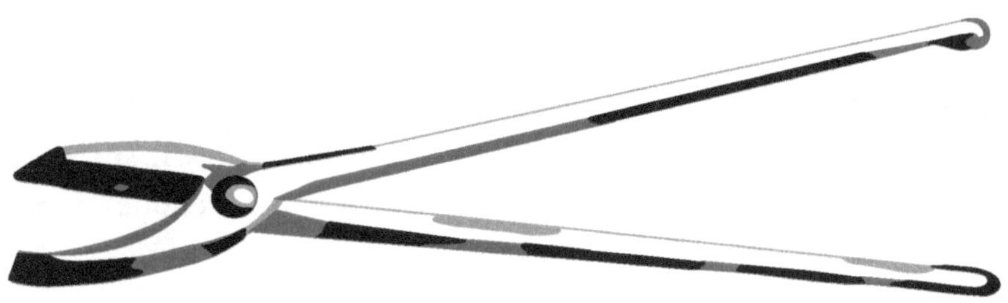

AFTER TWO DAYS OF work, we had finished crafting weapons for Elin, as well as rearming several Guards whose weapons and armour had been damaged or destroyed in the attack. As we packed up to leave at the end of the workday, Elin had a set of staves and a new sword.

"Elin," Edda said as she approached the smithy, "I invited Nassir and Malia to our dwelling for dinner, and I'd like to make a dish from Jezzine-on-the-Meander for dessert."

"You're making *jo-fahke*?" I asked. "Please tell me you're-"

"If I can get fruit," she told me with a laugh. "I know fresh fruit is expensive in the main market, but I was hoping you knew of somewhere else I could find some, Elin."

"You could just do what I did last time," he shrugged.

"What did you do last time? You were a bit vague... Did you steal it?"

"No," he laughed, "I just asked. The farmers who tend to the fields have plenty, and they're happy to share it. I can run and ask Samhid when we get home."

"Samhid?"

"That tall boy who worked beside us in the apple orchard? His family owns the field."

"Oh, wonderful. Before you go, I'll bake you something to give to them. Seems right, if they're going to just give us the fruit, to give the family something in return."

||

An hour later, Elin ducked back into the dwelling just as Edda was finishing up the cream for dessert.

"Whoa," Elin said as he took in the room, candles and curtains hanging that weren't there before, a nice cloth laying over the table, and an elaborate spread coming into being on the counter. "How many people did you invite, Mother? Because it seems like you have enough food to feed everyone in the city."

"She bakes when she's nervous," I said with a laugh.

"I'm not nervous, I just want to be a good host." She wrung her hands as she looked out at the table. "You think they'll like it, right?"

"Mother," Elin said as he rested a hand on her shoulder. "It's wonderful. Now, do you want me to help cut up the fruit? What are we making? What is *jo-fahke*?"

"Jewels and cream. It's a simple dessert, but it was a favourite back home— and I've yet to find a dessert in this city that actually has fruit in it, so I think it'll be exciting for them."

"It sounds wonderful," he told her, pulling a variety of fruit out from his satchel. He unsheathed his knife and she held up a hand to stop him.

"*Ex*cuse me," she said. "Kitchen dagger, not combat dagger. I don't know where that knife of yours has been."

"I was gonna boil it first," he grumbled under his breath, making a disgusted face as he took the blade Edda offered him. "And it's a dirk." In a warrior's hand, I knew the kitchen dirk felt unbalanced, heavy and flimsy at the same time. In the hand of an apprentice blacksmith, it must have been excruciating.

"Father, can you please teach me how to make one of these? **Better**?" he asked deliberately.

"We'll start tomorrow," I laughed as he and Edda worked side by side to cut the fruit up and mix it into the cream.

"Can you set this in the ice room to keep it cold?" Edda asked him.

He ducked into the room, and a moment later, I heard a cheerful, "Ruce!" from the doorway.

I turned to see Malia and Nassir at the threshold, smiling at us. "Good to see you both again, please come in. We're happy to have you."

Elin stepped back into the main room as I ushered them inside, my eyes locking onto a stave peeking out from his satchel. I quickly looked at him and subtly jerked my chin at the bag. "Your home is wonderful," Malia said. "It feels loved."

"Yes," I said, stepping into their field of vision as Elin quickly chucked his satchel into the ice room. "Many of the things we have were gifts, and that makes them mean all the more, doesn't it?"

"It does indeed," Nassir said with a smile.

CHAPTER FORTY-ONE

ELIN

"Rhis ij sho goog," Malia said through a mouth full of fruit.

"What?" I laughed.

She swallowed and glanced up at me with a smile. "This is so good. Your mother is a genius."

"No argument there," I agreed. "You've got some-" I touched my own face and she reached up to her cheek, her fingers getting touched with cream.

"Thanks," she giggled. She set down her now-empty bowl and looked out over the dark fields. We were sitting outside the ledge on the refugee cutaway, our legs dangling out into space as we chatted.

"Are you enjoying the city?" she asked me.

"It's beautiful," I answered honestly, "but..."

"But?"

"I don't know, it feels different. Not... not entirely like home, you know?"

"My father told me that your family lost a lot, before you came here. I'm sorry. I know from experience that it takes something from inside of you and leaves you a little bit hollow."

"I've never heard someone describe it like that, but that's exactly how it feels... I'm sorry about your mother."

She shook her head with a teary smile. "I'll always remember her voice, so... I at least have that blessing. You lost more than just your home, didn't you?"

"How-"

"I can just tell," she shrugged. "You and I can see through each other, can't we? Because we both understand what it feels like to lose people we love. Who did you lose?"

"I lost... more people than I want to count. The attack was- it levelled everything. Hardly anyone survived, and no one that belonged to me. I lost them all, my f-" I cut myself off. "My... friends," I finished.

"Tell me about them," she said gently. It didn't feel like prying or pushing, it felt like permission, and I couldn't stop my eyes from filling with tears as I cleared my throat.

"Miriam was the oldest. She was coarse, and protective, and bold. She was supposed to get married, before..." I shook my head. "She was- like a big sister to me. Ismael was the littlest, but he was really smart. He wanted to take care of animals when he grew up, and he could tell you everything about them— lions were his favourite, though. Fatima was messy and loud and *so* funny. She constantly had leaves stuck in her hair from climbing trees, dirt on her dress from playing ball. She could always make you laugh, even if you were having the worst day. And Pali was always there to hug you when you needed it. She was the sweetest girl I'd ever known, and she didn't-" my voice caught in my throat and I struggled to clear it. "She didn't deserve to die like that."

Malia put an arm around me, hugging me as we sat together. "I'm sorry, Elin. I hope you always remember their voices."

"I hope the same for you, and your mother."

CHAPTER FORTY-TWO

JOVE

"WE'LL PURSUE!" I SHOUTED to *Oren*. "Cut him off in the square!"

Oren turned down the right path, and Sergeant al Abbas and I sprinted after the assassin on the left.

"The square is full of people at this hour!" Sergeant al Abbas told me. "He could take a hostage!"

At that moment, we heard screaming up ahead of us. We pushed our bodies harder, trying to catch up, and as we exited the citadel, I saw the assassin holding a young woman at knifepoint. The square was in chaos. *Oren* was holding his hands up, speaking levelly to him. "Let her go, and you'll keep your life. If you tell us-"

I stumbled as a man fleeing the fight bumped against my shoulder. When I looked back up at the scene, I was making eye contact with Harun. "-we may make a deal," he told me.

"I'm protecting this city!" I shouted, stepping back as I drew the knife against my hostage's throat. Jazhara?

Sergeant al Abbas caught my attention, moving closer. "How is this going to end? Make your choice, Jove. It doesn't have to end this way."

"I'm not getting out of this," I told her quietly.

"I know."

Jazhara bit into my arm, drawing blood as she ripped herself out of my grip. Everything slowed down, then, as *Oren* lunged, his knife piercing my rib cage.

I gasped, stumbling, as I lost control of my limbs. I looked up, my head cracking against the ground, and saw the statue of Lady *Foria* above me. She was leering down, laughing at me. Her eyes glowed with power and lightning struck the sky as she reached down for me.

Her crushing grip turned the world black.

I bolted upright, gasping, a sheen of sweat clinging to my body. I desperately pushed the sheets off, standing more quickly than I should have as I rubbed sleep out of my face. "Just a dream," I told myself.

As I dressed for the day, I swear I could still feel the wound in my side.

||

"Your Majesty. I need to-"

"My daughter?" he asked weakly. "Did you relay my wishes to her?"

"I-" I hesitated, stepping forward with a practised grimace. "Yes, Your Majesty... I told her you wished to see her, but she would not listen. She said she could not bear it. Unfortunately, this is not the only news I have for you. Riadh has been largely absent, but when she *is* present-"

"What?"

"She has turned, almost... cruel. Unfeeling. After the attack killed one of our own, I tasked her with notifying their family. I recently heard from them that she..." I shook my head. "The way she spoke to them, without sympathy, it hurt. They said it made their loss feel even greater. She's just so bitter, that-"

"You... truly believe-" he broke into a fit of coughing. When it finally subsided, he dragged in a shaky breath. "She shouldn't become queen?"

"I am sorry, Your Majesty, that in your state of sickness she has shirked her responsibilities. I thought... knowing how important this city is to you, she would rise to the task, but I was wrong."

"Jove... when the time comes, I need-" he gasped for breath. "I need this city to be safe. *You* have to-"

"Your Majesty, I could not. It is not my right to take the throne."

"You... are the only one- that I can trust."

"I... if you are certain, Your Majesty, I can- I can have the papers drawn up to..."

"Please, Jove."

I bowed my head, rising. "I will see it done, Your Majesty."

I turned from the room, containing my smile until I had reached my study and I was alone. *Finally*.

When I first sought greater power, I was naive, mourning the death of my Captain. I thought of killing the king and taking the city for myself, but that would have been bloody. It was by happenstance that I learned of another way. A chat with a young woman in an eat house the night before my Immersion, someone who didn't know who I was or what power I held. She mentioned a venom, in the deserts near her home city, that had recently killed a soldier she knew. The poison, she told me, was interesting—it could be fatal, but only if so much was ingested. A smaller dose would not kill, but it would make the body deteriorate and wither away slowly over many years. She told me the only cure to this condition was reintroduction to the same venom that brought it about, but the venom was so difficult to procure that this was a near impossibility.

If not for that foreigner, I would not be standing here now, mere days away from becoming the heir to the throne— without any war at all.

It was, of course, a shame that Harun had to take the blame. That was never my plan, the boy was like a son to me... but when suspicion began to fall on members of the royal household, it was only a matter of time before people began to doubt me. Better someone else than me— and Harun was one of the few people who had access.

After I was done spinning my lies, he had motive as well.

In the Dark

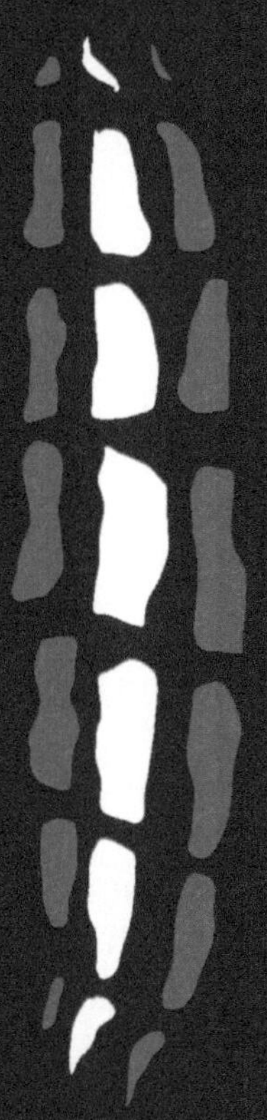

Chapter Forty-Three

Elin

I GRINNED AS WE crested the path that led up to the Sarigh cutaway, which felt more like home every day. There were lights in every colour, mismatched tables and chairs and cushions, food piled high on every surface. Musicians played and people danced and sang and laughed with each other. I couldn't have counted on both hands the number of cultures I saw here; song, dance, food, dress... It was like the entire continent had been stirred into one giant pot together.

"Oh, this is beautiful," Malia murmured. "To think, these people were able to come together like this in the wake of tragedies. You know what it reminds me of...?"

"The Day of Visiting?" I asked quietly.

"Exactly. Elin, where should we put these things?" Malia asked, gesturing to the piles she and her father carried.

"Uh..." I glanced around, catching sight of who I was looking for. "Basma, Tali!" They turned and approached, smiling at me in question.

I set a hand on Malia's shoulder. "These are friends of our family, Nassir and Malia Bayouth. They brought food to pass, and some spare clothing and blankets. Bayouths, this is Tali, the unofficial leader of this community, and her wife, Basma."

"Then I think these will be in good hands," Nassir said as the two women offered to take the gifts.

"Thank you," Tali said as they started away. "We can always use more to help our new residents settle in."

"Nassir, Malia!" Edda said, coming to greet them with Ruce on her arm. They embraced our friends tightly, smiling.

"Well?" Ruce asked, gesturing widely. "Not too shabby?"

"It is wonderful, and we are honoured to have been invited. Would you do me a favour, Ruce?"

"Anything except let you borrow my tools," he shot back instantly. Edda elbowed him in the ribs as Nassir gave him a confused look. "Continue," Ruce said with a pained smile, rubbing where the point of Edda's elbow had struck him.

"I... was hoping you might introduce me to some of your neighbours? Perhaps... that one, in particular?" he asked, pointing with his eyes at the pretty woman who was dancing in the crowd.

"Ah," Ruce said knowingly. "Yes, I think I can manage that. Malia, you're in charge," he said over his shoulder as he led Nassir away.

Malia rolled her eyes with a smile, turning to me. "Are you hungry?"

"Not really."

"Good; me either. I see a storyteller over there, though."

I sighed good-naturedly as she dragged me over to where a small screen stage had been set up— large enough only for the two puppets that currently danced on it. As a kid, I'd only seen shadow stories a few times. They were common in Stangauer, so we only got them when travelling players came through, or when an enterprising Stangrey uprooted their life to resettle in the city. There was a wax paper screen before us, with players behind it making puppets dance in the light of an orange lantern. It was a captivating story, and one that I knew well.

Malia and I settled onto cushions with the children to watch, and with a start I realised Edda had followed eagerly.

"Fan of puppet shows?" I murmured to her.

"This is your history, isn't it?" she replied, ducking closer to whisper in my ear. "Your faith? I want to learn more about it... Where we've lived, we put our trust in something unnamed, but I want to know your gods. Tell me, what is this story?"

"I've actually mentioned it before. You remember the goddess grapes?"

"Delicious," was her only reply.

"This is the story of how they were made." As I spoke, the shadows of puppets echoed my words on the screen. "*Setcha Gria*, the Goddess of seaming and medicine, was lost, hunted by monsters. She had been sent on a mission to collect a rare metal, but she couldn't find her way home, not in the dark. *Nora Gria*, who guards travellers at night, loved her dearly and had been watching over her. As the monsters gave chase, *Nora Gria* dropped stars to the earth to light *Setcha*'s way home. The goddess grapes grow where those drops of starlight once fell."

We watched in wonder as tiny, bright lights began to fall down the screen. "Wooooow," the kids murmured, scooching closer.

The *Setcha* puppet ran across the screen as *Nora* looked down on her from the heavens, and the monsters fell away into the distance as, all at once, a cutout of Lothforias popped up into view. *Setcha*'s head tipped up and she raised a hand, *Nora* coming down to meet her in a tender kiss.

"The end," the boy behind the screen called, standing and bowing dramatically. He looked to be my age, maybe a year or two older. A set of spectacles slipped down his nose as he bowed.

"That's not the end!" the kids shouted as one.

"It's not?" he asked, pantomiming confusion as he scratched his head. "Well, what happens next?"

"The Sentinel! The Sentinel!"

"**Ohhhh**," he sighed in relief, popping behind the screen once more and bringing it to life. *Setcha* now carried something in her arms, and she puppet-hopped across the stage to hand it to another figure who stood outside Lothforias.

"That's the Sentinel," I explained to Edda, "god of combat and blacksmiths. He was the Lady *Foria*'s Guard, but he was badly hurt and couldn't protect her anymore... so he sent *Setcha* on a mission to find living metal, and he crafted himself a new body so he would be strong enough to protect her from any threat."

"Why would he do so much?" Edda murmured.

"That's what you do when you love someone; you shape yourself into what they need. He loved her more than life itself."

On the screen, the Sentinel put on his new body, no longer human, but sharp and made of strength.

"That's your brand," she whispered to me. "His new face."

"He founded the Guard of Lothforias, so the city his Lady loved would always have someone to protect it, even when he was gone."

"Where did he go?"

"He died. Both of them did... They brought peace to the city, and then they vanished."

"I didn't know gods could die..."

"They weren't always gods... just people with a touch of destiny. That's how it all started. Someone believed in something so strongly that not even death could take it from them. And now they watch over us, their descendants, to guide us on our own journeys."

The story ended and the boy blew out the lantern, standing and stretching. The kids began to disperse and the boy approached the cushions Malia, Edda, and I occupied. "I must say, you three are older than my usual audience..."

"Young at heart," Edda promised. "You do beautiful work."

"Thank you. Rami," he said, offering a hand to each of us in turn. Edda and I introduced ourselves and he smiled at us, but when he reached Malia, his movements went jerky and uncertain. "Uh- hi," he said to her nervously, staring at her for a moment too long before blinking. "Uh... I'm Rami."

"Malia," she said with a playful smile. "Will you be wanting your hand back or can I keep it?"

He gaped at her, his face flushing as she laughed. He made no move to pull away, though, until Malia stood up.

"I'm starving," she declared.

I frowned. "I thought you said-"

"Rami, care to show a girl what's good?" she continued as if I hadn't spoken.

"Uh, uh- Yes, please."

He scampered off with her and Edda laughed, resting a head on my shoulder. "That girl has a fire in her."

"Ten minutes ago, she said she wasn't hungry," I told her.

"I don't think it's the food she's interested in, *hayati*. Maybe Nassir will be parting with some cows after all."

"What cows? Why-"

"Shh," she hushed, patting my arm. "Help your mother up. I'm hungry too."

I supported her as she stood, and she led me over to the table our families were sitting at. Rami and Malia were chatting, laughing already, their shoulders brushing, and I realised what Edda had been saying.

"***Cows***, right!" I said suddenly.

Of course, that earned me several strange glances as I sat down, and a quiet laugh from Edda.

||

"Elin," Edda called, "don't go yet! I'll be right out!"

"Of course, Mother!" I moved to sit at the dining table to pull on and lace my *lahat*, but Edda appeared and waved her hand.

"Hang on." She took something out of her satchel and held them out to me. "I made you these."

I turned them over in my hand, my eyes widening. "*Venaq*. How-"

"Another Guard asked me to make her a new pair, so when I learned the pattern..."

"The Lieutenant needed a new pair," I murmured.

"Uh- yes, it was Lieutenant al Abbas. How-"

"Thank you, Mother. These will be very helpful." I pulled them on and tucked my feet into my boots, feeling... settled. The familiar feeling was comforting, finally wearing *venaq* again.

"You're welcome, *hayati*," she said as she pressed a kiss to my hair. "Now, get to work."

Chapter Forty-Four

Ruce

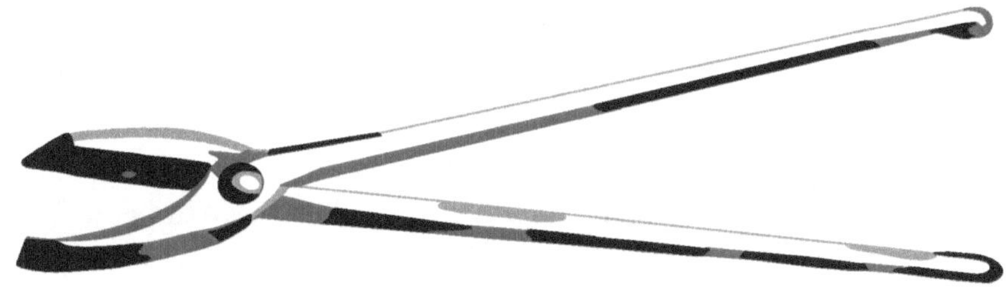

"You see them, Father?" Elin asked, jutting his chin towards the men carrying crates into the citadel.

"They're back," I noted. "Then I suppose you'll be admiring the citadel's craftsmageship today?"

"If you can get me a distraction. That Guard is watching me like a hawk— and she promised if she caught me sneaking again, it would be unpleasant."

"I can manage that. When do-" My voice died in my throat.

What the hell is he doing here?

"Father, what-" Elin followed my gaze to a man who had just entered the citadel and was directing the crate-bearers. "What's wrong?"

"You need to be very careful, Elin."

"I know, Father. I-"

I grabbed the shoulder of his shirt to stop him from moving away. "***No,***" I said into his ear. "You don't. That man there... I know him. We served together. We were- friends, once."

"He's from Jezzine-on-the-Meander? Why would-"

"I wasn't born in Jezzine, boy," I hissed. "That man is more danger-ous than you know." I took a breath and committed to the truth. "He's a Jewel of *Al majowan.*"

"The *Menagerie?*" he asked, his face turning ghostlike.

"You've heard of the Scorpion? The man who led the destruction of Cessiri?"

He nodded grimly.

"Good. So you know exactly what he is capable of."

"Father, you said that- You served with him. Does that mean you were-"

"I was born in Lithdreya, yes."

"That's not what I'm asking and you know it. Where did you-"

"Listen to me. *Al majowan* believe that they are protectors, that their mission is holy, and they will do ***anything*** to complete it. You go, you find out where they're hiding their weapons, and then you come and get me. Understood? You will not confront them alone."

"I understand."

"***Promise*** me."

He took my outstretched hand and clasped it tightly. "I promise I won't confront them alone."

"Good. Now go. When I cause the distraction, slip past that Guard and ***find*** *Al majowan.*"

"What will your distraction be?"

"You'll know it when you hear it."

CHAPTER FORTY-FIVE

ELIN

I reached the nearest asymmetrical hallway quickly, ducking into the Catacombs and closing the hidden door behind me as quietly as I could. Ruce's distraction, whatever the ungodly noise had been, was loud and messy enough that no one noticed me slip out of the craftsmages hall.

When the wall closed behind me, I was left in almost pitch darkness. I reached into my satchel and pulled out the candle I had kept there since the first day I saw the crates. They couldn't be too far ahead of me, so I had to be quiet.

In the light of the candle, I peered down at the ground, finding several footprints in the sandy section. The ground was peppered with spots of dust from centuries of wind and water eating away at the rock. Every once and awhile as I made my way down the tunnel, a drop of water would fall into my hair or onto my cheek.

"I'll find them," I promised, "and I'll stop them from hurting your people."

I moved through the Catacombs quietly, dizzying turns that would have disoriented me if I hadn't played in here as a kid. I had brought a piece of chalk with me, and for each turn I took, I slashed a small X and an arrow pointing back home onto the wall.

The bigger problem was tracking the raiders. As I got deeper underground, there was less sand to leave footprints on, fewer signs of disturbance. I reached a fork in the path and looked fruitlessly for signs that one had been more recently travelled than the other. There was nothing.

I sighed, glancing back the way I came as I wondered if they had actually come this way. Did I make a mistake? What if I had lost them? I-

Drip. Drip. Drip. Drip.

I turned, watching as water fell from the centre stone in the left tunnel at a rhythmic pace.

"Thank you," I murmured as I ducked into the tunnel, a playful drop of water breaking over my nose.

A few turns later, I picked up the trail again in the form of a scrap of fabric left hanging from an unlit sconce. It was the same white cloth those men had been wearing.

I quickened my pace, encouraged, and heard a shuffling some distance in front of me. I stopped, scanned the hall, and stiffened.

There, at eye level, was a small symbol drawn in chalk; a circle with a line hanging down. ***Riadh***.

I quickly blew out my candle and the tunnel fell into darkness. I quieted my breathing, praying that I hadn't been heard, that she hadn't noticed me— or that, better yet, that was an old marking, and she was far away from here.

A match was struck behind me and the hallway began to fill with the glow from a lantern. I winced, slowly turning around.

"Lurking in the dark, Harun?" Riadh asked. "What are you doing here?"

"I'd imagine..." I said slowly, "the same thing you're doing here."

"Arresting a traitor?" she hissed. "I don't think so."

She started forward, but I held up a hand. "Whoa, whoa. You're down here looking for the Lithdreyans who attacked the citadel, right?"

"How do you know that?"

"Because I followed them down here. I'm tracking them. They are more dangerous than you know, Riadh... They're Jewels and Initiates of the *Menagerie*."

"Inside our walls?" she asked in a dangerously low voice.

"I know... what you think of me, but I am trying to stop them and protect this city. If you want to prevent another attack, our best chance is to work together."

"Work with a traitor? That's funny." She launched herself at me, her knife slipping from its sheath, and I just barely brought a stave up in time to catch the strike.

"Riadh, we don't have time for this!"

She gritted her teeth and slashed at me again, but the strike glanced off my arm. The carapace was undamaged.

"How *dare* you use the weapons and armour of a Guard!" she hissed.

"I *am* a Guard, Riadh. That will never change. You are wasting time; we need to protect this city."

She stabbed at me, overhand, but I ducked out of the way and her blade bit into the stone wall. She yanked it out, now nicked, and we heard a rumbling above us as dust started to fall.

Riadh looked up in shock and I barely tackled her out of the way before the entire tunnel collapsed behind us.

I coughed as the dust started to settle, catching my breath. I lifted my head as my ears slowly stopped ringing, rolling onto my back with a quiet groan. Before I could take in the damage, Riadh was pressing her knee into my chest and her knife to my throat.

"You're under arrest," she hissed at me.

"Good luck with that," I shot up at her. "If you hadn't noticed, we can't go back the way we came, which means if you wanna take me to the dungeons, you've gotta walk me past the foreigners attacking the city—and unlike me, they *will* try to kill you. I wish you the best."

She hesitated, easing the knife back from my throat warily. "Temporary truce. We deal with whatever's down here, and *then* I arrest you."

"Counterproposal. We deal with whatever's down here, and then you give me a chance to explain— without knives."

"Chance to explain, **with** knives," she said coolly.

"'*Asabat.*"

"'*Asabat.*" She took my hand, pulling me to my feet. "If you stab me in the back-"

"I won't." She looked at me sceptically and I continued, "It wouldn't work. You're wearing a carapace."

She laughed before she could stop herself. "That's very reassuring."

"I try. Let's go find the invaders."

I started down the tunnel, crouching down to follow the trail left behind. We came to a fork in the road and I frowned, peering down both tunnels.

"You lost them?" Riadh asked. "Some help you are…"

"Just give me a minute, will you?" I knelt down, scanning the ground for any signs of which direction they went, but I could find nothing. I let my eyes fall closed and my head tip forward, quieting my breathing. "I'm trying to find them," I murmured, "but I need your help."

"What are you-"

"Shh," I hissed. "I'm trying to listen."

"Listen for what? Do-" She faltered as I pushed myself to my feet, glancing down the left tunnel. "What is it?"

"Listen. Do you hear it?"

She came to stand next to me, peering down the tunnel. Finally, she nodded. "Running water. But it doesn't mean they went that way."

"It hasn't failed me so far."

"**That's** how you've been 'tracking' them? By following random sounds?"

"By following water. **Faith our reservoir**, right? I swore to Lady *Foria* that I would protect this city. Maybe no one else believes me… but she knows my heart, and she gives me a path to follow."

I could see the anger on Riadh's face, but she said nothing. "Let's get moving."

Chapter Forty-Six

Riadh

"Ugh, why are the halls so full right now?" I groaned, jostling through the crowd of Guards and servants. "I'm going to starve to death right in this hallway."

"We could always take a shortcut?" Harun offered, laughing at the evil glint I got in my eye.

"Gimme a boost," I ordered, and I was already lunging towards him. He caught my foot on his interlaced fingers and propelled me up, then dashed towards the wall and kicked off, joining me in the air. The benefit of constantly being surrounded by Guards was there was always a surplus of broad shoulders to step on. Within moments, the hall was filled with complaints and curses and the occasional groan as one of our feet found the odd pressure point on our way to the dining hall.

"Come on, slowpoke!" Harun called over his shoulder.

||

I hated everything about this. Even his voice was the same— just a little bit lower and harder. The way he moved, the sound of his breathing, where he paused when he spoke... It was like being followed by a ghost. I shouldn't have needed to remind myself every five seconds that he was the enemy, that he was a traitor who had tried to kill my father, but I did anyways, because he wasn't an enemy, he was **Harun**. He had darkened his hair to hide himself, and his face had grown sharper and thinner in the past two years, but he was still Harun.

I heard voices echoing off the stone walls ahead and held up a fist. Harun fell into a crouch behind me, his hand falling to his knife instinctively as I peered around the corner. "Seven shadows," I murmured over my shoulder.

"Seven voices," he replied with his ear tilted towards them. I nodded shortly and began to creep out into the room, still crouched. I ducked behind a long box and glanced back at Harun, nodding. He rolled out from behind cover and hid next to me, peering out at the storeroom. It was poorly defined by the flickering light of the torches, and the shadows cast by the people working were almost dizzying.

"The men I saw aren't here," Harun whispered to me. "Neither are the crates. I'm guessing they're further in." He pointed to the arched doorway at the other end of the store room.

"How do you propose we get there? We can't sneak across the room, and we can't take out seven people without making noise— and we have no idea how many more there are down that hall."

"Are you wearing *venaq*?" he asked, glancing up at the ceiling.

"Always. Why?"

He nodded and I followed his gaze up to the thick wire tendons that were anchored into the walls. "Shortcut."

I had to stop myself from smiling at the inside joke. I quietly unlaced my *lahat* and he did the same. "Give me a boost," I ordered.

"You'll pull me up?"

"Just lift me."

He interlaced his fingers to make a hold. I stepped onto his hands and steadied myself on his shoulders before he pushed up, launching me into the air. I caught myself on the tendon above us, pulling myself up to lay across the two nearest tendons. The sounds of work and chatter would cover small noises, but I didn't want to take any chances.

I looked out into the room, making sure that the workers weren't looking and hadn't heard anything, and then I reached down to pull Harun up. I worked to stay quiet even through the exertion, and he joined me up in the air. We crouched on the tendon and Harun glanced at me. "Ready?"

"Go."

He raised himself up to stand, his hands out to the side to keep himself from swaying. He must have been out of practice—we'd stopped steadying with our hands entirely two months into single rope sparring. As he started towards the far door, slowly his hands dropped to his sides and he was moving the way I remembered.

I had to move more slowly, our scuffle earlier making me aware of the cut on my thigh, which still throbbed in pain. As I worked my way across the tendon, that fight in the alley played over in my mind; the determination in Harun's eyes, the stillness of his voice, the fear I felt when the knife went to my throat. I had been certain he was going to do it. Especially after the way he-

I have dedicated my life to finishing this mission. Nothing else matters.

My foot slipped and I felt the nausea of weightlessness as I started to fall towards the ground, but Harun sensed the tension of the tendon and spun around, catching my arm in panic. I hung there for several moments, only my knee hooked around the tendon and Harun's hand around my forearm keeping me suspended in space, and prayed I hadn't made enough noise to alert the workers below. I didn't dare move, letting my eyes flick to Harun, who was staring intently down at the room. Finally, he shook his head, glancing up at me. With his free hand, he waved a few fingers over his eyes.

They don't see.

Dreya, I hated him in that moment. It was like he was trying to mess with my head, to get me dazed and confused and keep me off-balance.

He carefully pulled me back up to crouch on the tendon, peeling his fingers from their tight grip around my arm. He looked me in the eyes, shrugged his shoulders, and tipped his head forward for a second. *Why are you so clumsy?* he was asking me.

I touched my hand to my thigh with a bit of venom, looking at him pointedly. **You**, I mouthed angrily.

His eyes fell and he turned back around, continuing across the tendon. He reached a pile of barrels near the door and glanced back at me quickly before tipping forward to catch the tendon next to us and drop down to the ground. He immediately crouched, waiting to make sure his move had gone unnoticed. When it had, he nodded up at me to drop.

I hesitated, perched on the tendon, as I considered the pain the impact would cause to my leg. Seeing my thoughts, Harun went to one knee, turned up his hands, and held out his arms in offer. I clenched my jaw, finally giving a curt nod. I watched the workers carefully, and when they were turned away, I dropped from the tendon into Harun's arms. The moment he caught me, I quickly rolled out of his arms and onto my knees.

I looked up at him bitterly and touched my shoulder with a faltering hand. **Thanks**.

He turned away again, some weird expression on his face, and rolled through the doorway into the next hallway. I quickly followed him, standing and stretching once we were alone. **He's almost the same height as me now**, I realised with a start. It ached.

"Are you okay?" Harun murmured to me as I rubbed my leg.

"You don't get to ask me that."

"Maybe you forgot," he hissed, angry for the first time since I had seen him in the alley, "but **you** tried to kill **me**. I was protecting myself."

"I didn't-" I stopped. Maybe I had wanted to kill him… "I was trying to protect my father."

"So was I," he murmured. "Riadh, **please**, just let me-"

A small boom shook the tunnel beneath our feet and our hands flew to our knives. We quickly moved down the hall as a foreign voice hissed angrily in Lithdreyan.

Harun leaned over. "'Careful, idiot. You'll blow your fingers off.'"

"Since when do you speak Lithdreyan?"

"Long story, Ri. Fill you in later."

His answer felt so normal, so friendly, that it hurt. I pushed it down as we reached the threshold of another room, three times the size of the first and supported by a series of columns. "What do those crates say?" I asked, nodding to the Lithdreyan words written on the sides.

"I don't know," he said with an unhelpful shrug.

"I thought you spoke Lithdreyan!"

"Yeah," he huffed in frustration. "I speak it, not read it. It was a working education," he said distractedly as he looked around the tunnel. Suddenly his face turned ashen. "Do you know where we are?" Harun asked.

"We're not-"

"Right beneath the palace?" He nodded.

I peered back out at the foreigners, trusting Harun's sense of direction. Even when we were kids, he always knew exactly where we were when we played in the Catacombs. The marks he left had been more for my benefit, honestly.

There was a barrel of black powder spilled out beneath the furthest column, with a black mark on the ground where one of the workers had dropped his torch onto a small cluster of it.

"They're going to collapse the chamber," I realised.

"They're trying to destroy the palace and kill everyone inside. We need to stop them!"

"How do you propose we do that? You said there was a Jewel of the *Menagerie* down here!"

"Scorpion," he said slowly. "Leave that to me. I should-"

"Don't you do this again. Don't tell me you think you can take a Jewel of **the Menagerie** in a fight."

"I've... had some exposure," he shrugged, "to similar tactics. I think I can at least hold him off long enough for you to-"

"Fine. We don't have time to argue. We go on three?"

"How about on go?"

"Fine. Go!"

I leapt out into the room, immediately sinking my knife into the shoulder of the nearest man. The room exploded into shouts and footsteps and blades unsheathing and screams of pain as Harun and I went to work.

I didn't have time to count the enemies before we went in, but within minutes, there was only one left standing, limping heavily. Nothing had challenged me, and I was wondering which of these novices could be the Scorpion.

"Riadh!" Harun shouted, but before I could turn, a heavy impact slammed me into the wall. As I fell into a heap, groaning, my head spun and screamed at me. Years ago, Harun had struck a blow against my head with a stave and left me dizzy for days. This felt a lot like that.

I weakly tried to push myself up, but I couldn't manage it on arms now shaking in pain. I struggled to refocus my eyes, finally catching sight of a blur of movement and light glinting off of swords. As the world came into focus, I registered what I was seeing.

Harun was facing off against a man who could only be Scorpion; he was tall and thin, but deceptively strong— from the way his attacks pushed Harun back— and he held weapons unique to his role. His sword was the same as that carried by every Jewel of the *Menagerie*, and as their Scorpion, he had a chain from which dangled a blade with a sickening curve that evoked a scorpion's tail.

He would alternate between lashing out with the chain and catching the knife in his hand to slice at Harun. He struck so fast that in my daze, I couldn't follow it... but it seemed like Harun could. As I watched the fight, I saw something incredible. Scorpion feinted with his sword, coming in just under Harun's ribcage with that small scorpion chain-knife, but Harun's stave was already in place to block the strike before it came, like he had anticipated it. He struck with the pommel of his sword, taking Scorpion across the jaw, and grinned as the man staggered into the wall.

"Let's move!" Harun yelped at me, voice full of adrenaline as he pulled me to my feet. I shook my head clear and joined him in front of the crates. We pried them open with our knives and my stomach dropped at the sheer quantity of black powder. There were eight barrels full around the room... The entire city centre couldn't survive that explosion, much less the palace. "Oh my god..." Harun breathed.

"What do we even do with this?"

"There should be an irrigation tunnel just through that hall. We could-"

"Harun, look out!"

With my warning, he ducked to the side just before Scorpion's knife bit into the wood next to his head. Scorpion yanked on the chain and the blade came free, starting its lethal pendulum once more. "You get the powder into the water, I'll deal with him!"

Harun spun to his feet and immediately met Scorpion's sword with his own, his knife crossed behind it to anchor himself against the strike. I grabbed the nearest barrel of black powder, rolling it towards the doorway Harun had pointed out to me.

I heard the roar of moving water as I neared the doorway, encouraged by the sounds of the Goddess. I finally caught sight of the irrigation tunnel and the roaring river it held, shoving the barrel forward to splash into the water.

"Thank you," I murmured to Lady *Foria*, knowing her power would render the black powder useless. Over the centuries, our people had learned that water was its only weakness.

I was on the seventh barrel when I heard Harun hiss in pain. I looked up from my task to see a gash open on his cheek, just below his eye. I had no reason to worry, because his opponent was sporting several more wounds— not that I **had** been worried.

He kicked out Scorpion's knee and the man staggered to the ground. Harun ran to me and took over rolling the last barrel, which I was grateful for because my muscles were groaning in agony. "I'll toss this one; you find us a way out of here once we're done!"

I sprinted over to the doorway against the other wall, peering down the tunnel to see a faded X at eye level and an arrow pointing right. "I found a way out!" I shouted, ducking back into the room to see Scorpion holding a torch as he moved towards the black powder that had been spilled next to a column— the column closest to the irrigation tunnel.

"No!"

Harun spun as the last barrel fell into the water, locking panicked eyes with me just before the torch dropped, and the world exploded.

"Harun!"

SEARCHING

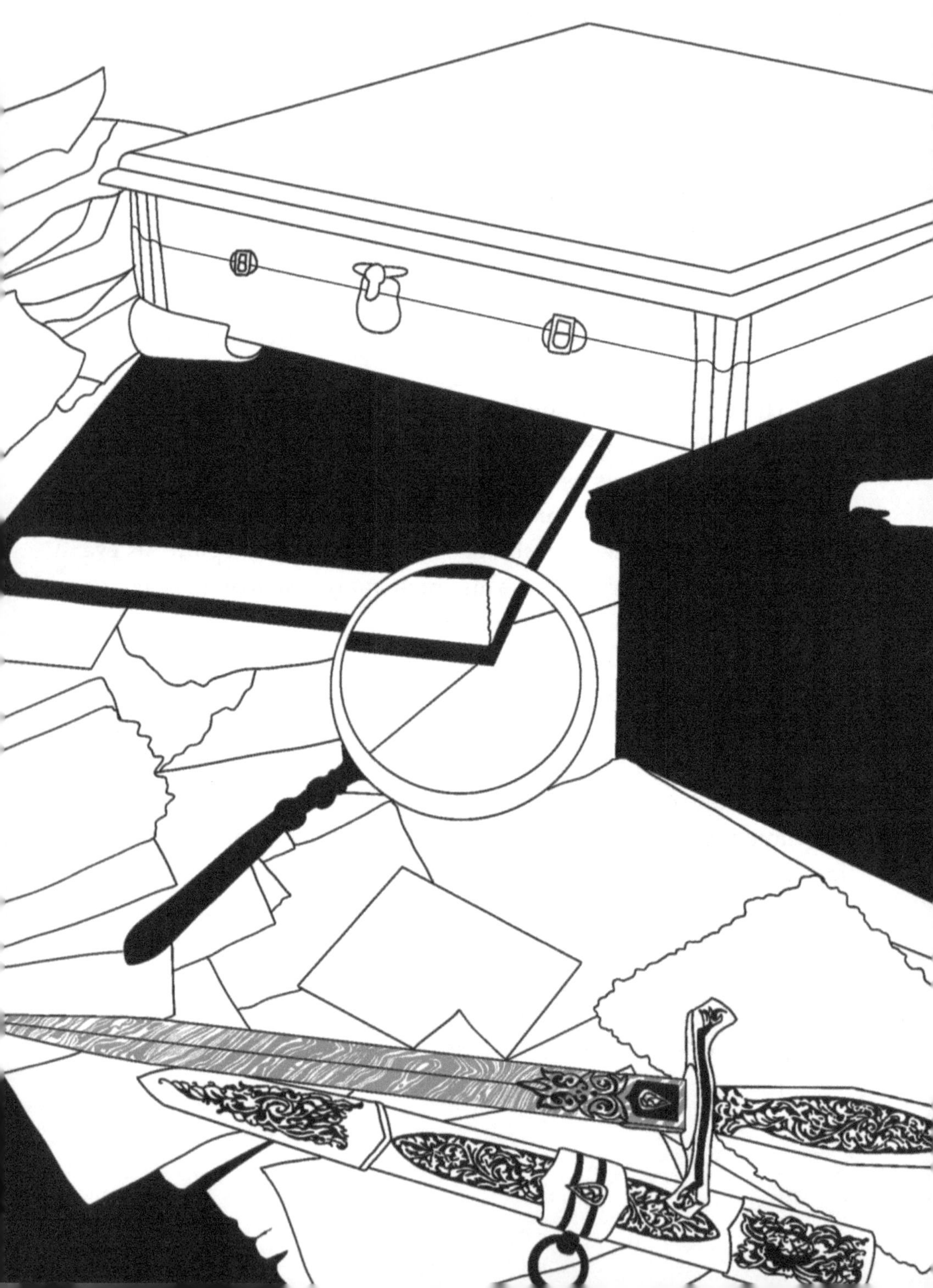

Chapter Forty-Seven

Riadh

When I came to, the air was so thick with dust that it looked like impenetrable fog. I coughed heavily, pushing myself up off of the wall to stand on shaky legs. My thigh wound had reopened, either in the fight or the blast, and I could feel blood soaking into the linen of my *shiwr*. I tore a strip of fabric from my *kara* to tie above the wound.

That was another *kara* Harun owed me...

Harun!

I stumbled over the uneven rubble as the dust began to gather on the ground. There was a small pool of blood on the ground near the doorway, but no body— Scorpion must have walked away from this. I knew it had been him because of the scrap of fabric still pinned under a fallen wall. The *Menagerie* believed in function and practicality above comfort, and much of their clothing often reflected it— rough, pitted for airflow, and absent of any dyes.

I continued towards the doorway into the irrigation tunnel, though that doorway was now less than half my height. I groaned as I ducked onto hands and knees to crawl into the tunnel, which was in even worse shape than the room I had just left. When my eyes adjusted to the relative dark, I saw nothing. Nothing but rubble. Even the flow of water had been stopped, which filled me with dread. The Goddess wasn't in this place anymore.

"Harun," I called into the echoing deep, but there was no answer. "Harun!"

CHAPTER FORTY-EIGHT

EDDA

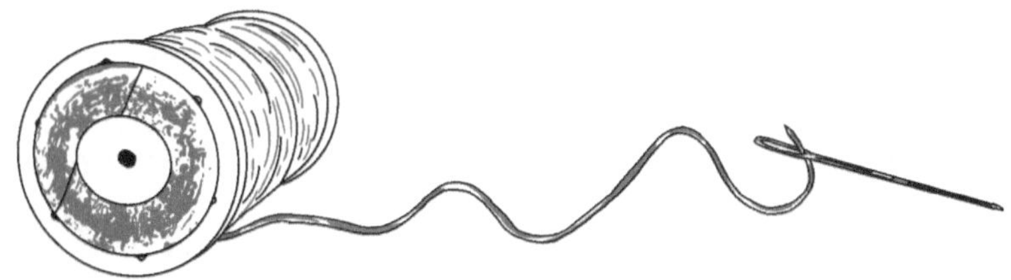

I WOULD'VE THOUGHT IT was an earthquake if I didn't know my Elin liked to go running after bad men. Knowing that, every second after the trembling stopped aged me ten years, shaking my hands and spiralling my thoughts. A bell began to ring, clean and high like water. It didn't stop.

The Guards of the city were at attention immediately, hands on their weapons and eyes hungrily roving over every foot of the citadel.

I crossed to the fountain, lifting cupped hands to my face and letting the water trickle down my cheeks, cool and refreshing.

"Please," I murmured, "***please*** keep my boy safe. Bring him home to me."

It was almost an hour before anyone knew what had happened. I looked up as sharp, raised voices echoed off of the marble. They followed the Lieutenant through the citadel, her orange uniform covered in dust and touched with blood, a scrap of fabric serving as a tourniquet on her thigh. She walked with purpose, calling out to the Guards in the hall of craftsmages.

"We're not under attack!" she informed them. "Not anymore... I discovered foreigners in the Catacombs with crates of black powder. They were dealt with, but a small store of powder went up and collapsed a tunnel."

"Foreigners?" one of the Guards asked.

"Lithdreyans," she nodded. "Including a Jewel of the *Menagerie*. Scorpion."

My blood went cold as the word left her lips. I fisted a shaking hand into my dress, feeling the rough scar that had run along my palm for thirty-five years and whispered that name at every touch.

"You defeated a Jewel of the *Menagerie*?"

She faltered, shaking her head. "He made his escape, when I found their hideout. Only eight of them stayed behind; you'll find their bodies in the Catacombs."

There were murmurs of praise from the crowd and I saw her brows pinch in discomfort. She drew breath to say something, but stopped, nodding to a messenger.

"I need you to tell Captain Owaines about the attempted attack, and that I'm taking a squadron into the Catacombs to make sure they've been driven off. There's no time to waste."

"Yes, Lieutenant!"

"End the workday; send these people home," she said lowly to another Guard. "Tell them work resumes as normal in the morning."

"Are you okay, Lieutenant? You're bleeding, and you look..." she didn't finish, but the concern didn't leave her face.

"I'm fine," Lieutenant al Abbas said shortly. "I just..." her face fell and her shoulders drooped slightly. "I'm tired."

The truth, but just a drop. Elin told me that the Goddess *Foria* carried the city on her back for three days before laying it down here. The Lieutenant looked like she was burdened by a similar weight.

"You should rest, Lieutenant. You're wounded."

She shook her head. "There's no time. I need to lead the squadron down to where we fought the foreigners."

"We?"

"I... I misspoke," she sighed. "Form up."

She started back the way she came, then stopped, turning and finding me in the crowd of seamsters. "Pardon, mother. I've ruined my *shiwr* and *kara* today. Would you be able to craft new ones when work resumes?"

"My pleasure," I stuttered out.

She smiled at me, turning back to lead the squadron of Guards, and the moment they were gone I sprinted to find Ruce and Elin.

Chapter Forty-Nine

Elin

I WAS IN PAIN when I awoke, but not the work ache I had grown used to. There was a dull throb in my cheek, and a burning on my arms and hands, but cool water moved along my body, soothing the pain. My head spun as I opened my eyes fruitlessly. There wasn't enough light to see my hand in front of my face, if I'd had the motivation to lift my hand that far. I didn't.

What I wanted most was to just let my head fall back and lay there, numb, but I couldn't. Mother would be worried, and I promised her I'd come home.

The texture of the ground under my hand was enough to tell me I was in a tunnel— not the same tunnel I had been in, I guessed, based on the darkness. I weakly pushed myself to stand, staggering forward as I put weight on my right leg. No broken bones, pain memory told me, but something had wrenched out of place, so it was hard to walk on. I couldn't help but limp as I started forward, following the flow of water downstream.

Almost delirious, I remembered how Ruce had told me to fake a limp when we first came into the city. ***Don't have to fake it now...*** I started laughing, my voice echoing off the round walls of the tunnel.

The further I walked, the lighter the tunnel got until I could see the evening sky reflecting on the water below me. As I stepped down from the tunnel into a stream, my eyes adjusted to the wavering light. I had emerged several feet from the olive orchards by our dwelling. I was alone, which I was glad for— I didn't know how to explain to anyone why I'd ended up bloody, bruised, and barefoot in an irrigation tunnel.

I turned, looking up at the road to the Mount Sarigh cutaway with something akin to hatred. It seemed so much longer than it ever had.

When I finally reached the cutaway and started up the stairs to our dwelling, I could see a figure pacing across the candlelight, their shadow stretching out of the mouth of the cave. At the sound of my uneven footsteps, the pacing stopped, and Edda appeared in the doorway. "Oh, Elin, where have you been?" she asked, peering out into the dark.

I drew breath to answer her, but slowly shook my head and brushed past her into the main room. Ruce was sitting at the table, his biceps three shades lighter where his fingers dug into them anxiously, but he stayed silent.

"What happened to you?!" Edda asked.

"Fell," I mumbled.

"***Fell***?! You fell where?!"

"Down."

"***Down*** where?!"

"Irrigation tunnel."

"***An irrigation tunnel***?!"

"Are you just going to keep repeating what I say in a louder voice?" I asked tiredly.

"Elin, we have been worried sick! ***Please*** tell us what happened!"

"Yell louder, Mother, I still have some hearing left," I said in a moment of belligerence. The pain and exhaustion were catching up to me.

"***Ooh***," she fumed, "I should've learned you better when you were younger! I just can't-"

She stopped short, looking up at me for a moment, her anger frozen on her face before she began to smile, and eventually laugh.

"Oh, Elin, sometimes I forget that-"

My eyes dropped. ***That you're not really my son***, my brain finished.

"-you weren't always my son."

I slowly looked back up at her, my shoulders sagging in exhaustion. "I'm so tired, *Ama*."

She pulled me into her arms, hugging me tightly and running her fingers through my hair. I let my eyes fall closed, let myself believe that the tears were okay if no one could see me. "It's okay, *hayati*. We're here. Tell us what you need."

"I- I don't... I don't know."

"Ruce, grab the medicine bag. I'll make something hot for you to eat, okay?" She stepped back and I wiped my eyes as she ducked down to meet my gaze, her thumbs still rubbing circles on my shoulders. She glanced down at me and frowned. "Elin, why are you barefoot?"

"Oh. I'm... I'm gonna need new boots," I said through a sniffle.

CHAPTER FIFTY

RIADH

"Excellent work, Lieutenant," Captain Owaines told me with a hand on my shoulder. "All the bodies have been recovered, and we've verified that they were all Initiates."

He crouched in front of one of the bodies to lift the sleeve, turning the man's wrist to show me the several scars that formed a beautiful pattern on his arm of dots, Vs, and lines. The ceremonial scarring of the *Menagerie.*

"All of them? There was... no one else?"

"What were you expecting?"

"I just- want to be sure they were working alone. You checked the irrigation tunnel?"

"Yes. All of the black powder was destroyed."

"That's... all?" I asked falteringly. "You didn't find anything else in there?"

"No. Are you sure you're alright, Riadh? The medics said you lost a lot of blood... and you took a nasty blow to your head."

"I'm fine."

"You're certain? Because I need to report to the king, but I will wait if you need me to manage the scene here."

"I've got this, Captain. Go." He dipped his head to me and I turned to the stoneworker who'd come down with me. "Was there any structural damage to the palace?"

She stepped forward, mindful not to jostle her arm in its sling. "Only one column was destroyed," she told me, "but it was there for support. You should all be vigilant around the interior wall of the temple for the time being. We'll need to shore up the support here to prevent a collapse, but I'm still recovering from the attack on the citadel, so I can't do the work we need, and I don't..." Her face fell. "I don't have an apprentice to help me anymore."

"I'm sure it will be fine until you recover. I'll let the other Guards know to stay out of the temple until it's repaired, and we'll move the washerwomen to temporary housing. Is that all?"

"Yes, Lieutenant."

"Excellent. I have something I need to do. Sergeant!" I called across the room. "Walk with me! New orders for your squadron!"

CHAPTER FIFTY-ONE

RUCE

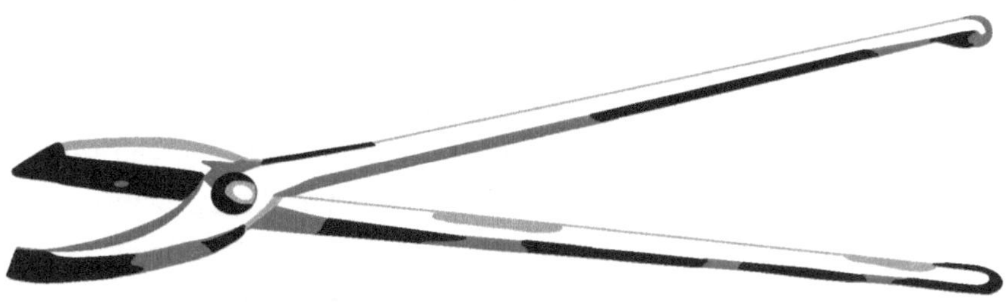

"You've been working on that dirk for three days," I said to Elin as I came up behind him. "That's a lot of detail in that blade, son. We get a special commission?"

"Not yet."

I watched him work for a minute, burnishing the small engravings on the handle and the sheath, before I was finally able to voice the question I'd been carrying around since the explosion. "Did you intend to break your promise to me when you made it?"

"What?" He stopped working and looked up at me. "I... I didn't break it, Father. I was going to come back to get you, but a tunnel collapsed."

"So you fought them on your own and nearly got yourself killed."

"No. I fought them alongside someone else... and, nearly got myself killed," he finished meekly.

"What happened, with Scorpion?"

He looked up at me, measuring how much to tell me. "We stopped him, for now... He had nine barrels of black powder, Father. He was going to take out the palace, the citadel, the city centre. I had to do something. You understand that, don't you?"

I didn't say anything, but I did. I understood what it felt like to see the *Menagerie* doing something that was wrong... and be unable to stand by.

I moved away to resume my own work, wondering what had happened to my old friend after the explosion... I wondered if Elin would tell me. I wondered if he knew. The boy had been a bit off when he finally came home. Edda had guided him to sit at the table to eat and let me take a look at the cut on his cheek, and every so often, his eyes would go unfocused and distant before snapping back to presence, just a little bit too wide. His jaw would clench and unclench as he played with the knife on his belt. I knew what it was; I had seen it all the time when I was his age. "Can't stop, can't start," the others would say. We'd get that way after a fight sometimes, or after a fright. Seemed like he'd had his share of both before he finally made it home to us.

"Lieutenant al Abbas gave us new orders."

I stopped hammering, leaning a bit closer to listen to the Guards on the other side of the smithy.

"We're going to every dwelling in the city and searching for a young man with a Sentinel brand. We won't stop until we find the traitor. Lieutenant says he's still here."

I dropped my hammer to the worktable, striding across the smithy to Elin and laying my hand on his shoulder. "They're looking for you," I murmured into his ear.

"Tell me something new."

"Alright. They're going dwelling to dwelling looking for any boy your age and checking him for a Sentinel."

"What?"

"You need to remove it, boy; that mark'll get you killed."

"You want me to-"

"Elin!"

We turned in unison, seeing Malia waving as she walked over to the smithy.

"Mal!" Elin jumped up and went to lean up against the counter. "What're you doing here?"

CHAPTER FIFTY-TWO

ELIN

"I JUST CAME INTO the city centre to do some shopping and bring my father a meal." She held up the basket at her side. "You boys hard at work?"

"Can't call it work when I enjoy it this much. I'm starving, though. Can't wait to go home for supper."

"Your family should come over to ours. I'm making *freekah* and chicken."

My stomach growled at the thought. "Don't play with me, Mal."

"Tell your parents I insist. It's been too long since we've all had a meal together."

"Five days."

"Too long!" she said with a laugh. "I expect to see you all at supper tonight."

"Stop mentioning food," I groaned.

She reached into her basket and set a small meat pie onto the counter, turning away with a wink. "Bye, Elin!"

"I appreciate you!" I called after her, the pie already halfway to my mouth.

When I turned back to the smithy, Ruce was still looking at me in concern. I shook my head, swallowing the pie in a hurry.

"I know you're worried," I told him, "but I can't remove my brand. I won't abandon my faith."

"But if-"

"I'll trust my Goddess. Whatever happens."

I sat myself down at the workbench facing away from him, my teeth grinding over each other against my will. "I will follow you," I hissed out, hoping Lady *Foria* could hear me over the sounds of the forge and Ruce's worry.

I held the dirk up to the light, slowly nodding to myself. "Father, when the city's Lieutenant comes and asks for a new blade, can you give her this one?"

He crossed the smithy, snatching it from my hand without looking at me. He turned it over with an irritated expression, then looked up at me shortly. "It's impeccable work. Start on the hatchery commission."

I turned to reach for a new piece of steel to fold, but knocked into the bucket of water we kept for dousing the fire. It skidded across the table and spilled its contents over the edge, right into the barrel of hot oil. Trying instinctively to catch it as I had been, my arm was immediately hit by hot oil when it exploded on contact with the cold water.

I hissed in pain, clasping a hand over my arm as I staggered back, falling to my knees.

"Elin, what happened?" Ruce asked, turning to me in shock at the clatter.

"Accident," I groaned through my teeth, "I'm fine." I pushed myself to my feet and reached for a clean piece of linen, but in my clumsiness I knocked it to the floor. I dropped back down to my knees and elbows and wormed my way under the table to grab it as Ruce hovered above me uselessly.

"Excuse me, father."

Startled by Riadh's voice, I slammed my head up into the table before scurrying underneath it.

"Elin," Ruce whispered, "what are you-"

"She needs a knife. Just give her the knife!" I hissed back.

He turned and I watched his legs move over to the counter. He cleared his throat. "What can I do ya for?"

"My side-knife was recently damaged, and your wife told me that you're the finest metalworker in the city. I was wondering if you could make me a new blade with your Jezzine steel."

"Uh... my son has just finished a wonderful piece, actually." I heard the quiet thud as he set it to the counter. "It's yours if you want it."

"It's beautiful," she murmured, dropping several *darai* to the counter. "Where is your son? I'd like to thank him."

"Oh, he's- around. I'll pass on your gratitude. Have a wonderful evening, Lieutenant."

"You as well, father."

When Riadh's footsteps receded into the distance, I finally released the pained groan I'd been holding in and ducked out from under the table, looking at the burn on my arm.

"Now, what happened to you, Elin?" Ruce asked in exasperation. "I turn around for one second and-"

I gaped, staring down at my arm, my pain momentarily forgotten. "It... it's gone."

"What?" He came over to stand next to me, medicine bag in hand.

"My brand..." I looked up at him, dumbfounded.

"The oil burned it away completely."

I gave a shaky laugh. "I guess Lady *Foria* agreed with you. The soldiers won't find me now, will they? Oh, that really hurts, though..." I groaned, doubling over in pain.

"Sit down. Let me bandage your arm."

I moved to sit at the workbench again as he laid out the supplies from the medicine bag. He mixed some honey and yoran root onto his finger and gently spread the mixture over the burn. I watched him work with a furrowed brow.

"You were one of them, weren't you?"

He stilled, his back to me where he had turned to grab the linen.

"You told me you were born in Lithdreya, but that's not all. You were a part of the *Menagerie...*"

"What makes you say that?"

"I beat him."

He finally looked back up at me, his expression unreadable.

"When I faced Scorpion, I knew how he would fight, because sometimes when we spar... you fight the same way."

"Maybe that's just how we're taught in Lithdreya."

I shook my head. "I've fought members of the People's Army; Scorpion was different. He was like-" I cut myself off, shaking the memories of my banishment away. "He was like you— dangerous."

He took a step close to bandage my arm, never breaking eye contact with me. "We should go find your mother, make sure she knows we've been invited to dinner."

I clenched my jaw as he started out of the smithy. I had no right to be irritated that he was dancing around the truth; not when he and Edda had to force every other word out of me. I knew I was right, though. I knew that sparring with him, with a former member of the *Menagerie*, had saved my life down in the Catacombs.

||

"Alright, Elin?" Malia asked.

I glanced up to see my family and Nassir looking at me around the dining table. "Yes, sorry, just enjoying the food. You were right, Mal. Five days *is* too long to go without your cooking."

She grinned at me and went back to her meal.

"I heard something interesting in the citadel today," Nassir said conspiratorially to Edda. "I'm friends with a court scribe, and she told me that the Captain of the Guard commissioned an order of succession testament. Those are only needed when the ruler decides to name a new heir. It sounds like the king is going to leave the kingdom to Captain Owaines, not his daughter."

"He can't do that!" I blurted. Everyone turned to me and I stammered, "Uh, the- Lieutenant al Abbas seems like a very capable heir. She was instrumental in stopping that attack, w- wasn't she? Why would Bazzeri pass her over?"

"No one knows," Nassir sighed. "Very few people are allowed to see the king; not even his daughter has permission."

"Do you think he's being lied to?"

"Who would dare deceive the king?"

I fell silent, knowing **exactly** who it was, but wondering what I could possibly do about it... There was no way I could get to the king— I'd had to put my efforts to cure him aside to focus on the raiders, and now that the Guards were sweeping the Catacombs... I hadn't been able to find a way through.

||

"Are you sure you're okay?" Malia asked, glancing over at me as we sat together up on the third floor. "You haven't said a word since we finished dinner."

I blinked, tearing my gaze from staring into space. I had been looking down two stories at the dining table where Edda, Ruce, and Nassir were chatting for twenty minutes. "No, I'm just... thinking about a problem," I said sadly.

"You know what *I'm* thinking about?"

"What?"

She laced an arm through mine. "Climbing trees with my best friend," she said happily. "It was my favourite thing to do when I was little... but I stopped doing it, after Fatima died."

I looked up at her in panic. "You-"

"I'd thought something about you looked familiar, the first night we met. You have the same eyes as her," she said gently.

"Then you-"

"Yeah. I know who you are... but I never blamed you for what happened to my mother. Even before I met you, I didn't believe what they said about you... and now that I've played *bita* with you, I'm certain you couldn't have poisoned King Bazzeri."

"I'm not *that* bad at cards," I grumbled.

"No," she laughed, "but you are hesitant, and gentle. You and I both know you could have won that game twice, but you didn't because you would've had to play cold-blooded. And even though you're capable of it, you didn't want to."

I slowly nodded.

"Ruce, on the other hand... I wouldn't want to be on **his** bad side."

I fell silent and she glanced over at me.

"I didn't... tell you about Fatima to make you worry or feel bad, I just wanted you to know that I understand what you went through, and that you don't need to lie to me to protect your family down there. Fatima was my friend, and **you're** my friend— you can talk to me about anything."

"I don't... even know what I would talk about. Everything... everything is everything, does that make sense?"

She leaned her head against my shoulder. "I feel like that a lot... You know the story where *Setcha Gria* stopped the sun in the sky, so she could finish weaving *Nora Gria*'s cloak of stars in time? Sometimes when I was younger, I wished I could stop the sun and just breathe for a minute."

"That would be nice."

"My *Ama* taught me a trick, though. Wanna see?"

I nodded and she set a hand over my heart, nodding to me.

"You can take a breath right now; you don't have to stop the sun. Breathe."

I slowly inhaled, then exhaled.

"Again."

Inhale. Exhale.

"You can **always** take a minute to breathe, and hopefully everything will feel a little less everything."

"Thank you."

"Thank you for protecting us, the other day."

I looked up at her in surprise. "Wh-"

"That was you, wasn't it? Or do you really expect me to believe— what did your father say— that you hurt your leg in a fall?"

"I did, though," I protested. "He just... didn't mention that it was into a tunnel in the Catacombs after an explosion," I laughed.

Malia joined me giggling and soon we sounded delirious. Eventually, we could breathe again, and she laid back, looking up at the touched glass as her feet kicked in open space through the staves in the railing. "Do you think they'll come back?"

I lowered myself down to lay next to her, my gaze tracing the story of *Setcha Gria* and *Nora Gria*'s love in the glass roof. "Not for a bit, at least... We scared them off, ruined their plan. And when they do come back, I'll fall down a tunnel again, don't worry."

"My hero."

I smirked, glancing over at her. "You really used to play with Fatima? I don't remember you."

She was staring up at the night sky through touched glass, her hair framing her face with pretty curls. "I don't think we ever met. You were one of those kids who played in the grove... and made swords out of sticks and pretended to be a warrior, right?"

"Yeah."

"Thought so." She shook her head. "We wouldn't have played with you. We were too busy **discovering far off lands**... We were going to sail around the world when we were older, you know. Fatima had a running list of everything we would need to pack; she'd learn to steer a ship, I'd learn to sing sea-songs, and we wouldn't come back until she'd seen everything."

"I didn't know that... I didn't know she wanted to leave the farm."

"She thought you were really brave, for doing what you wanted, even though your father tried to stop you... I did too."

I gave a weak smile and reached up to wipe my eyes. "I'm sorry we didn't play together when we were younger. I think we would've been good friends if I had known you back then."

"Yeah... It's a good thing our families didn't spend time together, though. I think if my father had seen yours walking around in the dirt barefoot and singing to his trees, he would've dropped dead right there."

I laughed. "Yeah. Your father is more..."

"Practical?"

"That's a better word. Let's go with that."

We laughed until we didn't have the energy anymore, and Malia rolled onto her side, smiling at me. "You laugh like Fatima used to... Can I tell you what I remember about her? I miss... well, all of it, I guess."

"Please."

"I remember one day in the spring, Fatima and I were running through your family's orchard, and she told me about how the apples were yellow because they were made of ***pure gold***, and we had been hired by the king to bring some back to the palace. But then, a dragon appeared, and we had to sneak through..."

Chapter Fifty-Three

Edda

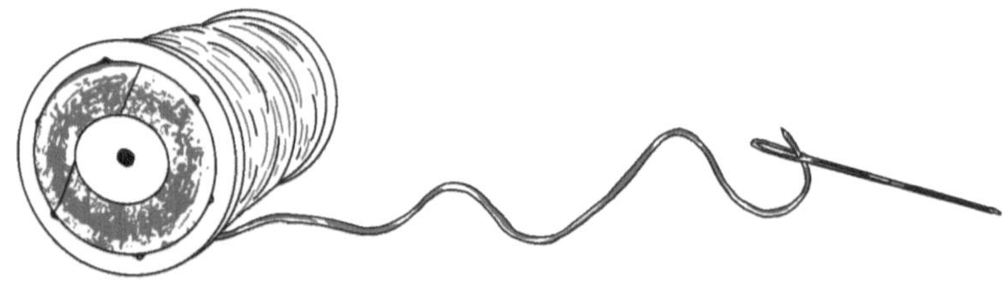

"I GOT SOME REJOHANESE tea at the market today; I thought we might expand our horizons," I said over my shoulder.

"Tea, Edda?" my husband asked me. "Are you trying to poison us?"

"Nassir swears by it," I laughed. "He said it has a robust and calming flavour."

"Well," Elin said, "it is important that flavour be robust."

"Oh, *essential*," Ruce agreed.

"If you don't like it, there's plenty of *kahve*," I promised as I turned to set the tray on our table.

"Excellent. Let's start there."

I laughed in exasperation. "I just thought-"

As shadow fell over the doorway and I froze, my heart stopping. Three Guards stood outside our dwelling, armed and armoured. And my boys had their back to the door.

"Hello," I said amicably, forcing down my terror. "To what do we owe the pleasure of a visit from three honoured **Guards**?"

Elin's shoulders tensed just slightly as he looked up at me, and Ruce's hand subtly tightened around the kitchen dirk he had been using to slice fruit.

"Apologies for intruding on your day, mother, but we are on official business. We were told a boy lives here, about twenty?"

"Yes, my son," I said levelly, fighting the rising panic. "May I offer you some tea, or sliced apples? *Kahve*? My family was just sitting down to have an afternoon break."

"We don't wish to take up your time, mother, we just need to ask some questions."

"Of course; please, come in."

"Are you sure you wouldn't like something to eat?" Ruce asked, offering the Guards a seat. The kitchen dirk he had been holding was nowhere to be seen. "You three must have been working hard."

"Thank you, Father. We appreciate your hospitality."

I busied myself serving our 'guests' and prayed that they couldn't hear my heart hammering in my chest. Were they here for Elin? If they had found him...

"What brings you here, Sergeant?" Ruce prompted politely, handing her a cup of tea.

"Well," she said, "we've received word that someone has slipped into the city disguised as a refugee, and we've been asked to investigate. A boy, around his age," she said, nodding to Elin.

I laughed. "Oh, our Elin's never been in the city before; none of us have."

"Where is your family from, mother?"

"We made our home in Jezzine-on-the-Meander, but we lost everything in the massacre... We were lucky to survive."

"I am sorry for the tragedy you three have endured. You seem familiar," the Sergeant said to Elin. "Have we met before?"

"I apprentice with my father in the hall of craftsmages," he said smoothly. "Perhaps you've seen us in the smithy?"

"You two are the Jezzine steelmakers," she said in realisation. "Yes, of course— I have heard wonderful things about your work. One last question before we leave you: could you roll up your sleeves for us?"

"Of course," Elin answered quietly, shifting in his seat. I stared at him in shock as he bared one forearm, then the other. But where his brand had been was a fresh bandage.

"What is this?" the Sergeant asked.

"My son was burned in the fire that destroyed our smithy," Ruce explained.

"Can you show us?"

"I'm sorry," Ruce sighed, "but you want us to **prove** that my son was scarred in the raid that levelled our village? What are you looking for?"

"We... I apologise, father, but I must insist."

"We need to change the bandage soon anyways," Elin said gently, stretching his arm out for Ruce to unwrap the bandage. Layer upon layer was unwound, baring a painful, splotched section of skin. It had been burned a dark, angry red, like it had been made by oil or pitch.

"The- the thatch on our roof caught fire," Elin explained shakily, "and it had been coated with pitch to make it waterproof..."

The Sergeant looked more uncomfortable by the moment, and she cleared her throat hurriedly. "Thank you three so much for giving us your time; I hope life in this city treats you well."

"You are too kind," I said to her, clasping her hand as she rose. The others followed suit and started towards the doorway.

"We'll take our leave; if you see anything suspicious, let us know, yes?"

"Of course," I beamed at them. "Anything to help."

The moment they were gone, I turned on my boys, slowly looking between them with a harsh expression.

"Well, that went well," Ruce said lightly.

"Swimmingly," Elin agreed.

"There wouldn't be something the two of you forgot to tell me about, would there?"

They glanced at each other, each frowning ignorantly, as though Elin's burn wasn't on perfect display in front of them. "No, nothing... nothing I can think of. You?"

"No. No."

CHAPTER FIFTY-FOUR

RUCE

"Keep your chin up, boy. You may have gotten lucky once, but that's no reason to get cocky. Stay in the moment."

"I'm here," he said through gritted teeth, his gaze constantly flicking from my sword hand to my knife to my eyes to my feet— did my shoulder just tense— and back as he bounced on the balls of his feet, filling the room with nervous energy. Over the past several nights, he'd taken to instruction eagerly, grateful for any advantage he could get over the opponent he'd faced in the Catacombs. I hoped he wouldn't need to put these lessons to use, but I knew better than to rest on hope.

"You must have drilled this over and over," he said as he blocked a sword strike, "when you were an Initiate. How did you and Scorpion match up?"

I huffed out a laugh as I brought my knife into his blindspot to take him by surprise. As I expected, he was able to deflect the attack, but it took up enough of his focus that his questions stopped for a moment.

"You were friends with him, weren't you?" he said eventually. "Were you evenly matched or was there a clear difference in skill?"

I locked the hilt of my knife against his sword and twisted, sending him sprawling and the weapon across the room in one swift motion. I leaned down to pick him up with a wolfish smile. "What do you think?"

"Ay!" Edda called from her chair in the main room. "How many times do I have to remind you his leg is still healing?"

Elin grinned back at me, the torchlight from the main room making the sweat on his face shine. "I think it wasn't even close. I think you swept the floor with him without even trying."

I ruffled his hair affectionately, then wiped my now-sweaty hand on his *kara*. "Eugh. Right answer. Now be quiet and focus."

"I can focus and ask questions at the same time; I'm supposed to be learning, aren't I?"

"How to survive a fight, not run your mouth. Your turn on the attack. Remember not to fall into patterns. Predictability is death."

Twenty minutes later, I was nursing a cut on my arm and Elin was holding ice to a bruise on his cheek as we sat at the table together. Edda was snoring loudly as she dozed in the bedroom.

"Did it hurt?" Elin asked quietly.

I looked up at him, the warmth of the fire making me tired and slow. "What?"

"Initiation."

I sat up and slowly unrolled one of my linen wraps to show him the ceremonial scars that covered my forearm. I hadn't bared them to anyone but Edda in thirty-five years. "More than anything I'd ever felt," I nodded. "Yours?"

He laughed. "I didn't want to cry in front of the other Guards, but I couldn't help it. It was over quick, but it hurt for days... Do you- do you regret it?"

"I don't have time for regret. I made a mistake. I won't make it again. Isn't that what matters, boy? That I'm different than I used to be?"

He was silent, staring at the grains of the table like they could answer.

"You don't have time for regret either, you hear me? Put it away, do better. That's the only option."

He nodded decisively and stood, moving to the pack he'd brought with him into the city. "Do you think..." he asked as he started back into the main room, "that you could make me a pair of these out of Meandering Steel?"

I looked down at the blade he offered me and barked out a laugh as I glanced back up at him. "Now... just where did you get **these**?"

CHAPTER FIFTY-FIVE

RIADH

I WOVE THROUGH THE crowd of Guards moving out of the temple, finding Hakim and his mothers quietly going over a list. I had put the Corporal in charge of the evacuation of the temple for several reasons, only two of them being the women who stood to his left and right. His mothers had served Lady *Foria* as washerwomen for years, honoured to attend to her temple and her protectors. The washerwomen oversaw the temple's care and cleaning, as well as the care of the Guards. All of our clothing, armour, bedding, and food was handled by the temple's attendants.

"Sita, Anjali," I called as I approached.

"Good morning, Lieutenant al Abbas," they said together.

"How is the evacuation going?" I directed this question to Hakim, who nodded quickly.

"All essentials have been moved out of the temple, and I've organised for the washerwomen to stay in several of the citadel's meeting rooms until the support can be repaired. I've divided tasks among our ranks to set up the rooms and move belongings. My mothers are confident work will carry on without delay."

"Excellent." I knew Hakim would perform the task diligently and with great attention to detail; he always did. The source of his drive may have annoyed me, but I was never one to argue with the results. Though I was far too busy these days to spend my time sparring with Privates and Corporals, I had seen Hakim in the practice courtyard on occasion handling a disadvantage of three opponents with ease.

"Sita, Anjali, I hope you both know that if there is anything you or the other washerwomen need, all you have to do is ask."

Sita beamed at me, taking my hands in hers. "Thank you, Lieutenant al Abbas. For you to come and check in during such a harrowing time means the world. I only hope that you are taking care of yourself just as well as you are taking care of your people."

"Yes, she's right," Anjali said. "You look tired, too tired. You deserve to rest."

"I'll rest when this is over. Corporal, report to me when the preparations are complete."

"Yes, Lieutenant."

||

I turned over the blade in my hand again, admiring the detail in the hilt as the candlelight glinted off of it. It had been polished till it shone, engraved with delicate hook flowers that were each darkened to a warbling black. The blacksmith's son must have taken days working on these tiny details, putting such care into his craft. It had earned the boy my respect, even though I'd never met him. His work spoke. I knew this weapon would serve me much better than the one I had damaged a week ago in the Catacombs, when I lashed out at Harun.

I tossed the dirk onto my desk in irritation as I saw his face once more. I began to pace back and forth across my bedroom, which took nearly twenty steps each way. My shadows grew long and misshapen from the distance between me and the walls of the room, but the space felt suffocating right now. Harun's body hadn't been recovered after the explosion, but after a week of searching, the squadron I'd sent out had found no sign of him in the city. They had searched every dwelling and they'd found no sign of him... What if he'd staggered away from the blast and bled out in some darkened tunnel? What if his body had been washed out into the desert and the sun was bleaching his bones, windswept sand the only burial he'd ever get? What if he'd still been down there, alive but only barely, and I just left him there, came back to the comfort of my bedroom in the palace?

I shook my head, sprawling onto my bed in exhaustion. "No," I breathed. "No, he's smart. They didn't find him... that doesn't mean-" *That doesn't mean he's dead.*

He made it so hard to hate him, especially when he kept maintaining his innocence, kept promising me he'd never hurt my father, that all he wanted was to protect the city....

I replayed the confrontation in my head, the moment I'd found him in the Catacombs. *I know what you think of me*, he'd told me, *but I'm trying to protect the city.*

That was when I lashed out, slicing his arm open— or I should have, but he was wearing...

I sat up, leaning forward on the edge of the bed. He'd been wearing a carapace, a green fabric that held up under my knife. I recognised that fabric; I had overseen delivery of it myself.

||

"Do you need an escort, Lieutenant al Abbas?" the Corporal at the gate asked, startled to see me exiting the palace before the sun had fully risen.

"You have your orders; follow them." I strode past her and into the citadel, weaving through the corridors until I reached the craftsmages hall. It was a rest day, so the only people here were Guards, but one of them would know which refugee settlement the Jezzine seamster lived in.

Half an hour later, I made my way up the cliff face to the cutaway on Mount Sarigh. I caught the attention of a nearby woman and asked, "Edda Lahd of Jezzine-on-the-Meander?"

She directed me up to a cave on the second level. "Miss Edda's in right now, just call out and she'll be happy to host you."

"Is this the home of the seamster?" I called as I ducked inside.

I saw Edda at the counter in the main room, cutting up some ginger for the breakfast she was preparing. At my greeting, she turned, smiling at me. "May I serve you, Lieutenant?"

"Yes, mother. I'm looking for someone, and I believe you sold-" I had been casting my eyes around the unfamiliar dwelling, but I caught sight of a *kara* hanging to dry. Grey, like the one Harun had been wearing— and a *kara* was a young person's garment. "Uh- Does a boy live here, about twenty?"

"Just my son, Elin," she shrugged, and turned back to her cutting board. ***The blacksmith's boy. Of course***. I almost let the matter drop, but the knife began to waver in her hands as she tried to continue chopping ginger. I couldn't understand why... Refugees had no reason to fear the city's Guards, and she certainly had no reason to fear me.

I drew breath to speak, but then a shadow passed over the cave entrance. "Mother, I got the apples you-"

I spun around and Harun's voice died.

"Riadh," he finally managed.

My hand immediately fell to my knife, my eyes narrowing. "So you've been hiding here all this time?"

"Mother," he said slowly, his eyes never leaving mine, "go find Father."

Edda shook her head, stepping between us and pointing an angry finger at me. "Now, I don't know what you're doing here, but my son has done nothing wrong. If you think I'm going to just-"

He turned and looked at her, his face hard. "Mother, I'll be fine."

CHAPTER FIFTY-SIX

EDDA

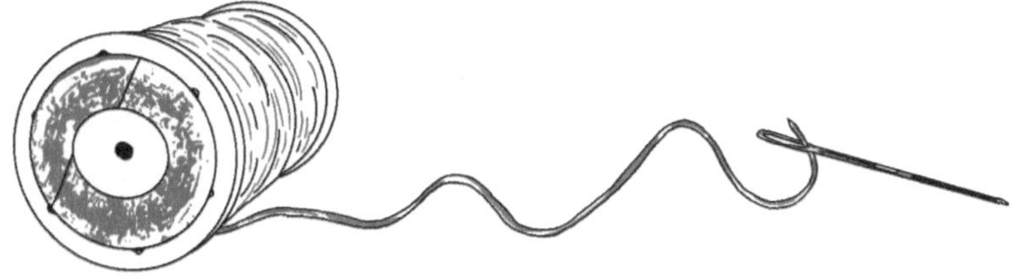

HE WAS LYING.

Chapter
Fifty-Seven

Riadh

"I'm not leaving you alone with-"

"*Ama*, I need you to go. Please."

Edda looked up at him for a long time before slowly backing out of the dwelling. Then she turned and sprinted down the road.

When she was gone, I said, "I lost you after the smoke cleared. I thought you'd been hurt."

"Were you worried, or relieved?" he asked over his shoulder bitterly.

"You tried to kill my father, Harun. Don't you dare ask me that."

"I d-" He looked up at me for a long time, and I saw his thoughts spiralling, heard his breath racing. Finally he turned away from me and set a hand over his heart, his breaths causing it to swell and dip several times as they began to steady. When he looked back at me, he was solid, grounded. "You promised to give me a chance to explain."

"Fine. Talk."

He crossed the room decisively and unsheathed his knife as he moved to the mud-brick fireplace. He levered a single brick out of place and reached into the hole it left behind. He removed from it a small glass bottle that hung on a cord, like it had been worn as a necklace, and slowly came to set it on the dining table in front of me.

"What is that?" I asked curtly.

"Four-fang venom. Tempered."

I grappled with that as I stared at the silvery contents. "This is where you've been?"

He stepped forward, leaning down to catch my eye. "I have **never** wavered, Riadh. I would give my life to protect the king."

"Jove- Jove told me what you did; why you did it."

He scoffed. "What did he tell you? Was I a fanatic? A traitor? An assassin?"

"The attack that killed your family— you believed my father knew about it before it happened. You snapped, put poison in his wine."

Harun shook his head. "No, that's not true. Your- your father is a good man; he protected his people. If he knew, he would've stopped it."

"You really seem to believe that... Were you always this good an actor?"

"I'm not the one convincing your father you're unfit to rule."

"What?"

"There are rumours in the citadel; Captain Owaines commissioned an order of succession testament."

"You're lying."

"You don't need to believe me... but take this." He held out the bottle to me. "This **will** heal your father, but **please** do not tell Jove that you have it."

"What, you think I'm going to just let you go? Forget that there is a couple here harbouring a traitor to the crown?"

Harun was instantly eye-to-eye with me. "I don't care what you do to me, but don't you **dare** threaten my family."

"**Family**? Harun-"

"Elin. My... my family calls me Elin." There was something earnest in his gaze.

I studied him for a long time with a furrowed brow. "And you prefer it. Why?"

"Elin," he explained, "protected his family, stood by them. He protected the city. Harun's family died because of him, because he abandoned them. *Oren*'s slip-up allowed your father to be poisoned. I'd rather be Elin than any of my mistakes."

"You really want to protect this city?" I asked deliberately.

"I took an oath, Riadh. That means something to me."

"Then here's your chance. Come with me."

CHAPTER FIFTY-EIGHT

RUCE

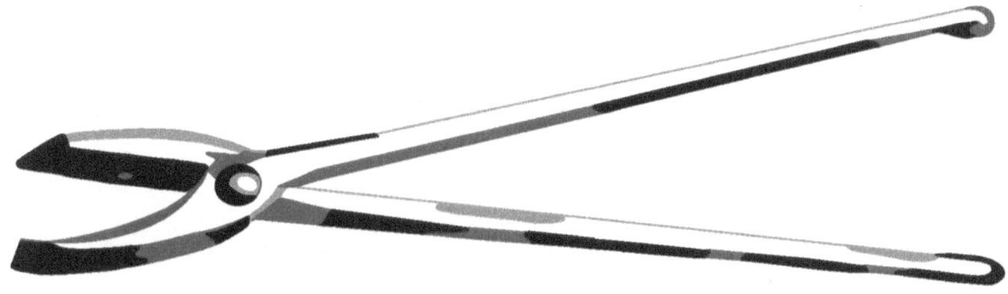

EDDA RAN INTO THE dwelling and I was pulled in after by her death-grip on my hand.

I had been cleaning broken crates and dead rats out of our new shop since the sun came up, trying to make it workable. I'd thought it would take at least a year for us to earn enough to buy our own shop, but Nassir—talkative, friendly, wonderful Nassir—had a friend. She was old and had no family, so her shop had sat empty for years, no use to her. Nassir introduced me to her last night to strike a deal, and all she asked in exchange for the building was a new dress. Blue aizome, please, to ward off mosquitos.

So I had set to work on the shop, kept going by the promise that Elin would come by later with breakfast and a set of hands to help. We would put the forge in that corner there, a workbench here... Edda could have this entire room here for her seaming, with all this wonderful light coming in. She'd love it. The shop was tucked into the bend of the river, just like ours had been in Jezzine, before the fire. It was perfect.

"Ruce!" Edda had burst into the shop, panicked and panting and her hair flying wildly. "You need to come home!"

When we ducked into the dwelling, it was empty. Elin was gone, and there was no sign he'd ever set foot in this place. His *venaq*, which sat up against the foot of his bed on rest days. His sword, tucked into the ice room. His *kara*, hanging to dry. Even the small glass bottle he'd tucked behind a brick in the fireplace when we first came here had been stolen from its hiding place. Everything was gone.

"He said she was an old friend, Ruce, but she was **so** angry. Do you think-"

"We both know what can happen between old friends," I said lowly.

"Scorpion," she murmured.

||

It had been thirty-five years since I had seen my friend, thirty-five years since I had carried the weapons of *Al majowan*. I would never forget the way he had looked at me... after I knocked the blade from his hands, stood between him and the foreigners we were told were the enemy. I'd betrayed him. That was all he understood.

He didn't listen to me, didn't give me a chance to convince him that our teachers were wrong, didn't stop to consider that the children shivering behind me were people just like us. I shouted at them to run, and then my oldest friend and I were grappling on the ground. We rolled in the dirt, and within breaths he was standing above me, sword in hand. He looked down at me with hatred, trembling with rage, and raised the weapon to kill me. I flinched, but the blade never struck me. A young woman jumped between us and caught the blade, wild curls flying as she panted.

"Get away from him!" she screamed.

I kicked out at his knee and he pitched forward with a choked sound. I leapt to my feet, grabbed the young woman's bloody hand, and started running as her city burned behind us. We didn't stop until we reached a small village in the bend of a river.

We didn't love each other, at first— Edda didn't even like me, and honestly I couldn't blame her. She would never know what had happened to her family, if anyone had survived the fires, because of *Al majowan*, and the scars on my arms were a constant reminder that I had held one of the torches.

As the years passed, though, we didn't just stay with each other out of necessity and obligation and no-one-else-could-understand. We built a new life, small and happy, and started to let ourselves heal. Eventually, our son was born, and Edda called him *Elin*, our new moon. He was our chance to move on, to make something better than what we'd had before...

||

I couldn't protect our boy in Jezzine. But I wasn't going to lose another son— no matter what I had to do to keep him safe. Edda couldn't take it again. *I* couldn't take it.

"Ruce-"

"We'll find him," I promised. "We'll find our boy."

THE WORK

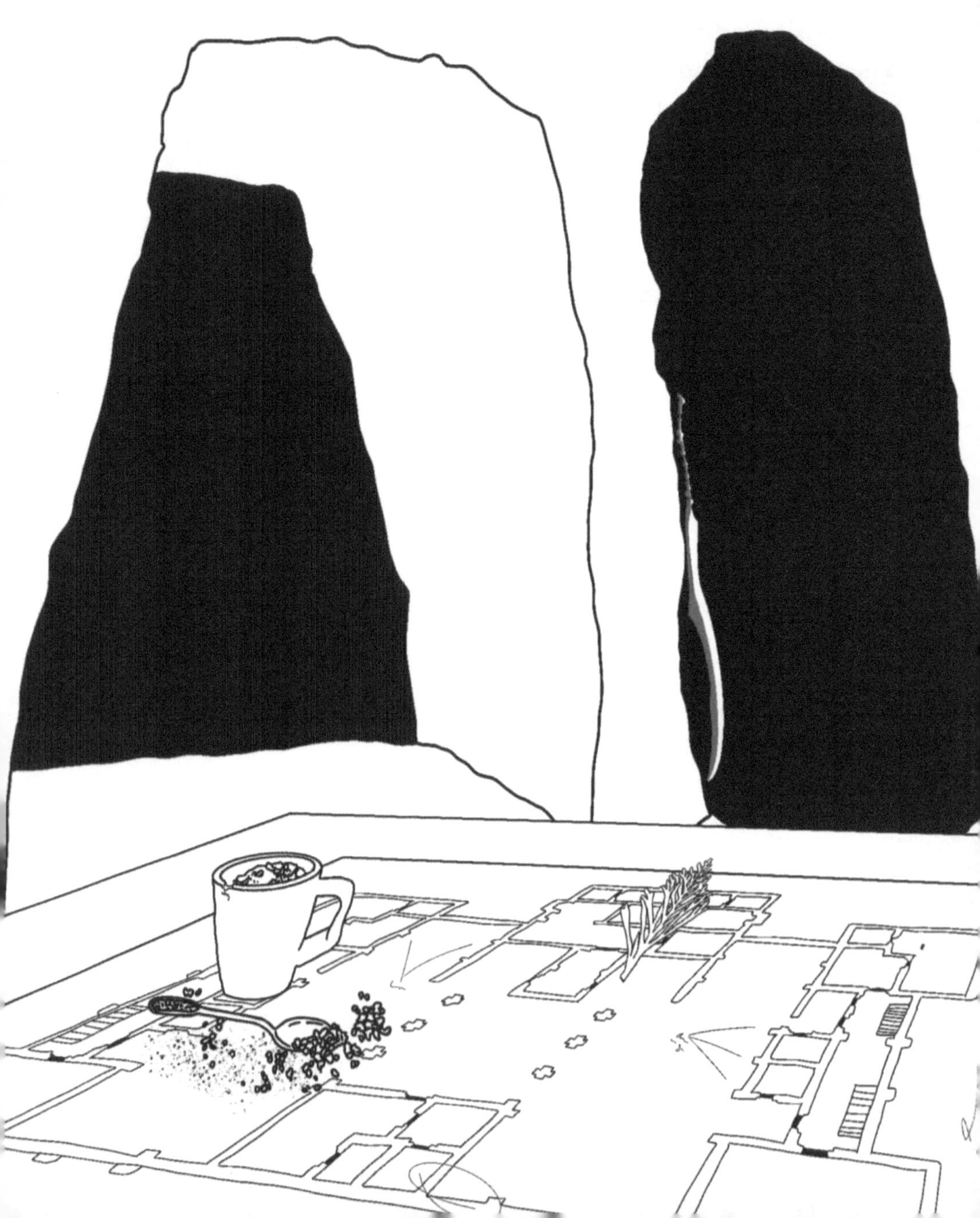

CHAPTER FIFTY-NINE

ELIN

EDDA AND RUCE WERE standing over the dining table, the candlelight making their shadows flicker and stretch out of the mouth of the dwelling as I approached. I ducked inside, squinting at the paper that was laid out on the table. In Edda's delicate handwriting, I saw the citadel laid out before me, entrances marked with a shaking hand and *bita* pieces playing Guards. Ruce had his sword strapped to his belt, and Edda's knuckles were white around a knife.

"What's going on?" I asked.

They turned to me in surprise, and Edda sprinted over to pull me into a hug. "Elin!"

Ruce was only a beat behind her, tilting my chin towards the light to see the bruise on my jaw. "Where have you been?!"

"I thought you'd been arrested, Elin!" Edda panted.

"I'm sorry that I scared you, Mother... but I took care of it. Riadh's going to leave us alone now."

"How'd you manage that?" Ruce asked, turning my arm to see the cut that had sliced clean through my carapace. I knew what he was thinking, that only two metals were able to cut through a carapace—we'd tested it thoroughly one slow workday. Stangrey blue metal, and Meandering Steel...

"I convinced her that I'm trying to protect this city too."

"Is that why you're bloody?"

"Surface wounds," I said with a shake of my head. "I'll be fine."

"Sit," Ruce ordered. Edda was already halfway across the room to her seaming kit by the time I fell into my chair.

As Edda began stitching the cut on my arm, I winced and my eyes were drawn down to the table again, at the map drawn from memory. "...Were you two planning to attack the citadel?"

"Of course not," Ruce said dismissively, rolling up the blueprints.

"You were. You were figuring out how to get in."

"Remember that next time you disappear," Edda told me. "You're our boy; if you're in trouble, we're gonna be there to get you out of it."

"You shouldn't-"

"Don't. Your trouble is our trouble."

"What if my trouble gets you killed?" I shot back angrily.

"What if?" she shrugged. "What if I fall down and hit my head tomorrow? What if I'm mugged in the street? What if a flowerpot falls from a balcony and kills me? What if," she said deliberately, leaning down to meet my gaze, "you were killed because I stayed out of this? Do you think I would prefer that? To know that I had lost my boy without even trying to protect him? Would you ask me to be okay with that, Elin?"

My eyes dropped.

Ruce sat across the table from me. "What happened today, Elin? Where have you been?"

"Just a skirmish," I shrugged. "Out past the farmland. It was nothing."

"How close is that to the truth?" Ruce asked without skipping a beat.

I looked up at him and he gave a knowing smile. "Not." My teeth gritted against each other. "We have work in the morning. I'm going to get some sleep."

Chapter Sixty

Riadh

I WAS PACING MY room again. I say 'again' like it had happened once or twice before. The truth is I hardly did anything else in this room now. Since Harun's betrayal— not a betrayal?— every eye had been on me, and this was the only place I could be alone, be myself. And my self was restless... I couldn't stand the silence, the questions that snapped at the back of my neck like wild dingoes.

Harun, Elin, whoever he was trying to be now, had followed me so willingly out of that dwelling. He'd had no way of knowing what I was going to ask of him, just that I believed it would protect the city, and he'd followed me without hesitation.

||

As we walked down the main road past the farmland, I told him that I had found cypress sprigs stuck to the boot treads of the several bodies that had been left behind after we fought the Lithdreyans in the Catacombs.

"Which means they were camped somewhere at the west edge of the city."

I nodded. "The only other cypress trees in the city are in the palace courtyard, and if they had access to the palace, they wouldn't have placed the black powder in the Catacombs."

"You're hoping the survivors are still out here, licking their wounds."

"I'm hoping you and I can fix that. Captain Owaines denied my request to take a squadron out here to search."

"He seems to be shutting you down quite a lot these days."

"Don't start that again," I practically growled. "You think I'm going to trust your word over his?"

"I think that used to be your first instinct."

"That was before you **poisoned my father**!" I had stopped on the road, gotten face-to-face with him in my anger.

He just looked at me like he was waiting for something. "Why did you believe him?" he asked finally.

"What are you talking about?"

"I don't care **what** evidence he gave me, if Captain Owaines had told me that you betrayed this city, I would have denied it to my dying breath because I **know** you, Riadh. I know what kind of person you are... I thought you knew me at least so well."

With that, he turned and started down the road again, leaving me behind as he scanned the outlands left and right.

||

I collapsed onto my bed, my fingers playing with the small vial he had given me, the vial that now hung around my neck. Captain Owaines had been searching for this for two years... All I had to do was give it to him, and he would help me save my father.

But Elin had begged me not to tell him I had it. Why would he give me the cure in the first place unless he was genuine?

I already knew that the contents of this vial would, in fact, heal my father. The moment I had returned to the palace, I'd barricaded myself in the library and learned how to tell what was real. Every treatise I'd found agreed: elixir made from the venom of a snake varied from yellow to white; the only exception was the four-fang, which had the strongest venom ever recorded. It was potent, almost black, but appeared coloured in the light, like oil.

I held up the vial to the candlelight, watching the colours wax and wane as I twisted it.

It was real. Elin had given me the only thing that could save my father, and he had told me to keep it hidden from Captain Owaines.

Could the Captain really not be trusted? After my mother's death, his Immersion had been auspicious. The water spraying off of the falls had mixed with the sunlight, sending out brilliant colours. Why would the Goddess give such an omen if the Captain were a traitor?

||

Early in the morning, I found one of the Guards who had escorted Captain Owaines to his Immersion, cornering her in a deserted hallway. "I need you to tell me about the omen you saw, when Captain Owaines finished his Immersion. Tell me about the coloured light."

She frowned at me, slowly shaking her head. "I... I wasn't there, Lieutenant. None of us were allowed to accompany him the last three miles of his trip. He ordered us to stay behind, so he might undertake the Immersion alone and have a chance to grieve."

"His Immersion lasted five weeks!"

"Yes, Lieutenant. We remained encamped as ordered until he returned. Though Captain Owaines told us of the wonderful omen that appeared above him, he was the only one who got the chance to witness it."

"Thank you, Corporal," I said slowly, turning away.

||

"Elin!" I called, jogging down the road to catch up. "Wait!"

He stopped, just for a moment, to give me time to fall into step beside him. "I've seen several sets of footprints on the road, and I think they split off from it there." He pointed some ways ahead of us, where a faint path had been worn into the sand by a group of people all walking the same way. He crouched to look when we got closer, nodding. "I see eight different sets of footprints— five men, three women."

I shook my head, sighing. "Then it's the wrong trail. The *Menagerie* only recruits men."

He gave a laugh. "That's a lie. There are just as many women in the *Menagerie* as there are men— maybe more."

"It's common knowledge, Elin, that-"

"I spent the last two years in Lithdreya searching for the four-fang. I fought Lady *Dwer-da* myself. The only reason everyone 'knows' women aren't recruited is because the *Menagerie* spreads that lie to allow their female operatives to do their work without suspicion."

"Do you think there are some here, hiding in the city?"

"I'm certain of it. And I'm certain that this trail is the one we're looking for."

"Why do the Lithdreyans hate us so much?" I sighed as we started off the road.

"The *Menagerie* doesn't speak for Lithdreya," Elin shot back. "Most Lithdreyans just want peace. The people we're fighting were raised to hate us."

"Okay, let's g-" I stopped dead. "I'm sorry, did you say that you **fought** Lady *Dwer-da*?"

"Yes."

"One of the dingoes?"

"Yes."

"A **Jewel** of the **Menagerie**?"

"Yes," he huffed. "I told you I had experience with the *Menagerie*. I'll tell you everything later, now can we-" He nodded to the trail we were following. "Please?"

"Lead the way," I sighed.

||

"Captain Owaines!" I called as I caught sight of him turning down the hall. "Might I have a word?"

He slowed, smiling at me, and nodded towards his study. "Please, join me. I have some trade reports to look over."

I sat in one of the plush chairs in front of his desk, watching as he poured out *sahlab* into two cups for us. I politely took a cup, ignoring the sinking feeling in my stomach as the warm smell wafted up to me. Harun and I had made a tradition of going for *sahlab* after long days of training.

He would always make a face after the first sip and sigh, "It's not as good as my mother's," before downing the entire cup.

He taught me how to make it, once. We'd snuck out of the barracks in the middle of the night and down to the palace kitchens. He'd shown me how to mix the warm milk and corn flour together and stir in vanilla. I'd asked him how much vanilla and he inhaled deeply, doing a little dance. "Feel it in your soul," he told me. Our laughter had almost got us caught that night. We barely had enough time to pull ourselves up onto the support tendons above the kitchen before the doors opened and a pair of Guards walked in, searching for the source of the laughter.

"What did you want to talk to me about, Lieutenant?" Jove asked.

I cleared my throat, taking a small sip of *sahlab*. "I've been thinking about the poison that was used to weaken my father. Wondering... if there was any other way for us to get hold of it. I don't- I don't know much about this poison, but you and I both know there is a black market in-"

"We won't find any in the city," he told me quickly. "The poison used against your father comes from the Lithdreyan four-fanged serpent, which makes it dangerous and difficult to acquire. No one is selling it, because it can only be found in the Lithdreyan desert. Most people who try to obtain it are killed, and the four-fang is rare. Even those who manage to survive the encounter need patience or luck to happen upon the snake."

"Then... how did Harun get it?" I asked innocently, tilting my head and furrowing my brow. "He never left the city in his life."

Jove blinked, taking a moment to stammer out something noncommittal about how, "Determined people find a way."

I slowly set down my cup of *sahlab*, now wary of the drink in front of me, and glanced up at him. "Yes... I'm sure they do. Thank you for answering my questions, Captain. I feel no less hopeless, but now I understand exactly what went into poisoning my father... and why we're having so much difficulty curing him."

I rose to leave and he held up a hand. "There should be a court scribe waiting outside. If she has arrived, would you send her in?"

"Yes, Captain." I turned from the room quickly, finding the woman sitting on a bench outside the study. "He's ready for you," I said with a bright smile. As I passed, I peered over her shoulder to peek at the document she was carrying. ***Order of Succession. Dereliction of duty. Unfit to rule. With mine own authority...***

The hallway turned three degrees hotter in my anger. I strode through the palace, ducking under one of my father's servants to snatch the key from his belt, and quickly made my way to the king's bedchamber. I locked the door behind me, my breath still shaky as the darkness of the room enveloped me.

"Riadh?" my father's weak voice asked. "Have you finally come to see me?"

"Father," I said with a start, turning to stand beside his bed. "Captain Owaines... told me you didn't want to see me. If I had known-"

He held a hand over mine, coughing. "You've come... because of my decision."

"Then it's true? You've passed succession onto Captain Owaines?"

"Not yet, but I have no choice, Riadh... You are not ready to rule."

"Why? What have I- He's been lying to you too," I realised, pulling my hand back from his. "He- he's convinced you that I'm... what? What have I done wrong? Has he not told you that I have served this city faithfully, that I am protecting it daily from raiders? It wasn't two weeks ago that I stopped Initiates of the *Menagerie* from destroying this very palace, and he has told you that I'm unfit to rule?"

"Riadh-"

I shook my head, slipping the vial from around my neck. "I am going to cure you, and you will see what I have done in your name, in your absence, Father."

"Is that-"

"Four-fang venom, tempered. It will restore your strength, but we were lied to... It was not Harun who poisoned you. He has been faithful, even in his banishment, searching for this cure the last two years. I now believe it was Jove who poisoned you, who snuck into the Lithdreyan desert when we believed him to be undergoing his Immersion. We have been deceived, and he is not to be trusted."

"Jove..." he said sadly. "I knew- He was angry, before-" he broke into a fit of coughing. "Before his Immersion. But... I thought-"

I raised the vial to his lips and he slowly drank, grimacing at the taste.

"Recover, Father, and you and I will walk through the city together again. Hide your condition from Jove until you have regained your full strength, and we will root out his treachery."

"Thank you, *hayati*." He weakly raised a hand to cup my cheek. "So much like your mother... I doubted you. I'm sorry I trusted someone more than my own child. When I recover my strength... show me what you have done."

I wanted to tell him that it was alright, that he was not to blame for the lies Jove had told him... but I couldn't convince myself of that. I was hurt by my father's belief in those lies, by the fact that he had thought so poorly of me even though-

Even though he knew me. Just as I had done of my oldest friend. I understood, now, the hurt Elin carried whenever he looked at me, the lengths he had gone to trying to show me he could be trusted...

CHAPTER SIXTY-ONE

ELIN

I SIGHED, SITTING UP in my bed once more. I had been restless for the past hour, unable to sit still but too tired to do... anything.

I pushed myself to stand, feeling like a little child as I decided a warm cup of *sahlab* would help me sleep. I ducked between the curtains that gave my room privacy, locking eyes with Ruce in surprise. "What-"

"Shh," he said gently, nodding towards the bedroom. "Your mother's sleeping. What are you doing up?"

"I... I was just going to make some *sahlab*. What are you doing up?"

"I'm wondering what kind of 'skirmish' you could've gotten into protecting the city... Wondering what shape you left *Al majowan* in."

I slowly sat down, nodding. "Those are good questions."

"Are they going to get good answers? Are any of my questions?"

"There..." I sighed. "There is too much that I don't know how to tell you. So many questions that I don't know how to answer."

"Then start small; tell me what happened today. I'll make us some *sahlab*."

"It was just a sandworm, Father."

He gave me an appraising look at the Lithdreyan phrase. "Tell me anyways."

I sighed, thinking back to this morning that felt years away. "Riadh had tracked the *Menagerie* out past the farmlands... We found their trail and followed it to their camp."

||

The trees, sparse at first, became denser and denser as we moved deeper into the outland. As the sound of voices grew closer, we ducked behind the cover of a healthy cedar tree.

"Three shadows," Riadh hissed to me.

"I think I hear four voices..."

She crept to the side, peering through the branches as they got thinner to examine the campsite. She held up four fingers, glancing over at me as she gestured. She split the air in half, pointing left and right. ***I'll take the two on the left, you take the two on the right***, she was telling me.

I nodded, unholstering my staves as she unsheathed her knife. She held up three fingers and began to count down, locking eyes with me once more. As she reached one, we both ducked out from cover to the left and right of the tree, sprinting into the campsite with our weapons drawn.

||

"Cinnamon and pistachios?" Ruce asked, glancing up from the two cups of *sahlab* he had just finished pouring.

"Just cinnamon."

He sprinkled the spice over top of our drinks and came to sit across from me at the table. "What happened, after you leapt out of cover?"

"The fight went by in a blink. Facing two Initiates each, we took care of them quickly."

"They were Initiates, all of them?"

"Yeah. But we didn't realise there was another party that had been out scouting when we found the camp. That fight was... different."

"He was there. Scorpion."

I nodded.

||

Riadh's shout was my only warning before the curved scorpion blade bit into the tree above my head. I spun, holstering my staves behind my back and drawing my knife and sword.

Riadh was engaged with two Initiates and doing her best to draw the attention of the third. Scorpion smiled as he yanked his chain-knife free and started to swing it in a small arc. "I didn't think you had survived that explosion... Make this interesting for me, will you?"

"I'll try."

He lunged at me, and the back-and-forth started. My practise with Ruce had made these patterns so familiar to me that the fight felt almost choreographed. He caught his knife to jab into my blindspot and I deflected. He used both weapons to lock my sword in place, but before he could twist it out of my hands, I ducked free and immediately struck out with my knife, catching him in the side, and he cried out.

"I thought something about you was familiar, boy... You fight like your father," he growled.

"Interesting enough for you?" I asked as I knocked the chain from his hands. The knife skidded across the dirt some ways away from us.

He pressed me back against the tree with his sword, hissing. "I was hoping your father was dead."

"Funny. He wished the same about you."

"Next time I send someone to kill him, I'll tell them to make sure he's inside before they set fire to the smithy."

The implications of that, that Scorpion had ordered the attack of Jezzine-on-the-Meander and killed Edda and Ruce's son, caused my focus to slip, and Scorpion levered my sword from my grasp, knocking me off balance. He pressed the advantage in my moment of weakness, slamming his fist to my jaw and sending me staggering. He grabbed my wrist to twist the knife from my grasp and slashed at me wildly, cutting clean through the carapace on my arm. Within moments, he was on top of me, pressing my own knife down towards my throat. My tiring grip on his wrist was the only thing keeping the blade back.

"After I kill you," he snarled, "I'm gonna tear this city apart until I find your father, and I'm gonna rip him to pieces. Did he stay with that hag from Cessiri? Maybe I'll track her down too, finish what I started..."

I struggled to push my free hand over the ground, searching for something to give myself a fighting chance. Riadh was still engaged with two of the Initiates and too far to rely on for rescue. My fingers closed around a cold metal chain and I worked it through my hand, trying to reach the handle of the knife but failing. I kicked my knee up into his ribs, targeting a cut I had given him in our last fight, and used the momentary lapse in pressure to stretch further and grab the blade. It sliced through the pad of my finger before I could wield it, making the handle slippery with blood. Finally, I gained purchase and forced the blade up into Scorpion's ribcage with a harsh exhale.

He gasped quietly, his breath turning wheezing. As his eyes shuddered closed, his arms gave out and he slumped forward.

Chapter Sixty-Two

Riadh

"Elin!" I shouted, lashing out at the last Initiate and sending her bleeding to the dirt. I sprinted over to Elin and hauled Scorpion's body off of him, staggering back. "Are you okay?!"

He looked up at me in a daze, panting. "I'm... Yeah. Yeah."

I took his hand and pulled him to his feet, frowning at the ugly bruise forming on his jaw. "I'm... I'm glad."

He turned and looked down at the body beside us, Scorpion's head turned towards the city's wall. "The city's safe for now... at least from the *Menagerie*."

"I already told you-"

"I'm not trying to convince you, Riadh," Elin said curtly. "If you don't believe me, that's fine. I ***know*** that Jove is a traitor and I'm going to prove it on my own."

He turned away, starting back into the city, and I glanced over at the dead Jewel of the *Menagerie*.

Elin never hesitated when the city was in danger. He was unwavering, even in the face of taking a life. It had always been this way. Nights that I had been restless, after protecting the city and being forced to kill, Elin slept without trouble. He had done his duty, kept our people safe. Nothing else mattered to him.

I started after him, watching his shoulders set in certainty as he walked.

"Remember our deal," he called over his shoulder. "You don't come near my family."

"If I need your help again-"

"You know where to find me."

"Standing over the forge in the citadel?" I asked.

He glanced back and grinned at me. "Or hiding under the table..."

"That's where you were?!"

CHAPTER SIXTY-THREE

RUCE

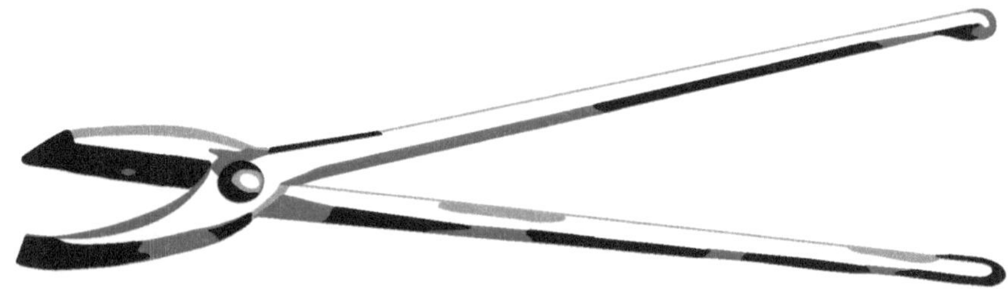

"So Scorpion is-"

"Dead," Elin said as he locked eyes with me over the rim of his *sahlab*.

"And you're... okay?"

"Should I not be?"

"After killing a man, it's understandable if you're not... Most people wouldn't be."

"I'm not most people. I know it was the right thing; he would've killed everyone in this city if he had the chance."

"You can know something is right and still feel guilty."

"He threatened you and Mother," Elin said darkly. "Why would I feel guilty?"

I didn't respond to that, watching the steam rise from my *sahlab* in silence.

He finally spoke again, itching in the silence. "My father would have had something to say to me... would have told me that violence, that killing, is always wrong. But everything I didn't know about the soil, he didn't know about war."

"Do you think it's over, then?"

"Do you?" he shot back, looking up at me. "You stood next to them. You know they're not gone. Hate can't be killed so easily... We just delayed it. Even if it takes years, it's years they have. They'll raise up new warriors to infiltrate our borders, won't they? There were kids younger than me fighting by his side, and that won't change."

"Then how do we stop it? Find peace?"

"I don't know," he sighed. "Ask the farmers."

Chapter Sixty-Four

Riadh

"Riadh, doll, tell me you look better than the other guy," Tor said with a grin as he approached with outstretched arms.

I embraced him gingerly, smiling. "I'd say so. I'll tell you all about it; please." I nodded for him to come sit at the table with me.

He waved his finger and a servant stepped forward to pour tea for us. When he reached me, I held up a hand. "None for me, thank you. My stomach is... a bit off."

"We live in stomach-churning times," Tor said philosophically as he sipped at his tea. "So, I told you I would speak to my informants about Lithdreya and their little zoo. I regret to say it's borne little fruit. Mere rumours of the presence of a Jewel in the city."

I waved a hand gently. "That's actually... been dealt with."

"Oh?" he asked, sitting forward and crossing his legs.

"You wanted to hear about the other guy..."

"No," he cooed. "Tell me everything."

I recounted to him their numbers, their hiding place. "Once we had tracked them to the edge of the city-"

"We?" he interrupted in curiosity. "I thought you said your Captain didn't sanction the mission. Who was with you?"

"I-" My voice caught in my throat as my mind raced. As useful as Tor may have been, I didn't trust him completely, and I was hardly reconciled with the truth about Harun— Elin. I couldn't tell Tor the truth, but he was waiting eagerly for my answer. I needed something sensational enough to keep his attention and prevent him poking holes. I leaned forward, lowering my voice so he pressed closer to hear. "This is not to leave this room, you understand."

"Of course, doll."

"You're right that Captain Owaines didn't sanction it, so I went off alone. When I tracked the *Menagerie* to the outer city, I was rash. They saw me and attacked. But I wasn't the only person who tracked them there. I thought I was dead, when a man wearing a mask came to my aid."

Then I told him about the battle, embellishing details where I could, just a little, to feed his desire for gossip. I recounted to him my fear, where my strikes landed, how long it took for them to surrender. The only thing I didn't exaggerate was how much my companion's fight both terrified and impressed me. Watching him go head-to-head against a Jewel of the *Menagerie* and win was the most incredible thing I'd seen in my life.

"And then he vanished," I lied.

"Did you recognise him? Who was it?"

"I wish I knew," I answered. That wasn't a lie, not fully. I didn't know if I would *ever* fully understand my old friend. "But it's over now. We don't need to worry about the *Menagerie* in the city anymore..."

"Riadh," Tor said, catching my hand as I moved to get up. "I'm-proud of what you've accomplished, but... You may wish to hear about the rumours."

I slowly sat back down. "What? What is it?"

"The rumours weren't about Scorpion."

"How do you know?"

"Because the Jewel that they've been talking about... they said *she's* been in the city for years."

I slowly exhaled, looking around the room in a daze. "He... he said that-" I turned back to Tor. "If your informants hear **anything** else about this Jewel-"

"You'll be the first person to know, doll."

"Thank you, Tor. Oh, when will this all end? I feel like I've been awake for three years."

"It feels different now, doesn't it? Like something big is coming, like the air around us is holding its breath?"

I looked at him in surprise. I had always thought him aloof, oblivious to the world around him beyond parties, gossip, and good food. "Yes... Yes, it does."

"I worry about what Lithdreya will do, knowing that the *Menagerie* has infiltrated your city. I worry for you and your people. If there's any-thing Stangauer can do to aid you in this fight-"

"I've been thinking, actually, about something a friend said to me recently. He told me that... that most Lithdreyans hope for peace. That only the *Menagerie* is fighting this war against us."

"And how does your friend claim to speak for them?"

"He lived in Lithdreya for two years, worked side by side with them. I think it's possible that-"

"I don't think you should trust them, Riadh." He slowly shook his head. "After your mother's death, I- I thought you would be more wary of them. How much more damage will you let them do to your nation?"

I pushed myself to stand, shaking my head. "You think continuing this war is the better option? You think **violence** will protect us? It only fosters more hate. Shouldn't there be a better way?"

He stood and moved closer to me, clasping my hand. "I admire you for wondering, but... There are thousands of years of hatred between you."

"And you want me to let it live forever. Goodbye, Tor. I have business to attend to."

He let go of my hand as I turned away, sighing. "*Ha det*, Lieutenant. Good luck."

"Thank you," I said over my shoulder.

CHAPTER SIXTY-FIVE

ELIN

IN THE MORNING, LIKE every morning, we went to work. The work was good for me, grounding. I'd told Ruce I didn't feel guilty, and I didn't. Guilt twists, knowledge just... has weight. That was how I felt, as I hammered steel in the smithy; heavy.

The weight lifted in fits and starts, like it had to, like rocks taken from a bucket until it was easy to carry. Over the next few days, there were whispers around the hall of craftsmages, but they were no longer furtive like they had been in the weeks since the attack. There was joy and safety in them as people told each other how Lieutenant al Abbas and a masked hero had driven the *Menagerie* from the city.

A masked hero. Really, Riadh?

Ruce and I didn't speak to each other much, but there wasn't a gap. We didn't use words because we had learned how to work with each other without needing them. Delicate teamwork in silence came easy. I would turn to ask for a tool and find it already being offered. He would draw breath to speak, and I'd already moved to stoke the fire. I had to imagine this was the kind of rhythm he'd had with the Elin of Jezzine, before losing him. Every reminder of their Jezzine boy sent a chill through me, reminding me of the night I'd come home to find Edda and Ruce preparing to risk everything for me.

You're our boy; if you're in trouble, we're gonna be there to get you out of it.

As scared as I was of losing them, they were of losing me.

"Working on multiplication?" a friendly voice asked.

I looked up, breaking myself from my daze and my scowl, and smiled at Riadh. "Lieutenant al Abbas," I said with the respectful distance of a craftsmage to a soldier. "How may I serve?"

"We've had a rounding error in our supply lists, and the shoesmiths are out of iron. Any to spare?"

I ducked my head in a nod, turning to where Ruce had stacked our deliveries of raw materials. As I set the iron onto the counter, I leaned close to ask, "How's your father?"

She gave me a warm smile. "Stronger every day, thank you. And yours?"

"Waiting on a set of hands," he called from the forge.

"Coming!"

Riadh laughed as I scampered over to Ruce's side. "Goodbye, Elin! We'll have to get *sahlab* sometime."

"We'll be working on the shop this weekend, if you want to stop by!" I called back to her. "*Of Steel and Thread,* on the meander, at the intersection of the Craft and Olive districts!"

"I'll bring ka'aq!"

Ruce swatted me gently upside the head and I turned my attention back to the forge. "Sorry."

"I'm glad to see you making friends, Elin, but I'd be more glad to see you making progress on this order," he said dryly.

I stoked the fire and held my hand over the heat, murmuring a well song to find the right temperature. I had to pull my hand out a few seconds too early. "Wait a minute, then it's good," I told him.

I had always loved the well songs. They were ancient, older than our language, but they helped us tell temperature. You held your hand over the heat source and sang the well songs. The sooner you had to pull your hand back, the hotter it was. If you were baking bread or making glass, you wanted your hand out by the first chorus. For bricks or a sword, you'd want to make it a full verse.

Chapter Sixty-Six

Ruce

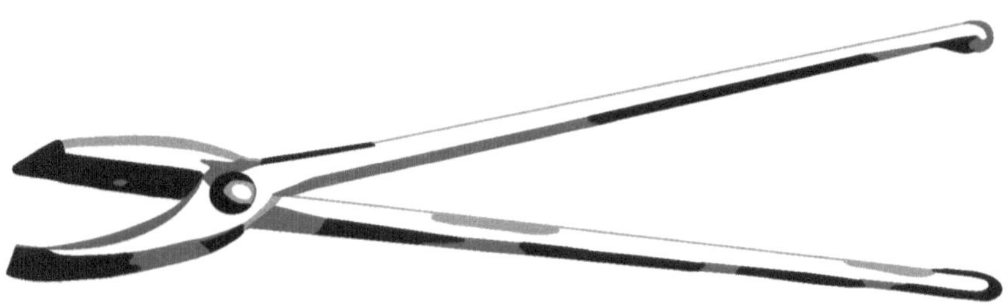

"Tali," I called as we crested the cutaway on Mount Sarigh.

The community leader turned from her conversation and beamed at us. "Morning, Lahds!"

Elin and I approached her and set our bundles at her feet. "You said our fellow refugees could use our skills; I broke out some old moulds and put my boy to use."

Elin opened his bundle and held a bowl up to Tali. She peered at our treasures and laughed. "Oh, wonderful. We have some new families settling in, and I know they'll appreciate it. Thank you, boys."

"My wife also sent a few dresses along; she said you were running low on clothing for little girls?"

"You three are a blessing, honestly. Oh, my wife was actually thinking of you last night... One second." She ducked into the nearest dwelling and emerged with something wrapped in cloth. "Sweet bread, for your family."

"Tell your wife I would die for her."

"I'll pass on your compliments," she said with a laugh.

||

"Elin, pass me another nail. Elin!"

"Sorry!" he called, jumping up to cross the room. It was a bit difficult, as our shop was still a mess of construction and repairs.

He bent down to hand me a nail and I leaned close. "Again, I'm glad you have friends, but I'd like it if your wits didn't leave you when they came around."

"I'll be more attentive," he promised. And I knew he would be. He always took direction well, never made the same mistake twice— except for this one, but I suppose for two friends I would give him two chances.

"Sorry," Malia called, "am I doing more harm than good?"

"No, of course not, dear. You're always welcome— especially when you bring refreshments."

She beamed at me, coming to offer me another cup of pomegranate juice. She'd wrapped a block of ice in several layers of cloth for the walk over, so the juice was fresh and freeing on the hot day.

"Thank you, Malia."

"You know, I can do more than look pretty. I could start on painting that wall, if you'd like."

"Edda has yet to decide on a colour, but thank you."

She lifted a piece of paper from the counter. "'Ruce—honey yellow.'"

I sat up and scratched my head as I took the note from her. "Now, where'd that come from? I don't suppose she put paint with it..."

Malia shook her head with a knowing smile. "You'll want to go to Anders's stall around the corner. Tell him you're a friend of the Bayouths; he'll take good care of you."

"Thanks. You're in charge while I'm gone."

"What?" Elin asked indignantly.

I opened the door to the shop to come face to face with the young woman about to knock. "Lieutenant al Abbas."

"Oh; hello," she said awkwardly. "I brought ka'aq." She held up the loaf of wrapped bread.

"I see you did. The kids are inside; I'm just running to the market-place."

"The kids?" she muttered to herself as I started down the road.

CHAPTER SIXTY-SEVEN

ELIN

RIADH DUCKED INTO THE shop a moment after Ruce left, smiling at me. "Hi. I-" She frowned at Malia. "Who's this?"

"Oh, this is Malia Bayouth. She and her father are friends of my family. Malia, this is Riadh al Abbas. She's my oldest friend."

"Pleasure to meet you, Lieutenant," Malia said with a smile. "Elin's told me a lot about you. I can't imagine facing down the raiders like that..."

"Right," Riadh said, shifting awkwardly in the doorway as she looked at the small blanket of snacks on the floor between me and Malia. "You made new friends. It's good that you made new friends."

"Are you jealous?" I asked with a grin.

"Of course not."

"Then sit down and stay awhile."

"Oh... No, I can't. I just came to give you this. Sort of an... 'I'm sorry for trying to kill you' ka'aq loaf."

"Customary," I nodded.

She set the bread onto the blanket and rushed out of the shop before I could stop her.

"Riadh-"

Ruce walked through the door, glancing behind him in confusion as he waved the container of paint. "I was gone two minutes, what did you do?"

I shook my head. "I wish I knew."

Malia set a hand over mine and smiled at me gently. "You should go after her; make sure she knows she hasn't been replaced."

"I'll be back."

Ruce clapped me on the shoulder as I passed. "Don't come back until you fix it; I like that girl."

"You just like that she brought food."

He glanced up from the loaf of bread he'd already started cutting into. "I don't know what you're talking about."

"Mhm. Riadh!" I called as I jogged out of the shop.

I caught up to her a few blocks into the inner city, turning onto the street that led to the city centre. When she heard me coming, she slowed and eventually came to a halt.

"Hey. Are you okay? Did I-"

"You didn't do anything," she sighed, "I just... I wish we could go back to before everything went wrong. I'm sorry, Elin. I should never have trusted Captain Owaines over you... I-"

"You made a mistake. You won't make it again."

Tears pricked her eyes and she shook her head at the sky, unwilling to meet my eyes. "Elin, you can't just forgive me and-"

"Neither of us have time for regret. We put it away; we do better. No other option."

She looked down at me doubtfully. "Yeah?"

"Yes. Now will you *please* come back and meet my friend Malia? *Really* give her a chance? I think you'll get on well."

"You two aren't...?" She made a vague gesture.

"No," I groaned. "Why does everyone think that? We're friends; partners in shenanigans and enemies in *bita*."

"You played *bita* with her?" she asked as we started back towards the Olive district. "You hate cards! I don't think I've ever seen you win a game."

"I know. We were at the Bayouths' for dinner and my mother made me. It was a bloodbath."

Chapter Sixty-Eight
Edda

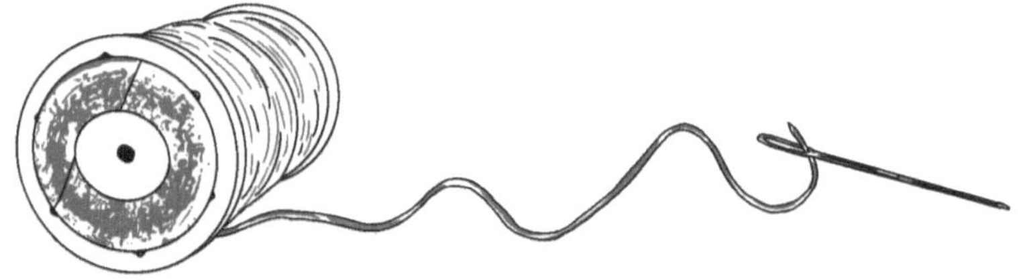

"Malia said that the shop is coming along," Nassir told me as we worked.

"Yes, she spent the weekend helping get things in order; she's quite diligent, and well-loved by my boys. Oh, and thank you for helping Ruce make that deal."

"I'm just a friendly guy; I know people. Oh," he said conspiratorially, leaning closer. "For example, I'm close friends with one of the king's private attendants, and *she* told me that his colour has been improving over the past week."

"What does that mean?"

"She thinks he's finally recovering."

"Is that possible?"

"Well, we know very little about the poison used against him, but she says he looks healthier every day."

"Really."

"It's wonderful news, if it turns out to be true." He managed to work in silence for not two minutes before he was saying, "Oh, Malia has been experimenting with a new flavouring in some of her dishes. Your family must come over tonight to try them."

"I'll tell the boys at the end of the workday."

||

The moment I did so, Ruce beamed. "I will never refuse that invitation. Can we go right now?"

"Nassir is still packing up his things," I laughed. "Give him a minute. Oh, he told me something earlier. Apparently there's a rumour circulating that King Bazzeri is recovering."

"What?" Elin was suddenly looking at me in rapt attention, like he'd been struck by lightning, though moments ago he'd been lazily chasing a bug across the counter with a piece of straw.

"The king is healthier than he used to be; his attendants think he's healing from the poison."

"And everyone knows this?"

I nodded. "Nassir told me."

Without another word, Elin leapt the counter and was sprinting across the hall.

"Elin, what-"

CHAPTER SIXTY-NINE

JOVE

HE'D GOTTEN TO HER. That was the only explanation. There was no way the boy could have infiltrated the palace... no way *he* could've given Bazzeri the antidote.

I left my office, my head knocking around on my shoulders with each step. Loud, too loud. Thundering.

And yet the signs were there. His pallor was gone, his breathing had lost its rasp. Whispers flew around the citadel. If Riadh had given her father the antidote without telling me, in secret... there could only be one reason.

Harun had told her.

I needed to know for sure if Bazzeri were hiding his health from me. I reached the end of the hall, dismissing the Guards from the doors of the king's chambers with a flick of my wrist. I opened the doors without announcing myself, half-expecting— hoping— that I would find Bazzeri still lying weak in his bed, in the throes of sickness.

He was standing in front of the mirror, tying the waist sash of his robe. He stretched his fingers, working the muscles in his arms in test. He spun to me in surprise as the doors hit the wall and rattled, his features struggling to arrange themselves before he gave me an uneasy smile. "Jove."

The doors slammed closed behind me and we were alone in the dark room. My hand fell to close around my sword. Cold. The metal was cold against my fingers.

"Your Majesty. You've recovered. It's a miracle."

CHAPTER SEVENTY

RIADH

I MADE MY WAY down to the Catacombs, where we'd had to store the bodies of the *Menagerie* raiders due to the sheer number of them. Over the past few days, I'd been given far too many tasks to touch base with the squadron I'd sent to recover the bodies from the outlands. As I reached the large chamber, I was hit by the smell of preservative spices, not death. Even though they were enemies, I had insisted that each of their bodies were cared for in the way their culture deemed fitting for warriors.

As I approached, the Sergeant came to attention. "Lieutenant al Abbas!"

"What did you find? Any signs of other spies in the city, plans?"

"We recovered the seven bodies from the camp and went over their belongings. They-"

"Seven?" I asked, stopping his story in its tracks.

"Y...es. Seven bodies were recovered."

"Show them to me."

He nodded and one by one, his Corporal pulled back the shrouds that covered their faces and I shook my head in horror, stepping back. "No, no, no, no. Where is his body?"

"Lieutenant?"

"He must have survived... I need to warn Elin."

"The blacksmith's son?" the Corporal asked, confusion crossing her face. "He was looking for you earlier, said it was important."

"Where is he?"

"It was the end of the workday, Lieutenant," she said. "We... sent him home."

"What? Why?!"

"He doesn't have the right to a direct audience with you on a whim... Unless- unless he does?"

"If he ever needs me again, you are to bring him immediately, understood?"

"Did he-" She fell silent.

"Speak," I ordered.

She drew in a slow breath. "You said you were aided by a masked warrior... Is-"

I cut her off. "Perhaps it is best you keep your thoughts to yourself." I directed my next order at her Sergeant. "Tell Captain Owaines I'm going on patrol."

Damn Tor. At this point, everyone in the city knew about the 'masked warrior'. By tomorrow, he'd be the Sentinel reincarnated, with how the rumours were growing.

I started up the steps into the citadel, and then the bells began to ring.

Chapter Seventy-One

Elin

"Elin, is everything alright?" Edda asked. "You just ran off earlier, and-"

"I needed to talk to someone, but- It'll have to wait. Let's just enjoy dinner, and then I'll... I'll deal with this later."

"Elin, if something's wrong, you can-"

"Mother, just-"

We all flinched as cacophonic bells began to echo from the citadel. Edda and Ruce hunched together in fear, but I knew them well. I knew what they meant.

My knees hit the dirt.

"Elin?" Edda asked.

My fingers dug into cool soil, tight and unforgiving and not painful enough. Nothing that my eyes landed on had any meaning.

"Elin," Ruce said, "what happened?"

The king was dead. The other Guards weren't to know this; all they knew was that they were under attack. They were coming to attention, thundering up stairs, strapping armour into place, patrolling with vigour. Only later would they come to know what had already sunk into my bones.

We had failed.

BEFORE

Chapter Seventy-Two
Harun

I stepped through the swinging doors, the floorboards creaking under me as my eyes adjusted to the dimness of the bar. As I walked, dust fell from my boots to swirl about the air I disturbed. The watering hole was built on a wellspring, and it was the nearest reliable source of water to the *Denuda* Wastes, the region the four-fang was native to. Like every source, life had been built around it, and I'd become familiar with the workings of Tunder Village over the last several months. One thing you could count on was that the price of water was always going up.

"How much will this get me today, Ateri?" I asked hoarsely, tossing my last three coins onto the counter. I wanted to clear my throat but couldn't. The last two days had been like this, since my water had run out.

The woman in front of me narrowed her eyes as she took in my dishevelled form. The tops of my cheeks were sunburned, my lips dry and cracked, my fingers scraped raw. My clothes were torn and faded from the sun, and blood had dried in several places. "Look, kid. Your safest bet is to take this coin and book a ride out of this place before it kills you."

"That advice come free of charge? How much water are you going to sell me?" I reiterated coldly. That might have seemed counterproductive, but Ateri respected bluntness. I had learned that the first day I walked into the watering hole looking for information on poisonous snakes. She was the one who had eventually scribbled out a few circles on my map and told me to start my search there— after a few coins made their way into her hand.

"I was just trying to help, but if you've got a death wish, this'll buy you a skin. No more."

"What if I fight her?" I nodded to the poster on the wall. Its text was faded, but from the style, I knew it was boasting about a champion fighter— something called Big Rini. I'd seen a number of fights in my time here, and I'd learned how this worked. Lithdreyans always wanted to watch a good fight, and they were willing to pay for the experience.

"What if you jump into a pit with rattlers? You die."

"How much would you pay if I win?"

She leaned over the counter and grinned as she pointed to my coins. "I'd pay you ten times this, but when you get killed, I'm not gonna send a penny to your family."

"Ten times." I held out a hand and she shook it, then slammed her fist onto the counter several times. Around the bar, patrons looked up from their sickly-coloured drinks, cheering— or jeering. It was hard to tell with this crowd.

"We've got a fight, everyone!"

||

Twenty minutes later, I strode out of the bar with three waterskins slung over my shoulder, money in my purse, and a few bruised ribs. "Gotta love Lithdreyan culture," I chuckled to myself, the movement making me realise those ribs might not just be bruised. "Nh- Something honest about it."

My mount was waiting, clicking impatiently as she looked around the town. When I'd first gotten here, the *kisa* had unnerved me. Those glittering scorpion eyes, devoid of the kindness I was used to in horses back home; the rolling plates of armour that stretched down its back, glinting like swordsmetal; the sharp beak where the muzzle should be; and that deadly, curling tail. I didn't know if they were monsters, like the old legends, but I knew this: we didn't have scorpion-horses back home. Honestly... they **still** unnerved me, but they were the best navigators for tramping around the desert, so I didn't have much choice.

I swung up onto my *kisa*, mindful of the pain in my ribs, and nudged her with my knee to start out of town. My knuckles were cracked and aching as I worked the reins, but I had grown used to the feeling. As I started back into the *Denuda* Wastes, I unstoppered one of my waterskins and took a sip, savouring the moment's respite from the dryness of the desert.

CHAPTER
SEVENTY-THREE

EDDA

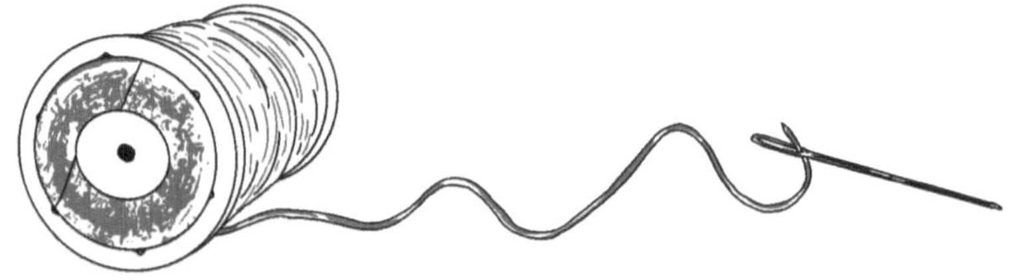

"Elin!" I called, "you'd better be getting up! Your father was working the forge an hour ago, and you know how he gets!"

"Coming, *Ama*..." he groaned. When he blindly stumbled down the ladder into the kitchen, his jet black hair was a wild mess. "It's his fault for waking with the sun, anyways..."

"Or yours for sleeping with the moon," I chided, always amused by the petulant way he kept his eyes closed for as long as possible when he woke, as though it wasn't really morning if he couldn't see it. "When did you get home this morning, *hayati*?"

"Couldn't sleep, *Ama*. I just-" he yawned, "went for a walk. And then... all of a sudden— there's the sun. Oh, Victoire wanted to have dinner together tonight. Is that meat?" he asked, sniffing the air with his eyes still closed.

"You can eat on the way. And take this to your father," I said as I pushed two bundles of warm food into his hands.

"Thanks, *Ama*." He started out the door and I reached up to catch him by the back of his shirt.

"Boots, Elin."

He looked down at his bare feet and grinned. "Oh, right." He stuffed his feet into his boots and started out the door, his untied laces clacking on the front stones as he started through the village. "Love you!"

Chapter Seventy-Four

Ruce

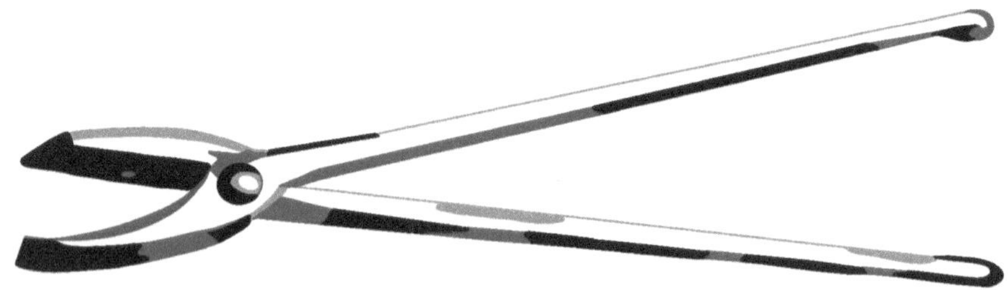

"Heat the oil, will you?" I called.

"How did you know I was here?" Elin asked as he stepped into the smithy.

"It's an hour after you were supposed to be here. Right on time," I said dryly. "Oil."

"Mr. Aqaba asked if we could-"

"Make him a new kitchen dirk. He came by earlier to ask me, in case you forgot again."

"He needs to let that go," he said with a roll of his eyes. "What're we working on now?"

"That Guard from the capital that's working with the town sentries commissioned a new sword. After I lattice this, I want you to take over."

"Are you sure?" he asked. "Because-"

"Just keep your focus. You know what to do when you don't get distracted; and I'll be here to help if you forget the order."

"Okay. Oil's heated."

"Good job, son." I touched his hair fondly as I dipped the sword into the oil to cool.

Chapter Seventy-Five

Harun

"Three skins," I said as I stepped up to the counter. Ateri grinned at me.

"You're not dead yet! Tell ya what, kid, I underestimated you... You know, if you're gonna keep going into the Wastes— not that I think you should— tricks'll be worth more to you than skins."

"What tricks?" I asked.

She turned her palm upwards and looked to the rafters absentmindedly. I rolled my eyes and pressed a few coins into her hand. "Try cutting open a cactus or two," she said as she lifted one of the coins up to study.

"That's it?"

She counted the other coins into her purse. "Bugs are your friends... and trust the stars instead of the sun."

"Thanks for nothing," I scoffed. "Three skins."

"Remember my tricks," she called after me as I carried my water-skins out of the bar. "Save your hide, kid!"

"Yeah, thanks for the cryptic riddles and life advice."

I tried to push my foot into the stirrup of my *kisa's* saddle, but it took me several attempts. Oh, how I missed my *venaq*. I hadn't been allowed to take anything with me when I was banished but the clothes on my back, and my *venaq* were sitting in my quarters with all of my weapons except for Pierre, having been freshly polished.

The sword I now carried had been paid for through manual labour and gambling on fistfights. It was far inferior to the blade I had carried as a Guard of Lothforias, but I took that philosophically, because it was my mistake that had allowed the king to be poisoned. I had been stationed outside of his rooms that night, and somehow I had allowed an assassin to slip past me and put the poison in his wine. I wasn't fit to carry that sword anymore, so this one suited me fine.

As I laid down to sleep, I agonised over the details of that night just like I had for almost a year now, trying to remember **anything** that would explain how I had messed up, what I had missed.

The stars were so much clearer than they had been back in the city. There was no need for a fire to be able to sleep; at first, I had used one for warmth, but it always attracted predators. In the first few months, I saw several traders selling thick pelts and I'd gotten one for myself, and now the temperature was bearable enough for sleeping.

Trust the stars and not the sun. What had Ateri meant by that? Had she meant anything at all or just felt the need to spout something off in exchange for my coin? She'd been helpful— some— in the past, but like everyone else in this desert, she was crazy and untrustworthy.

I had almost fallen asleep when I heard the wolves begin to howl.

Chapter Seventy-Six

Riadh

"Careful, Sergeant," Captain Owaines called from the edge of the ring, "I need some of my Guards left when you're done with them."

"Then tell them to train harder," I said angrily, swinging my sword even harder and sending Hakim to the dirt. He immediately pushed himself up and was ready to go again, and I would have been impressed if his fire hadn't been lit by his **hero**, Harun. Instead, that incensed me further and this time, I sent him down bleeding.

"Riadh!" Captain Owaines said sharply. "A word?"

I threw my sword to the ground for one of the Privates to pick up and followed Captain Owaines down the corridor. "Yes, Captain?" I asked stiffly.

"You seem tense," he said lightly. "I know your father's health has not changed in the past four months... I'm sorry for what you're going through."

"What do you want? You're not the sympathetic kind."

"You wound me, Riadh. But... I do have an offer. You seem listless, after Harun's betrayal... I think you need purpose, and I want to give it to you. My Lieutenant, Eschel, is ageing, and his war wounds are taking their toll... Would you consider taking his place?"

"You- you want me to become Lieutenant?"

"You're ready, and the responsibility would be good for you. You need something to do; you need to know you're helping this city. Am I wrong?"

"Can I... can I think about it?"

"Of course. I'll leave you to your thoughts. But... Riadh?" he called after me.

"Yes?"

"Please try not to break your fellow Guards. We do need to have **someone** left to defend this city, after all..."

CHAPTER SEVENTY-SEVEN

HARUN

I STAGGERED, THE SAND catching my ankles with every step. I could hear the wolves behind me, but they were distracted by my *kisa*, which bought me time to run away. I had nothing with me but my pelt, my sword, and the waterskin I had been drinking from while I rested. The rest of my water, my food, and my money was all next to my mount, which was currently being torn to pieces by the predators of the desert.

I lifted a shaking hand to the shallow slashes on my cheek. I had dived out of the way when the wolves came for me, but I wasn't fast enough to avoid their claws entirely. The movement sent daggers into my shoulder, pain emanating from the gouge marks left in my flesh by teeth. There was some sickly green stain in my wounds and it burned like acid... I'd seen that same verdant tint on their fangs, and I almost gave up then and there... The wolves here were venomous. Of course they were, because this desert *hated* me.

I glanced back at my campsite at a particularly loud snarl and pitched forward into open air, rolling down the steep windward side of a sand dune. My bones jarred as I rolled, landing with a mouthful of dirt and a ringing in my ears. I groaned, spitting fruitlessly, and sacrificed a swig of my precious water to clean out my mouth. I looked back to the top of the dune, but I saw no sign of the wolves, and their sounds had faded into the distance. I was safe. Well...

I glanced around the dark expanse of desert that stretched out all around me. There was a buzz of poison in the air, rattlesnakes and spiders and scorpions all lying in wait.

Safe for now.

||

I had forgotten how to blink, after two days walking under the hot desert sun. My water had run out halfway through the first, and now blinking was more of a leftward looking motion, my eyes rolling back into my head as my eyelids trembled.

I staggered so frequently that my walk had become a shuffle-stumble-step because I knew that if I stopped to let myself catch my balance I wouldn't start again. My only protection against the vengeful sun was the *keffiyeh* I held above my head, but even now my fingers and cheeks were starting to blister. The buzz in my head only grew louder during the day, and I could actually see it rising off of the sand. I could *hear* the heat around me.

The venom had slowly run its course through my body, sending me shivering or retching or hearing voices with no remorse. It had left me weak, and I knew in this state I wouldn't last long in the desert.

In the haze that warped the world in front of me, I started to see something moving. At first, I thought it was another predator, but she shook out her hair and started towards me.

"Riadh?" I tried to ask, but it came out in a dry croak.

She had come. She had forgiven me for my mistake and come to help me. She held a waterskin in her outstretched hand and I started running towards her, desperate for relief. "Harun!" she called out as I approached.

Finally I reached her and grabbed for the waterskin, but my hand passed right through her, and then she was gone.

My momentum took me to my knees and I caught myself on my hands, gasping. I began to sob, but there was so little water in me that I had no tears to spare.

"She's not there," I panted, my vision fracturing in exhaustion. "Of course she's not there."

I collapsed face-first into the hot sand; laid down to die.

Chapter
Seventy-Eight

Edda

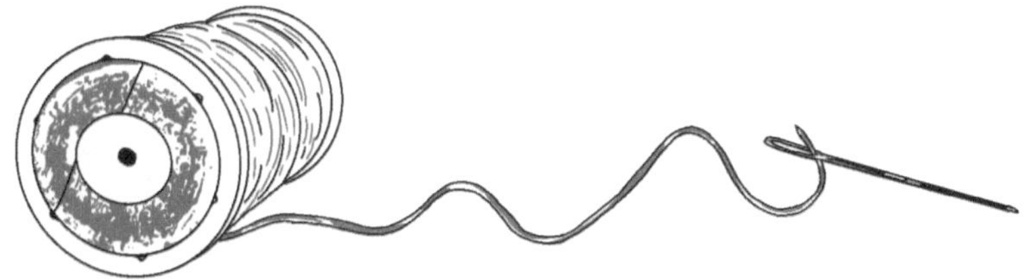

I moved through the desks, occasionally pausing to look over at a student's seams. This was one of the best batches of seamsters yet. I had been hesitant, at first, when the headmaster had asked me to come back and teach, but I'd fallen into it naturally, I admit. The students took to me well and I found great satisfaction in passing on my skills.

"Oh, Lila, watch the loop there. That's better, yes."

"Miss Edda?" Sebastien asked. "Can you help me?"

I came to sit next to the boy, smiling down at him. "You seem to have trouble with steps sometimes, yes?" He nodded morosely. "It's alright, Elin's the same. What we find works the best is to make it a sort of game, or a story. If your needle is a character, make each step a task they need to complete. Then it'll be easier to remember. So, your…"

"Warrior?"

I gently took the needle from his hand and started through the steps. "Your warrior. Once he goes... to the top of the tower to fight the evil princess... then he has to go down to the cave to rescue the dragon. Got it?"

"**Oh**... Thanks, Miss Edda."

CHAPTER SEVENTY-NINE

JOVE

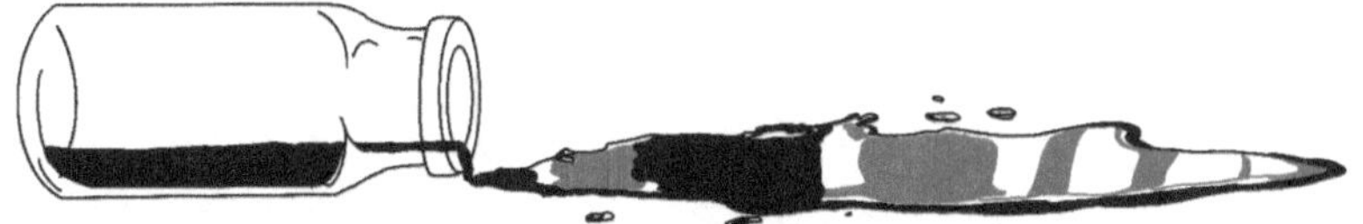

I STEPPED BACK FROM the balcony, nodding to Riadh as I did. "Eschel taught you well, *Lieutenant*. The recruits are drilling perfectly."

"Thank you, Captain," she beamed.

"How are you finding your new responsibilities?"

"I think it suits me. I've been busy, but... It feels right. I won't let you down."

"I know you won't. I'll leave you to it."

I turned down the hall and started walking. Out of habit, I made it all the way to the temple before I realised what I was doing. I had to stop this... I had long been sick of praying in a temple to a god who never listened, but sometimes my feet carried me here anyways. In the days after Jazhara's death, I had almost thrown the portrait of *Lady Foria* from its place behind my new desk, across the room into my fireplace. The only thing that had stopped me, in the moment, was that some decorator had the foresight to nail it down.

In the months following, I threw all manner of insults at the impassive figure looking over my shoulder, but never once did she answer or hurl bricks down to smite me or pull me down to the watery depths for my insolence. She just stood there, like paintings are inclined to do.

||

Four months after Harun's banishment, I made my way down to the *sahlab* shop by the marketplace, the same as I did on the first of every month. It was a favourite of the Guards, and so close to the city gates, a foreigner wouldn't be out of place here. Ateri slid into the seat across from me with a grin as I passed her a mug of steaming *sahlab*.

"Well met?" I asked cordially.

"Better if with coin," she said brusquely.

As always, I found the Lithdreyan's personality grating, but I forced a smile to my face as I passed the pouch of money beneath the table. I recoiled as her filthy fingers brushed mine in the exchange, but she didn't seem to notice— or if she did, she took no offence.

"Tell me of the boy."

"Don't get your hopes up," she told me. "Far as I know, he's still alive."

"I hired you to fix that."

"You hired me to send him down the wrong path, and I did that; I'm not an assassin."

"You're Lithdreyan!" I hissed. "What's the distinction?"

She bristled, eyeing me coldly. "Watch yourself, **Captain**. A girl's feelings can get hurt. What'll you do if I turn around and tell your boy exactly where to find his little snake?"

She started to rise and I quickly caught her hand, giving a placating smile. "My apologies, Ati... I just know how capable you are. Can't we... come to an agreement and find a solution to my problem? You know, I don't think I've been considerate. I'm not paying you what you're worth, am I? Let's sit down and talk about it..."

She considered me, twirling her matted and braided hair as she sat back down. "I'm listening."

"I know you can't stop selling him water, but... Can't you gain his trust, tell him you've heard of a place he can find the four-fang and just... lead him into a trap? Send him into a dangerous part of the desert."

"Every part is dangerous."

"Yes, I remember. Some do their work more quickly than others... That's what I'm paying you for, yes? Peace of mind? Please, the next time I see you... bring the news that he's dead."

"I've asked this before... but what is it exactly this boy did to deserve death?"

"He's a traitor to the crown, and he's plotting against my kingdom. You'll be doing a service to the people."

"**_Your_** people. Mine would probably give him a medal. He's the one who poisoned your king, isn't he?"

"I understand you have no loyalty to Lothforias, but he betrayed the trust he was given... Isn't that what matters?"

Ateri looked at me for a long time, but I knew that I had her. Lithdreyans had a funny thing about broken oaths and trust. I didn't care why, but it did come in handy...

"I'll see it done," she told me, though she sounded sad about it.

CHAPTER EIGHTY
RUCE

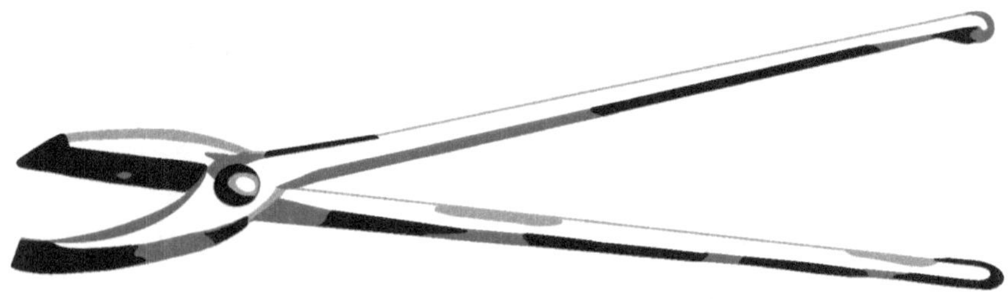

"Wonderful to see you, Victoire. How's your family?" Edda asked as she and Elin's fiance set the table.

"Hard at work, with the harvest coming soon."

"Already? Has it really been a year? I remember you two announcing your engagement at the harvest festival last fall. Has so much time really passed?"

Victoire beamed at Elin, laying a hand over his. "I can hardly believe it myself. It feels like I just blinked."

As we shared our meal and talked, Elin's fingers were drumming a constant and chaotic beat against Victoire's palm. He'd never been able to sit still, but she didn't mind it like so many of our neighbours. Every so often, she'd glance down at his jittery fingers and smile to herself. She was good for him, I had to admit.

When he'd first started bringing her around, maybe... two summers past, I had done my best not to like her on account of a long-standing grudge between her father and I over some "borrowed" tools that never seemed to find their way home. Eventually, I'd given up on their return and crafted new ones, but Hener Mayelson had made an enemy for life.

Unfortunately, his daughter was vibrant and friendly and utterly without malice— and she made Elin happy, which was all that really mattered... Though if Hener had insisted on returning the tools as a sort of dowry, I wouldn't have refused.

"More bread?" Edda asked sweetly, poking me in the ribs under the table and drawing my focus back to the conversation.

"No, thank you, *Habi*. Sorry, I'm just a bit tired."

"Old age," Elin said to Victoire through a mouthful of food.

"How was the smithy today?" Victoire asked me before I could retort. "I heard you received a commission from a capital Guard."

"We did, yes. I actually had Elin do the..."

Chapter Eighty-One

Harun

Whatever gods were in this place must have hated me. Why else would I have been woken by a mosquito biting my arm?

I blearily lifted my head, swatting at the bloodsucking bug to no avail. It simply moved further up my arm and began its work anew.

Bugs are your friends, a voice whispered in my head.

Yeah, I wanted to say, *well, friends don't bite each other.* I would have, too, if my throat hadn't been so dry. As it was, the thought made me laugh like a madman.

I pushed myself up on my arms, feeling the cool breeze of the night touch my face. The mosquitos had found me because, after dark, I had the only warmth out here for miles. They would drink their fill and then fly off to wherever they hid during the hours of blistering sun...

Wherever they hid... I sat up, scanning the world around me. They had come from somewhere, and they didn't live in dry places. They needed water, just like me.

I staggered to my feet, the sand clinging to me as I started walking like the desert didn't want to let me go. Mosquitos and flies buzzed around my ears on occasion, and I knew I was getting closer. Finally, I crested a dune and saw the dark form of lush vegetation... and this time, it was no mirage. The heat of the desert had faded hours ago.

Branches scratched my clothes as I moved through the brush, but I didn't care, because I could hear the bubble of a spring somewhere in the centre of this little oasis. When I caught sight of the pool, I flung myself into the water without care for pain or grace. Relief, relief, relief. I knew that drinking too fast would make me sick, so I pushed myself up to my knees in the pool and slowly drank from cupped hands. When I finished, I took another portion and spilled it over my hair. "Thank you," I sobbed. "Thank you. Faith my reservoir," I reminded myself.

I smacked my neck, my hand coming away bloody with the mosquito I had killed, and I reflected on the bug smeared across my hand. I had followed these pests here, to water, to safety...

Bugs are your friends.

Ateri had meant something after all. I stood and waded through the pool that soothed my burned skin, finding one of the many cacti among the brush. There was a drawing of this kind on the wall in the bar above the menu; Ateri must have used some part of them in her cooking. She had told me to try cutting open a cactus or two, and I was hungry enough to do it.

Five minutes and several finger-pricks later, I had cut open the red fruits of the cactus and my fingers were sticky with juice. I had never tasted anything so good. When I had eaten my fill, I drank some more from the pool and filled my empty waterskin.

The last piece of advice Ateri had given me was to trust the stars, not the sun... and I was starting to realise what she meant. If I wanted to make it out of this wasteland, I had to get moving.

I took a moment to remember where the sun had set to orient myself, and then I trudged out of the oasis and started walking towards the south, where I would eventually come to the safety of Tunder Village. My instinct was to travel by day, sleep by night... but Ateri had warned me not to trust the sun. I was realising how much safer it must have been to sleep during the hottest hours and travel during the coolest. It was such a simple solution that I was mad at myself for not thinking of it sooner.

Ateri's advice was going to save my life.

Chapter Eighty-Two

Riadh

I knocked on the door of Captain Owaines's study, entering at his reply. "Lieutenant," he said with a glance up from his paperwork, "what can I do for you?"

"The emissary from Stangauer is here to discuss the new terms of the treaty, and I wasn't sure... Well-"

"Yes?" he asked dryly.

"Is it my duty as princess, or yours as Captain?"

He gave a twisted smile, like he was trying to hold it in. "As acting commander of the city, the duty falls to me... but I would like to send you to the meeting."

"Sir?"

"I have faith in you, Lieutenant. You've been trained for this, and you're good at it. Report back once Djanson has departed."

"You just don't want to go to the meeting, do you?"

"I can't stand the man, Riadh... I don't trust him as far as I can throw him. And as your commanding officer, I'm ordering you to do it."

"Yes, Captain."

I strode from the study, making my way through the corridors of the palace until I reached the citadel. Guards from both nations flanked the meeting room doors, bowing their heads to me as I entered.

The Stangrey emissary was already waiting inside, and I noticed him the moment I entered. Like any self-respecting Stangrey, he aspired to be the most brightly-coloured thing in any room, and in this one he certainly succeeded. His attire was almost gaudy with its garish colours and ruffles. I crossed the room to where he stood, studying the painting that was hung on the far wall.

"Beautiful work, isn't it?" I asked him, lying through my teeth. This painting was just as gaudy and garish as the man beside me, but that wasn't the diplomatic thing to say. "It was a gift to our people from your benevolent king."

He turned, smiling widely as he came to shake my hand. "It is indeed quite wonderful. Tor Djanson, emissary of Stangauer."

"Riadh al Abbas, Lieutenant of the Guard of Lothforias and princess."

"An honour, doll. Please; let's begin. Tea?"

CHAPTER EIGHTY-THREE

HARUN

I WOKE TO A gentle humming, slightly distant, and the pungent smell of what I had come to recognise as yoran root. It was commonly used in Lithdreya and the outlying Lothforian settlements as a healing salve. I weakly raised my hand to my cheek where I felt something stuck and found bandages covering the claw marks I had suffered near a week ago.

My eyes opened unevenly and lazily scanned the room around me. It was small, lit only by a trio of candles, and piled high with crates like those used for bottles at the watering hole. The humming grew closer and turned into words. I could make out the tune of a lullaby I had heard once or twice in my time here. It was in Lithdreyan, so I only understood every third word and couldn't make sense of the song. Something about the sun.

I gingerly pushed myself up to sit, stiff and sore. How had I gotten here? The last thing I remembered... I was walking through the desert. I threw the blanket off, setting my unsteady feet to the floor and preparing myself to st-

"I wouldn't do that."

I looked up in surprise as Ateri ducked into the room stirring a small jar of something.

"Stay off your feet for a bit, yeah? Thought you were a ghost when you wandered into the village."

"I'm not," my voice cracked. "Thanks to you."

She grinned crookedly. "Told you them tricks would come in handy. What happened to you, kid?"

"Sandworm," I muttered.

She laughed at the response. "You're going native."

'Sandworm' was local slang for 'nothing,' just a tiny bump in the road... but Lithdreyans were funny, in that sometimes what they said was the opposite of what they meant. 'Sandworm' was a way of brushing off the big stuff, a way of saying, 'Everything that could go wrong did, but let's not dwell on that'.

"Drink this," Ateri ordered, holding out the jar she'd been messing with.

At this point, she'd had several chances to kill me, and I didn't have much to lose, so I downed it in one.

"That tastes awful," I groaned as it burned down my throat.

"'S how you know it's working. Medicine isn't supposed to taste good, is it?"

"You found me when I collapsed in the village?"

She shook her head, flopping down to sit beside me on the bed. "Big Rini did, came in the bar looking for a doctor or something. I told her I'd take care of you."

"Out of the goodness of your heart."

"You wound me, kid. I thought we'd bonded, you and me, but if you don't want my help-"

I caught her arm as she stood. "Sorry, Ateri... Thank you, for helping me. I just... I'm not good at trusting."

"Good. Stay that way. You'll live longer. You hungry?"

"I don't have any money; I can't-"

"Did I ask? You'll pay me back later; I know you're good for it."

She shuffled out of the room and I carefully pushed myself up to follow her, steadying myself against the wall as my head spun. As I slowly moved through the apartment, I recognised the internal architecture of the bar.

"Are we above the watering hole?" I asked as I stepped into a cramped kitchen.

"Thought I told you not to get up, sandworm."

"Yeah, but then you said food."

Ateri rolled her eyes as she carried two plates of food to the table in the corner and I followed, careful not to knock into any of the books or boxes that were piled around. It seemed like she had tried to fit a large life into a small home, or like she had an addiction to collecting pretty but useless things— I didn't know her well enough to tell the difference. The table was levelled on the bottom by a stack of books holding up one of its legs, but it still wobbled a bit.

"Eat up," Ateri ordered. "You must be starving."

I had never been so happy to obey an order in my life, and she hadn't finished speaking before I was digging in.

"I don't think," I told her as I ate, "that I'm making much progress. I feel like I need to talk to someone who... I don't know, there are people who hunt snakes in this country, right? I was hesitant to reach out to a stranger, but think I should talk to them to figure out where to look next."

"You're really gonna go back out there?" she asked quietly. Her question seemed devoid of emotion, but Ateri was always like that. I had to imagine that she cared, sometimes, about people. And who was to say I wasn't one of them? "You nearly died, sandworm."

"I have to. I made a mistake, and this is the only way I can fix it. My Captain told me that if I bring this venom back, I can come home."

"Your... your Captain," she said slowly. "He's the one who sent you out here?"

"He trusts me, Ateri. He believes that I can do this, and I won't let him down... So I can't give up. I can't leave this desert until I find the antidote."

There was something in her expression, something searching, when she looked up at me. "That's what you need it for? A cure?"

I gave a faltering nod. "I... I failed to protect someone, and now this is the only thing I can do to make up for it. My Captain... he's like a father to me. He gave me a second chance, and I need to show him I deserve it."

Something changed in her face and she was silent for a long time, picking at the food on her plate. She wasn't looking at me when she finally spoke. "I'll help you."

"You will?"

"I know some people in the business, even a few who've sold four-fang venom before. I'll ask them to teach you what you need."

"What's the catch?"

She grinned at me and shook her head. "No catch. You've earned my respect, sandworm."

"Mhm."

"Tell you what... You've heard the story of my god's betrayal?"

I nodded. "Lithdreyan myth says that the God of Lithdreya and the Goddess of Lothforias were once lovers, king and queen of a great nation. One night, they argued, and *Foria* fled in the night, throwing acid in *Dreya*'s face to keep him from following her. She tore the great city out of the ground and carried it on her back for three days. Where she placed it became Lothforias, and their land was fertile and prosperous. The people left behind rebuilt and created Lithdreya, but the land had been changed by acid. Mountains now spewed sulphur and the water became toxic around the ruins of the city, because the bond of their gods had been broken. That's why... our peoples hate each other."

"It's why my people take oaths and trust so seriously... because nothing is more important to Lord *Dreya*. So when I promise to help you find this serpent and get home..."

"You mean it."

"Come on, sandworm. Finish eating. When you're done, I'm going to teach you how to survive."

"I thought that's what those tricks were..."

"Not how to survive the desert. How to survive people." She stood and dusted herself off as she started out of the kitchen. "And... not all of my people hate yours. The men and women raised by *Al majowan* may speak more loudly, but they don't speak for all of us. Some of us..." she trailed off into her own thoughts. "Some of us just want peace."

CHAPTER EIGHTY-FOUR

RUCE

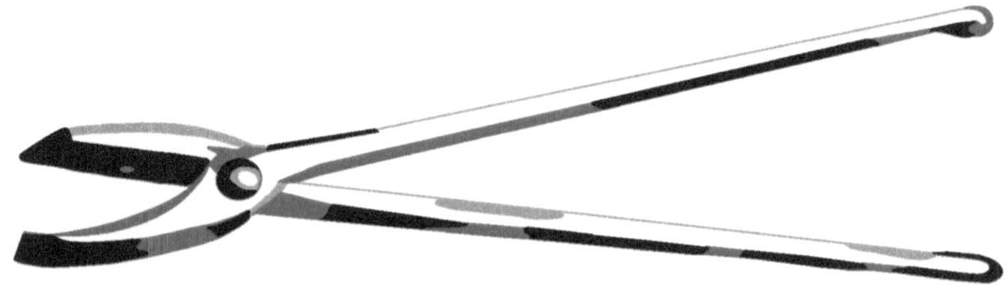

I WAS HAMMERING OUT the shape of the blade before me, Elin watching over my shoulder ready to help as needed, when Steth Henerswif sprinted into the smithy.

"Ruce," she panted, "Hener got stuck under the plough and we need to take it apart to get him out! Can you help?!"

"Elin," I said, "take over here. I'll be back." He took the hammer from me and I grabbed my bag of tools, following Steth through the village quickly. "Victoire!" I called as we drew closer. "Go to the academy and tell Edda to bring her seaming kit and some yoran root!"

When I reached the field, I understood why Steth was so panicked, but I knew it wasn't as bad as it could have been. Hener was caught under the plough, with one of the blades driven down into his leg, but it hadn't hit the main artery. He was awake and talking and, clearly, in a lot of pain.

"Hey, Ruce," he said weakly, trying to keep his voice light and friendly even as it wavered. "Fancy seeing you here."

"Yeah, you're just lucky I made a new set of tools, Hen," I said dryly. "Steth," I called as I began to work the bolts loose, "I'm gonna need you to grab some extra hands to help get the parts clear. I think Old Woman Tri and Mr. Parri should be around; go bother them, would you?"

Minutes later, they ran up with Edda close behind and helped me sort out Hener's leg, carrying him to the house carefully. Edda stitched him up neatly and covered the sutures in yoran root.

"Thank you," Steth said, "who knows how long it would have taken for the doctor to get here..."

"We all know it's a long walk from the pub, 'specially when you're cross-eyed," Old Woman Tri cackled. "Good one, Edda. Well, boy?" she said to me.

"Master Tri," I said with a smile. "Always a pleasure."

"I was wondering why my old apprentice saw fit to summon me. Efficient work," she told me, turning away without another word. The praise still set me beaming.

"I've gotta get back to the forge," I said to Steth, waving in farewell. "Hen, hate your guts."

"I smile when you suffer, Ruce," he called after me with a laugh.

I ducked into the smithy and dropped my bag of tools to the table, glancing up at Elin. He looked miserable. "What's wrong?"

"I messed up, *Aba*. I got the steps wrong and it's ruined."

"Lemme see this." I stepped up behind him to study the blade he had been working. He was right; the metal had been bent too far out of shape to continue. Even now, almost thirty-five years after I had left *Al majowan*, there was a voice in the back of my head screaming, an instinct to flinch. I had to remind myself that failure wasn't the end of the world.

"See?" he mumbled.

"It's alright, son. The good thing about metal is it can always be reworked. When we make mistakes, we can always start again. There's no point regretting; just move on and try to do better next time, yeah?"

"Yeah," he said quietly. "Thanks, *Aba*."

"Heat the forge. Let's fix this together."

CHAPTER EIGHTY-FIVE

JOVE

MY FOOT TAPPED IMPATIENTLY as I looked furtively around the shop. Steam had stopped rising from my two cups of *sahlab* an hour ago, and Ateri still had not shown. She had never been late before.

Finally, I refused to wait any longer and made the short trip back to the citadel, finding Eschel in the armoury. I quietly instructed him to go to the shop and order a cup of *sahlab*, keeping an eye on the table in the corner in case Ateri had been held up. I myself could not be seen loitering for the rest of the day while there was work to be done, but Eschel was a Guard in little more than name at this point, slowly ageing out of service, and he trusted me implicitly when I told him she was aiding me in my efforts to cure the king.

In the evening, he returned to my study with the news that she had never arrived. I was worried, then, about what could have stopped her.

Perhaps she had been delayed, and wouldn't be allowed into the city for another month. But perhaps she had been discovered… and dealt with. If Harun had realised his life was in danger, he would have acted decisively. It was possible that Ateri was already dead.

CHAPTER EIGHTY-SIX

HARUN

"YOU SURE YOU'RE FEELING up to it?" Ateri asked as she studied me. "If I were you, I'd stay in bed at least a week after a sandworm like you had..."

"I don't like sitting still. Work quiets my mind. Now are you going to show me what you've got in that bundle or not?"

She grinned, unrolling the small pack she'd brought down the stairs with us. She'd insisted that I hold her arm the entire way down, though I was perfectly capable of managing myself. I appreciated that she wasn't being overly kind to me, though. Every act of care was accompanied by an impatient taunt or a friendly jab. I limped over to stand next to her, looking down at the weapons she spread out on the table. "Tada! Lithdreyan peasant daggers!"

"They're so... little," I said mildly, trying not to sound disappointed.

"That's the trick," she told me as she held one of the knives up for me to study. It was the middle of the restday, so we were alone in the bar. I was sweating from the heat, so I was grateful. The privacy meant I could bare my arms without fear of being discovered. Ateri was standing next to me in long sleeves, in case I had been wondering whether she was harder than me. I hadn't, by the way. She moved like she didn't even feel the heat. "No one ever expects something small to be dangerous."

"That's the motto of the *Menagerie*, isn't it?"

Her face darkened for a moment, but it was gone so quickly I wondered if I'd imagined it. "*Hin al majowan ef.* 'The small kills quietly.' Yeah, that's their philosophy. Scorpions, snakes, spiders... children," she murmured. "I would think a kid like you, as dangerous as you are, would understand that just because something is small doesn't mean it's harmless."

"I'm almost nineteen!" I complained.

"Yeah," she shrugged, "an infant." She pointed with her bottom lip at the peasant dagger between her fingers again and I took it, turning it over in my hands.

It was thin, very light, and smaller than any blade I'd held before. It was shaped like a diamond that someone had stretched on one end, with a thin piece of slightly sticky ribbon wrapped around the handle, which ended in a ring. On instinct, I slipped my finger into the ring and spun the knife, catching the handle before the blade began to spin too quickly. "***Oh.***"

She grinned and nodded at me. "Starting to see the light? I haven't even shown you how to sheath them yet..."

"Sheath them? I want to ***use*** them; are they for throwing or close combat? Do you use one or do they work in pa-"

"Slow down; you've barely gotten back on your feet, sandworm..."

"I really don't like that nickname."

||

"Hey, Ateri?"

"Mm?" she asked, turning her head to me as her eyes continued to scan the bar's inventory sheet.

"There were wolves in the desert..."

"You know, I've heard that before..."

"Aren't the Jewels of the Menagerie the dangerous animals of the desert?"

"They are, kid. Keep your voice down."

"Why isn't there a Wolf?"

She sighed, glancing up at me and dropping her papers to the counter. "For the same reason there's no Lion; the title is passed on in death."

"What does that mean? Does that mean there *is* a Wolf out there somewhere?"

"Not one that answers to *Al majowan*. You've never heard this story?"

I slowly shook my head, setting down the broom I'd been using as I came to lean against the counter across from her.

"What do they teach in Lothforias?" she muttered under her breath. "At least tell me you've heard of the burning of Cessiri?"

"My Captain was there... Said it was the scariest thing he'd ever seen."

"Yeah, he wasn't the only one who felt that way. All of the favourite Jewels of the *Wani*— that's the Quiet of *Al majowan*—" she informed me before I could ask, "were sent to the city. Lion, Viper, *Tannin*, *Dwerda*, Scorpion... they were all there. But then-"

"Where were the others?"

"Minding their own business, now don't interrupt."

I struggled to bite back the other questions I had and Ateri nodded curtly.

"He can be taught. Good. Now, that night, something happened that had **never** happened before. A Jewel, a favourite blade with a holy mission, **walked away...**"

"What? What do you mean? They just left?"

"The Lion vanished that night, and hasn't been seen in almost forty years."

"Surely they're dead..."

"Maybe. Maybe not— the *Wani* isn't sure... And until proof is found of his death, the title cannot be passed on." She held up a hand before I could speak. "You asked about the Wolf; I know. A few years after the Lion's betrayal, another Jewel walked away from *Al majowan*. The Wolf."

"Why? Where are they? What happened?"

"Do you always have to ask three questions at once?" she huffed in irritation.

"What? I do that? Are you sure?"

Ateri rolled her eyes to the sun and shook her head, muttering something in Lithdreyan about 'teenagers'. "**Anyways**... *Al majowan* doesn't know where the Wolf ended up. If they did... they would do whatever it took to pass on the title and erase a traitor from their history."

"Even people in the *Menagerie* want peace..." I murmured.

"Not all of them," she said with a sad smile. "...But some."

Chapter Eighty-Seven

Edda

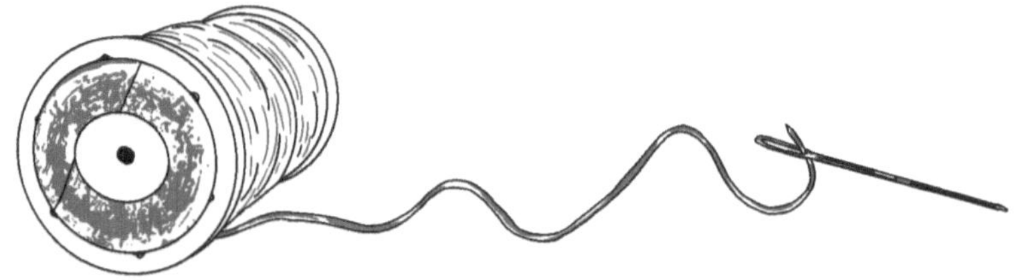

I OPENED THE DOOR and smiled widely as Victoire's family stepped through the door, Hener supported by a heavy wooden crutch. "Steth, you look lovely," I said as I embraced her. Victoire helped her father inside and the boys piled in behind her until the main room of our house was happily crowded. Happily, of course, for everyone but Ruce—if you took his word for it.

"Hener," he glowered, "I see you're healing well."

"Sorry to disappoint, old timer," he barked out in a laugh.

"We'll fight to the death one day," Ruce promised as he pulled out a chair for Hener to sit in.

"*Aba*," Elin called, "when you're finished chatting with your friend, can you help me bring dinner from the kitchen?"

Ruce spluttered. "We're not- He's not my-" He grumbled and joined Elin in the kitchen without another word.

I moved to sit at the table, setting a hand on Victoire's. "Elin mentioned you've started talking about the wedding. This summer, you were thinking?"

"It's my favourite time of year."

"You'll be a beautiful bride. I would be honoured to make your dress, if you'd-"

"Oh, yes, Edda, thank you!"

||

"Ruce, hand me that pin?"

"Here, *Habi*."

"Thank you."

Victoire was standing in the centre of my workroom, beaming down at me as I worked. "Oh, it's going to be beautiful, Edda." She swayed side to side and the layers of fabric in her skirt swished.

"Hold still, girl— you're as bad as Elin."

"What about me?" my son asked, popping his head into the doorway. "Did you- Oh, wow..." He moved further in, grinning at his fiance. "Tori, you look- Wow."

"Thank you very much," she said with a curtsy.

"Still," I ordered again.

She froze, laughing quietly as she and Elin made eye contact.

"Thank you. Elin, you look tired."

"No, just-" he was interrupted by a yawn and he smiled at us sheepishly.

"Did you get into my *kahve* again?" Ruce asked gruffly. "You're the only person I know who needs a nap after a cup of *kahve*. I- Hang on... There wasn't much *kahve* left when I-"

"Well," Elin grinned, "unrelated, I'm off to the market. See you later." He struck with speed, pecking a kiss to Victoire's cheek before he was gone.

"Oh, that boy," I laughed. "Are you sure you want to commit to living with him?" I asked Victoire.

"No question," she answered instantly. "I've never loved anyone like I love him..."

Chapter Eighty-Eight
Harun

I carefully pulled my filthy shirt over my head, still mindful of the wounds that peppered my body. I caught sight of myself in the mirror in the corner of the room and slowly stepped forward, taking in my reflection.

My body was covered in scars, bruises, and wounds all in various stages of healing. Tightness trailed through every muscle, pain and resolve and something broken. My chin was touched with shadow and my face had lost any of the softness it once had.

When did I stop looking like a boy?

I drew a dagger, stepping close to the mirror to clean my face, and when I was done, I pretended that I recognised the person staring back at me.

I looked around the cramped attic room— **my** cramped attic room, at least for now— full of boxes, crates, and barrels all piled high and left to gather dust.

I moved gingerly, picking up a crate that was flimsy from age and full of nothing more than scraps and old broken bottles.

There was a word I hadn't used in so long, a word I was so afraid of that I didn't even dare think it... But this little room was mine, and I wanted it to feel like... well, I wanted it to feel like-

"Sandworm," Ateri called. "You coming or what?"

"Uh- yeah," I yelled, my voice carrying down the stairs. I quickly set the crate back onto the pile and grabbed a clean shirt. "Yep, on my way!"

||

"Keep your eyes up; don't watch my feet," Ateri ordered, lunging at me with her daggers.

"You know, there's a draft upstairs," I told her as I ducked out of reach.

"Old building," she shrugged. "We can fix it up."

"I- I was also thinking I might clear out some stuff from the room you have me in, if that's alright."

"'S your room, kid. Whatever makes it feel like home. You're telegraphing," she said as she jumped forward and punched me in the face.

"What?" I asked, looking up at her from the floor as I rubbed my cheek.

"Before you jab with your left, you pop your chin up, just a bit. Tells me it's coming; break that habit before someone breaks you."

"The only one breaking me is you, Ateri."

"And I'm going easy," she said with a grin. "Imagine someone **really** scary."

"How am I gonna learn if you hold back? Let's go faster."

"Fast is the opposite of what you need right now," she told me as our knives locked. "You're still healing, Sandworm."

I shoved her back and caught my breath, steeling myself for what the scholars would call 'a stupid decision'. Then I launched myself at her without mercy, doing my best to carve her head clean off her shoulders.

She gave ground for a moment, but recovered quickly, matching my strikes and jarring my arms when our knives came together. We moved so fast that I knew the moment my focus slipped, it would be over, but Ateri wasn't grinning at me anymore. She was focused, which meant she had finally stopped holding back.

She began to rain blow after blow down on me, and I struggled to keep up, barely managing to stop her from cutting me or knocking me off my feet.

The end came without warning as I brought one blade up in front of my face to parry an attack, blinding myself to the second for a moment too long. I saw the strike coming and flung myself out of the way. As I dove to safety, I felt several stitches in my side pull and blood well up anew. I fell to my knee, gritting my teeth at the pain as I pressed my arm into my side.

Instantly, Ateri resheathed her knives and was grabbing her seaming kit. "I told you, you need to heal. You're moving too fast."

"No, I was too **slow**," I huffed as she pulled me to my feet and helped me lean against the table to look at my injury. "But I'll block your strike next time."

I dug my fingers into the dry wood of the table as she deftly restitched and bandaged the wound. "All done."

"Let's go again."

She sighed in irritation. "Sandworm-"

"I'll get it. Again."

||

My army was almost dead. Ateri's forces were scattered all across the tabletop, surrounding me.

I'd never been a fan of *bita*, but Ateri insisted on it in between sparring sessions.

She had asked me to take time to heal and learn how to protect myself before I went back out into the desert. The only reason I agreed was because she refused to introduce me to any of her snake-catcher friends otherwise.

Ateri dropped a misfortune card to the table sadistically. "My troops are surrounding your last stronghold, and I just threw a dead cow over the walls to lower morale and spread disease... You're circling loss, kid. What's your move?"

I studied the board carefully, my eyebrows lifting as I decided on my strategy. Ateri's troops were downwind... and I had a misfortune card. The only problem was, her territory was heavily forested all the way to the coast, and there were several cities behind her armies full of innocent people.

"Think faster, kid," she prodded. "Oh, and if you lose, I'm making you clean the bar after closing every night for a week."

I stared at the pieces on the table for a long time. Every piece represented ten thousand soldiers or villagers. Ten thousand lives... and the board was heavy with them. Finally, I committed to my decision and set my chosen card faceup in front of her.

"I set fire to the forests west of my position, and they don't stop burning until they reach your coast. My victory."

She stared at the board for several seconds. "Wow, Sandworm... I didn't think you had it in you. At the very least, you crippled my nation, and at most, you razed it to the ground. Good work."

"I don't want to play like that, Ateri."

"I don't care if you play like that or not, just that you know how to. Not everyone plays the game with your heart, and sometimes winning means destroying your enemies. Understand?"

I looked down at the board again, picking up a city. "...I think I'm starting to."

||

"Table Three," Ateri instructed as she handed over a tray of food. I lifted it up onto my shoulder and wove through the patrons easily.

Their patterns had become familiar, over these last several months working with Ateri, and I hardly ever spilled food now. Alcohol was a different story, because when the workers came in during the evening, after the workday, they usually drank until it made them clumsy and stupid. Tonight was no exception.

"Oi, oi," a patron called, waving his hand for my attention. "Kid, you interested in some medicinal snake oil? Fair price!"

His friend elbowed him conspiratorially. "Leave Ter's nephew alone! You think she pays him enough to afford our cure-all?"

I leaned closer, smirking at them. "You know, gentlemen," I said lowly, "you might wanna change your pitch. Eventually, people are gonna realise that the snakes native to the *Denuda* Wastes don't actually **produce** oil, and you're gonna be run out of town at knifepoint. What is it really, huh? Red pepper and olive oil? I doubt it could even cure my thirst."

They smiled at me nervously. "Uh- eh, you're a good kid, you know? Sharp. I like you," the patron said, giving me a gap-toothed grin. "Give you a special discount."

I rolled my eyes with a laugh, adjusting my grip on my tray and moving on once more.

I had almost reached Table Three when a drunkard— some migrant merchant— staggered into me. It happened too quickly to stop it. He flailed, hoping to catch his balance, and grabbed me for support, pulling my sleeve up in his desperate struggle.

I quickly pushed him away, but not before the fabric slipped up enough to bare my brand to the tables closest to me.

The noise in the room dulled to a murmur as people glanced at each other, whispering and studying me with new interest. Suddenly, Ateri was there driving her knife down into Table Three, sending the room dead silent.

"Anything I can do for you?" she asked coldly.

"I didn't see anything," one of the patrons muttered.

"I have a horrible memory."

"I'm very drunk."

"I'm blind," another promised.

"I was studying this table. Quite interesting..."

The room fell quiet again as Ateri looked around threateningly. "Good," she said finally. "Keep it that way."

She quickly steered me behind the bar, looking at me in annoyance. "I thought I told you to keep that covered."

"I was trying. I know you always wear ten layers, but some of us actually feel the heat."

"Oh, you'll feel it if *Al majowan* gets word about you, Sandworm. A little suffering might keep you alive." As she spoke, she hastily tore a scrap of fabric from the hem of her tunic and wrapped it around my wrist, keeping my sleeve flush against my skin and immovable. "That's your new best friend unless you wanna get killed."

||

My gaze raked over the three warriors in front of me. Rejohan, Lithdreya, Stangauer. Ateri was having a laugh outside the ring, I was certain. She always told me to be prepared, to be adaptable... And now she was setting me against three strong warriors who all had different styles of fighting.

Big Rini and I were frequent sparring partners, and though I usually won our bouts, she made it hurt. She was thick and beefy, a former member of the People's Army and well-trained with a longspear. Markos had grown up in Stangauer as a member of their mounted forces. He carried a long cavalry sword and his tactical awareness was unparalleled. Sakura was a wanderer from Rejohan, one of the few who had defied the travel ban. They had come to Lithdreya with nothing but the clothes on their back and their curved sword. *Katana*, they called it. Fighting the three of them at once would be quite difficult, especially because Ateri had taken my weapons. I would have to get in close to do any damage, and they were all armed with long weapons that provided an unfair advantage— my teacher's intention, obviously.

I'd been training with Ateri for almost a year now, and my wounds had fully healed a while ago, but I'd lost some of my urgency to go back out into the *Denuda*. Every day, I learned, and every day I got stronger and sharper. My sword had been too noticeable, too clunky for working the watering hole or fighting in close quarters, so it sat tucked under my bed. Instead, I had taken to carrying my peasant daggers, and Pierre, the long dirk that rested against my hip. The way Ateri was teaching me to fight was realms different than I had ever learned back-

There was that word again.

Stay focused. Sakura. Big Rini. Markos.

"Fight doesn't end until you win," Ateri called up to me, "or until you ***lose***."

She was a harsh teacher, always too willing to send me to the mat bloody and bruised, but I respected it. If I wasn't on my game, I paid for it. It pushed me to fight harder, smarter. Months ago, I'd broken several bones in my hand in a sparring match with Ateri, and the next day, she had made me get back in the ring with Markos. I'd gotten bloody, but I had adapted to that weakness. I only had one hand to work with, so I made sure I hit Markos hard enough that he wouldn't get up.

When we finished sparring, we would always sit together, icing and bandaging our injuries. It was a strange sort of friendship, made even stranger every time I was reminded they didn't know my name, but friendship nonetheless. Big Rini told me it was the highest honour to bear scars earned by locking blades with strong opponents, which I **think** meant she liked me… and which meant she would forgive me for hurting her.

I lashed out with my foot, kicking out her knee. She grunted in pain, but all I did was throw her off balance for a moment. She was thrusting her spear at me a second later and I barely dodged out of the way in time, feeling the air as the spearhead drove past me. Instinctively, I ducked, and Sakura's *katana* passed through the space my head had just occupied.

My only chance was to make my opponents get in their own way. They each had long weapons; time to make them regret it. I hurriedly backed into the corner of the ring, watching as they pushed forward, coming shoulder to shoulder. There was that moment of confusion, of elbows jamming into ribs and navigating each other's space, and I took the opportunity to strike out at Markos with a left-handed jab. Hand-to-hand had never been my favourite, until I met Sakura. They taught me the satisfaction of feeling a good punch connect.

And **that** was a good punch.

Markos staggered back, dizzy and unbalanced, and the motion drove his sword towards Big Rini. She ducked out of the way, but it cost her dearly. I put all of my strength into a second kick at her knee, and the way she cried out told me I had done **damage**. She was out of the fight.

Seeing their team dispatched, Sakura quickly gave ground, retreating into the centre of the ring, where they had enough room to swing their sword.

I carefully edged around them, making sure to put them between Markos and I. He might recover, and it wouldn't pay to have him in my blindspot when that happened. I had learned **that** lesson the hard way.

"Condition, Sandworm!" Ateri called. "Momentum!"

I rolled my eyes. She loved to do this to me, to give me sudden rules for the way I won the fight. She wouldn't be satisfied now unless I used Sakura's momentum against them.

Sakura's swing sliced my cheek open without warning and I fought the instinct to squeeze my eyes shut. If I hadn't, I never would have seen the thrust they followed up with. I swayed to the side, grabbing their wrist as the sword swished past me, and I knocked the sword from their hand with my other hand, twisting their wrist and sending them to their knees with a **crack** as I broke bone.

I staggered back as they gasped in pain. Markos was slowly regaining his feet, digging the tip of his sword into the mat to hold himself up. "Timeout, kid," he panted. "Timeout."

"You know there are no timeouts in my ring, old man," Ateri called, her arms crossed.

"Oh, make an exception."

"Would you have made an exception for my boy here, if you were in his shoes?"

He looked up at me, sighing. "Nope."

With that, he launched himself off of his back foot, his sword coming up in a violent arc.

Instinct told me to duck, to move out of the way, but Ateri called, "Condition! Disarm!"

I huffed in exertion, flexing my fingers in preparation, and then lunged forward, catching Markos's wrist in both hands, stopping his swing cold. I wrenched the sword from his hand, whirling it and bringing it to rest against his jugular.

"Good boy," Ateri said with a sadistic grin. "Alright, you three, pick yourselves up. Sandworm wins, which means the three of you get to do his chores this week."

Markos helped Big Rini to her feet, letting her lean on him as she limped out of the ring.

"Sorry, Rini," I said as I dropped down to the floor.

"Nah, kid," she laughed. "Makes me feel young again. And it's a pleasure watching you fight. I'd say you're ready to get back out there."

The other two murmured agreement as they each nursed their wounds.

I looked over at Ateri, blood running down my arm and dripping to the floor. I didn't even remember getting cut there... "Well?" I asked her.

She slowly nodded. "...I think you just might survive, Sandworm."

||

"Sandworm, meet Pips. Pips, Sandworm."

"Do you really have to introduce me that way?" I asked.

"I could call you by your real name, if you prefer." I fell silent at that and Ateri laughed. "Sandworm it is, then. Pips is the best snake-catcher who... isn't currently out working, so he's who you get."

"Touched, Ter," he said with a roll of his eyes. "She is kidding. You that *loro* stumbling around the desert looking for poison?"

"That's me. You any good at your job or is there a reason you're in here bumming drinks off of the bartender?"

"I am one of the best in the business, kid," he hissed through his teeth.

"Prove it. Tell me how to find a four-fang."

He laughed, leaning back in his chair as he shook his head. "You are even crazier than she said. Know what we snake-catchers call a four-fang?"

"How much will it cost to keep it to yourself and start teaching?"

He looked at me with a hard but amused light in his eyes as he measured me. "Alright, tell you what. Step into the ring with me; you last three minutes, I will give you the friends and family discount. You do not, you walk away and find some other way to get yourself killed."

I slowly started to smile as Markos, Sakura, and Big Rini began to whoop animalistically, egging me on. "You might come to regret that offer."

As I ducked up onto the raised platform to stand opposite Pips, Ateri slammed her fist onto the bar and called, "We got a fight!" She moved to me and ruffled my hair. "Be careful, yeah?"

"Ateri-"

"I need him alive when you're done."

I broke into a grin. "Deal."

"Remember. You're small. Kill quietly."

||

"No, bet is off," Pips protested as he nursed the dark bruise on his jaw. It had taken him half a minute to wake up after the fight was over, and I couldn't bring myself to feel sore about it. "I was not properly informed. Ter did not tell me-"

"I didn't tell you to make a stupid bet," she scoffed as she came and set a drink in front of him. "You promised the friends and family discount."

"That was just if he lasted three minutes," Sakura called happily. Markos and Big Rini laughed. The three of them were cleaning the watering hole, sweeping the floors, wiping down tables, restocking the bar— the work *I* usually had to do. Ah... life was good.

I touched my chin thoughtfully. "Oh, yeah. It was over so fast, we never discussed the price if I kicked your sorry-"

"Alright, that is not fair, you are all ganging up on me," he huffed. "Fine. What do you wanna know, kid? You really going after your own death?"

"I'm going after the four-fang. I want you to tell me how to find it, and how to survive when I do."

"That is more... on the job training. I am heading back into the *Denuda* Wastes in three days. Tag along; I will teach you what I can. On the house— for family."

"Thank you."

"You hungry, Sandworm?" Ateri asked as she set a plate in front of me. "Been hard at work."

"I really don't like that nickname."

"Yeah, yeah, eat your lunch." She swayed away as she continued her job delivering plates and drinks to the other patrons.

"I really did underestimate you, kid," Pips said quietly as he stole a piece of *labneh* off of my plate. "Should have known better, you being Ter's nephew... *Hin al majowan ef*, and all, right?"

"...Right."

"Where did you come from anyway? I didnt even know Ter had a nephew."

"Near and far; keep eating my lunch," I snapped playfully. "Heading out in three days, you said?"

"At sundown. Edge of town. Don't be late— and bring those little knives of yours."

"Expecting a sandworm or two?"

"Never hurts to be prepared," he shrugged. "Well, I am off to cause trouble. Tell Ter I will pay her back tomorrow."

"Mhm," I said dryly as he strode out of the bar.

"Oi, where'd he go?" Ateri asked me as she pulled up to our table with a tray of empty plates in hand. "He owes me money."

The door swung open and she turned in irritation.

"Yeah, you'd better be back to-"

Her breath caught as a tall woman deliberately walked into the watering hole, her eyes shifting back and forth across the room as she moved. Her hair was thick, braided in some places like Ateri's, curling around her neck and beaded with gold. An ugly scar went from her temple down the side of her neck. She was dressed all in white, her clothing rough and pitted and touched with blood in several places. A sword hung from her belt, and as she walked, a looped metal wire shivered against itself at her hip.

Two men stepped inside after her, one slightly taller than her and one slightly shorter, both dressed the same as she was, and I knew who they were.

Dwer-da. The dingoes.

Most Jewels of the *Menagerie* were singular, lone, but the dingoes travelled in a pack. They hunted together, and they revelled in the blood and fear they incited. I knew better than to make eye contact— Ateri had warned me— but in the moment, I couldn't stop myself from staring at the proof that the *Menagerie* recruited women.

The moment the lead *Dwer-da* caught my gaze on her, she leapt forward and yanked me to my feet by my shirt, snarling when we were face to face. "Something to say, boy? There a reason you're gawking at me?"

"N- no," I stammered out, fighting the instinct to break her wrist and instead forcing my shoulders to hunch and my eyes to dart. "I- I'm sorry, I didn't mean to-"

She threw me down, knocking over the table and chairs and sending plates of food flying. As she stepped over me, she told Ateri, "Three drinks— the strongest you have."

"Yes, Lady *Dwer-da*. This table is free; I'll-"

"No," *Dwer-da* said flatly. "I want **this** table." She pointed in my direction. "Have your boy clean it up for me."

"Yes... Lady *Dwer-da*."

Ateri shot me a wary glance as I began to right the overturned furniture. I took the broom that was standing against a nearby column and started sweeping away the spilled food.

"Good. Get chairs for my boys," *Dwer-da* ordered.

I followed directions quickly and meekly, aware of Ateri's hand moving underneath the bar, where I knew she kept her blades. She didn't draw them, but her eyes never left the *Dwer-da* and I don't think she breathed, either, until I was behind the counter with her.

"Careful, Ateri," Lady *Dwer-da* said, "you'd better teach your boy better. You wouldn't want to lose another one... would you?"

Ateri looked ready to jump over the counter and attack her until I grabbed her wrist, catching her eye. She looked down at me and slowly exhaled, turning back to Lady *Dwer-da* with a controlled expression. "Sage advice, Lady *Dwer-da*."

Lady *Dwer-da* gave a reptilian smile as she sipped her drink. "Always a pleasure."

Chapter
Eighty-Nine

Riadh

I ENTERED THE MEETING room, smiling at the emissaries from Stangauer who were waiting inside. I bowed first to the woman I had not met, then to the emissary familiar to me. "Tor Djanson," I said as I bowed my head in greeting. "It's good to see you again."

"You as well," he smiled as he clasped my hand, "though I so wish it were under different circumstances. My mother, architect Djan Sminsdottir. Mother, Lieutenant Riadh al Abbas."

I quickly shook her hand and we moved to sit at the table. "Our people heard how devastating the most recent attack was," she said quietly, "and we are mourning with you. Our king has sent us to offer our support as you rebuild."

"Thank you, Emissary-"

"Just Djan, please."

"Djan. Our people are grateful that you stand with us. This attack was... one of the most brutal we've seen in years. The explosions were set off in the marketplace in the middle of the day, and many lives were lost. I know three of your own people, traders and visitors, were injured in the blast. How are they recovering?"

"We are monitoring their conditions closely in your hospital," Tor said, "but my king wishes us to focus our efforts in repairing the damage and reopening the market as quickly as possible. This is why my mother has come, to assist in rebuilding. You have our full support in this, Lieutenant al Abbas."

"Thank you, Tor. I would love to stay longer, perhaps enjoy tea together, but-"

"But there is no time for tea; I understand, Riadh. Don't worry, next time I'm in the city, we'll have a social visit, and maybe one day, in a time of peace, you can be a visitor in my country. I will introduce you to the Stangrey Circus and we will walk the Halls of Bertrain... Please, tend to your people's needs. *Ha det.*"

"*Ha det*, Tor, Djan."

I took my leave as quickly as was polite and then made my way out of the citadel. The marketplace was full of Guards and healers and craftsmages. I started towards Hakim, who was checking a list.

"Corporal, report."

He continued reading through his list, murmuring to himself, until I moved into his line of sight.

"Corporal."

He looked up in surprise, giving me a nervous smile. "Sorry, Lieutenant. Still getting used to that... I didn't realise you were talking to me. I've taken stock of the damages and casualties, and I've started a list of the materials we'll need to rebuild."

"Did anyone ask you to do that?"

"Uh- No, Lieutenant, but it needed doing, and my Sergeant is occupied with shoring up defenses. I just-"

"Good work, Hakim. I appreciate your diligence. Continue with your work, then report to me this evening."

"Lieutenant," he said with a duck of his head.

Chapter Ninety

Harun

A QUIET VOICE STIRRED me from sleep, and I rolled out of bed, padding out of my room to seek its source. The apartment was gently lit by a flickering candle, and as I got closer to it, Ateri's voice became more clear. She was singing that lullaby again, like she was trying to soothe herself. Living with Ateri and working in the watering hole downstairs had made Lithdreyan come naturally— sometimes, I even spoke it in my dreams now— and understanding the words was like getting hit by a mace.

Little sun, little sun, Mama is here. Little sun, little sun, standing in the shade. Little sun, little sun, just put your little hand in mine. Little sun, little sun, never be afraid.

I inched closer, hearing her voice waver. She was hunched over on a stool, a soft stuffed crocodile pressed to her chest as she ran her fingers over the fabric.

Little sun, little sun, I will be brave for you. Little sun, little sun, I'll keep you from harm. Little sun, little sun, I'd raise my sword for you. Little sun, little sun, safe in my arms.

"Ateri?" I asked hesitantly, making her jump and turn to me in surprise.

She hurriedly wiped her eyes and threw the stuffed animal down to the ground. "I thought you were asleep, Sandworm."

"Are you alright?"

"Always," she answered instantly.

I gingerly moved to sit on a cushion next to her, looking up in question. "You know... you don't **have** to be. When you lose someone, it's okay to falter. Don't they deserve that space in your heart?"

She laughed as her eyes watered again, turning away to wipe them. "He would be almost eleven, now."

You'd better teach your boy better. You wouldn't want to lose another one... would you?

"...Your son," I realised. "You had a son. What happened?"

"*Al majowan* takes what they want," she spat bitterly. "He was hardly three when they came and snatched him away from me..." She ran her hands over her long sleeves anxiously. "They destroy whatever they touch, and they killed my sweet boy."

"You think he's dead?"

She was silent for a long time, staring out the tiny window to the village like it could answer for her. "I hope so," she breathed. "He'd be better off that way..."

"Is that why you agreed to help me?"

"You think I decided to save you because I couldn't save him? You think because no one was looking out for you, I felt sympathy? You think you remind me of my son?" She spat every question into my eyes with venom, but her hands were tight, every line in her body tense and electric.

"Do I?"

Her eyes fell from mine and she hugged herself again. "Eight years I've been alone, and I've never missed him so much... I wonder what he would have looked like, if he ever got to be as old as you. What he would sound like, if his laugh would still sound the same... He used to get this... this **giggle** when he was tired— really tired— where he just couldn't stop." A smile came across her face. "It was the best sound in the world... I can hardly remember it now."

She fell still, so far away, wisp-like and intangible. "Ateri?" I asked.

She suddenly stirred, looking up at me like she had forgotten I was there. "What is it, kid?"

"You said all the dangerous animals of the desert are Jewels."

"I do recall mentioning something along those lines... Why?"

"What about the four-fang?"

"Of course. But we call them *S'Qidah*. It's Lithdreyan for-"

"Four-fang, I know. It's not bone surgery the way you name your warriors."

"No-" she started, trying not to laugh. "Well, yes, the names tend to translate easily, but *S'Qidah* does not mean four-fang. It means 'king'."

||

"You've got everything? Did you double-check?" Ateri asked as she fretted over my pack and my knives and the new clothing she'd gotten me from the market.

"I have everything, Ateri. You should relax, or I might think you care about me."

She looked up at me, a smile playing across her lips, and I knew she was thinking about our conversation last night. "Well, we can't have that, can we, Sandworm?"

I shouldered my pack and started out of the watering hole, but she caught my shoulder. "Be careful out there, kid. Pips is the most trustworthy snake-catcher I know... but he's a snake-catcher, and you don't get good at that job unless you learn to think coldblooded, like your prey. You remember what I told you?"

"That I'd live longer if I didn't trust people?"

She nodded curtly and pried her hand off of me, trying to feign ease. "Right. See you when you get back. Tell Pips he owes me money."

||

Pips was waiting for me where he said he'd be as the sun began to set. I tugged my *kisa* along by the reins and he nodded in greeting.

"You sure about this, kid? No shame in not dying."

"Are you that horrible a teacher?" I shot back.

He bristled for a moment, then shook his head with a grin. "You really know how to hurt a guy's feelings."

"We're wasting moonlight, aren't we?"

He nodded and swung up onto his mount. "Let's go, kid. See how much the desert likes you."

||

With Pips's guidance, it took less than a week for me to find my first snake. Cobra, black scales that shifted in the light, unsettling rasp of a voice.

He taught me how to catch it, how to immobilise and drain it of its venom. Once it was in your grip, getting the venom was the easy part. It was finding the snake that proved most difficult.

We were out there for almost a month before we finally got a lead on a four-fang. Pips told me sometimes it took twice as long just to figure out where one had been, much less to pick up a viable trail.

The four-fang trails were distinctive, he said, because of the extra markings. Every snake left the curve of its tail in the sand, but the four-fang had stubs coming out of its sides, like it was trying to grow legs. Like it was trying to turn into something else.

One afternoon, when we were sitting down to eat under the shade of some trees surrounding an oasis, he asked, "You ever heard the legend of where these damned things come from?"

I shook my head.

"After *Foria* fled to the coast, she could still hear *Dreya*'s screams from the mountains. They shook the earth, scared away the birds... She took pity on him, and she sent her closest friend to ease his pain. The seamster Goddess could not heal him completely, but she was able to draw some of the acid from his wounds. Where the drops fell, four-fanged serpents slithered out of the earth. They were full of his poison, but they were also full of his rage. That is what makes them so dangerous— not the venom, the hatred. Cobras, finicks, rattlers, even vipers can be caught. The four-fangs, though... you cannot stop them unless you kill them, and even then they will spend their dying breaths struggling to get to you. That is why in our business, we call them Dreya's Furies."

I shook my head and huffed. "I didn't wanna know that. Why did you tell me that? We're less than a day from catching up to one of those things. I don't need that in my head."

"Good sense?"

"Fear," I said solidly. "It gets in the way."

"I gotta say, you are the weirdest kid I have ever met."

"What sane kid would talk to you?"

He laughed, laying back as a cool breeze filtered through the brush. "Fair enough. I am gonna take a short one. Wake me when the sun sets." With that, he tugged his wide-brimmed hat over his eyes and began to snore.

||

I pictured the little stuffed lion Ismael had always been playing with, the soft fur, the stitched whiskers, the eyes full of love...

Had the person who made that ever seen a real lion?

It paced in front of us, a low rumble in its throat as its tail flicked back and forth. Its tail— of course its tail had a morningstar on the end; this desert couldn't stop looking for ways to kill me. Its maw was streaked with blood, its fur matted and gouged from fighting, and one of its eyes was scarred shut. I recognized that scar: I had several of my own from my encounter with the wolves... Their venom left pockmarks in whatever it touched, stippling across skin carelessly like a child playing with a stick in the dirt.

"Do not. Move," Pips breathed to me, his breathing coming shallowly. We had been packing up our camp as evening came, brains still muddled from sleep, and we hadn't noticed the lion until it was right in front of us, growling and pacing. I had instinctively reached for my sword, but Pips had caught my wrist in fear, holding us both in place like statues.

"Pips," I ordered in a low voice, "let go of me."

"You are going to get yourself killed before we even find your damned snake," he hissed as I wrenched myself free of his grip.

I stared the lion down as I drew my sword, walking forward deliberately. "Are we going to do this, or what?" I asked the beast.

"What the hell are you doing, *loro*?!" Pips yelped in panic.

The lion roared angrily, taking a step forward and drawing my attention to its flicking tail, to that club that could break my ribs so easily... but I refused to step back, instead pushing myself closer and swinging my sword. "Go on. You might kill me, but I'm taking you with me," I growled, my eyes stone.

It felt like the desert stopped breathing for a moment to watch. The wind slowly stopped throwing sand and whistling around our ankles. For an eternity, the lion and I stared each other down, until without warning I lunged forward, shouting and stamping my foot. The beast flinched, its conviction wavering. It was a predator; it was **the** predator. Why wasn't this clawless, vulnerable creature scared?

Finally, the lion decided I must be a predator, and a dangerous one to stand so steady... and it turned tail, warily stalking away from us.

"You... are insane, kid," Pips moaned, backing away even though the lion was already leaving.

I glared at its retreating back. "No; I'm tired."

Pips started towards his *kisa* and made a weak sound, his shaking legs giving out and sending him to his butt awkwardly. "I'm just... gonna sit here a minute," he told me.

||

"There it is, you see it?"

"I'll never stop seeing it. That's gonna haunt me in my nightmares."

Pips chuckled. "You remember what needs to be done, yeah?"

"Do you? I'm ready when you are, old man."

He punched me in the arm somewhat lightly. "Let us go. I will take left."

We both moved, unsheathing our knives and spreading out to come at the snake from both sides. I don't know if it heard us, smelled something, or just knew we were there, but the snake hissed and immediately lunged for Pips. He scrambled, yelping, and I threw one of my knives. The blade nicked the serpent's side, but it didn't seem to notice. It just kept going for him as its sickly yellow blood soaked into the sand.

In the back of my mind, I was wondering about the serpent's name, because from what I could see... it only had two fangs. I pushed the thought down as I moved towards Pips, but then he shouted, "Behind you!"

I spun, seeing oily black movement, and threw my knife with deadly precision. As the snake died, I watched it wriggle and struggle to gain purchase with its stubs.

"W*aah*!" Pips called, and as I turned, I realised he meant it as a warning. The first snake had abandoned its hunt for Pips and had started towards me. As it neared, I could see in its eyes the hatred of an undying god.

And both of my knives were laying in the sand several feet away. Too far.

I reached into my pocket and pulled out the only thing I hadn't left on my saddle— the glass jar of a snake-catcher.

Knowing the snake would be on me in moments, I said a prayer and made the first move, diving towards it. I got it by the neck— is there any part of a snake that *isn't* the neck?— and for a moment, it seemed to be looking at me in surprise. I guessed no one had ever lunged for it and grabbed hold like it was a wayward child's hand. I forced its fangs through the cloth cover of the jar and pressed down on the back of its head, dark venom slowly dripping out. It writhed, scratching my arm with its stubs, but I gritted my teeth and held fast.

Finally, as I was tiring, the drip of venom stopped, and I let go. The snake shook loose, snapping at the nearest thing— which happened to be my hand.

I swore and threw it off, but the pain was inconsequential. No burn of acid, no blood-curdling venom coursing through my veins, just a little snake bite.

"You're dry," I said belligerently, kicking sand at it as I stood. It looked at me for a moment like, **Why aren't you dead?** And then it slithered off.

I moved to the other snake, lifting the dead scaly thing to add its venom to the jar. I watched as it barely came up to reach the tiny scratch Ateri had etched in the glass. "You need at least this much," she had told me. "Otherwise, it won't cure anyone."

I turned to Pips, tossing the dead snake at his feet. "You didn't think to warn me they travel in pairs?" I scoffed.

"I... I did not know," he panted, staring at it in shock. "I did not know."

"Ateri told me you sold four-fang venom before!"

"I did! But I did not actually- I just *found* the venom! I never hunted a four-fang, it is a death sentence!"

"You just figured it'd be *my* death sentence and *your* payday?"

"Nothing personal, kid... It worked before."

"Oh, so you 'found' the venom on someone else's body?"

"I- look, kid," he said as he stood and dusted himself off, "I am good at this, okay? One of the best in the business. But *no one* goes after a four-fang and survives it. You were determined to try, and I thought..."

"You thought it was easy money," I spat.

"I- Look, come on. We got it, alright? And there is enough for both of us to become very wealthy..."

"Yeah, there is."

"Hey, it is a good thing Ateri taught you how to survive, right? Gave you those knives? Came in real handy."

"Yeah," I said slowly. "She, uh... she teach *you* how to survive the desert too?"

"Who do you think taught her?" he grinned.

"Good."

I slammed my palm into his nose and he staggered back, blood trickling through his fingers as he reached up in shock.

I struck the back of his *kisa* and it sped off, startled. "Don't hurry back."

I pulled myself up into my saddle and squeezed my knees, urging my *kisa* forward.

As I rode south, I heard a furious, "You are dead, kid! When I find you, you are dead!"

||

"Ateri!" I called breathlessly as I pushed my way into the watering hole.

She jumped and put a hand on her chest, turning to me. "*Foria*, kid!"

"Sorry," I said with a heavy exhale, wiping my forehead. "I need help. Fast. You told me you know someone who can temper this, right?" I asked, setting the snake-catcher's jar onto the counter.

She held it up, turning it over in the light, then ruffled my hair with a grin. "You really did it, huh, Sandworm? You know, I'm-"

"Yeah, I'm proud of me too, but can we hurry? I don't know how fast Pips'll be able to get back."

"What'd you do?"

"I suggested he might prefer to walk back, get in some exercise."

"Oh, yeah, we'd better hurry." She pulled her headscarf off its nail in the wall, leading me out of the watering hole. "How angry was he?"

"Murderous," I shrugged.

"Old Dwy works with all the snake-catchers, has since I was a kid," she explained as we walked through the village at a brisk pace. "No one knows tempering better— and she lives like a monk, so you can rest knowing she won't sell you out for profit."

We reached a small dwelling and she marched in without knocking. "Dwy!" she beamed as she caught sight of the old woman hunched over a desk.

"How many times I tell you to stop tracking sand in, Ter?"

"Clearly not enough. My friend Sandworm, here, is in need of your services— fast as you can provide them."

She pointed towards Dwy with her bottom lip and I offered the glass jar. Dwy whistled appreciatively. "What fool did you steal this off of?" she asked, giving me a smile that was a few teeth shy of full.

"Didn't. I had the pleasure of meeting a four-fang pair myself."

She glanced up at me with an appraising eye. "It's the second one that gets ya, huh?"

"Never saw it coming."

She moved to a small table-fire and began pouring the venom into a small pot, mixing it with odds and ends from around the room.

"The four-fangs, they mate for life, y'know? Hunt in pairs all their days, never apart."

"Do you work faster when you talk?"

She gave a crackling laugh. "Places to be. I can respect that."

After about a half-hour of work, she doused the fire and carefully poured the concoction into a small glass vial she then hung from a leather cord.

"For safe-keeping," she informed me as she handed it over.

"What do I owe you?"

She shook her head. "Ter, get this kid out of my space. Nice to meet you, **Sandworm**," she cackled as I was guided out of the dwelling.

||

Ateri and I were standing across from each other at the bar, leaning on the counter as I played with the cord of the vial that sat between us. I had packed my few belongings into the satchel that now leaned against my leg, and Ateri was having trouble meeting my eye.

"So," she finally said into the quiet, "you're leaving now."

"I'm leaving now." Why did that hurt so much to say?

"You know, it- it hasn't been unbearable, having a kid to help around the watering hole. You could stay, a bit longer... if you wanted. Your room's not going anywhere. And Pips'll get over it if I give him free food; a month or so should do it."

I was silent for several seconds, fighting how much a part of me wanted that. "Ateri... I-"

She shook her head. "It's fine. Go on, Sandworm."

I held the vial up to her. "I've been looking for this for **two years**... I can fix everything. I- I **have to** fix everything."

She nodded. "I know... I wasn't really expecting- Take care, kid."

She started to turn away, but I pulled her into a hug. It was a bit awkward over the counter, but she immediately returned it, sniffling just slightly. Finally, she pushed me away by my shoulders and gave me a smile that was definitely not accompanied by tears. "And- and remember, Sandworm, to be careful who you trust. Not everyone's good, like you, yeah?"

"Or like you?"

She shoved me away gently and lifted her hand to brush hair out of her face. "Get out of here; if you miss this wagon to the river, the next one isn't for two days."

I was trying to leave, to turn and walk out of this place for good, but it deserved the hesitation. I'd felt more at home here than I had any right to... and I was going to miss Ateri.

"Sandworm..." she said falteringly. "Before you go, I- I need to tell you something."

"What is it?"

She shook her head in anger. "You're probably going to hate me for this... but I-"

The doors slammed against the wall as Big Rini ran in, out of breath and favouring her injured knee. "*Dwer-da's* here," she told Ateri, "and they're looking for your boy."

I clipped my sword scabbard to my belt, squaring my shoulders and releasing a tense exhale as I started towards the door.

Ateri caught my arm in panic. "What the hell are you doing, kid?!"

"They're after me," I told her levelly. "Not you. I've already brought enough trouble to your door, and I can't possibly repay your kindness."

"I can't let you fight them alone, kid."

"What happened to your son was not your fault, Ateri. You don't need to get hurt for me."

"They will **kill** you."

"Probably," I sighed harshly. "But I'm not gonna find out standing here." With that, I bolted out of the watering hole, leaving behind that home that wasn't mine.

||

The village was quiet, the streets empty, as I moved through the dark. The moonlight was occasionally blocked by patchy clouds, the bugs buzzing in the background and setting my teeth on edge.

I slipped the cord of the vial around my neck as the fingers of my other hand drummed against the pommel of my sword.

"I know you're out here, boy," a sing-songy voice called as I heard footsteps off to my right. "There've been some rumours about you... and a certain mark on your arm. Stop hiding and I promise we'll make your death quick," Lady *Dwer-da* hissed. I could hear the sadistic smile in her voice.

"Yeah," one of her boys guffawed, "it'll be over in a second."

I quietly moved towards that voice, knowing that if I faced them as a pack, I'd walk away broken— if I walked away at all. Better to separate them, take care of them quietly, one-on-one, before the others knew what was happening.

I heard footsteps growing closer, heavy, a bit uncoordinated. That would be Tall *Dewr-da*. I'd noticed in the watering hole that he walked with a slight limp.

I gingerly turned down the alley, squinting in the dark. I could see movement, but it was unclear. I silently crept forward, flexing my fingers in preparation, when suddenly the hairs on the back of my neck stood up.

I spun, watching two figures step out of shadow and block the way I had come. Behind me, Tall *Dwer-da* scratched his blades against each other in anticipation. They had hunted me as a pack, and now I was trapped. I'd never seen a Jewel fight... and it was an experience I wasn't looking forward to.

The three of them advanced, but Lady *Dwer-da* held up her hand and the others froze obediently. "I want to play with my food," she said deliberately, savouring each word in her mouth as she stared at me hungrily. She unhooked the coil of wire from where it hung by her hip, slowly feeding it out as she stalked towards me. She stretched the wire between her hands and my stomach leapt into my throat as I realised what it was. ***A garrote***.

There was nothing defensive about that weapon— even a sword could be used to block an attack, but the garrote was designed only to kill.

She gave me a sweet smile as she approached, like I was a lost child. "Poor thing..." she cooed.

"Please," I sobbed, meekly holding up my empty hands, "please, I- I don't know who you think I am, but-"

"Save it," she spat. "I'm not falling for that again. You think I'll get close, underestimate you? I know you bear the Sentinel brand, boy... and I know that ***traitor*** has been teaching you. I'm not letting my guard down around you again."

I let the act drop with disgust. "Fine. Let's get this over with, then."

"Ooh," she laughed. "***There*** he is... Make this fun for me, will you? I haven't had a good fight in ***ages***." She said it like she ached, playing the wire through the air with tension throughout her body.

I silently unsheathed my peasant daggers, watching as she moved towards me like a desert cat. I needed to strike, hard and fast.

I thrust at her without warning, but she wrapped her garrote around my wrist and pulled it taut, catching my strike before it could hit her. If I hadn't had that extra fabric around my sleeve from hiding my brand, the wire would have sliced into my flesh. Lady *Dwer-da* twisted my arm behind my back, sending me to one knee and throwing my dagger across the alley. I elbowed her and the garrote slipped from around my wrist. If Ateri hadn't insisted on teaching me to defend against a garrote, I wouldn't have reacted quickly enough when *Dwer-da* threw the wire around my neck and crossed her wrists for extra leverage. As the wire dug into my throat, I turned my body to take pressure off of my windpipe and slammed my palm into her ear.

Lady *Dwer-da* staggered, her ear ringing, and the garrote fell from her clumsy fingers. I quickly kicked it into the dark.

She drew her sword and I just had time to draw Pierre before she brought it crashing down. I caught the blade with my knives in an X, gasping at the jarring impact it sent up my arms.

"Not too bad, little boy," Lady *Dwer-da* sneered, pushing closer to me until we were eye to eye. "But I'm getting bored. Why don't you-"

A strangled *hrrk!* from behind me stopped her silent as she looked away, peering into the darkness. "*Habi?*" she called. "*Taré?*" **Husband? Brother?**

How sweet. They were a family of murderers.

"*Toré!*" Short *Dwer-da* called. **Sister.** "Someone moves in the dark!"

Lady *Dwer-da* shoved me back, searching angrily. There was a crash behind her and she turned just in time to be pelted in the face with sand. Ateri leapt out from shadows, kicking high and striking Lady *Dwer-da* across the jaw, sending her to the dirt.

"I've been looking for you, kid!" Ateri panted angrily. "You're insane!"

"Do you think the two of us can beat her?" I asked as a dazed *Dwer-da* got back to her feet.

"Maybe," she panted, "but we're not going to find out. I got you an opening; now run, and don't stop until you get on that wagon out of town."

"No! I'm not leaving you! We can-"

"Don't go straight to the ferry," she continued as if she hadn't heard me. "Who knows how far they'll go to find you. Stick to back roads, be patient. Now **go**." She emphasised the order with a shove. I stumbled, gaping up at her.

"Ateri-"

"Go on, kid," she said. She started to grin as she turned back to Lady *Dwer-da* and drew her peasant daggers. "I'm looking forward to this."

"I can't-"

"Go! I'll be fine! Get **home**, get your life back!"

I hesitated a moment longer and the moon came out from behind the clouds, its light tracing over the scars on her arms. I'd never seen her bare arms before, I realised, or I'd have known... She was trained by the *Menagerie*. That must have been what she'd wanted to tell me, before I left.

"Go!" she pleaded, her eyes filling with tears as she looked back at me one last time.

I turned and sprinted to the couriers' station, forcing myself to keep running even as I heard Ateri cry out in pain.

Thank you, Ateri el Din.

I clutched at the vial around my neck as I thrust a few coins into the hand of the driver and jumped up into the wagon.

"It will be a few minutes," she told me. "I am still-"

"No! We go now!" I ordered, shoving several more coins at her.

"Yes, young sir. We go now." Within moments, the wagon was trundling down the road away from Ateri and the mess I'd gotten her into.

CHAPTER NINETY-ONE

EDDA

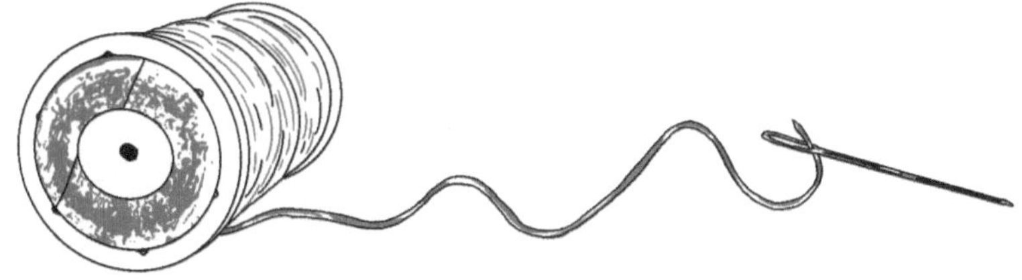

RUCE HAD THOUGHT THE flowers would be too much, too bright, too overpowering, but interspersed with candles and torches, they looked like warm fire themselves, bathing the entire clearing a beautiful orange.

There was a large circle of cobbled stone where the two of them would stand, ringed by cushions for the guests. Each had been sewn by one of my students and were embroidered with prayers and well-wishes for my boy and his bride.

Business had been good— very good— for the past several years, and what was our wealth for, if not to make our son's wedding **warm** in his memory?

"It looks beautiful, Ed," Ruce said as he came up behind me, putting an arm around me and pressing a kiss to my hair. "You've done it again."

"Again? Our wedding wasn't nearly this beautiful... We had so little, then."

"Wasn't it? All I remember from that day is the way you looked..." he interlaced his hand with mine and spun me back and forth a bit, evoking the feeling of the dance we had shared.

"How's Elin?"

"Nervous as a rooster on a roof."

"Is that quite nervous?"

"Well, chickens are flightless birds, you know... They're probably scared of heights."

"He's still frustrated about the card?"

"I told him it's fine; it's hard to give vows from memory for anyone... Lord knows I messed mine up."

"Oh, really?"

"Yeah, I meant to say that I would love you in dark days and light, in cold feet and loud snoring... or something like that. I can't quite remember."

"Well, it was thirty years ago, now."

"Can you believe I've put up with you that long?" he laughed.

"I can, actually. I'm quite enchanting."

"Quite. Oop. You'd better get to work."

I stepped forward as Victoire's family entered the clearing, greeting them with a wide smile. "You all look wonderful. I've set aside cushions for you there— Old Woman Tri had a fit, but— yep, just off to the left there. Wonderful."

||

Her dress was beautiful, just what she had asked for. She stepped into the clearing, her hair touched with delicate yellow flowers that matched her dress.

Elin entered from the opposite side, beaming at her. His hair had been tamed— as much as was possible— and he was dressed in grooms' red. ***It's a miracle I finished those clothes,*** I thought to myself with a laugh. Elin had been fidgeting and bouncing the entire time, asking questions as his mind galloped from one thought to another.

They joined each other in the centre of the circle, kneeling face-to-face. They were beautiful; sunlight and blood.

Mr. Parri stepped forward, coming to stand above them. "We've come together to see the joining of souls. Like the roots of neighbouring trees, they will intertwine and become inseparable. Elin Lahd?"

He drew the card from his pocket and cleared his throat, his thumb bullying the corner of the paper in anxiety. "Tori, you calm me. You silence my mind and steady my hand. When you look at me, I know love. I will love you in dark days and in light, and all that come in between."

Victoire beamed at him, her teary eyes scrunched with her smile.

"Victoire Henersdottir?" Mr. Parri asked.

Victoire reached into her pocket— of course her dress had pockets, I wasn't an animal— and pulled out a card to read from. Elin looked up at her in surprise and she winked at him. All at once, his nervousness faded.

She drew a gentle breath and started to speak, her eyes scanning the card slowly. "Elin, I love to watch you wander, and I love to see you come back to me every time. When you hold me, somehow it feels like freedom. You excite me and show me how to dream. I will love you in dark days and in light, in sleepless nights and in comfort."

Elin rose and offered his hands to Victoire to pull her up, and all of us rose to follow them. They moved to an empty space at the edge of the clearing, where Mr. Parri had set out two spades, a jug of water, and the seed of an oak tree.

They each took a spade and knelt to the ground, working together to dig a small hole. Elin placed the seed and covered it, and Victoire carefully poured water onto the freshly turned dirt.

They interlaced fingers covered in dirt and stood together, smiling sheepishly as we cheered for them.

"As the rings of this tree grow every year, so will their life together." Mr. Parri beamed as he looked at Elin and Victoire. "Now they have bound themselves to each other."

CHAPTER NINETY-TWO

JOVE

I GLANCED UP AT the knock on my door. "Enter."

Eschel ducked into the study, closing the door behind him quickly. He was slightly out of breath. "She's here."

"What?"

"The Lithdreyan... She's in the *sahlab* shop."

I pushed my chair back and stood, my mind racing as I followed him through the maze that was the city centre. As we entered the dimly lit *sahlab* shop, I caught sight of Ateri tucked into the corner. There was a deep cut across her temple and several bruises along her jaw and cheek, but it was her.

I nodded to Eschel. "Thank you. I will deal with this. You may return to the citadel."

He bowed his head and exited the shop without another word.

I crossed the room to slide into the seat across from Ateri, who was looking up at me with amusement. "How've you been, Captain?"

I took a sip of the *sahlab* set before me to wet my throat. "It's been eighteen months since your last report. Where have you been?" I snarled.

"Sorry, business has been good. I've just been busy." She spoke casually, leaning back in her seat.

"Fine," I huffed. "What of the boy?"

"Oh, he'll be here soon enough."

"Pardon?"

She leaned forward in her chair, baring her teeth in something like a smile. "He's on his way... and he's got the cure."

"You were supposed to ***take care of him***."

"***You*** were supposed to take care of him. That boy trusted you with his life... You know how my people feel about broken trust. You're just lucky I couldn't get poison into the city," she seethed.

I stopped sipping my *sahlab* and winced. "Ateri... the situation is complicated. You don't-"

"Don't I? I've spent the last two years with him. I know he is ***nothing*** like you claimed, and you're not going to be able to stop him. This city's going to find out exactly what you are, and you're going to drown in your lies."

She stood and walked out of the shop with a venomous smile.

CHAPTER NINETY-THREE

HARUN

I COULD HARDLY KEEP my eyes open when I finally reached the river. I had spent the past several weeks moving from one travelling caravan to another, slowly making my way across the Lothforian border and to the ferry station.

I thanked the traders for the ride and they wished me well, insisting that I owed them nothing for common kindness. I separated from the group to kneel by the river, taking my first sip of water in hours. After glancing around to ensure I was not seen by anyone, I tipped the rest of my water onto the crown of my head.

"Thank you, Lady *Foria*, for bringing me home. Faith my reservoir..."

I stood and moved to the dock, stepping onto the skiff with a nod to its captain.

I played with the vial around my neck, unable to keep my mind from wandering to the city at the end of my journey, to Riadh and Captain Owaines, to the temple fountain and the barracks that I once called home... the *sahlab* shop at the corner of the market, the Catacombs where Riadh and I had played, the courtyard where we sparred.

I sat against the wall of the skiff and pulled my hood down to cover my eyes, finally allowing myself to sleep.

||

I was tired from playing in the grove when I walked into my family's dwelling, but it was the happy kind of tired that comes from a day well-spent. Maybe... sleepy. I was sleepy when I got home from the grove.

"Harun, is that you, *hayati*?" my mother called from the kitchen.

"No, *Ama*, I'm a brigand come to rob you."

"Well," she said philosophically, "I still expect you to wipe your feet. Have you seen Miriam?"

"She was in town with her boy," I said in disgust. "Do you want to play some *bita* together?" I asked as I stepped into the kitchen, beaming up at her.

"Oh, I can't, honey... I have to take care of the laundry for tomorrow. It's Pledging Day, and our family needs to look its best."

"Let me take care of that, *Ama*," I said, reaching for the pair of *shiwr* in her hands. "You've been really busy."

"No, my love, it's fine. I've got it."

I held up a firm hand as she tried to take the pants back. "Mother, I know you wouldn't be so cruel."

"Cruel?" she asked with a laugh.

"Cruel. To not let me help you and show you how much I love you."

"Well," she chuckled, leaning down to kiss my hair, "I can't be cruel. How about we do it together? That way, we'll finish in half the time, and maybe we can play *bita* before supper." She held out her hand.

"'*Asabat*," I said, shaking her hand firmly.

"'*Asabat*."

She came to stand next to me, picking up one of Pali's dresses and folding it. We worked in silence, until my mother playfully jogged me with her hip.

"I love you, Harun, you know that?"
"I know, *Ama*."
"That's all I need."

Chapter Ninety-Four

Ruce

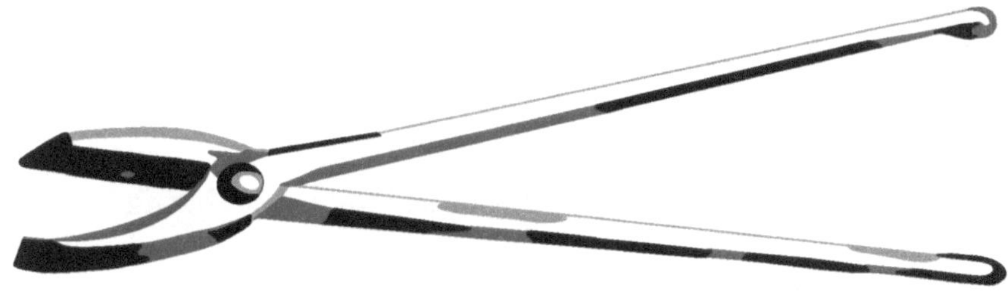

ELIN AND I WERE working side-by-side in the smithy to make new horse-shoes for Hener and Steth's mare. The sound of hammers, rhythmic, had glazed over my mind and the work became instinctive, not guided by any thought but instead by muscle memory and training.

"Elin, would you grab the new bottle of oil from the storage room? We're running low."

He nodded and quickly moved to complete the task, murmuring, "Oil bottle, oil bottle," over and over again like it was a mantra.

"Do you smell that?" I asked. "Someone must be building a fire..." I continued working, stopping when I heard a distant voice. "What, Elin?" I called.

"I didn't say anything."

"Then who-"

There was a flash of movement from the window and I turned, hearing raised voices and the sound of horses. All around, screams erupted and threw the world into chaos. I could hear my neighbours, my friends, crying out, begging for mercy. Among them was another voice.

"Leave nothing standing!"

Scorpion.

Al majowan had come.

"Elin!" I shouted. "Elin, we need to go!"

I found myself coughing as I moved towards the storage room. Fire began to creep into the smithy, licking up the walls and eating through the thatch with a vengeance.

"*Aba*, I can't get out!" His voice was touched by fire and smoke, rasping and weak. He slammed against the door, but it would not budge.

"I'm coming, Elin!" I reached the door and pulled fruitlessly. "It's stuck! The fire warped the wood, hang on!"

I grabbed my axe, levering it out of the log it was biting into, and readied myself.

"Stand back!"

I struck the door with the axe-blade, biting in and cracking one of the planks. A flaming support beam fell across the door and I staggered back, coughing.

"Elin, I'm here!" I promised. "I'm going to get you out!"

I worked with the axe, eating away a hole in the door. I stumbled, my head spinning from the smoke, but I kept trying.

"*Aba*, go!" Elin gasped. "You can't-" He took in a wheezing breath. "You can't get it open!"

"I'm not leaving you!" With a hard strike, the hole was finally large enough for me to see him through. His eyes were wet, wide, but his jaw was clenched and hard.

"*Aba*, you need to go." He was weak, holding himself up on a shelf. "You-" he coughed heavily, falling to all fours.

"I'm not leaving you, Elin... I-" I blinked, shaking my head as it filled with fog. "There's gotta be..." I stumbled, falling to one knee, sucking in harsh breaths that only coated my lungs in smoke. "I won't..."

||

It was raining as we finished burying the bodies. The charred husks of houses still smoked all around us, trees burning in the distance. There had been almost two hundred people in this village...

I stood, wiping my forehead, and looked at the small group left. Two hundred people... and we had buried all but five.

Edda sobbed next to me, her shaking hands patting the dirt over Elin's body firm. One of the Stethson boys— the *only* Stethson boy, I realised— stood over the graves of his family. Mother, father, sister, brother, brother. My old master crouched in front of the dirt that cradled her wife, wearily untying the delicate black ribbon she wore in her hair and laying it on the grave. One of Edda's students just stood behind us, hugging himself and shaking. His eyes were so distant... I didn't know how to comfort him.

I cleared my throat, stepping forward to pull my wife to her feet. "I... I found this, in our house," I murmured to her, holding out a smooth river stone on a cord. "I thought-"

She just nodded, burying her head in my shoulder as she clutched the necklace our son had made for her.

"We can't stay here, Ed."

"I know," she murmured. "I- I know..."

||

"Let's rest for a while," I called to the group, moving to set my pack against a tree. "Ed," I asked quietly as I came to rest a hand on her shoulder, "how are you doing?"

She managed a smile, nodding up at me. "I'm alright. I can keep going. I don't know about Sebastien, though... His leg's been bothering him."

"Okay. I'll check in when we get moving again."

"Boy," Old Woman Tri called.

I moved to join her on the fallen log where she was resting. She had never been gentle, while she was teaching me how to work metal, but she had been a good teacher, and I had great affection for her. "Master Tri. How's your arm?"

"Burned," she cackled. "I can hardly feel a thing. Listen, kid... there's a ferry nearby. It stops at a village close to the capital. I think we should go there, seek help."

I shook my head. "The smartest move is to keep going until we reach the capital. They have resources, protection. Anything less is still at risk from raiders."

"I don't know if we're going to make it to the capital..." she sighed. "At least, not all of us."

"What are you saying?"

"I'll take the kids. Sebastien and that Stethson boy, they're tired. We'll stop at that village and let them rest. The two of you..." she glanced up at me and Edda. "You should keep going."

"I don't think we should separate. We don't-" My voice caught. "We don't have anyone else, Tri. We were the only people who survived the attack on Jezzine, the only people who understand what we went through."

She shook her head. "The capital is full of refugees. You'll find a new home there. Go, make a new life, honour your boy's death. The city could use you. I'll look after these two, find them a quiet place to grieve. It'll be alright."

||

We stepped off of the skiff, saying our quiet goodbyes to the boys and to Tri. "You could still come with us," Edda said sadly.

Tri shook her head and Sebastien spoke up. "I'm tired, Miss Edda... I just want to stop moving."

The Stethson boy— I could never remember his name, with all his siblings— nodded. Erik? Ansel? Lars? I knew it wasn't Victoire. "I don't want to go to the city. I want to find a quiet farm and... and keep going with my family's work."

Edda wiped her eyes, giving both boys a tight hug before she stepped back. "Okay... Okay. But you know, if you ever change your minds, or if you need our help... You can always come find us."

"Goodbye, Miss Edda."

"Ruce," Old Woman Tri said stiffly. "Do our craft proud, won't you?"

"Yes, mother."

She swatted my arm with a laugh. "That makes me feel old."

"You are old."

"Bahh!" she scoffed, starting down the path to the village with the boys at her heels. "I'm in the bloom of youth, and I have half a mind to knock you on your ear."

"Yes, Master Tri," I said with playful obedience.

As they faded into the distance, we hesitantly moved towards the path that led to the capital.

"We're really doing this, then...?" I asked.

"We've got no choice; we have to keep going. We'll find purpose again, won't we, Ruce?"

"We certainly don't give up easily."

Everyone was milling about and turning down their respective paths, except for a boy standing alone at the edge of the clearing. He was gazing out towards the capital, a look on his face somewhere between mourning and longing.

"Another refugee, you think?" I murmured to Edda, nodding in the boy's direction.

"He looks... stuck," she said finally. "Turned to stone. You think he'll ever move?"

"Go give him a poke, help him on his way."

Edda stepped forward and set a hand on his shoulder. "Excuse me, son. Are you travelling to the city?"

He turned, almost startled, and looked down at her with a wistful smile. "I am, mother."

"You're welcome to walk with my husband and I..."

BETRAYAL

Chapter Ninety-Five

Elin

It was so quiet out here.

The wind gently blew past me, through the trees, up the side of the mountain. The graveyard was always quiet. No one much liked spending time here...

I sat beneath my father's gravetree, hiding in its shade. The rest of my family stood on either side of me, their leaves gently swaying in the wind.

I couldn't bring myself to come back here when I first returned to the city. I couldn't face them until I had fixed my mistake...

There was no chance of that now, and I owed my family the visit. Soon the king's body would be laid under the earth, just like theirs, and a sapling would be planted over him. Riadh had already been forced to bury one parent, and now... because of me-

"Can I join you, or is this strictly solo brooding time?"

I looked up at Malia in surprise as she approached. "What are y-"

She stepped forward and set a handful of flowers against Fatima's gravetree. "Your parents told me where they thought you'd be. They went to dinner— you know, at my dwelling?"

"Right, dinner," I said in a daze. "I... I forgot."

She plopped down beside me and set the basket she'd been carrying between us. "That's why I'm here. Well, that, and to make sure you're okay..."

"You've heard, then?"

"The news reached us an hour ago. I'm sorry, Elin. I can't imagine..."

"It's my fault. I was supposed to *fix this*. I- I was supposed to protect him, and- I failed."

She immediately put a firm hand on my shoulder. "This is not your fault. You couldn't have saved him."

"No, but I still should have. If I- if I had been more careful, if I was **better-**"

"Better?" she scoffed. "Elin-" She shook her head and sighed. "I don't think 'better' than you exists."

"What are they saying?" I asked, turning away from her and quickly wiping my eyes. "How do they say he died?"

She shook her head. "Captain Owaines was supposed to make an announcement earlier. Our parents went, but I came to find you. I- I assumed the poison finally took him..."

"No," I said darkly. "It didn't."

"How can I help, Elin? Let me help."

"I don't know what I need, Malia... I just-" I closed my eyes, letting my head fall back against my father's gravetree.

"Well, whatever you need, whenever you need it, you know where to find me, yeah? You can always come to me."

I laid a hand over hers. "Thank you, Malia. I don't- I don't know what to do, now that..."

"You'll figure that out later. For now, we can just sit together." She looped her arm through mine and rested her head on my shoulder. "For now, just breathe."

CHAPTER NINETY-SIX

EDDA

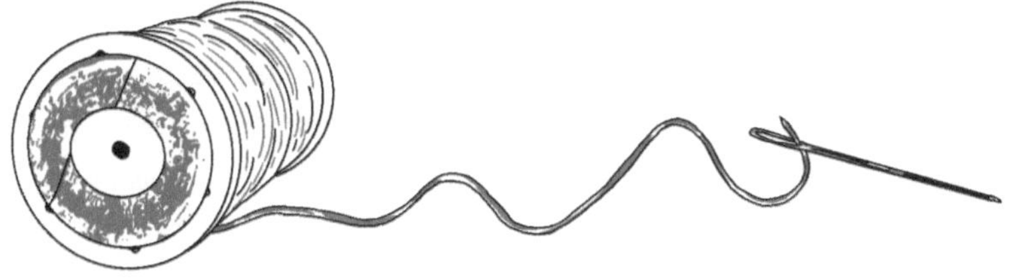

"It is with a heavy heart," Captain Owaines called down from the balcony, "that I stand before you tonight. I am sure you have all heard whispers of King Bazzeri's death, and it sorrows me to tell you they are true."

A gasp went through the sea of people gathered in the square. Then the whispers started, chaos running through the crowd, shoving and cruel.

Captain Owaines held up a hand and the noise dwindled. "However, that is not the end of the news I have for you... Nor the worst of it. We have identified his killers. We have learned that the traitor Harun has returned to the city, and we have learned why. It was our own princess, Riadh al Abbas, who convinced him to poison her father two years ago. She coveted the throne, and last night, when she learned that her father was to change the order of succession, she told Harun to strike. He has succeeded in murdering our king, and we now need your help to uncover his hiding place. My Guards will be scouring the city, and we will not rest until he is caught or killed. Anyone who is found to be harbouring him or the princess is a traitor, and will share his fate."

Ruce turned to me, whispering lowly. "We need to get home."

I nodded, taking his hand and pulling him towards the edge of the square. "Nassir," I murmured as I caught his shoulder, "I'm feeling faint. Thank you for dinner, but we must call it a night."

"Rest, Edda," he said in a kind but heavy voice. "I think we're all going to need it."

||

I looked up as Elin ducked into the dwelling, his eyes red-rimmed and tired. Ruce squeezed my hand under the table in encouragement.

Elin started towards his room, then stopped and looked up at us. "Is... is something wrong?" he asked, moving closer to the table.

"Sit down, Elin," I said quietly. "You promised to tell us the truth one day; that day's come."

He took a step back, shaking his head. "Mother, I-"

"Sit down, Harun."

He froze, the rise and fall of his chest stopping as he stared at the ground. He swallowed thickly and slowly moved to sit down, like it was the last thing he would ever do. A mix of emotions swirled over his face when he finally spoke. "What... did you hear about me?" he murmured, his eyes never leaving the table.

"Lies."

His face pinched, but he still wouldn't look at me.

"We know you," Ruce said. "We know the kind of person you are, and you did **not** do the things they say. But we can't help you if you don't tell us the truth."

He bit his lip, shaking his head. "I- I don't want the two of you getting hurt because-"

"They accused you of murder," Ruce said darkly. "The entire city is after you; you're in over your head, kid, and you know it."

"Talk to us," I pleaded.

He pushed himself to his feet, turning away from us as his breathing started to pick up. "I- I can't, I-"

"Elin, we're your family."

I could see him fighting himself, and eventually he won. He pressed his hand over his heart and worked to slow his breathing. He inhaled shakily and then forced out, "You're right. I need help."

"Tell us what's going on. Everything."

He finally turned back to us, meeting my gaze for the first time since he'd come home. "Then... we're gonna have a long night."

||

"How do we fix this?" Ruce asked. He kept his voice low and level so as not to wake Elin, who had fallen asleep leaning on the table.

"We'll figure it out," I murmured, looking down at our son's sleeping form. His hair took its time making its way across his face, in dips and curls that tickled his cheeks. As we sat there, I gently dragged my fingers through them all.

"We're going to need to deal with that Captain of his, somehow..." Ruce sighed. "None of this can be put right until he's-"

"Caught?"

He was silent for a moment, then smiled at me. "Sure. Caught. Let's go with that," he said lightly.

With a start, I pushed myself to my feet, moving to grab the floorplan we had made of the citadel.

"Idea, Ed?"

"Elin said he'd been unable to use the Catacombs to reach the palace because they were so heavily guarded, yes?"

"That is what I heard. Idea?"

"That spineless Captain said his Guards would be 'scouring the city'."

"I heard that too."

I rolled my eyes and turned to face him. "If they're searching the city, they won't be guarding the Catacombs anymore."

His eyes widened in realisation. "If we could reach a passageway, we'd have a straight shot to the palace... But how do we get in?"

"I have an idea," Elin said sleepily, sitting up and stretching. "But I don't think you're gonna like it."

CHAPTER NINETY-SEVEN

JOVE

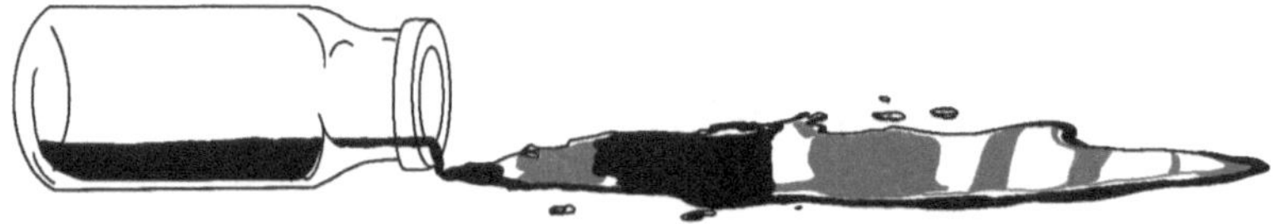

MY MOST-CAPABLE GUARDS STOOD before me at attention, waiting to be briefed. I looked over them for a moment, revelling in the power, in how close I was to taking command of the entire city.

"You have honoured Lothforias and Lady *Foria* with your service, but now you are called to save it from the worst threat we have ever faced. Harun and Riadh have colluded, under our noses, to kill our king, and now we must root them out. You will be sent out into the city to search; understand that you need to be prepared to use lethal force. These-"

"Hang on," Corporal Sadir said, stepping forward as he held up a hand doubtfully. "You're telling us that **both** Harun and Riadh are traitors? I **can't** believe that." He shook his head, glancing at his companions. "They have always been the best of us. When King Bazzeri was poisoned, you told us Harun was an assassin, that he blamed the king for his family's deaths... and I stood by and watched him become our villain. I will **not** watch you do the same to Lieutenant al Abbas. She is **good**... and I think Harun was too, when you cast him out." As he spoke the last, he looked up at me boldly, his chin out in defiance.

"Then you are not fit to stand among us. Blinded by sentiment, unable to do what must be done... Lady *Foria* no longer needs your service, Hakim."

His eyes widened and he stepped back in horror. "What?"

"Pack your belongings and leave," I spat deliberately. "You are no longer a Guard of Lothforias."

There was a stirring in the group, whispers that passed between them, but no one spoke up.

"You can't do this," Hakim murmured. He looked as though he had been struck. "I have been loyal, I have served this city well. You're going to dismiss me for trusting my fellow Guards?"

"Perhaps that is not a harsh enough sentence for you... I have chosen to let you remain in the city. Do not force me to consider banishment."

He clenched his jaw, fighting his anger, and dipped his head in deference. "Yes... **Your Majesty**," he seethed as he turned to leave.

"Now that that's taken care of," I sighed, "if any of you have information that may help us locate Riadh or Harun, speak up now."

There were several moments of silence as my Guards glanced between each other before one of them falteringly raised her hand. "Riadh has... she's been spending time with the blacksmith's son."

"Yes?"

"I-" she hesitated, then finally spoke. "I believe this may be Harun in disguise."

"Do you know what he is calling himself?"

"Sir, do you think it's possible Hakim is right? Could he still be loyal to the city?"

"Sergeant," I said sharply. "Do not make me doubt your loyalty as well. **Do you know what name the traitor goes by**?"

"I... I can tell you where he lives, Captain."

Chapter Ninety-Eight

Elin

I WAS PACING IN the ice room, waiting for Edda to return and tell me that she and Ruce had been successful. They had ordered me to stay out of sight, in case the Guards came looking in the refugee camps again.

In my hands, I nervously toyed with a *bita* piece. A palace, fittingly... I kept thinking back to my games with Ateri. *Not everyone plays the game with your heart.*

I knew what she would do... what Riadh would do, what Ruce would do. What *Jove* would do. And as much as I paced trying to find another option, I knew that I didn't have a choice. I had to be cold. This wasn't a game... and I couldn't afford to lose. *When someone has the upper hand,* Ateri liked to tell me, *you break it.*

Suddenly I heard heavy footsteps as someone sprinted into the dwelling. I ducked behind the ice room door, gripping my sword tightly where it hung sheathed at my hip.

"Elin?!"

"Riadh?" I stepped out into the open in surprise. "What are you doing here?"

"They're after you. They-"

"I heard. I'm laying low, and-"

"No, they're on their way here! Someone made the connection, and they told Jove where you live!"

"What? No, I- I don't-" I wasn't ready. Edda hadn't come back, Ruce wasn't in position... "No, no, no, I need more time."

"You don't have it. We need to go somewhere safe; now." She started back out of the dwelling and I caught her arm, thinking of the loss she had suffered last night.

"Riadh. I- I hope you always remember his voice. I know that..."

Her face scrunched for a moment, but she shook her head. "We don't have time right now. Where should we go? The shop?"

I shook my head. "It's connected to my family by name. No, we need somewhere they wouldn't think to look."

"Where does your girlfriend live?"

"She's not my-" I shook my head. "Come on." As I started out of the dwelling, I pulled one of Edda's headscarves from its hook and wrapped it around myself to cover my face as much as possible.

I quickly led Riadh down the path to the inner city, pulling her into an alley as footsteps thundered towards us. We held our breaths as a dozen Guards raced past, moving as a unit up to the refugee cutaway.

Riadh started out of hiding before I could catch her, running directly into the last man. I cursed mentally as I realised that Riadh, never having run from our city's Guards before, was not used to countering their tactics. Every patrol had a straggler who followed several paces behind the others for just this occasion— to catch criminals unawares as they ducked out of their hiding place, thinking they were in the clear.

A shout went up as soon as the last man recognised Riadh, and the dozen Guards on the road up to the cutaway turned and immediately locked onto us. Riadh looked at me in panic and I grabbed her hand, lowering my shoulder to drive the last man to the ground and make us an opening. We sprinted down the street, around the corner, being chased by the sounds of boots on cobblestone and weapons drawing.

I yanked Riadh into a cramped alley, immediately locking my fingers together to make her a foothold. Without hesitation, she planted her hands on my shoulders and stepped up. I propelled her up and she caught a support tendon that stretched between two dwellings with both hands. She pulled herself up and sat on the braided wire, flipping upside down to offer me her hands. I jumped up and took them and she pulled me until I was close enough to grab the tendon myself. She shimmied onto the roof of a dwelling and I quickly joined her.

We shucked off our *lahat* and stretched for a moment to get used to the freedom of our *venaq*. Then we were moving, sprinting across rooftops, nimbly moving across support tendons as the Guards chased us in vain. They simply couldn't keep up with us as we took our shortcut, and within minutes, their voices had faded into the distance. We ducked down onto the surface of a roof with a shallow angle, peeking over the crest as we waited.

Finally, after the Guards ran past, scanning the rooftops for us, we pushed ourselves up to crouch.

"We need to get to Malia's, as quickly as possible," Riadh whispered.

"No, we need to go back for our boots."

"Elin-"

"My mother already had to buy me a new pair after the fight in the Catacombs, I'm not losing these boots."

"If you get caught, you'll be arrested— and probably executed."

"I like those boots! And we wouldn't have been spotted in the first place if *you* were better at running from the Guard."

"Sorry I'm not a ***properly***-trained criminal! We still shouldn't risk going back."

"If we walk through the city without boots, people ***will*** notice us."

She rolled her eyes and huffed, gesturing for me to lead the way. We moved back across the rooftops as quickly as possible while ducked down to avoid being noticed, and finally we reached the chimney where we had tucked our *lahat*. We laced them back up quickly and Riadh nodded at me to start moving.

I leapt from the roof, catching a support tendon to drop from. Riadh did the same, and I caught her before she touched the ground, remembering the wound on her leg that had already been re-sutured several times in the past few weeks.

"Thanks," she murmured. "Where's Malia's?"

I readjusted my headscarf, which had loosened during the chase, and casually started out of the alley with Riadh close behind. Within minutes, we reached the Bayouths' dwelling, but Riadh caught my arm.

"Wait! What do we say? We can't tell Malia the truth."

"She already knows who I am," I said as I swatted her arm.

"She does?"

"Yeah, she was friends with my sister."

"Which one?"

"One of the dead ones," I huffed. "Pretty sure you don't know her. Can we please get out of sight before someone stabs us?"

"Okay, be that way..." she muttered. "Forgive me for trying to chat. I haven't seen you in two years."

I ignored her, stepping close to the door and knocking. It opened almost instantly and Malia deflated in relief. "Get in!"

She pulled me and Riadh into the dwelling, closing the door immediately. She took a breath, turning to us.

"Elin, my father told me about Captain Owaines's announcement. I was so worried, but you're okay, and- You are okay, aren't you?"

"For now," I nodded. "But this isn't going to just go away. I'm going to need your help."

"Anything."

"Hey, *hayati*, do you-" Nassir faltered as he came into the main room and caught sight of me. "What is your boyfriend doing here?"

"He's not my-" Malia huffed in irritation. "Nevermind. We were going to play some *bita*," she lied easily. "He's been demanding a rematch for weeks."

"Ah. Well, I was wondering if..." He stepped closer, focusing on Riadh in confusion. "You look l-" His eyes widened, and then he looked in between her and I. "You-"

He started towards the front door, but Malia cut him off, pressing herself up against it.

"Let me through," he said tersely. "They're murderers."

"No."

"Malia-"

"You're going to hear me out, *Aba*." She looked at him with stone, refusing to back down. "Elin has done **nothing** wrong."

"**Harun** got your mother killed!"

"That's not true. He is good, and he is protecting the city. We need to help him."

He shook his head. "I refuse to just blindly trust that-"

I stepped forward, raising my hands placatingly. "Just let me explain. Let me tell you what happened... what **really** happened."

He looked at me for a long time, at war with himself. Finally, he sighed, "Fine. Tell me your story; but trust that I can read a liar."

"Thank you, Nassir."

CHAPTER NINETY-NINE

RIADH

MOMENTS AFTER I HEARD the stairs creak, Elin ducked into Malia's room, slowly nodding at me as I looked up in question from the spot where Malia and I lounged on her bed. "Nassir... has decided to give me the benefit of the doubt, for now. He said he'll wait downstairs for when my mother finds her way here. It shouldn't take long, once she realises I'm not at- at home..." I finished quietly.

"Then what? You have a plan, don't you? We're not just hiding, right?"

"I have a plan. I'll tell you all about it when my mother gets here."

Malia pushed herself up to stand. "You both must be hungry. I'll make something."

"Thanks, Mal," I called after her.

Elin stepped out of the doorway to let her pass and leaned against a bare wall, sighing.

"Are you alright?" I asked.

He slid down the wall to sit wordlessly. He looked up at me and opened his mouth to speak, floundering. He shook his head and finally said, "I- I'm sorry. It's all my fault. I should have-"

I immediately realised what he meant. "You've taken the blame for enough," I hissed, practically breathing fire in my rage as I sat up. "We both know whose fault this is."

"Elin?!" Edda called.

||

In between bites of *ka'aq*, Elin explained the plan. Edda chimed in occasionally and he took the opportunity to keep eating. Anyone who was impressed by his skills with his sword had never witnessed his appetite. Eventually, they both fell silent, Edda's hand absentmindedly running through his hair as she stood behind him, her shoulders hunched with worry.

"That's it?" I asked. "That's what we're counting on?"

"It's all we've got," Elin sighed. "I can't think of another way in. The irrigation tunnel I came out before is collapsed... and the farther we get from the citadel, the less I know the tunnels."

"Okay, but once you're in, what are you going to do? Any Guard that catches you will kill you."

"That's... where you come in. You already told me that not all of the Guards believe you're a traitor. One of them even warned you to flee."

I nodded, remembering the moment this morning when I had walked down the palace stairs into the citadel, coming face-to-face with Hakim as he emerged from the barracks. His eyes had widened and he'd hurried to me, clasping my arms. "You need to go, now! Jove is trying to turn them against you. He told them you arranged your father's death, and as I was leaving, someone told him where Harun lives."

I had turned and sprinted from the city centre without another word.

"That's true," I told Elin. "What do you need me to do?"

"If we're going to earn back this city's trust and expose Jove, we need to start there. You're..." His voice caught and he looked up at me sadly. "You're going to be queen, Riadh. You need to make them see that, get them on our side, or none of this is going to work."

"I'll leave immediately. Good luck on your end. Give me five hours, then make your move."

He hugged me tightly, then turned back to the table. "Nassir; tonight, we're going to put your people skills to work."

||

I slowly moved through the market, my hair wrapped up in one of Malia's delicate scarves, its tail across my face so everything but my eyes was covered. I wasn't very fond of green, but it did its job. I pondered the jewellery in one of the stalls and, out of the corner of my eye, watched the Guards on patrol. Finally, I approached one of them, a girl named Nadia that I had trained with. She had always been popular among our peers, not only for her good looks and skill with a sword, but for her honesty and kind intentions. I had overseen some of her training myself, happy to find a friend in a girl my age.

"Excuse me," I said in a soft voice that was starkly foreign from mine, "would you help me? I'm new to the city, and I've lost my way."

"Of course, sister. Where is your family staying?"

"The... The lake dwelling?" I said meekly. "I believe that's what it's called."

"Lake district. I can take you there."

She started into a side street and I followed her eagerly. "Oh, thank you, Corporal!"

As we turned the corner and the sounds of the market faded, she glanced over at me. "I am Nadia. I'll get you where you need to go, I promise."

"Thank you, Nadia," I said in my own voice as I unwrapped my headscarf. "I'm in desperate need of your help."

She whirled on me in surprise, her hand hovering over her sword, but she didn't draw it... She just looked at me, waiting for me to make the first move.

"Jove told you I'm a traitor, didn't he?"

She gave a faltering nod. "He did, Lieutenant... I don't want to believe it. Please, give me a reason not to believe it."

"You know me."

She was silent, staring at me— through me— for a long time, before she let her hand drop to her side. "I do. I know how much you loved your father... But I still can't believe that Harun-"

"Don't. He's been working side-by-side with me to protect this city."

"The 'masked warrior'?"

"Yes."

"Then tell me the truth. Tell me what really happened and I will believe it."

"You would trust me that much?"

"I would trust you with my life." She pressed her forehead against mine, then dropped to her knee. "You are my Lieutenant and my queen. Tell me what has happened. Tell me how I can help."

"I'm going to tell you a story, and you will share it with the others. I need them to know who is really protecting this city."

CHAPTER ONE HUNDRED

EDDA

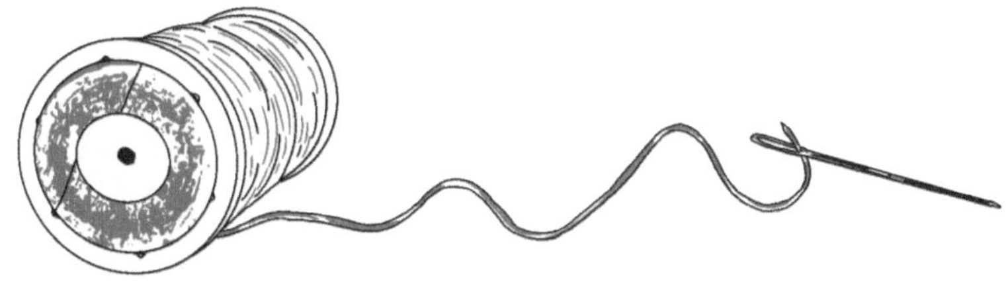

ELIN HAD BEEN PACING in the main room since Nassir left to complete his task. His usually steady hands were shaking, fingers moving and toying with the hem of his shirt and drumming on the pommel of his dagger.

"Elin," Malia said, pushing herself up to stand and moving to him. She caught his shoulder, forcing him to still and face her, and placed a hand over his heart. At the direction, he nodded and shakily inhaled and exhaled until he stood more firmly.

"Thanks, Mal."

"You have a plan, okay? Everything's going to work out... We're all doing our part, and we're going to help you. We've got this."

"I know. I just... there is so much I can't control, so much I can't guarantee... What if the Guard doesn't believe Riadh? What if she's been arrested? What if Jove has her and he's just waiting for me to walk into a trap?"

"Would *you* believe her?"

He nodded, unclenching his fists and exhaling. "Yes."

"Then so will they. She *is* their queen, and they will see. They will believe her, and they will do what's right; that's who Guards are, isn't it? They're people like you."

"You think so?"

"I do."

He started to speak, but there was a knock on the front door. Nassir peeked through with a friendly smile as he caught sight of us. "I'm so glad you're still here," he told us. "I've found somewhere safe to hide you. Please, come with me."

Elin clipped his sword to his belt and we followed him outside. The moment I stepped out into the fading sun, I saw the glint of met-al— everywhere. The dwelling was surrounded by Guards with drawn weapons.

"*Aba,*" Malia said in horror, "what have you done?"

"This is him! This is the assassin!" Nassir shouted to the Guards, pointing directly at Elin.

They started forward and Elin immediately unsheathed his sword. I moved towards Nassir in fury, but two of the Guards caught me by the arms and held me back. "How could you?!" I screamed. "We trusted you!"

"You should never have trusted me to help a *murderer*," he spat. "They have promised not to arrest you or your husband. Please, Edda. Don't fight. Let them take him. It will be better."

Elin attacked, but against a dozen Guards, he was quickly over-whelmed. He was sent to the ground with a bloody lip, his sword skid-ding across the cobblestone as it was flung from his hand.

"You are going to rot for what you've done, Harun," Nassir told Elin.

"Thank you, father. Lady *Foria* is honoured by your loyalty," one of the Guards told him.

"What loyalty?!" Malia screamed. "You betrayed us!"

Elin was pulled harshly to his feet, his arms held fast as he fought.

"Take him to the citadel."

As Elin was dragged away, bloody and dazed, I locked eyes with one of the Guards that had him by the arm. If I didn't recognise my husband's eyes under that helmet, I wouldn't have had any idea he wasn't one of them... He played the part perfectly.

"How could you do this to us?" I sobbed loudly and fell to my knees as the Guards rounded the corner. "I thought we were friends!"

As soon as they were out of earshot, I sat up, wiping the tears from my face.

"Give me a hand up, will you?" I asked, reaching out to Nassir.

"Of course, dear." He pulled me to my feet, grinning at me and Malia. "That was some excellent acting from the two of you... Real tears, Edda? I'm impressed."

"Elin told us to be convincing, didn't he? Now comes the hard part."

"Yes," he sighed. "Now, we sit, and we pray that they are successful. *Kahve*?" he asked kindly.

"I'll put a pot on," Malia offered. "I'm guessing it's going to be a long night."

Chapter One Hundred One

Ruce

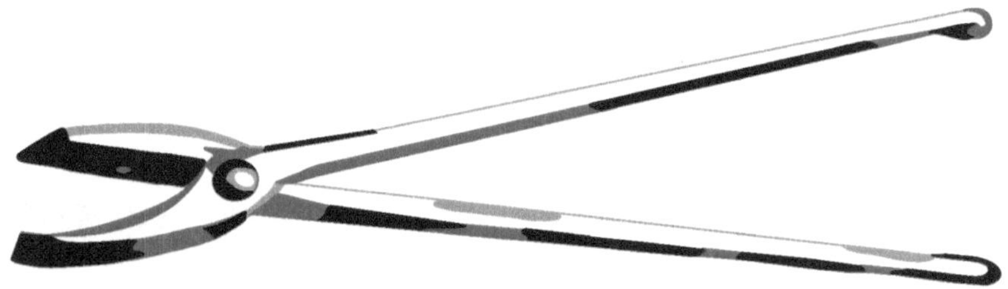

WE TURNED THE CORNER, moving down a thin staircase to the prison at the centre of the citadel. The shackles around Elin's wrists clanked with every movement. They had confiscated his dirk, his staves, and his sword, so he was, by all appearances, unarmed.

As we reached the bottom step, Elin stumbled, falling to all fours with a quiet, "Oof!"

Lithdreyan peasant daggers, first used by the People's Army, were designed to be carried discreetly while brushing shoulders with nobility. As such, the sheaths that held these blades went on the inside of the forearms, and were thin enough to go unnoticed under long sleeves.

The Guard next to me huffed and leaned down to pull Elin to his feet. As he did so, Elin leapt into action, drawing one of his daggers from its sheath hidden at his wrist. He stabbed the blade through the Guard's carapace at the shoulder and it bit into the wall, pinning him in place.

He turned, kicking out at the knee of the Guard guiding us, who was still drawing her weapon. Elin drew his other blade as the Guard's knee buckled, holding the knife to her throat. "Keys," he ordered.

"Kill me," she seethed.

"That's a bit drastic, Anahid," he said casually as he pushed her against the wall by her shoulder, snatching the keys from her belt.

I drew my own sword to keep her in place as he resheathed his knife to manoeuvre the keys.

"I don't want to hurt you. I'm actually..." he stopped unshackling himself for a moment to look at her. "I'm actually trying to help." Careful to avoid my sword at the Guard's throat, Elin shackled her right wrist to her companion's left through the railing support, effectively trapping the two of them in place. "Would you do me a favour and wait a minute before you start shouting?" he asked as he freed his dagger from the wall and the Guard's shirt.

Anahid sucked in a large breath and yelled, "Help! The prisoner's escaped!"

Elin nodded philosophically as footsteps thundered down the stairs. "I expected that. Bye, Ana!"

He sprinted down the hall and I followed, glancing back at the shackled Guards. "It would have been more efficient to knock them out," I told Elin. "That way they wouldn't have warned the others."

"Trust, Father," he said with a grin as he looked over at me. "I need them to know I'm not their enemy."

"They can know that while they nurse a bump on their heads," I grumbled.

"Speaking of bumps, did you need to hit me so hard?" he asked as he touched his bloody lip. "I'm gonna feel that tomorrow."

"You-" my voice died in my throat as we ran headlong into a Guard as we rounded the corner.

Her eyes widened, but before Elin could speak, she started walking past us, whistling a quiet tune to herself as if she'd never seen two intruders.

Elin glanced at me and grinned. "Riadh did her job. Who knows how many of them she got to, though, so we need to move fast."

He turned down a dead-end corridor and I looked behind us. "Elin, we can't afford mistakes. They're right behind us."

"Gimme a minute," he huffed as he analysed the walls. He reached for a torch, just like any other, and pushed. The wall swung inward, revealing a narrow staircase that led down into a dark, dank tunnel. "Let's go."

The wall slammed shut behind us as I followed Elin down into the tunnel.

"You have the candle?" he asked, holding out a hand and touching my arm.

Slipping the wax from my pocket, I blindly grabbed for his hand and placed the candle in his grip. In moments, a small flame was flickering between us. In this low, harsh light, his face almost looked like a skull—like he was already dead.

"Elin," I started in a level voice, trying to mask my concern, "are you sure about this plan of yours?"

"Father," he said simply.

"Right. Sorry. Not arguing or doubting."

"I should hope not," he said dryly. "Let's go."

He guided us through the Catacombs, which he had described to me as a 'labyrinth'. From what I could see, he was certainly correct, but he led me down tunnels and around corners like it was as familiar as our own dwelling. Though, I suppose, to him it probably was. He told us he and that girl— the mean one that I liked, Riadh— had played down here as children.

My eyes caught on a scrap of fabric stuck on an empty sconce and I snatched it. Rough, pitted for airflow, absent of dyes... I shook my head and let it flutter to the ground, telling myself that it was paranoia. Scorpion was dead.

Finally, Elin started up a set of steps and gently pulled on the wall, peeking out through the crack that formed. When he saw that it was clear, he nodded to me and started into the hallway.

The palace was made of delicately carved bricks of sandstone. Beautiful, but those iron bars on the windows could have been made without that ugly join in the metal, and it would have taken hardly fifteen minutes of grating to get that bump down. Lazy work.

Soldier today, I reminded myself. I shook free of my metalworker mentality, following Elin as he crept deeper into the palace. As we reached a brightly lit hallway, he held up a fist and I stopped, peeking around the corner over his shoulder. Two Guards stood in front of a set of large double doors, armed with spears.

"Ooh," I murmured with a wince. "I made those spears... Good weapons."

"Not. Helping," Elin hissed over his shoulder as he peered down the hall. His fingertips turned something over and my eye was drawn to the tiny pebble he toyed with. Without warning, he drew his arm back and flung the pebble down the hall and past the double doors.

It clattered on the stone floor a few times and drew the attention of both Guards. One of them started towards the source of the sound while the other turned to supervise. Elin gestured towards the hallway and I followed him, the two of us creeping towards our targets. As we drew nearer, Elin mimed snatching something and glanced back. I nodded, and when I was close enough to the nearest Guard, I rose up and pulled her into a chokehold, covering her mouth to keep her silent.

Elin kept moving, hurrying to reach the other Guard before he turned back to his post. He quickly silenced him, restricting his breath until he collapsed in Elin's arms. He quietly set the Guard against the wall and I did the same.

As he came back to me, I whispered, "I thought you didn't want to knock them out."

He jerked his head towards our sleeping Guards. "I couldn't risk them warning him. Also, they were mean to me in training."

"Ah. Well, if they were mean to you," I said reasonably.

He smirked and shook his head, moving to stand in front of the doors. He raised his hand, and then hesitated, his hand shaking before he set his jaw and exhaled resolutely. He knocked, and a carrying voice called, "Enter."

He opened the doors and stepped inside as I closed them behind him, turning to keep watch.

CHAPTER ONE HUNDRED TWO

ELIN

I STEPPED INTO THE familiar study, where Jove sat looking over supply manifests. "One moment," he said without looking up. "This needs my approval as soon as possible."

"Ah, the duties of the king," I lamented.

He looked up in shock, immediately reaching for his sword, which hung from the belt slung over his chair. He stood, unsheathing the blade, and levelled it at me.

"You're not happy to see me?" I asked, feigning sadness. "I thought I was like a son to you. Is- is my visit not welcome, Captain?"

"How did you get in here? Guards!"

"If you were really trying to keep me out, you should've had more than two Guards stationed outside. They're not coming."

"Harun, let's-" He held up his hand that wasn't wielding a sword in a placating gesture, as if that would make the blade any less sharp. "Let's just talk."

A few years ago, I would've been wary of any weapon in my mentor's hands, but my time in the desert had changed me in ways he had never been changed. He'd stayed in the shadows, hiding like a snake in the ground... and I'd gotten good at hunting snakes. The trick was to get them before they got you.

"Let's talk, Harun," he pleaded again.

"Yeah," I replied. In an instant, I swept forward, pushing into his personal space in an action most people would call reckless. I grabbed his hand and twisted his sword from his grip, sending my palm into his nose and making his head snap back. He stumbled back into the wall as I threw his sword across the room, metal grating against stone. "Let's talk."

As he stemmed the flow of blood, supporting himself against the wall, I kicked the chair in front of his desk to an angle, sitting down and putting my foot up on the desk. I unsheathed one of my peasant daggers, picking at the dirt under my nails. "So. How've you been?" I asked casually, gesturing with the knife for him to sit in his own plush chair.

He shakily lowered himself to sit, his eyes scanning the room rapidly. "I didn't **want** you to be blamed..." he started. "It wasn't my intention. But when people started asking questions, I didn't have a choice."

"No, Jove, you had a choice. You had... so many choices," I laughed, counting off with the knife on my fingers. "You had the choice not to search for the four-fang venom. You had the choice not to poison the king, the choice not to frame me. You had the choice to put things right when you saw me in the square. To let the king live. You had the choice to do **anything**, and you chose to become a murderer and a traitor."

"Say what you like about me, Harun," he sighed wetly, "but I am not a traitor. I have done... what I thought I had to do in order to protect this city. The reason I-"

"I don't really want to hear your reasons. I think I know. I think after Captain Jazhara was killed, you wanted to go to war. I think the king was determined to try for peace. I think you saw him as weak. I don't know when your motives changed, but they did. As soon as you stopped wanting to protect this city, as soon as you desired to rule it, you lost my respect. You're not going to convince me your cause was just."

"I loved her, Harun," he said shakily. "And she was taken from me... What would you have done, if someone had taken Riadh from you?"

"Why does everyone think we're in love?" I huffed. "And if you really cared about Jazhara... you wouldn't have killed the man *she* loved."

"So, what are you here for? To arrest me? To drag me in front of the city and tell them all the bad things I've done?"

I set my foot back to the ground and slowly looked up at him, running my fingers over the blade of my dagger absentmindedly. I hadn't talked about this part to my parents. They hadn't needed to know. "Is that what *you* would do? After all... you taught me everything I know."

He paled, swallowing thickly. "Harun-"

"Is that what you would do in my position?" I repeated, leaning forward. "Make an arrest? Or would you ***deal with the problem***, right there?" As I asked the question, I dug the blade into the pad of my thumb. Blood and barely-contained anger dripped onto the stone floor, but I didn't flinch. I didn't break his gaze.

"Harun, I-"

"I spent two years in the desert pursuing one thing. You... cannot imagine," I laughed, "the things that I went through, the things that I learned. And after ***everything*** I did to save the king, you just... took it away. I think it's my turn to take something, don't you?" I stood with such force that the chair I had been sitting in slammed to the ground. Jove leapt to his feet, pressing himself against the wall.

"Please, Harun. Listen to m-"

He was interrupted by a boom that shook the palace, that sent books flying from their shelves and threw us to the ground. We staggered to our feet, looking at the dust filtering down from the ceiling in surprise, and Ruce pushed the doors open. "The citadel is under attack!"

When I looked back at Jove, he had retrieved his sword, but I was in no danger. He was moving towards the door, our troubles forgotten. His instinct, like mine, was to protect this city— even if he viewed it as a possession, a tool for revenge. I could deal with his treachery, his desire for power, later. For now, we would need every warrior we could find.

The three of us sprinted through the upper level of the palace to where it joined the citadel. Jove pushed the doors open and ran out onto the battlement at the top of the citadel. We followed closely, scanning the city centre below. The night was dark, except for the fires the Guard kept burning... and the other fires. I peered down at the blackened ground in the square, where several small bombs had gone off and thrown the once-bustling crowd into chaos. People were screaming, sobbing, running, fighting back desperately with whatever they had in hand.

In the square, in the central courtyard of the citadel, on the battlement around us, Guards were locked in combat with figures clad in rough, pitted clothing. Without a word, we went to work, our movements perfectly in sync from muscle memory as the three of us joined the fight.

As swords clashed all around me, I heard a loud, barking laughter. I spun in shock, my eyes locking onto what must have been a mirage. He couldn't be here. He was dead.

"Scorpion."

GHOSTS

CHAPTER ONE HUNDRED THREE

JOVE

THE BATTLEMENT WAS IN chaos. All around, my Guards were fighting for their lives against Initiates. Grappling lines bit into the parapet as Initiates started the climb up to join the fight.

I immediately joined the fray, locking swords with an Initiate who was standing over one of my Corporals. I flung the Initiate away and pulled my Corporal to her feet. "You alright, Anahid?"

"Yes, Captain," she panted. "Thanks."

I nodded, chasing down the Initiate and finishing her off. As I looked up into the chaos, I was thrown into a memory. A night just like this, a city on fire. My first real exposure to the *Menagerie*, my first real understanding of the hatred they had for us. I had seen some of them, that night. Their precious Jewels. I had watched their young Scorpion laugh as he slaughtered innocents. *Tannin*, their Crocodile, had left the experience scarred on my face. The *Dwer-da* hunted and cornered children like prey. Viper had leapt down on unsuspecting people from rooftops, her eyes crazed as she did her work. I had watched the beautiful city of Cessiri fall.

I was not going to let that happen to Lothforias.

Around me, my Guards were losing heart. With a majority of their companions still on their way back from the search for Harun, they were outnumbered and fatigued.

I pushed forward, disarming an Initiate standing over one of my Guards, catching the attention of the group that was nursing their wounds. They looked up at me in exhaustion, but also a flicker of hope. I was their hero, their leader, and they needed me right now.

"Every one of you has honoured this city, today," I told them. "You have done our people proud; but they still need our protection. If the citadel falls, the *Menagerie* will raze Lothforias to the ground. No matter what, we cannot let this citadel be taken. We must trust in each other and ***never*** stop fighting, to our last breaths!"

They roared in agreement, encouraged by my speech, and as more grappling lines were thrown up to latch on the parapet, we charged forward as one.

Chapter One Hundred Four

Elin

I STAGGERED BACK, LEANING against the parapet to catch my breath. A grappling line came to dig into the stone right next to my head with a harsh thud and I spun, quickly slicing through the line and sending several Initiates to the cobblestone below.

I caught sight of another woman to my right, working her way up the side of the citadel. Unlike the others, though, she had no grappling line. She simply dug the knives in her hands into the gaps between bricks and hauled herself up with nothing but her own strength keeping her from falling. She was climbing the wall like a-

Like a spider.

When she flipped her grey hair out of her face, I froze. I recognised this woman, I knew her. As she inched closer, I remembered Nassir's shopkeeper friend, that woman who had sold us my bed. *Nala*. She had been so kind, so unassuming... and it had all been an act. Those Initiates I fought had been just like her, living peacefully in the city, waiting for their orders.

She pulled herself over the parapet with a grunt, turning to face me. She was dressed in pitted Lithdreyan clothing, with several knives sheathed along her legs and arms, two across her abdomen. On the inside of her wrists, she wore the same sheaths I did, but hers didn't hold the weapons of a Lithdreyan peasant, and they weren't hidden by sleeves. Her daggers were longer, slightly curved— military. She casually stepped towards me, grinning. "So, you're the little Lothforian causing us so much trouble? Honestly, from the way Scorpion described you... I expected more. I certainly didn't expect the little boy who walked into my shop a few weeks ago."

"You... you're the Spider, aren't you?" I asked meekly, staggering back.

"Why don't you find out?"

I launched myself at her with the sword I had taken from a fallen Initiate and she caught my arm easily, throwing me back. *You're small.* She struck me across the face and sent me sprawling, the sword skidding across the ground. *Kill quietly.*

I pushed myself up onto my elbows and looked up at her as she advanced on me, letting fear cross my face. She smiled sadistically and drew one of her knives. "Please," I pleaded, my lip trembling. "Just- just let me go."

She scoffed, pulling me up by my *kara*. "Poor boy..." she purred. "We're not letting anyone go tonight. But maybe, if you beg, I'll kill you quickly rather than letting my poison do its work." She held her knife up to me to show me the sickening green sheen to it.

"Please..."

"Only the weak beg," she hissed through teeth bared in a smile.

"And only a fool lets their guard down," I murmured, slipping one of my peasant knives from its sheath and driving it under her ribcage without hesitation.

She gasped, staggering back and losing her grip on my shirt. The light left her eyes as quickly as her breath and her legs gave out, sending her backward. She toppled over the edge of the parapet, and as I turned back to the battle, the sound of her body hitting the cobble below made me flinch. I allowed myself that moment; she was a murderer... but still a person. I quickly wiped her blood from my peasant blade, scanning the battlement.

I caught sight of Ruce, still in the armour of a Lothforian Guard, fighting back-to-back with Riadh. I started towards them, but then a familiar face stole my focus. Scorpion locked eyes with me and tauntingly spun his chain-blade. I clenched my jaw, moving decisively and drawing my second peasant knife.

He was bleeding, heavily, but if he felt it, I couldn't tell. He moved towards me like a charging bull, blood soaking into his white clothing in several places. The worst was the wound I had given him— the wound I **thought** had killed him.

This time, I would make sure.

No playing with him, no quiet. He wouldn't underestimate me again. I only had to hope that his wounds slowed him down more than mine did me. A harsh wind passed me, chilling the blood on my clothes and re-minding me how badly I had been hurt during the fight. They had chosen the perfect time to strike— the Guard was distracted and scattered across the city, searching for me. It was less than an hour since my 'capture,' and many platoons must still have been on patrol, not having heard.

There were, at most, fifteen Guards here to fight the dozens of Ini-tiates still swarming over the walls, and almost twenty lying dead or wounded around me. Ruce, Riadh, and I were well-trained, but skill can't negate overwhelming numbers.

As I caught Scorpion's sword strike with my daggers carefully locked in an X, I realised that no one had sounded the alarm. No one outside of the city centre had any idea the onslaught we were facing.

I glanced back at the bell tower, but that moment cost me. Scorpion shoved me backwards with his sword and swung his chain-blade in a wild arc, slicing open my thigh. I groaned, my leg buckling, and struggled to get back to my feet.

I was lacking my usual speed, as hurt as I was, and Scorpion kicked out my knee, sending me to the ground and throwing one of my knives across the battlement. I attacked with my last blade, but he slashed at me with his sword and it flew several feet away. Too far to reach.

He pressed his foot to my chest, pinning me to the ground, and raised his sword. I struggled, but I was too weak to push him off. He stared down at me, waiting to see my fear, waiting for me to beg. My breath was coming hard and my body ached all over. I was exhausted. I **was** scared, but my hatred of him was stronger. I stared right back, waiting.

As the sword came down, I saw the flash of movement and fabric as two swords met.

CHAPTER ONE HUNDRED FIVE

EDDA

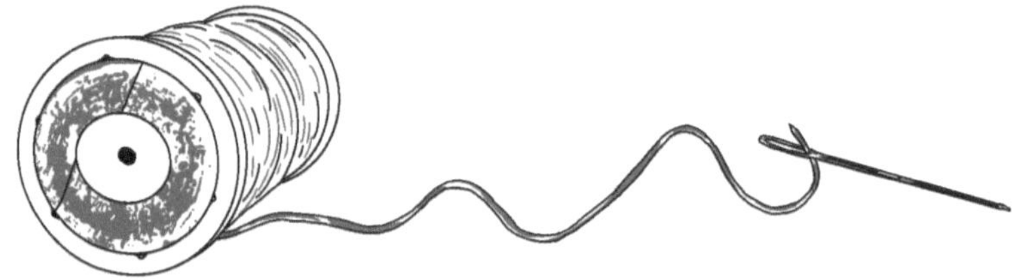

I CAUGHT SCORPION'S BLADE on Elin's sword, which I had carried with me from the Bayouths' when I heard the sounds of fighting.

Scorpion's sword skittered down mine, catching on the hilt. He growled at me, distracted, and that gave Elin the opportunity he needed to push Scorpion's foot off and struggle to his feet. He snatched his peasant dagger from the ground as Scorpion stepped back, spinning his sword threateningly.

"Mother," Elin said hurriedly, "the bell! Sound the alarm, tell the Guards the city is under attack!"

I turned, searching the unfamiliar battlement until I found the tower. There were two Initiates guarding it and I started towards them before I gave myself time to think. As I approached, they stared at me in shock, the nearest barely having time to block my strike as I swung my sword at him.

As I fought, I cursed that the last time I had picked up a sword was over thirty years ago. I held my own for a minute, but their training would quickly overwhelm me.

Suddenly, my husband appeared at my side, slashing at the ankle of my opponent and sending him to the ground. "What are you doing here?!"

"Helping; I need to ring that bell!"

"Best start climbing, then. I'll handle this one, *Habi*," he said with a nod at the girl between me and the ladder. The Initiate lunged towards him in anger and I ducked past, hauling myself up to the bell tower's platform. I panted, jerking the rope that hung from the bell and sending it sounding in a pendulum.

It echoed through the city, glancing off rooftops and filling the air. From my vantage point, I could see platoons in the streets surge towards the citadel to answer the call.

I turned back to the battlement, catching sight of my son fighting a losing battle. Scorpion was armed with a sword and that sickening blade on a chain, while Elin had only a single dagger less the size of a butter knife.

"Elin!" Lieutenant al Abbas shouted, unclipping her own dagger from her belt and sending it across the ground. Elin rolled out of the way of one of Scorpion's attacks, snatching the dagger up and unsheathing it. Riadh's dagger was much longer— a dirk, Ruce would correct me, as though it made any difference. The blade was almost three times the length of Elin's peasant dagger.

As he felt the weight of two knives in his hands, muscle memory from Ruce's training kicked in. He spun the blades in his hands into an overhand grip and his arms crossed over his chest, one above the other to guard.

Before Ruce began training him, I hadn't seen that stance for some thirty years. It was the Lion. Armed with a weapon of Lothforias in one hand, and a weapon of Lithdreya in the other, Elin went to work.

I heard shouting and spun, seeing platoons of Guards in the square forcing their way past Initiates and into the citadel. The tide was turning.

There was a cry of pain as Elin drove the dirk into Scorpion's side, blood rushing from his body like a waterfall. Elin staggered back in exhaustion, falling to one knee, as Scorpion's limp body thudded forward onto the ground.

As the life faded from his eyes and left them unseeing, I felt no shame at the cold smile that crossed my face. That monster had taken everything from me, from Ruce. He deserved to die bloody.

Slowly, steadily, as Guards flooded the citadel and the Initiates realised their Jewels were dead, the sounds of fighting fell quiet.

LION'S DEN

Chapter One Hundred Six

ELIN

As the last of the Initiates were captured or killed, a stillness fell over the battlement. I felt the eyes of dozens of Guards on me, and I knew how conflicted they must be. They looked at Riadh the same way.

I could tell instantly which of them Riadh had talked to, which of them knew the truth. For them, the struggle was over almost instantly as they replaced the lies that had been told to them with the truth that stood before them.

In the city square below, I could hear cheering. The civilians who had been in the city centre before the attack were safe, grateful. I could see Nassir and Malia among them, helping to bandage wounds and pull people to their feet.

Riadh stepped up onto a crate and cleared her throat as she addressed the Guard as one. "We need to tend to the wounded, bury the dead. I know you are tired, but our job is not yet done. I promise that when this is over, we will celebrate, and we will rest. But for now, report to your Sergeants for orders, look out for your companions."

"Yes, Your Majesty!"

I felt a hand on my shoulder and turned, expecting one of my parents, but instead seeing Jove. He was cut up and bloody, but grinning like a fool. "That was something, my boy. You said I taught you everything you knew, but I don't think that's true anymore... That was something," he repeated.

"Do you think I've forgiven you? Forgotten what you did to this city?" I hissed, pulling my shoulder out of his grasp. "You may have helped us today, but you have a *lot* to answer for."

"I... I know," he said quietly, his eyes falling from mine. "Could we speak privately? I just... There are things I need to say to you. Afterwards, I will go peacefully, you have my word. A private moment in the temple, that's all I ask."

I nodded, following him down the nearest spiral staircase. He led me into the temple, holding its gate open for me.

We passed the Guard's private baths and made our way to the central fountain in the courtyard. Jove glanced at me, sighing. "I have made mistakes, Harun... You were right. I've been cruel. But my intention was *always* to protect this city."

He paused to reach forward into the fountain, cupping water in his hands and sipping. He stood, letting the rest fall onto his hair, and I moved to perform the ritual myself. I leaned on the fountain, drawing out a handful of water, when suddenly there was a hand on the back of my neck and I was being shoved under.

CHAPTER ONE HUNDRED SEVEN

RUCE

I watched Lieutenant al Abbas give orders and direct work as I shucked off the Guard's armour that had acted as my disguise. As the armour came off, wind rushed past me, cooling the sweat that clung to me and chilling me to the bone.

"We could set up medics in the temple," one of the Privates offered.

Lieutenant al Abbas quickly shook her head. "The Catacomb supports under the temple are still damaged; we can't know how much weight they can take. I don't want to risk the ground shifting or giving way."

Edda appeared beside me, bloody and carrying Elin's sword. She spoke breathlessly. "You'd better teach me how to use this," she sighed. "I have a feeling it's going to be necessary with that boy of ours…"

"I have a feeling you're right…"

"Pardon, father." We turned to see a boy a few years younger than Elin coming towards us hurriedly. "You're the blacksmith, yes? You're…" he seemed unsure. "Elin?" he pronounced carefully. "You're Elin's parents?"

"We are."

"Hakim!" Riadh called.

The boy glanced away, then turned back urgently. "Jove took him into the temple, and… and I have a bad feeling. Elin doesn't know— he thinks Jove still worships the Goddess, but he doesn't. The temple means nothing to him."

"That slimy Captain of the Guard?" He nodded. I picked my knives up from the ground and resheathed them, nodding for him to speak. "Where?"

"The gate, at the bottom of the stairs."

"Hakim," Riadh called. "I need you."

He looked away, his face pained. "I- please just make sure-"

"We will," I told him.

We wove through the citadel, down the stairs, and to the temple gate. Edda forced it open and I ducked through, sprinting into the central courtyard. In the dark, unlit temple, it was hard to make out the distant figures. The Captain, I saw, was standing over the fountain, but it was blurry, uncertain. It wasn't until I was five feet away that I could see Elin, scrabbling for purchase against the fountain as Jove held his head down in the water.

I lunged, drawing my knives and slashing at Jove. Instinct struck at his ankle and his wrist, and he cried out, staggering back bloody. I kicked him to the ground, putting myself between him and a gasping Elin. Edda caught our boy as his legs gave out in exhaustion, helping him sit against the fountain. His face and hands were bloody from scraping against the stone. Water dripped from his sopping wet hair and *kara* as he shivered, his eyes distant and his chest heaving. Edda held him up, fussing over his cuts and bruises, and I turned back to Jove with my knives bared like fangs. As I stepped forward, his eyes widened in recognition and he scrabbled to his feet, sprinting down the stairs into the belly of the temple.

I started after him, then stopped, glancing back at Elin. He just nodded, panting, and cast his weak gaze in the direction Jove had fled.

I didn't hesitate, immediately making my way down the stairs. Jove's running footsteps echoed off the bricks.

Chapter One Hundred Eight

Jove

THE LION WAS HUNTING me.

I turned the corner, slipping in my haste. It had been years since I'd set foot in this temple and my memory failed me. After Jaz's death, I'd come to hate this place and the Goddess it served, and I had forgotten the twists and turns of its corridors.

I could hear the Lion's deliberate footsteps, his knife scraping along the stone walls in a jarring, discordant threat. Somehow, while he was wandering the Lithdreyan desert, Harun had found himself a Jewel of the *Menagerie*, and from the looks of it, the Lion would have no qualms about killing for him.

I turned, trying to find somewhere to hide, and ran into a dead end corridor. With a start, I realised I'd cornered myself by running to the heart of the temple. There was a slow drip of water coming from the ceiling; I was right underneath the ritual fountain.

I spun around and watched the Lion's shadow stretch and warp as he stalked closer. I staggered back, catching myself on my hands.

Drip. Drip. Drip.

"Mercy! Please," I begged as the Lion turned the corner, predator's eyes locked on me. "Mercy!"

"You tried to kill my boy," he growled darkly, adjusting his grip on the Lothforian dirk in his hand. "You don't get mercy."

I scrambled back in terror as he came closer. Suddenly, the ground beneath us shifted with a horrifying *crack* and water began to flow down the wall from the fountain, pooling behind me.

"Look," I panted, making a last-ditch effort. I knew the Lithdreyans worshipped *Foria* just as my people did. "It's a sign from the Goddess! Please, let me live. It's a sign!"

He slowly cast his gaze up to the flow and something shifted on his face. "You're right... I shouldn't bloody a gift from my son like this." He slowly resheathed the knife.

I sighed in relief. "Thank y-"

Suddenly, the Lion grabbed me by my tunic and hauled me into the pool, forcing my head underwater and holding me there, never breaking eye contact.

I struggled and scratched, fighting desperately to breathe as I looked up at those predator's eyes through the water rippling with bubbles. His grip was unrelenting and I felt my head growing fuzzy, stretching and spinning and clawing at my throat. I watched the bubbles stop, and all at once the water went still.

SETTLING

CHAPTER ONE HUNDRED NINE

ELIN

I BECAME AWARE OF the world around me once more, hearing the buzz of Riadh's voice at the edge of my awareness. I was sitting on a bed in the infirmary, my parents beside me as a medic tended to my wounds. I didn't know for how long.

"...Found his body in the shrine under the temple," Riadh was saying. "I don't know if he went down there to hide or pray for forgiveness, but we know what happened when he did. His weight must have been too much for the damaged supports in the Catacombs to take, and the earth shifted, causing a crack that went all the way up to the fountain. He must have slipped and hit his head, drowning in the pool of water. It was the will of the Goddess," she sighed.

"The will of the Goddess," Ruce agreed in a low rumbling voice.

Riadh locked eyes with him and a moment of understanding passed between them. We've never mentioned it again.

"You should go home, Elin," Riadh continued, tearing her gaze away from my father. "Rest, let yourself heal. I think the city can take care of itself for a while. Oh—" she said, catching herself as she turned to leave. "Your banishment has been officially rescinded. You are welcome in the city."

"Oh, good, I was worried," I said with a tired grin.

She set her hand on my knee, smiling at me. "Heal. We'll talk soon."

||

I ducked past Lieutenant Owaines as he turned down the corridor leading to the temple. If he saw me sneaking into the palace, I would **definitely** get in trouble— no matter how much he liked me.

Once I was sure I was alone, I looked up at the palace wall with a climber's eye. My family had lived just west of Mount Sarigh, so I had years of practice climbing on rough stone— and mountains didn't even come with handholds. I dug my hands and feet into the cracks between bricks and hauled myself up at a spider's pace.

Riadh was at a fancy dinner with some wealthy family from the Silver Mountains, and she would surely be dying of boredom when she got back, just like I had been laying in my bunk in the barracks. I finally reached the balcony, tumbling over as my muscles ached.

"Worth it," I muttered to myself, standing and dusting off my pants.

I was lounging on her bed when she walked in twenty minutes later, huffing in irritation. Her father had made her wear The Shoes, clearly. Nothing else annoyed her so much.

She didn't notice me at first, tearing her hair out of the complicated tower someone had crafted it into and throwing the pins carelessly onto her desk. Her shoes were kicked off next, and then stabbed into the floor with her dagger in anger.

"What did those shoes ever do to you?" I asked, laughing when she startled, spinning to me.

"Harun!" she yelped, quickly catching herself and lowering her voice with a glance to the doors, where two Guards stood outside at all times. "What are you doing here?" she whispered.

"I'm rescuing you, princess, from that stuffy dinner."

"My hero," she said with a tired laugh. She stepped behind a screen in the corner of her room to change and I laid back on her bed, shifting until I was even more comfortable.

"Your bed is so much nicer than mine," I complained.

"Some of us deserve nice things," she tossed over the screen. "And then **some** of us track dirt into my room."

I lifted my head, taking in the patches of dirt on the floor that led right to the bed I was laying in. "Uh, that wasn't me. Some... other guy broke in and kicked dirt all over, then left. I told him it was very rude."

"Mhm," she said with a smirk, emerging in a simple *kara* and a pair of *shiwr,* and crossed the room. "Scooch over."

"Get your own comfy bed!"

"This **is** my bed," she laughed, shoving me in a very un-royal way so she could plop down next to me. The bed was so cushy that the impact launched me into the air.

"How did you get in here?" Riadh asked, resting her head against my shoulder.

"Front door," I lied. "The Guards are very incompetent."

"Mm. Someone should get on that," she said through a yawn, curling up against me.

||

"Careful, Elin, you're not fully healed yet. Remember, I'm here if you need me to take over."

"I'm fine, Father," I sighed happily. "This feels... good. Normal."

I glanced around the smithy, which had been quiet for the past few days. Riadh had ordered a few rest days, in response to the latest attack. As it was now, we were the only people in the citadel aside from the Guards. Actually, we might have been the only people in the city who were working— other than Edda and her assistants. With the coronation tomorrow, Edda was working tirelessly on a dress.

"It is good to get back to the work, isn't it? My hands itch when I don't have anything to do."

I sat back, letting the grinding wheel come to a stop as I looked over the dagger in my hands. In my fight with Scorpion, the blade had been scratched in some spots, and I wanted to repair it before I returned it to Riadh. We had been working on it for the past hour, and finally, when I held it up to the light this time, I couldn't tell the blade had ever been damaged.

"I'll be back, Father," I said as I stood.

"And you'll be careful, yes? No straining your injuries."

"Of course, Father."

||

I grunted in exertion, hauling myself up over the railing of Riadh's balcony. I caught my breath as I leaned against the wall, remembering how much easier that climb had been when I **wasn't** injured. I missed those days... Ah, to go back to a week ago. Or... six months ago? A year? I shook my head, realising I couldn't remember the last time I hadn't been hurt.

I gently levered open the lock on the touched glass doors with one of my peasant daggers, stepping into Riadh's room. I moved to the desk, setting her dirk in its gleaming sheath on top of an open journal.

"I never could figure out how you used to sneak in here..."

I jumped, turning to see Riadh sprawled on her couch reading a book. "Riadh!"

"Only you would climb up the palace wall," she said with a roll of her eyes.

"I just... wanted to return your knife," I said quietly.

"Thank you. A close friend made it for me, and I'd hate to lose it."

I smiled at that and started to turn back to the balcony.

"The coronation is tomorrow, you know."

I nodded, unable to bring myself to look her in the eye. "You're becoming queen."

"You'll be there?"

"If you want me there..."

"I do. I also wouldn't refuse if you wanted to sit with me for a while... I mean, I **still** haven't heard about your vacation to Lithdreya."

"Vacation?" I scoffed as I turned to her, coming to sit on the other side of the couch. "Is that what you think it was?" I laughed, shaking my head at the audacity.

"Well, I haven't heard about it. Maybe I'm wrong. Tell me a story, Elin."

Chapter One Hundred Ten

Riadh

I was knelt on a dais at the front of the city square, thousands of people watching as the crown was lowered onto my head.

I stood, the fabric of my gown shifting and catching the wind, and a cheer went up from the square. "To the health of the Queen!" they yelled. Tor was standing just off to my left, as was his privilege as an emissary to the Stangrey king. At the front of the crowd, I could see Elin and Malia, their hands cupped around their mouths and cheering louder than anyone. Their families were there beside them, Elin's parents and Malia's father, and the sight made me as happy as it did sad.

I swallowed and pushed my feelings down as well-wishers stepped forward, clasping my hands and offering me blessings.

"I don't suppose you'll be visiting anytime soon, will you, doll?"

I turned, embracing Tor as he stepped forward. "No, unfortunately I won't. I'm needed here. Peace talks with Lithdreya aren't going to be easy."

"Peace talks?" he asked in shock. "Riadh, your people are still re-building from your last ***talk*** with Lithdreya!"

"The *Menagerie* doesn't speak for their country, Tor, just for their upbringing. Based on your reaction, I'm guessing you won't want to take part in our treaty negotiations..."

"I really must be getting home, Riadh," he said diplomatically, though I knew he was angry at me. "Perhaps I'll take you to the circus another time. *Ha det.*"

"I wish you steady hands as well, old friend," I said, trying not to let sadness tinge my voice. I was sensing a growing tension between our nations before he had even let go of my hand.

As the crowd slowly began to fade, I felt a hand on my shoulder. "Your parents would be so proud of you, Ri," Elin murmured in my ear.

I turned and hugged him tightly, shaking my head. "You always see right through me."

Malia appeared by his side, beaming at me as she offered me a bou-quet of wildflowers. "You look beautiful, and ***so*** strong," she told me. "I'm honoured to have you as my Queen."

"As honoured as I am to have you as a friend, Malia."

"We'll leave you," Elin said gently. "I know you have matters to attend to." They turned and started towards the edge of the square.

"Captain," I called, "you need to pack for your Immersion."

I saw Elin glancing side to side, wondering which of my Guards I had named Captain.

"Elin," I laughed, "I'm talking to you."

He spun in surprise, a grin breaking out on his face. "You-"

"What? It was only a matter of time, wasn't it?"

"The blacksmith's son?" one of my Guards murmured.

"He's adopted," another informed him with a swat to his arm. "He's the one who saved the city!"

"***Ohhh.***"

||

"Report, Sergeant," I ordered as I strode into the room.

Hakim glanced up from his list, nodding to me. "Your Majesty. Every body has been treated with spices and wrapped in shrouds for the journey home. They are currently being laid in wagons for transport."

"And you have ensured-"

"Every tradition has been followed to the letter, yes."

"Excellent. What about-"

"Your offer of friendship. It's been translated, written, and is just waiting for your seal."

"Excellent work as always, Hakim."

"My mothers asked me to thank you for helping the washerwomen return to the temple once repairs were completed."

"Say hello to them for me. Now, I must go see off my new Captain."

CHAPTER ONE HUNDRED ELEVEN

ELIN

As we followed the turn in the road that took us out of the forest, the wind of the plains hit us, rippling our clothes and filling our lungs with fresh air. I caught sight of the Goddess Falls in the distance, grinning at the Guards riding behind me. "Almost there," I told them.

As we got closer, my fingers played over the pendant Edda had given me before I left. She'd told me its history, how it was a gift from her son... But she'd said the strangest thing. Before she could stop herself, she'd said 'your brother'.

I hadn't known how to feel about that at first, at being put next to him in her memory like that... but I had decided to take comfort in it. I wasn't the son she and Ruce had lost, but in their eyes, I was a son just the same.

I dropped from the saddle, taking in the beauty of the Goddess Falls for the first time. The mountain in front of us had four peaks— the Four Arms of *Foria*— breaking through the waterfall that fed into a large pool. The water was perfectly clear, and it sounded almost like a child chattering happily. Water sprayed off of the rocks as we approached, and the moment I knelt in front of the pool and dipped my cupped hands in to drink, the light caught it and sent colours shooting across the ground.

The Guards behind me gasped, staring up in wonder. I sipped from my hands, spilling the rest above my head. "Faith my reservoir," I murmured.

I turned to my envoy, clearing my throat. "What are we standing around for?" I asked playfully.

"Sorry, Captain," one of them stuttered out, and they quickly set into motion, unfolding bedrolls and setting up tents.

Eschel approached me with a small smile. He was no longer a member of our Guard, but he had asked to accompany me on my Immersion, and I had been grateful to have his experience. Few Guards had ever been on an Immersion before, and only one had actually accompanied the incumbent Captain to the Falls.

"Do I look like I know what I'm doing?" I murmured to him with a small smile.

"You're a natural, Captain," he laughed. "I have never seen the waters and the light mingle like they did just now. It seems you are everything your predecessor claimed to be and more."

"Eschel... I know that Jove was your friend-"

"His lies were my friend," he said firmly. "Bazzeri and Jazhara, **they** were friends, and he has dishonoured their memory. Go; bathe, commune with the Goddess. We will watch over you, Captain Lahd."

"Thank you, Eschel."

I gingerly approached the tent Anahid had set up for me, toying with the tie of my *kara*. I felt every eye on me, and it was paralysing.

"Why are we gawking like school children?" Eschel called harshly. "Anahid, make yourself useful and fetch some firewood. You two, get started on a fire and a meal. And you— don't give me stink-eye, boy— you get first watch. Perimeter, go!"

As those sharp gazes left me, one by one, I turned to Eschel and nodded gratitude.

"What are you looking at me for?" he asked with fake venom. "I just hate seeing young people stand around and relax."

"Thank you," I reiterated, and he shrugged sheepishly.

"Once you get back home, you'll have a Lieutenant for that sort of thing, but I thought I'd fill in for now. Now, get in the water, boy; it's not gonna get any warmer."

I laughed, unwrapping my *kara* and setting it on the floor of my tent. It felt strange, baring my body, the map of everything I had been through, everything I had learned, freely for the first time since I was banished.

I waded into the water, sighing as the cool water soothed my saddle aches. I pulled the necklace I wore over my head, lowering it into the water. "My mother asked me to give this to you... so you know to water his gravetree and help him find comfort in the afterlife." I let go my grip on the stone, and the current instantly swept it away, down into the depths beneath the waterfall.

"Thank you, My Lady," I murmured. "Thank you for trusting me, and for guiding me when I needed you."

A particularly violent spray sent drops of water onto my cheek and I smiled.

"I feel your presence everywhere I go, but here... It's like I can hear you clearly. Your city is safe now, My Lady, and I promise to always protect it to the best of my ability. I will follow your guidance wherever it takes me."

||

"Captain!" Eschel called out over the water. "If you want to make it home before dark, we should leave soon!"

"On my way," I answered, looking back at the Goddess Falls. "I would stay longer than a week, My Lady... but our city is healing, and I want to be there to see it. Besides... you're not just here, you're wherever I need you, aren't you?"

The waters here were addictingly pure, and I couldn't resist taking one last sip from cupped hands before I poured the rest into my hair. "Faith my reservoir," I promised.

I emerged from the pool, quickly drying myself and pulling my clothing on. Eschel approached as I tied my boots, holding the reins of both of our horses. "My Captain. You look different," he noted with a small smile.

"Yeah?" I asked with a laugh. "Transformed by my time here?"

"There's something, I know it."

"He's right," Anahid agreed. "Did you get taller?"

"No. Now get on your horse and let's go."

"I think so," she told Eschel as I swung up into my saddle. "I think he's taller than he used to be."

As I started leading the way back down the trail, I heard my Guards gasp, whispering to each other. I glanced back to see what they were looking at, and I watched as the entire sky above the Goddess Falls was transformed into a mirage of colour. The tones waxed and waned, almost sparkling in the mist.

I smiled. "Let's go home; we've got work to do."

||

"Captain," Riadh called, grinning as she ran down the steps. "*Dreya*, a week feels like eternity. How did it go?"

"It was fine," I told her. "An enjoyable trip, but unremarkable, really."

"You call **two** coloured omens 'unremarkable'?" Anahid asked, askance.

"No one tried to kill me," I shrugged. "It was actually kind of boring."

Riadh rolled her eyes, looping her arm through mine. "Well, tell me how boring it was while we walk. I assume you remembered that you need to choose a Lieutenant now?"

"Of course I did. I was thinking-"

Riadh frowned, glancing over at me with a strange expression. She looked me up and down and then down at herself and back several times. "Did you get taller?" she asked.

"What? No. Anyways, my Lieutenant-"

"I think you got taller," she continued.

"I was only gone a week, Riadh."

"You didn't used to be taller than me."

"Maybe your shoes are shorter. My Lieutenant."

"Right. You have someone in mind?"

"What was that boy's name? The one who I-"

She rolled her eyes at me again, grinning at me as she shook her head. "You are so predictable. He's in the courtyard."

Riadh dragged me through the citadel to the Guard's barracks and beyond. We emerged into the training courtyard, where several of the younger Guards were sparring— five against one.

"Hakim!" Riadh called.

His opponents stopped their assault and resheathed their swords as he turned to us. "Your Majesty?" he asked, reholstering his staves as he jogged over to stand with us. "Captain! You've returned from your Immersion. Do you have need of me?" he asked, planting his fist over his heart in salute.

"You've been keeping up your sword skills, I hope."

"Yes, Captain," he said immediately.

"Good. Let's spar." I unsheathed my sword, moving to stand in the centre ring. "Do you remember what I expect of you?"

"Captain?" he asked in confusion.

"You'd better land two hits on me."

The corner of his mouth ticked up just slightly as he stepped into the ring gingerly, resting his hand on his sword. "I'm always ready for a match, but... don't you have more important things to do right now?"

"Oh, this is of the utmost importance; don't worry."

"How so?" he asked as we started to circle each other.

"I'll tell you if you succeed. Oh, but— one condition. Use your right hand."

"You're trying to give me a disadvantage?" he asked, tossing the sword into his other hand. "That's not very sporting."

"Your enemies won't be worried about fair play. You have two minutes to get two hits in. Got it?"

"Yes, sir," he said solidly.

"Good. Let's begin."

No sooner had I spoken than he was launching for me. I moved to block his strike, but it was only a feint, and he quickly reversed his grip, swiping at my legs. I just barely jumped back in time to avoid the cut.

"Oh," I said with a grin. "This is gonna be fun."

Hakim didn't answer, his eyes picking apart my every move. *Focus.* I respected that. How would he fare on the defensive?

I struck with blinding speed, driving my sword toward his chest in a thrust. He quickly spun his blade around mine, using my momentum to send me past him and slicing my cheek open in one fluid motion.

I turned back to him, laughing. "That was nice form; your footwork could use some work, though. See how your toe's pointed?"

"My footwork is fine," he said, refusing to fall for it. "Why are you still going easy on me, Captain?"

I didn't answer, instead letting my sword apologise for holding back. He kept up with my strikes, slowly giving ground, before suddenly leaving himself open to my slash at his arm and swinging his sword in a wild overhead arc. I ducked the attack easily, just in time for his elbow to crack across my jaw.

I staggered back, my shoulders shaking with laughter as I took him in. "Not bad, kid... Not bad. But you let me get a hit on you."

"That wasn't part of the rules; I needed an opening, and I got one."

"You *let* me cut you so you could win?"

He gave a one-armed shrug, the barest hint of smile playing across his features. "Now; are you going to tell me why you took time out of your day to let me hit you?"

"We've got a lot of work to do before the Day of Visiting," I told him, resheathing my sword. "Come on, Lieutenant."

He gaped at me as I turned and started out of the courtyard, Riadh by my side.

"Is he still just standing there?" I whispered to her with a grin.

"Well, you can't blame him; you had the same expression on your face when *you* were named Lieutenant."

I glanced back to take in the look on his face. "Did not. We're walking, Sadir!" I called more loudly.

Within moments, he was by my side, standing straight like pride was holding him up, and he struggled to keep a smile off of his features.

"Did you cut your hair or something?" he asked as we started into the Hall of Craftsmages. "You look different."

"I thought he was taller," Riadh said to him conspiratorially.

"That could be it," Hakim nodded.

"I am not any taller than I was when I left," I grumbled.

Ruce shook his head with a smile as we approached the smithy. "No, you're taller."

"Definitely taller," I heard someone say through a mouth full of food. I turned, scanning the smithy until I saw Malia lounging in a chair with her feet propped up.

"Wh- That's my workbench! Get your muddy feet off it! What are you doing here, anyways?"

"Ruce is making a present for my father."

"She's helping," Ruce said deadpan.

"I'm helping," she agreed, taking another bite of her apple. "Who's this?" she asked, nodding to Hakim.

"Malia, this is Hakim Sadir, my Lieutenant. Hakim, this is Malia Bayouth... She's helping my father."

"Hey! I *happen* to be one of his best friends," Malia told Hakim indignantly. "And you think he'd be nicer to me, considering I'm leaving soon."

"What? Where are you going?" I asked.

"No. You were mean to me; I don't feel like telling you about it anymore," she said with an indignant huff.

I rolled my eyes. "Hakim, gather the Corporals. I'll be there in a minute."

"Do you need the Sergeants as well?"

"No; I don't want to take eyes off of the districts for this, and they already know what to expect."

"Captain."

I ducked into the smithy, kicking Malia's feet off of the workbench to sit there, crossing my arms. "I missed you, you know."

"Oh, was it boring, playing in a waterfall for a week? I told you to let me come with you."

"You know only Guards are allowed on the pilgrimage. Now tell me what's happening," I groaned, nudging her.

"Well..." she beamed, sitting forward in excitement, "I am now the proud owner... of a galleon."

"That's amazing!" I said, smiling at her as she danced around in her seat. "What is that?"

"It's a ship," she laughed. "A three-masted sailing ship, and she is **all mine**. As soon as Her Majesty signs my papers, the Bayouth Trading Company will be open for business."

"Trading company?" I asked in surprise. "When did you decide on this?"

"Oh... I'd been thinking about it for awhile, honestly. Years. But recently I realised that I want more adventure than this city can give me. It was actually spending time with you that reawakened that in me. You... you've seen so much, learned from so many different people and places. I want to travel the world... just like Fatima and I always dreamed."

"What about Rami? Weren't the two of you starting to...?"

"Well, he's actually sailed before, and when I mentioned it to him... he told me I should go for it, and that if I had any interest in a navigator, he'd come with me in a heartbeat. I've already learned some sea songs."

"Wow. How- How long are you gonna be gone?"

"Oh... just a few weeks, the first time. A little voyage, to test the ship and the crew."

"That's 'little'?"

"There's a whole world out there, Elin... And I'm gonna see it all."

"Well, then you'd better plan some downtime to tell me all about it whenever you come home from a journey. When do you leave?"

"As soon as the festival is over."

"That's only three days from now!"

"We'll have dinner before I leave. And who knows? Maybe someday I'll need to bring an awkward Captain of the Guard on one of my voyages?"

"Dinner, I can promise. Getting on a creaky old ship... we'll talk. I'll see you later, Mal. Father," I said, touching his shoulder as I passed.

||

"We are hosting the first Day of Visiting this city has seen in years, and we need to make sure everything goes well," I told my Corporals.

Each of them oversaw a squadron of ten soldiers. "Lieutenant Sadir will be overseeing the schedule," I said with a nod to Hakim, "but first we need to understand how this is going to work. When you are not on duty, you do not need to wear full armour, but I expect every one of you in carapaces, armed, and with your eyes open. You are all going to be assigned shifts of duty throughout the day; three squadrons during each shift."

One of the Guards in front of me groaned quietly, but not quietly enough to avoid my notice.

I drew breath to speak, but Hakim was already stepping forward. I reminded myself that, as Lieutenant, it was his job to mediate, and bit my tongue.

"How old are you, Corporal bin Fousa?" Hakim asked calmly.

"Uh- twenty six, sir…"

Hakim's voice was stone. "Then stop acting like you're nine."

The Corporal looked up in surprise, but his eyes dropped almost immediately.

"Any older," Hakim explained, "and you would remember the last Day of Visiting; how many lives were lost. Look me in the eye."

Corporal bin Fousa hesitantly looked up, meeting Hakim's gaze.

Hakim waited for a moment, making sure he had the attention of every Guard in the room. Finally, he spoke, his voice deliberate but not harsh. "Are you okay with letting people die so you can have a day off?"

Something clicked in the Corporal's eyes and he straightened, stepping forward. "No, sir!"

"Then what are you going to do?"

"I'm going to remain armed and in carapace on the Day of Visiting," he answered. "And my squadron will take the first shift."

"Thank you, Tariq," Hakim said kindly.

Nadia stepped forward to join him. "I'd like to volunteer my squad for the first shift as well."

Anahid nodded, coming to stand between both of them. "As will I."

"Excellent," Hakim said. "Each squadron will work one shift throughout the day; those of you who do not already have a shift, please come to me."

As the Corporals moved, jostling eagerly to be at the front of the line to volunteer for a shift, I caught Hakim's eye, nodding once. The corner of Hakim's mouth twitched in response.

||

"The square is beautiful, Elin," my mother told me. "You were right..."

"This was my favourite time of year, when I was little. I'm glad to bring it back."

"I'm glad Basma decided to make her sweet bread," Ruce sighed happily.

"Hey, save some for me," I huffed, snatching a piece of the sticky bread.

"You're lucky I love you," he shot back.

"Riadh was coming, right?" Edda asked, glancing around the Hall. "I haven't seen her."

"I don't know," I answered sadly as I spooned out some *majedra* for myself. "She... she doesn't have anyone to visit with anymore."

"Oh, nonsense," Edda tutted. "We're here. Oh, there's our girl!" she laughed, moving to go embrace Riadh. "How are you doing, *hayati*?" she asked. "You look beautiful."

"As do you, mother. May I sit with your family?"

"You're a part of that family too, you know," Edda said as she pulled out a chair for Riadh to join us.

"Thank you."

||

I looked up at a strange sensation, like someone had gently poked my forehead. Then another. Another. Drops of water began to fall on my face faster and faster, until I was looking up into the rain.

Around me, people were standing up, some of them shrieking, some laughing. Children ran around wildly, sticking their tongues out to catch drops of rain and splashing in puddles. Somehow the rain made everything look all the more vibrant. Clothing, flowers, sunlight...

Malia laughed beside me, singing happily as she spun in the rain. People in earshot were quick to join her, and soon there were dozens of voices.

People began to spill out into the city square, dancing together and cheering. Everyone was soaked to the bone, their hair plastered to their face... but none of them seemed to notice. Compared to their joy, it was inconsequential.

||

Nassir stood at the mouth of the harbour, pretending that his face wasn't screwed up with emotion as he watched his daughter lift her belongings up to the waiting hands that leaned over the side of her ship. Its name, *The Cloak of Stars*, was painted onto the hull in a warbling gold. Finally, her things were all on board, and she started up the plank that connected the ship to the dock.

"Mal, hang on," I called as I jogged up to her. She stopped, turning to smile at me.

"Come to see me off?" she asked cheerfully, but there was a sadness to her voice too.She stepped down to me and then swayed slightly, gripping the railing.

"You okay?"

She pressed a hand against her stomach, nodding. "I've just been a bit nauseous. I'm still getting my sea legs, you know?"

"Well, don't let me keep you. I've just come to give you a farewell gift." I held out a bundle and Malia beamed, reverently taking it out of my hands and unwrapping what was inside.

"Oh, Elin, it's beautiful..." she murmured as she turned over the dirk. "You know, I was wondering why Riadh got a dagger and I didn't," she said haughtily.

"Dirk."

"No, I'm not naming it that. I think something exotic, like... **Seraphina**. Yeah. I like that."

"The kind of dagger," I laughed. "It's a dirk. If you want to get a scabbard made, that's important to tell the leatherworker."

"Ah. Wow, this is-" she gaped at the knife, looking closer. "Is this the orchard?" she asked, her voice getting small and high as she studied the burnished engravings.

"So you have something of Fatima, on your journeys... and something of me. I'm not gonna be there to get you out of trouble, you know, and-"

"Sorry," she laughed. "Who gets **who** out of trouble?"

I rolled my eyes. "That's fair enough... Well, I just wanted to give you this before you left; don't let me delay you."

Malia kissed my cheek before pulling me into a tight hug. "Try not to burn down the city while I'm gone."

"Oh, only because it's you asking." I stepped back, waving up at Rami. "Don't fall in!" I called to him.

He smiled, nodding to me in farewell.

"Oh," Malia huffed, "can you please bring this to my father. He won't come any closer than that to the ship," she said, nodding to his distant position. "Like if he gets too close, I'm really leaving."

I gently took hold of the box she handed me, looking in her eyes one last time. "Good luck."

"I'll see you soon," she promised.

I turned, weaving through the crowd until I reached Nassir, whose eyes were misting. "Your daughter wanted me to give this to you," I told him, holding the box out.

He took it wordlessly, unlatching the lid and letting it swing open. Inside, there was a beautiful silver compass and a note. He gave a quiet laugh, reading it aloud to me. "'*Aba*, you taught me to find my own way. Trust that I will always find my way home.' Oh, that girl," he sighed, wiping his eyes. "I am so proud... but I am going to miss her dearly."

"Me too, Nassir," I murmured, watching as the *Cloak of Stars* left port, two tiny figures waving at us from the deck.

"Where are you headed, young Elin?" Nassir asked, turning to me. "Because I recently heard of a wonderful shop that opened in the bend of the river— Of Thread and Steel. Perhaps you've heard of it?"

"You know," I said with a grin as we started back up through the Barrier Ridge Pass and into the city, "I think I might've heard something about that."

As we turned down the street, I felt a soft touch in my hair. I reached up, finding the familiar texture of a hook flower. Turning, I smiled as Riadh winked at me.

"Nassir, I'm sure you remember my friend Riadh... Normally, she acts far more regal, I promise."

"Good morning, Your Majesty," Nassir said with a playful bow of his head.

"Won't you ever let me find peace?" I asked Riadh, throwing the flower at her unsuccessfully.

"Nah, you'd get bored. Where are we going?"

"My parents opened their shop today."

"Ooh, exciting," she said, looping her arm through mine. "*Sahlab* on the way? My treat."

"Well, if Her Majesty insists."

"Her Majesty does. Oh, and Hakim wanted me to let you know that the stack of paperwork on your desk isn't getting any smaller just because you're ignoring it."

"I quit."

The Sentinel Reborn

Elin

I SIGHED, PORING OVER the map once more. "There's gotta be something we can do."

"All of our reports come in too late," Hakim told me. "By the time we form up and arrive at these villages, the bandits have already moved on."

"All we need is one chance... and we could send them packing."

"What if we sent out scouts, dressed as normal travelers?"

I slowly shook my head. "No, we'd need to have some local force, even *if* those scouts could get to us. Remember, most of the villages that were attacked, the residents were taken hostage until the bandits were ready to move on."

I glanced up at the gentle knock on the door of my study.

"Enter."

Anahid stepped through the door, ducking her head to us in deference. "Captain, Lieutenant, a young man was causing a disturbance at the city's gates. He seemed quite panicked, and he asked to see the Lahds... I thought you would want to speak with him."

I nodded. "Bring him in."

She poked her head out of the room and beckoned, and two more of my Guards escorted a boy, maybe fifteen years of age, into the room. He was filthy and bruised, his clothes torn, and Anahid was right. The only thing in his eyes was panic.

"Our Captain of the Guard," Anahid said in introduction.

"S- Sebastien," he supplied, looking around furtively.

I stepped around my desk, holding out a hand to the boy. "Elin Lahd."

His eyes widened and a mix of fury and disbelief crossed his face. "You're a liar! You're lying!"

My breath caught as I realised who this boy must be.

The Guards moved to restrain him as he raged, but I held up a hand. "It's alright," I said in a rush. "Leave us." I glanced at Hakim. "You too."

"Captain," he said instantly, ushering the others from the room before closing the doors behind him.

As the sound echoed off the walls, the boy stepped back, eying me warily.

"Sebastien, your name was?" I asked gently.

He nodded, hesitant, suspicious.

"You wanted to see my parents, I assume? Edda and Ruce Lahd?"

"You're not him! You're not!"

"You're a survivor from Jezzine... aren't you?"

"You're. Not," he seethed deliberately.

I slowly shook my head. "No, I'm not the boy you must have known. But his parents took me in. They kept me safe by giving me his name when my own would have gotten me killed."

He faltered. "That... that sounds like something they would do, but-"

"Will you take a walk with me to my family's dwelling?"

"I'm not going anywhere with you."

"It's almost dinnertime, and I imagine you haven't eaten in awhile..." I said innocently. "I wonder what Edda's cooking."

Sebastien wavered, and I knew I had him. "Alright, fine. Lead the way, fake."

⬚

"Mother," I called as I ducked into our dwelling, "we have a guest." I say 'our,' though I hardly spent two nights here each week anymore. There was so much work to be done that I'd started sleeping in my study, until Riadh had insisted I take Jove's old quarters.

Edda turned in confusion, her hands covered in flour. "Malia isn't supposed to be back for-"

"Miss Edda!" Sebastien shouted, stepping forward and hugging her forcefully.

She laughed, embracing him back and covering his hair and his shirt in flour. "Sebastien! What are you doing here?"

Ruce stepped out of the bedroom, scratching his head. "Did I just hear- Oof!"

The sound was forced out of him as he was practically tackled by a mess of hair and gangly teenage limbs. "Ruce! Oh, it's so good to see you both!"

Ruce patted his hair fondly, smiling. "And what are you doing here, kid?"

Sebastien stepped back and his face fell. "Our village... it's in trouble. Old Woman Tri was hoping you knew someone who could help, so she helped me escape."

"Well, you're in luck," Ruce answered, coming to rest a hand on my shoulder. "Our boy here is the city's Captain of the Guard. Think you can lend a hand?" he asked me.

"I'll have a team ready by morning," I nodded. "What's the trouble?" I asked the furious boy in front of me, though I had a suspicion I already knew.

"You... you really did just replace him," he muttered. "It's only been a year."

Edda shook her head sadly, stepping closer to take his hand. "No one's replaced him, Sebastien... We still feel his loss every day. But I'm a mother, and the river led me to a boy without one. Tell me it isn't fate to try and make ourselves whole again."

He pulled out of her grip, shaking his head in anger. "Fine. Convince yourself of that..." he said bitterly. Turning to me, his expression steel, he said, "***Captain***, there is a group of men who came to our village under the guise of refuge, two days ago. When we allowed them into our homes, they started ransacking. They've taken over the village, and they kill anyone who disobeys. We can't last like this."

"We'll make short work of it," I promised him. "These raiders have been a thorn in my side since I took over as Captain. How many were there?"

"Over a dozen, all of them armed."

"I'll tell Hakim to ready two squadrons."

"Can we steal you for dinner?" Edda asked. "I'm assuming you'll lead the mission, and I won't see you for at least a week."

I slowly shook my head. "I can't even spare the hour, Mother. If the raiders know he escaped, we don't have much time before they shore up defenses, and they never spend more than a week in one place anyways. You can stay in my room for the night," I said to Sebastien, nodding to the curtain on my left. "I'll be back for you in the morning." I pressed a kiss to Edda's hair, stepping back. "I'm sorry."

"When you come home, then," she promised, giving me a sad smile. I hated disappointing her... but there was work to be done.

⬚

"So, ***Captain***, what's your brilliant plan?" Sebastien asked from his horse, which trotted slightly behind mine.

"I was thinking I'd go into the village alone, pretending to be a merchant... get an idea of their numbers, their capabilities, where they're keeping the villagers, then flee into the woods before they can grab me."

"Solid plan. You're good at pretending to be someone you're not." The remark was biting.

I turned to him sharply. "I'm assuming we have a problem?"

"No, of course not," he spat. "No problem... ***Elin***."

"I didn't choose the name," I shot back. "The Lahds gave it to me to protect me. I didn't choose it."

"No, but you wear it just fine," he huffed.

"Yeah. With honour. You aren't going to make me feel shame. Not for something I was given by people who chose to love me. Now, this is going to be dangerous. Are you capable of obeying orders or do I need to leave you behind?"

"You said you'd help us!"

"I'll rescue your village; it's whether or not I let you come with me that's in question."

"They're my friends!"

"Then don't get them killed; do what I say."

"Yes, sir," he said sharply, squeezing his knees and pushing his horse to ride in front of me.

⧠

"That's the leader," Sebastien said, pointing carefully so as not to expose our position. We were facedown in the grass, peeking over the hill that overlooked Arbor Village. More than twenty men were patrolling, digging through chests of jewelry, rifling through pantries for food.

"Sayyid Oman," I nodded. "A member of the People's Army in Lithdreya, until he built up a band of raiders and started pillaging our countryside."

"That's where most of the villagers were," Sebastien told me, drawing my attention to a large storehouse on the outskirts of town. "There were two guards standing outside the door."

"Only one door?"

He nodded.

"Then how did you escape?"

"There's a window, in the loft. Old Woman Tri made sure no one was looking at the back of the building, drew their attention, and I slipped out."

"You think the two of us could reach that window? If we can get in and talk to the villagers without alerting the bandits to my presence, that would be better..."

"I think we could do it, but there's no guarantee we could get to the window in the first place. These guys may be dumb, but they're not stupid. They have a perimeter patrol."

"I may have a way to get their attention... Let's get back to the others."

⧠

"You're sure this will work?" Sebastien asked skeptically. We were hiding in the forest, as close to the storehouse as we dare with those perimeter patrols.

"Trust me; I've done this before."

"I won't '**trust you**,'" he said in a deep voice. "But... I need you. I can't help my village alone."

A woodburt call rose up, three notes, then one, then two, which told me it was Anahid. Real woodburts sang three, one, and three times.

"That's the signal; get ready."

I pictured, in my mind, Ana laying on that hill with a mirror in her hand. She'd aim at the sun, then slowly tilt the mirror down until she saw the beam it reflected on the ground... and she'd guide it towards the dry pile of hay in the centre of the village. The sun was bright today, and it wouldn't take long for a flame to catch.

"*Igyak! Igyak!*" ***Fire! Fire!***

"Go," I whispered, and then Sebastien and I were sprinting to the storehouse. As we approached, I gave thanks that buildings were shorter in the countryside. I didn't know why that happened consistently, but at the moment I didn't care, because it made our task that much easier.

Sebastien locked his fingers together so I could step up, and then he pushed me up so I could catch the ledge. I pulled myself over the side, then turned back the moment I was on solid ground to hold my hand down to him. He leapt up and I caught his arm, hauling him up to join me. We ducked down, catching our breaths and listening for any sounds of alarm. Were we spotted? Had someone found a footprint? Had Ana's light given away her position?

Several minutes later, we finally moved, creeping down the stairs to the main floor. Villagers began to startle as they noticed us, but I held a finger to my lips and shushed them urgently.

They cast furtive glances towards the door, then visibly relaxed when they saw Sebastien behind me. Several of them ran up and hugged him tightly, but an old woman walked towards me. Her entire left arm was covered in burn scars, but I would have recognised her anyways—she wore Ruce's favourite unimpressed expression. She **had** to be Master Tri.

"And who might you be?" she asked lowly.

"Captain of the Guard in Lothforias. I was Ruce's apprentice for the better part of a year, and when they heard your village was in trouble, they asked me to come."

She looked me over with a raised brow. "How many times do you fold Meandering Steel?"

"Three," I shot back instantly.

"And two well-songs to temper a sword, yea?"

I grinned at her. Ruce had played the same trick. "No, just one."

"What kind of grind would you use for a training sword?"

"Convex, to dull the edge. Personally, I like to pair it with a double fuller to decrease weight without losing strength, but that's a matter of preference."

She nodded curtly. "I see the boy hasn't been slacking. What's your name, Captain?"

"Elin," Sebastien said mockingly. "They call him Elin."

Master Tri raised an eyebrow and I waved my hand dismissively. "It's complicated; I was banished, the Lahds hid me in their home, and eventually it stopped feeling like we were playing pretend."

She nodded, seemingly satisfied. "Well, Elin, I hope you have twenty more soldiers tucked into your pockets, because these *loros* aren't going away easily— especially not now that they've sent for reinforcements."

"Reinforcements?"

"There are smaller bands nearby, and after they realised Sebastien was gone, they were worried that he'd bring help. They sent a messenger this morning."

"I'll have Tariq send a scout to hunt him down before he can get there..."

"Where's Ansel?" Sebastien asked, pushing his way through the crowd of people.

Master Tri's face drew tight. "That damned chief of theirs is keeping some of our young people around him, as leverage."

"Who's Ansel?" I asked.

"He's my- my best friend."

"He's from Jezzine?"

Sebastien nodded tightly. "We have to save him."

"We will," I promised. I brushed my chin thoughtfully as I started pacing. An idea was coming to me, but it would be complicated.

"Well, boy? You have a plan?" Master Tri asked.

"Depends. Are you still a metalworker or have you retired to doddering old woman?"

She cackled. "Give you one guess."

"Good. I assume your forge is far from the foodstores and the farms? I'm going to need some armour."

"About a mile outside of the village; people'd bother me too often if the walk was any shorter. What are you thinking?"

"They're expecting reinforcements... I'm going to give them some."

⬚

Getting Master Tri out of the storehouse was no easy task, but eventually we were able to craft a ladder out of branches and vines from the forest with hooks on the end, so it could rest over the windowsill, and with the materials, it could go unnoticed when we hid it in the forest.

"They check on us at dawn," Master Tri murmured to me as we started down the path. "I need to be back by then."

"We'll get you back. Ana, how long until Tariq's team is back, do you think?"

"They found the messenger's trail, said he couldn't be more than three hours ahead. They'll be back by tonight, I assure it."

"Good. It wouldn't pay to have actual reinforcements show up and ruin our game..." I stopped short, and the rest of our party glanced back at me.

"Captain?" Ana asked.

"Of course... I can't walk into the village alone, and I need people who can pass as Lithdreyan to sell it, which will be hard if anyone speaks to you... Dammit, I wish Hakim was here."

Ana touched my shoulder. "My squadron all speak Lithdreyan, Captain. Lieutenant Sadir has been teaching us."

A smile broke onto my face. "He has?"

She nodded. "In preparation for the visit from the High Seat of Lithdreya. He thought it would be prudent for more of us to speak their language, to make negotiations go more smoothly."

"He really does think of everything."

This might actually work... but in order to sell it, I needed Sebastien. My mother would kill me if I let a kid-

"Hey, Sebastien, how old are you?"

"Sixteen."

Oh, I did **way** more dangerous stuff when I was sixteen. **That'll do**, I thought.

"**What**?"

Out loud. Thought out loud.

"Uh- I need your help, if we're gonna do this."

"You have it," he answered instantly.

"Okay; your friend Ansel, would **he** help us?"

"If we give him the chance, definitely. Why?"

"There's a... tradition... among the Lithdreyan raider bands that I'm hoping to make use of."

Lithdreyan raider bands collected all sorts of people, and they weren't exactly organised, so there was no strict manner of clothing. They all wore a mixture of Lithdreyan styles, and very few would ever lay claim to a full set of armour. It was more likely to find a tasset here, greaves there. That served my purposes well, as Master Tri would never be able to outfit my soldiers if every one required a full set of armour. I myself only had a pauldron over my left shoulder, secured by a strap across my chest, and a pair of mismatched bracers around my forearms.

Raised voices started as I strolled into the village. It felt strange to be wearing Lithdreyan armour, but I knew I looked the part, especially with Sebastien chained up behind me and four Lithdreyan raiders flanking me.

Sayyid Oman emerged from the chief's hut, which he had taken as his own, at the shouts. "Who goes there?" he roared in Lithdreyan, drawing his sword.

I played my tongue around for a moment to prepare, then called out in kind, "Is that any way to greet someone who brings you a gift, Sayyid?"

He stepped forward, squinting in the sunlight, and I shoved Sebastien forward, knocking him to his knees. He looked slightly beaten, and from the way he wriggled around when I had scuffed and dirtied his face earlier, you would have thought I had tortured him.

Several members of the band stepped closer to listen, interested.

"This boy came upon my party on the road, shouting for help. I figured you wouldn't want him reaching his destination."

All at once, Sayyid recognised him and gave a dark grin. "This is the one who fled in the night. I will be glad to clean his blood from my blade."

He stepped forward and I instantly came between them, willing my heart to stop racing. "Where is your hospitality, Captain?" I jeered. "My people and I have ridden hard for several days. Are you not even going to offer us food and water? You're lucky we're no longer in the desert, or you would be committing a grave offence."

"My apologies..." he reached out for my name.

"Malach al Djen," I said easily.

"Captain al Djen. Please. Your people must be tired... We will eat and rest, and then we will discuss the split of this village's resources. I was..." he said slowly, "expecting there to be more of you, though."

"After I found this," I said, yanking the chain Sebastien was bound by, which caught him off-guard and sent him sprawling because he didn't speak a word of Lithdreyan, "I wanted to be sure no one else had fled for help. The bulk of my forces have been scouring the forests and lowlands, but I thought it prudent to bring my most trusted here straight away. Your messenger was quite panicked, Sayyid," I said patronisingly. "I was worried the little farmers had proved too much for you."

"I... appreciate... your frankness, Captain al Djen," he said through gritted teeth. "Now, if you will give me the boy, we can-"

I laughed sharply. "Were you the one to capture him? To chase him down and subdue him? No, you were the one who let him escape. *I* caught him, Sayyid, and that makes him my property now. He is mine, as is anyone else my people find fleeing. I will not have you killing him out of anger and wasting a good slave."

He struggled for a moment to control his expression, then quietly said, "Very well. Bring your people, I will have beds made up and food brought."

We ate like kings, and I made a mental note to have Hakim send supplies to this village when this was all over. They were being eaten out of house and home.

Sebastien kept making worried eye contact with a beefy boy who looked a year or two older than him. Ansel. Ansel, himself, moved timidly, flinching every time Sayyid gestured wildly. He had clearly learned from experience.

"I cannot say I am familiar with your name, Captain al Djen," Sayyid said to me.

"Oh, I am quite well-known in Tunder Village and the surrounding *Denuda* Wastes."

"Is that so?"

"I trained under Pips Torred and Big Rini. Perhaps you are familiar."

"Rini... Yes, I served with her briefly, I think. Terrifying mountain of a woman?"

"So you do know her."

We shared a laugh and Sayyid raised his glass. "To friends, old and new, and to terrifying women!"

"I will drink to that."

In the middle of our meal, Sebastien bumped into Ansel and murmured to him. They shared a tense moment of conversation that I couldn't hear, but I knew what was being said. Sebastien was passing on instructions for Ansel to frustrate Sayyid, to make him angry. Ansel shook his head vehemently, probably saying something along the lines of, "No, you're crazy!" But Sebastien pushed and got through to him.

As they separated, I lazily struck Sebastien across the face, sending him to the floor. "Keep your head down, boy," I spat in accented Forain. "Do not plot."

"As I was saying," Sayyid continued, "my people subdued and took control of this village, so we are entitled to a larger share of the profits."

"And as I already told you, anyone who sends a messenger crying for help can't be **too** entitled."

His face reddened once more, as it had been the entire meal, and he huffed out, "I am getting sick of the way that- Aah!"

He cried out in pain as Ansel tripped and spilled hot soup into his lap. The next words out of his mouth were unnecessary to translate, though I must say they were quite creative. He swung his fist angrily and Ansel meekly ducked out of the way, murmuring an apology.

"Perhaps we should table this discussion, Sayyid," I said sweetly, "until you are no longer dressed in broth."

"Very well," he spat. "Get out."

"Boy," I called in Forain as I started out of the hut. Sebastien quickly fell into place with me, and I felt a flash of guilt as I saw the welt on his face that was already starting to bruise.

⧠

I was shown into a nice— but not so nice as Sayyid's— dwelling, glancing around impassively until Sebastien and I were left alone. I knew that by now, Ana would have fetched Master Tri again and she would be hard at work armouring the rest of my Guards, who had instructions to trickle into the village over the next day.

I took a moment to remind myself how it felt to speak my native tongue and then glanced up at Sebastien. "I hope I didn't hurt you too badly earlier," I said as I began to take off my armour.

Sebastien rolled his eyes. "I'd already agreed to it. Besides; you hit like a child."

"Glad to know my gentleness was appreciated."

"What were you saying to that guy, anyways? He was red as a cabbage."

"Oh, just poking and prodding... I wonder what it will take to get him angry enough to hit me."

"You... **want** him to hit you?"

"Kind of depending on it, actually. Preferably in public."

"Okay. Maybe I should have asked this before, but how exactly does your plan end?"

"With your village free and the raiders scattered. Isn't that what you wanted?"

Sebastien looked up at me impatiently and I grinned. "Okay, that tradition in Lithdreyan raider bands. Do you know how their leaders are chosen?

"Ugliest and meanest guy in the bunch?"

"The strongest lead. If you want to control a band, you must kill their leader in single combat. That's my plan."

"You-" Sebastien huffed and shook his head in exasperation. "And what happens to my village when you get yourself killed?"

"Please," I scoffed. "Did you see the way he held his sword? **You** could probably take it from him."

"When you die, maybe I'll have to."

"Trust me, kid," I said as I flopped down onto one of the cots. "I've faced a lot worse than Sayyid out there. I give him thirty seconds— if I go easy on him."

"You're cocky," he muttered, sitting down on the other cot.

"I'm good at what I do; there's a difference." **He's going to need reassurance**, Edda murmured to me. I rolled onto my side, looking up at him earnestly. "I've been trained to fight since I was ten. I've mastered every weapon I carry, and I've learned from several teachers. It's not arrogance... it's experience." He looked at me skeptically and I sighed, playing my victory card. "Last year, I fought and killed the Scorpion and the Spider of the *Menagerie*. Sayyid will be easy."

Sebastien turned to me in surprise, looking like he'd been struck by lightning. "**You're** the reborn Sentinel?"

I rolled my eyes, laying back. "I do not know how that rumour got started. Some loudmouth spreading fantasies."

"But you **are** the warrior who saved the city? The only person to ever be named a mage of the sword?"

"That's me."

"I've heard stories, but I didn't realise-" he shook his head. "Maybe we **will** get out of this."

I turned to the table, unsheathing my sword and laying it down to oil it. It was far more humid here than in the city, and I didn't want it to rust.

Suddenly Sebastien said, "I'd **heard** the Sentinel was the son of a blacksmith."

"Adopted," I said with a laugh.

"You know, I think he would've liked you."

"Hm?" I asked, glancing up from the table.

"Elin." I stilled. "I mean... you **couldn't** be more different, but you-you wear his name well."

I turned, crossing my legs as I scooched forward on my cot. "They don't talk much about him... What was he like?"

Sebastien smiled at some memory. "He was the kindest person I'd ever met. He always wanted to be helpful, even if he had no idea what he was doing. He ended up making a lot of messes that way, but no one got mad at him because he was so sincere about it. And he would play with me and the rest of Edda's students all the time."

"Edda was a teacher?" I asked in surprise.

He nodded. "Jezzine Silver Academy for Seaming. Best teacher I've ever had..."

"I believe that. And Elin, he was apprenticing with Ruce?"

"Yeah. He wasn't very good at it, though, he always said. Too forgetful, too excitable."

"How old was he?"

Twenty-two that fall. His birthday was just a few days before the wedding, actually."

"He was married?"

"Yeah, for... for about a week," he said quietly. "Before the attack."

"I didn't know that..."

"He actually married Ansel's sister, Victoire. Their dad was Ruce's best friend."

"Did he steal Ruce's tools?" I asked, realisation dawning on me.

Sebastien laughed. "Yeah. Ruce always said he held a grudge about that, but I didn't believe it. They were just playing. What about you? Tell me about you... Who did you used to be?"

"I was... I was a lot of things, Sebastien," I said slowly. "A lot of mistakes, a lot of failures."

"But you're a hero."

I laughed, suddenly realising the need to wipe my eyes. "Heroes make mistakes too." I sniffled and smiled at him. "Okay: me. My best friend is a queen, and she's tried to kill me twice. I accidentally became a famous snake catcher-"

"Yeah, you're nothing like him," Sebastien laughed.

"I'm a horrible card player, and... and I'm gonna be twenty-two this spring."

We locked eyes and Sebastien sighed. "It's scary, isn't it? Knowing that one day you're gonna be older than the people you've lost?"

"I don't want to be older than my dad..." I confessed. "Is that childish?"

"I get it. In a few years, I'll outgrow my big sister. It doesn't feel right."

"We should both get some sleep," I said gently. "We've got a lot to do tomorrow."

⧠

"You know what to do?" I murmured to Sebastien as we started out of the hut.

"I'm tripping a guy; it's not surgery."

"Okay, okay," I relented. "Just checking."

We started into the large building the raiders had been using as a meeting hall, but Sebastien caught my arm just before I opened the door. "Don't... Don't die, okay? I've already lost enough friends."

"Promise. Now, get moving, boy!" I shouted in an accent as I pushed the door open.

I shoved Sebastien inside and he stumbled quite convincingly. "Good morning, everyone," I called cheerfully in Lithdreyan, my accent back in full swing. Several teenagers, villagers from their clothing and the tension in their faces, roamed the room serving food to the raiders. "Someone cool down Sayyid's coffee for him before he spills on himself again," I laughed.

"I did not spill! That- that *boy*-"

"Blaming children," I sighed dramatically. "How fearless and brave our leader."

He pushed himself up from his seat so angrily the chair slammed back to the ground. "You are insolent!" he hissed.

I ignored him, weaving through the tables and picking grapes from random plates as I made my way over to a seat across the room. Sayyid followed me angrily, waving his finger as he fumed.

"Who are you to show up here and mock me? What gives you the courage to-"

He yelped as Sebastien stuck his toe out and sent him slamming his face into the wood floor. I laughed, glancing over my shoulder. "And so clumsy, too. Is this seat taken?" I asked the woman next to me.

She shook her head, struggling to hide her amusement. It was clear that Sayyid was not loved, and that it had been a while since someone provoked and stood up to him like this.

Sayyid pushed himself to his feet, tracking me down as he strung curses together like I had never heard before.

"What do you think of his *teguro* impression, huh?" I asked my neighbour conspiratorially. "Personally, I think he could be a little more red."

From across the room, someone guffawed at the comparison. The *teguro* was a fat little lizard that flushed red in the heat, and at the moment, it bore quite the resemblance to our leader.

That was the last straw. "Stand up!" Sayyid shouted at me.

"Is there *ka'aq*?" I asked, glancing around the table. "I'm going to need my energy if I have to listen to this one scream all day."

"Malach al Djen! Stand up, I tell you!"

There we go. Getting warmer.

I gave a painfully long sigh before pushing myself up to stand and turning to Sayyid. "Yes?"

He raised his hand to strike me, but I caught his wrist firmly as he swung. "Are you going to hit me, Sayyid?" I asked in amusement. "You'd better be sure of your choice, because if you strike me, I am going to kill you. Make it a good one."

I let go and he wasted no time in closing his hand into a fist and punching me. I felt his ring scrape across my eyebrow and slice it open, but I didn't let myself show the pain. Instead, I laughed.

"You did hear me tell him to make it good, yes?" I asked the man closest to me. "No matter."

It mattered. Sayyid looked like he was full of black powder; volatile, acrid, about to explode. "Out. Side," he spat deliberately.

Finally. "My pleasure, fearless leader."

There was a stirring in the group around me as they realised the significance of it all. As Sayyid and I started out of the hall, I saw people scrambling to down cups of *kahve* and shove bites of food into their mouths as they scrambled to follow us. *Lithdreyans always love a good fight*. Sebastien gave me an encouraging smile as I passed.

Sayyid strode out into the centre of the village, turning to face me as he tore off his shirt. I was forced to hold back a childish snigger as I watched him throw it to the ground. He drew his sword, swinging the blade through the air like he was trying to cut its head off.

"Take out your sword!" he screamed at me.

I glanced left and right as the other raiders formed a loose circle around us, joined by several wary villagers. Catching Sebastien's gaze, I winked and unsheathed my peasant daggers from under my sleeves.

My sword might be faster, sure, but in order for this to work, my victory needed to be *devastating*.

"You think to beat me with butter knives?" Sayyid scoffed.

"Would you rather I kill you with my bare hands, Sayyid?"

He didn't waste any more time on words, instead charging at me and roaring like a bull as he attempted to drive his sword through my rib cage.

I deflected the attack with contempt, his momentum sending him past me as I knocked the sword from his hands. He staggered, catching his balance, and I stepped back. "Go ahead," I prompted. "I'll let you pick it up."

He scooped up his sword, seething with rage, and came at me with a serious of rapid fire attacks, but there was no pattern to it, no thought—just blind rage. I caught his sword on my crossed knives and elbowed him in the face, swiping up the sword as it fell from his numb fingers.

"I might keep this, after I kill you. It's a decent enough toothpick."

I had dragged this on for long enough. I took a single breath and leapt forward, my training slashing at tendons, arteries, soft spots. When I stopped moving, Sayyid fell to the ground gracelessly, already dead, and I could feel blood dotting my cheeks.

A hush fell over the village as the raiders stared at their leader's dead body.

Give it a moment... Steady voice. I stepped forward, catching their attention once more, and called out in clear and carrying Forain. "My name is Captain Elin Lahd, Reborn Sentinel of the Guard of Lothforias, and as the victor of this fight... you all belong to me."

In the wake of that, I heard and saw several emotions passing through the raiders. Shock. Anger. Awe.

"I'd rather not waste my time killing you all," I continued, "but I can't have you pillaging my country either. I will give you three options: die, return to Lithdreya with your lives, or-"

One of them suddenly poured all of her strength into a sneak attack, which I sidestepped, driving one of my knives up into her ribcage without hesitation. As the fell to the ground, I sighed, wiping my blades on my trousers and resheathing them.

"As I was saying. Die, return to Lithdreya, or commit yourself to my Guard."

It seemed like the entire village was holding its breath, until finally someone stepped forward. She was almost as tall as Big Rini. I watched, fighting the urge to sigh in relief, as she fell to one knee. "I answer to strength... Captain Lahd, and you have proved yours. I will follow you."

Almost half of the band in front of me followed suit, their voices mixing together as they pledged their loyalty.

Emotionlessly, I looked around at the others. "And... the rest of you?" I asked boredly, my hand resting on my sword.

A young man stepped forward, slowly sheathing his sword. "We... we will accept your offer to return home, Captain."

"Very well, but listen closely. If any of you raise a weapon to harm one of my people again, I will personally hunt you down, and on that day there will only be one option."

I let that hang in the air until they were shifting nervously.

"Ana," I called sharply. "Take your squad and escort them to the border. The rest of you are going to help me put this place to rights."

I walked towards Sebastien, who was still staring at the bodies in the centre of the group in shock. "Wow..."

"How would you rate my service?" I asked playfully.

"Thank you, Elin," he said earnestly, grasping my hand in his.

Ansel slowly approached, leaning down to Sebastien. "Did- did he say his name was **Captain Elin Lahd**?" he asked in a daze, as though he had imagined the last five minutes.

"Yeah," Sebastien sighed. "Don't ask."

"You know I'm gonna ask."

"I'm adopted," I said at the same time Sebastien said, "He's adopted."

"Efficiently dome, boy."

I turned, seeing Master Tri with her arms crossed behind her back.

"I will see to it that you are paid for your work, Master."

"I won't hear of it."

"You will not deny me the honour of thanking a friend for their help," I said with measured sadness.

She glared at me for several seconds, then finally gave in. "Fine. Give it to the other families here."

"I'll make sure. And we will be sending builders to help you repair, as well as food to make up for what the raiders took."

"Do they have maps in that fancy city of yours?" she asked.

"They do."

"Remind my apprentice that one can use them to visit old friends."

I grinned at her. "I will make sure to do that, Master."

"Thank *Foria* you don't call me 'mother,'" she muttered to herself.

"I'd never dream of it."

◻

"Don't be a stranger, okay?" Sebastien asked as I swung up onto my horse.

"Roads travel both ways. I'd better be seeing the three of you in the city to come and visit soon. I'm sure Ruce and Edda would love to show you the new shop."

"The city?" Master Tri cackled. "You won't make me."

"Then I'll be back to bother you soon. Good harvests," I called over my shoulder.

"Even trails," Sebastien answered.

Turn the page for a sneak peek at Blood and Water Book Two: The Spider of the White Desert!

CHAPTER ONE

ELIN

THE DELEGATION WAS AN interesting party to watch parading through the city. First came the Lithdreyan emissary with whom Riadh had been negotiating for the better part of a year, and her staff. Next was a retinue of translators and advisors, followed by members of the Vigil. These were the warriors who guarded the crater city of Bayt-Wun and the palace. Why, then, it's tempting to wonder, were they passing through the market district of Lothforias?

Behind them, astride a *kisa* and dressed in fine white clothing touched with gold, was *S'Qidah*, the High Seat of Lithdreya. His name was Dreythin, but it would have been a great offence to call him by anything but his title. To his right rode a thin but muscular woman with piercing eyes, no more than a year or two older than me. The Vigil were all armed, and I knew *S'Qidah* had been trained in the *Menagerie*, but something about the easy way that young woman swayed with her mount's movement told me that of every person in this party, she was the most dangerous. She was dressed simply, in a white linen *shiwr* and bandeau, with high brown boots. Her overshirt was an almost sheer material that moved easily with the breeze. Something about the several knives sheathed along her body was familiar, but I couldn't place it. I was sure we'd never met; I would have remembered those amber eyes. As if on cue, she turned and her eyes caught on me. All at once, I was back in the desert fighting for my life against one of *Dreya's Furies*. That was the level of hatred I saw there.

I lost her attention as Riadh stepped forward, addressing *S'Qidah* with a welcoming smile. "We are honoured to host you, Your Majesty, though I only wish our first meeting could be under better circumstances."

His voice was deep and rich as he spoke. "As do I, so I hope you forgive me if we table the pleasantries in favour of solutions."

"Agreed; this illness has plagued both of our people for long enough. Please. We will talk inside."

S'Qidah dismounted and he and his advisors followed Riadh into the citadel. Inside, I knew, a meeting room had been prepared with Lithdreyan delicacies as a gesture of good faith. Our negotiations had been on rocky enough ground before the plague struck our nations, and anything we could do to strengthen bonds could make the difference between peace and death.

The Hall of Craftsmages was a sight to behold. Lithdreyan scorpion-horses grazed in the same stables as Lothforian stallions, their riders mingling together and sharing food quietly. There was an air of tension, but that was understandable... Not only had we been enemies for thousands of years, but the city centre was almost a ghost town. Hundreds, thousands of people were bedridden with the plague, and cities weren't meant to be this quiet. There were meant to be children in the streets, vendors shouting in the market, sounds of hammering coming from the Hall of Craftsmages...

The only good thing to come from this illness was that it had brought our two nations together. The sickness had been carried between our peoples, and our best chance to find a cure was working as one. It was comforting, to see Lithdreyans and Lothforians sitting and sharing apple slices and dates like old friends. No one here wanted to kill anyone else.

"***You!***"

I turned at the shout, the armed woman from earlier launching herself at me, a dagger in each hand. Before I'd even had time to think, my dirk was out of its sheath and blocking the strike. I staggered back from the force, hearing raised voices all around. The world was a blur as I defended myself against her rage, and then we were being pulled apart. Hakim steadied me as the woman was dragged backward by two members of the Vigil, still shouting and swearing at me and struggling to break the hold. I panted, adrenaline surging through me as pain flared in my body.

"Friend of yours?" Hakim murmured to me breathlessly.

I wiped my bottom lip, now bloodied by a hit from her elbow. "I've never met her before in my life..."

"Stand down!" a rich voice shouted in Lithdreyan, and the woman fought herself, slowly calming as she turned to the speaker, bowing her head obediently.

I spun, seeing Riadh and *S'Qidah* striding through the citadel. "Oh, good," Riadh said deadpan. "...You two have met."

"Your Majesty," I said quietly. "Negotiations going well?"

"We have come to a decision," *S'Qidah* answered. "Your queen has shared with us intelligence that the cure to this plague likely lies in the White Desert, far to the south. We have agreed to send a team, two of our most trusted, to retrieve this. Captain Lahd... meet your new ally. My Spider."

My stomach dropped. ***Spider***. That was why she was familiar... I had killed the last woman to bear her title.

"No!" The Spider shouted in anguish. "Your Majesty, he-"

"You will work together," he reiterated coldly, his eyes boring into her.

The Spider glared at me like she was about to burst into flame, and I can't say I was much happier about the prospect.

"And you will protect each other with your lives," *S'Qidah* ordered.

She clenched her jaw, slowly lowering herself to one knee. "I... I promise, *S'Qidah*."

Riadh looked over at me, lifting her eyebrows in question, and I made eye contact with her as I wiped blood from my lip again, nodding once.

"Excellent," Riadh said diplomatically. "There is no time to waste; once you are supplied, the two of you will leave at once."

I rested a hand against my chest, taking a moment to calm myself. Then I turned, keeping my face impassive, as I made eye contact with The Spider. I held out a hand to her diplomatically. "Elin Lahd."

"Spider," she said coolly in reply, crossing her arms.

"I'm not calling you that."

"That is my name, Lothforian." With that, she spun to follow *S'Qidah* and glared at the city square in front of us.

"This is going to be a long journey," I muttered to myself.

Glossary and Pronunciation Guide

Aba— papa/daddy

Al majowan (ah-l Mah-jo-wah-n)— the name the Lithdreyan assassins gave to their order; translates to "The Silent Death" and is a reference to their motto, "*hin al majowan ef*"; also called The *Menagerie*; A*l majowan* is made up of Initiates, Jewels, and The Quiet

- *Dwer-da* (d-w-air-duh)— the Dingoes; the only Jewel made up of a pack of three; the *Dwer-da* hunt together and act as a singular unit, bonded as closely as family

- Initiates— those who serve as foot soldiers; they are taken from their families as young children and raised in the Cavern; trained to use the sickle-sword of *Al majowan* and given brief training in the styles of the Jewels; upon the death of a Jewel, an Initiate is raised to a status of honour to replace them; Initiation is shown by ceremonial scarring on the forearms

- Jewels— Those warriors given names and a place under The Quiet; they are each named for the dangerous predators of the desert and trained in distinctive fighting and killing styles

- Lion— a Jewel trained with dual fang-daggers and a flail evocative of the morningstar-tail of a lion in their homeland

- The Quiet— *"Wani,"* the leader of *Al majowan,* who is chosen from the Jewels and answers only to the king

- Spider— a Jewel trained in stealth and patience, wielding poison and hidden weapons against their enemies; trained with *sikyh* knives

- *S'Qidah* (s-kee-duh)— the Four-Fang; their name translates to "king" or "queen"; this Jewel is chosen from the Initiates of *Al majowan* to become the ruler of the country

- *Tannin* (tah-neen)— the Crocodile; Jewel trained with a *ter-jt-u,* a weapon studded with crocodile teeth; this Jewel is also well-versed in grappling

- Viper— a Jewel trained to use their enemy's movement and weight against them; their weapon is a *haladie*

- Wolf— a Jewel trained to cut down an opponent quickly by striking at vulnerable points and arteries; unlike the other Jewels, this warrior is trained mainly in hand-to-hand combat and does not have a distinctive weapon

Ama— mama/mommy

Asabat (ah-sah-bot)— "pledged"; uttered when making a deal or an agreement

Bayt-Wun (bye-t Woon)— the capital city of Lithdreya; built in the crater left behind when Lady *Foria* took Lothforias out of the ground and carried it away

Bita (bee-tuh)— a board game popularised in Lithdreya and Lothforias for its focus on hypothetical war; players pit their armies against each other

Carapace— a fabric that has been imbued with protective magic; worn by the Guard of Lothforias; named for the protective shell of beetles because of its purpose and the fact that, just like a beetle's shell, a carapace has a slight shine or shimmer to it due to the magic stitched into it

Cousa soup (coo-suh)— a Middle-Eastern dish made with *cousa* squash, beef or lamb, tomato juice, long-grain rice, and spices

Craftsmages— people who work as skilled laborers such as: blacksmiths, farmers, cooks, stonemasons, healers, or seamsters

Darai— a unit of money

Dreya— the god of the sun and vengeance, who founded Lithdreya and wanders the desert in the form of a lion

Foreyn— the language spoken in the nation of Lothforias; bears similarity to *Lithdreyan* because they are descended from the same language

Foria— the god of falling and flowing water, a stoneworker, carried the city of Lothforias to where it stands today and built up walls around it; watches over the nation

Freekah and chicken— a Lebanese meal made with the ancient grain *freekah*, chicken, herbs, and toasted nuts roasted over an open fire

Ghalem (gah-lem)— a manmade symbol of vengeance and the dangers of power; a creature of legend said to be formed out of clay and brought to life; can also refer to a person who does not know who they are or "is not fully formed"

Gria (gree-uh)— a title put after the name of a god; similar to Lord or Lady, denotes godhood

Habi (ha-bee)— "my love"; a term of endearment to a spouse or partner

Ha Det (ha day)— a *Stangrey* farewell translating to "steady hands"; a wish for the other person to stay strong and certain

Haladie (ha-la-dee)— a double-ended knife wielded by the Viper

Hayati (hai-yuh-tee)— "my life"; a term of endearment from a parent to a child

Hin al majowan ef (heen ah-l Mah-jo-wah-n ef)— the motto of *Al majowan*; translates to "the small kill quietly" and signifies the belief that some of the most dangerous things are those which do not look dangerous, such as predators like spiders and snakes, and children

Jo-fahke (jo-f-ah-k)— "jewels and cream"; a desert from Jezzine-on-the-Meander made by mixing fresh fruit into cream

Kahve (ka-vay)— coffee

Kara (ka-ruh)— an overshirt that wraps around the body and ties at the hip; bares one's arms

Ka'aq (ka-ack)— a flat bread filled with white-brine cheese and covered in sesame seeds

Keffiyeh (kef-ee-yuh)— a Middle Eastern garment; a swath of fabric that can be worn in multiple ways, such as around the head for protection from the sun and the stinging wind, around the neck as a scarf, or over the mouth as a mask

Khopesh (ko-pesh)— the sickle-sword carried by Initiates and Jewels of *Al majowan*

Kisa (kee-sa)— scorpion-horses

Labneh (lob-ne-h)— a soft Middle-Eastern cheese made from straining yogurt

Lahat (la-hot)— tall boots worn frequently by warriors and craftsmages for their strength and aid in movement and control

Loro (low-row)— a *Lithdreyan* phrase for someone who is deranged or reckless

Mages— Craftsmages who become so skilled at their mundane magic that they are recognised by the gods

Majedra (muh-je-dra)— a Middle-Eastern dish of lentils and ricem-topped with caramelised onions

The Mark of the Sentinel— a brand worn on the inner forearm of a Guard's sword hand in a stylised image of the Sentinel's metal head; beneath the mask is a series of horizontal lines showing how many years a Guard has been in the service of Lothforias

Menagerie— The vernacular term for *Al majowan*, which finds its origins in *Stangrey*; translates to "collection of strange animals"; used in *Stangrey* and *Forain*

Mundane Magics— a Forain term for crafts or skills such as: blacksmithing, seaming, combat, healing, stonemasonry, and cooking

Nora—the goddess of the stars who watches over travellers at night; married to *Setcha*

Oren— the god of blacksmithing and swordplay; also called "The Sentinel"; guarded Lady *Foria*

Sahlab— a middle eastern milk pudding drink made by mixing warm milk, cornflour, and vanilla; can be topped with cinnamon and pistachios

Sandworm— a *Lithdreyan* phrase which translates to "nothing"; used ironically as a way of making light of a bad situation

Seamster— a person who is skilled and employed in "seaming," or the production of clothing and other wares made of fabric

Setcha— the goddess of seaming and healing; married to *Nora*

Shiwr (shee-wur)— high-waisted baggy pants which gather at the ankles

Staves—brass cylinders used in combat and held in the hand to lend power to a strike, or wooden rods/slats like those used in railings and barrels

Venaq (veh-nack)— trapeze "boots" with a hole for the heel and the toes to come through, worn for balance and climbing

Yoran Root— a root vegetable filled with a watery sap commonly used in Lithdreya and outlying Lothforian settlements as a healing salve; *yoran* translates to "soothing tears"

ACKNOWLEDGEMENTS

This story is very close to my heart, because its questions are mine. One of the most important questions I needed to ask was "what is family?" and through this process, I have found my answer.

Family is Nonny and Aunt Linda reading several drafts of my book and staying eager and patient as the narrative changed day to day. Family is my mother getting past her distaste for fantasy to read it and give me the hard truths I needed to hear about the story. It's my fiancé— previously referred to in my Acknowledgements as my "best friend" because I didn't know I was in love— constantly encouraging me and putting up with my bursts of energy and inspiration at 3 a.m. Family is the support I've found in other writers and readers during my struggle to finish this book.

I feel the need to thank every librarian who has ever put a book in my hands and encouraged me, opened my eyes to the magical worlds I could escape to, if only I had time and a comfortable corner to curl up in. Without them, I would not have nurtured my love for reading, nor would I have discovered this beautiful language I can use to reach people going through the struggles I once did.

I also feel so grateful to the authors who held my hand as I grew up, who taught me how to swing a sword and cast spells and stand up for myself as I was figuring out who I am. Chief among them is John Flanagan, who brought an entire universe to life that has captivated me since I was big enough to pick up a chapter book. His stories were my inspiration, and without them I would not be the person I am today. (Can you find the reference I made paying homage to Will Treaty in this book?)

Finally, I need to thank my readers. Each one means the world to me, and all I hope for is that something in my books touches you, makes you smile or cry or laugh out loud or shiver... Without you guys, I would have no purpose.

PUBLIC SAFETY NOTICE

Parker Atlas Yaw should never have been released from their enclosure, and their escape was the result of a level four containment breach. We at Orange Door Books recognize the danger of having a domesticated author loose on the streets, and we urge the public to aid us in his swift capture.

Last seen in Malone, New York, the subject has had very little socialization, and will likely stand out. During captivity, subject expressed interest in "education" and may be found roaming local college campuses studying English, Education, and Anthropology.

Subject is likely to be found:

- Binge-watching Power Rangers and sobbing

- Looking for pretty rocks

- At the McDonalds drive-thru between the hours of 1 a.m. and 3 a.m.

- Talking to himself

- Thinking about ghosts

- Trying to understand human nature through writing science

fiction and fantasy, dealing with non-human and superhuman characters to push the struggles that come with love, morality, and discovering your identity to extremes in ways that leave you reeling and desperate for a true emotional connection, wondering if you really can choose your own family and heal from your trauma

- Playing Fortnite

- Wandering the lights section of the nearest hardware store

- Speaking in an English accent (they are not English)

WARNING: If you see the subject, do not engage. All contact should be made through orangedoorbooks@gmail.com for your protection.